D1308269

# THE INFORMATION OFFICER

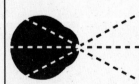

# THE INFORMATION OFFICER

## MARK MILLS

**THORNDIKE PRESS**

*A part of Gale, Cengage Learning*

GALE
CENGAGE Learning™

Detroit • New York • San Francisco • New Haven, Conn • Waterville, Maine • London

GALE
CENGAGE Learning™

**LIBRARY OF CONGRESS CATALOGING-IN-PUBLICATION DATA**

Mills, Mark, 1963–
    The information officer / by Mark Mills.
        p. cm. — (Thorndike Press large print historical fiction)
    ISBN-13: 978-1-4104-2581-2
    ISBN-10: 1-4104-2581-9
    1. World War, 1939–1945—Malta—Fiction. 2. British—Malta—Fiction.
3. Murder—Investigation—Fiction. 4. Malta—Fiction. 5. Large type
books. I. Title.
PS3613.I569164 2010
813'.6—dc22                                                        2010008037

Published in 2010 by arrangement with Random House, Inc.

Printed in the United States of America
1 2 3 4 5 6 7 14 13 12 11 10

*For Caroline, Gus, and Rosie*

*You have killed a sweet lady,*
*and her death shall fall heavy on you.*
*— from Much Ado About Nothing*
by WILLIAM SHAKESPEARE

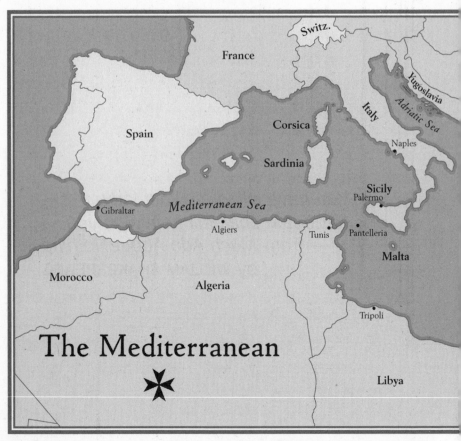

France
Switz.
Italy
Yugoslavia
Adriatic Sea
Corsica
Naples
Spain
Sardinia
Sicily
Palermo
Gibraltar
*Mediterranean Sea*
Algiers
Tunis
Pantelleria
Malta
Morocco
Algeria
Tripoli

# The Mediterranean

Libya

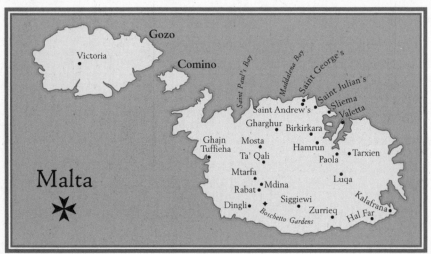

Gozo
Victoria
Comino
Saint Paul's Bay
Maddalena Bay
Saint George's
Saint Julian's
Saint Andrew's
Sliema
Valetta
Gharghur
Birkirkara
Ghajn
Tuffieha
Mosta
Hamrun
Tarxien
Ta' Qali
Paola
Mtarfa
Luqa
Rabat
Mdina
Dingli
Siggiewi
Kalafrana
Zurrieq
Hal Far
*Boschetto Gardens*

# Malta

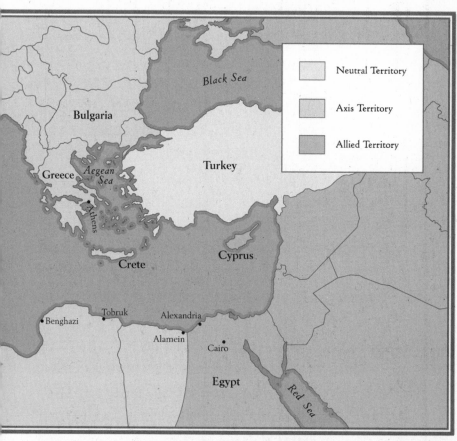

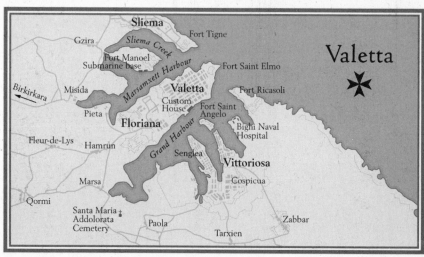

# LONDON
## MAY 1951

Mario was in a good mood.

This wasn't saying much; he was often in a good mood. It was a legacy from his father — a simple, hardworking man who had drilled into his children the value of giving daily thanks for those things that most people took for granted.

Mario cast an approving eye around the restaurant. A prime site a stone's throw from the Ritz, and after just four short years, a reputation to match the very best in town. Not bad for the son of a shoemaker from a small village in northern Italy. Not bad at all.

The place was empty, just one lone customer at the bar, but the restaurant would be heaving within the hour, even in these austere times. He checked over the reservations book, memorizing the names and the table allocations. He prided himself on not having to refer to it once the first diners had arrived. There was the usual smattering of household names with strong views about where they sat. Juggling their wishes was about as hard as his job got.

Table 7 was the first to show. The man's face wasn't well known to Mario — one of the birthdays-and-anniversaries-only crowd — but Mario remembered him as a generous tipper. He wore a good-quality suit, its looser cut suggesting one of the new tailors just off Savile Row. He informed Mario that his wife would be arriving separately and requested a dry martini to keep him company in the meantime.

The wife was obviously a romantic, because a special order had been placed earlier in the day for a bottle of wine to be brought to the table as a surprise. It was a white wine from a small French house, and it had arrived by taxi along with written instructions and a generous contribution toward corkage.

The bottle was already on ice, ready and waiting behind the bar. Mario tipped Gregory the wink before taking up a discreet position behind a bushy palmetto to observe the reaction.

The man smiled at the appearance of the ice bucket, but the moment Gregory revealed the bottle to him, he fell absolutely still, the blood draining from his face. He looked up at Gregory, speechless, and then his eyes darted wildly around the restaurant. They came to settle on the only other customer — the gentleman seated at the bar. The man's back was turned to table 7, but he now swiveled round on his stool.

It was impossible to read the look that passed between the two men, but it crackled with a strange intensity. Poor Gregory was flummoxed. He offered to pour the wine, was ignored, then wisely chose to retire as the gentleman at the bar made his way over, clutching his cocktail. He was tall and balding and walked with a lazy grace.

Another thing Mario prided himself on was his absolute discretion, but this was a conversation he wanted to hear. He drifted toward table 10, out of sight behind the high banquette but just within earshot. He arrived as the balding man was taking a seat.

"You look like you've seen a ghost."

There was a soft but unmistakable American lilt to his accent.

"Where's my wife?" said the other man.

"Don't worry. She's just fine."

"Where is she?"

"At home. She thought we should talk."

"I don't believe you."

13

"It's true. Call her if you'd like. Cigarette?"

"I have my own."

"Try one of these — they're Russian."

Mario heard the cigarettes being lit and then the balding man say, "What's your secret?"

"My secret?"

"You've barely aged in ten years."

"Nine."

"It feels longer."

"Does it?"

"I miss Malta."

"I doubt that."

"You don't seem very pleased to see me."

"What did you expect? The last time I saw you, you tried to kill me."

Mario almost toppled a wineglass on table 10.

"Is that what they told you?" asked the balding man.

"They didn't have to. I was there, remember?"

"You're wrong. I could have killed you. Maybe I *should* have. I chose not to."

The other man gave a short snort of derision.

Mario was well out of his depth now and regretting his decision to eavesdrop. Help came in the form of a large party of diners

14

who blew in through the door on a gale of laughter. Mario couldn't see them from where he was lurking.

"Isn't that the actor everyone's talking about?" said the balding man.

"I think so."

"I'm not sure a fedora and a cloak suit a fellow that short. He looks like a kid playing at Zorro."

*Definitely table 2,* thought Mario, swooping from his hiding place to greet the new arrivals.

# MALTA

## MAY 1942

She knew the cemetery well — not every gravestone, tomb, and mausoleum, but most. She certainly knew it well enough to tread its twisting pathways with confidence, even on a moonless night such as this. Before the blackout restrictions, she would have been assisted on her way by a constellation of flickering candles, but with the deep darkness as her only companion, she still walked with confidence and purpose.

The mellow scent of pine sap came at her clear on the warm night breeze. Tonight, however, it did battle with the rank odor of decay, of putrefaction. Two wayward German bombs — or possibly Italian, now that the *cicci macaroni* were back — had smacked into the hillside the previous night during a raid, reducing family tombs to rubble and wrenching coffins from the thin soil. Corpses in various states of decomposition had been scattered in all directions, their

16

rude awakening like some dress rehearsal for Judgment Day.

It was Father Debono who had drawn this parallel for their benefit at early-morning Mass, and while it was the sort of observation for which he was known, and the sort that endeared him to the younger members of his flock, his willingness to flirt with irreverence was a source of ongoing distrust among the more elderly. Many had furrowed their brows; some had even tut-tutted from their pews.

She knew where her sympathies lay, though. She knew that it was Father Debono, not old Grech and his wizened holier-than-thou sister, who had spent that day in the thick of it, toiling through the pitiless heat and the inhuman stench to ensure that all the corpses were recovered and reburied with all the proper rites.

Judging from the smell, Father Debono and his small band of helpers had not been able to complete their grim task before nightfall, and she picked up her pace a little at the thought of the rats feasting on flesh nearby. She had always hated rats, even before the war, before the stories had begun to circulate about what went on beneath the rubble of the bombed-out buildings.

She saw a light up ahead: a flickering

flame . . . the vague contours of a face . . . a man lighting a cigarette. Then darkness once more.

She slowed, more from respect than fear. With the cemetery doing a roaring trade, it was not the first time she had come across some grieving soul while making her way home from work in the early hours of the morning. She had once heard deep male sobs in the darkness and had removed her shoes so that the unfortunate person would not be disturbed by her footfalls on the paved pathway.

"Good evening," she said quietly in Maltese as she drew level.

He was seated on the low stone wall to the right of the path, and he responded in English.

"I think you'll find it's morning, Carmela."

She didn't know the voice, or if she did, she couldn't place it.

"Did you make good money tonight?" he asked.

He not only knew her, but he knew what she did, and she was happy he couldn't see the color rising in her cheeks.

"Yes, not bad."

"Oh, but you are, and you know it."

It wasn't so much the words as the slow,

easy drawl with which they were delivered that set her heart racing.

His small laugh did something to soothe her building apprehension.

"I was only joking."

He drew long and hard on his cigarette. In the dim glow of burning tobacco, she could just discern that he was wearing khaki battle dress: shirt and shorts. This didn't help much. All the services had adopted it recently, and she was unable to make out the shoulder flashes.

"Who are you?" she asked.

"Ah, now I'm insulted."

It could have been Harry, or Bernard, or even young Bill, the one they all called "little Willy" (before invariably erupting in laughter). But she didn't feel like laughing because it could have been almost any one of the officers who passed through the Blue Parrot on a typical night, and this man remained silent, enjoying her confusion, her discomfort, which was cruel and uncalled for.

"I must go."

He was off the wall and seizing her arm before she had taken two paces.

"What's the hurry?"

She tried to pull free, but his grip was firm, viselike, painful. She let out a small cry and attempted to twist away. The maneuver failed miserably, and she found herself trapped against him, her back pressed into his chest.

He clamped his free hand over her mouth. "Ssshhhh," he soothed.

He spat the cigarette away and put his mouth to her ear.

"You want to know who I am? I'm the last living soul you'll ever set eyes on."

She didn't need to know all of the words; she understood their meaning. And now she began to struggle in earnest, her thoughts turning to her home, her parents, her brothers, her dog, all so close, just a short way up the hill.

He repaid her efforts by twisting her left arm up behind her until something gave in her shoulder. The pain ripped through her, carrying her to the brink of unconsciousness, her knees starting to give. In desperation she tried to bite the hand gagging her cries, but he cupped his fingers away from her teeth. His other hand released her now-useless arm and jammed itself between her legs, into the fork of her thighs, pulling her back against him.

His breathing was strangely calm and measured, and there was something in the sound of it that suggested he was smiling.

# DAY ONE

"Tea or coffee?"

"Which do you recommend?"

"Well, the first tastes like dishwater, the second like slurry runoff."

"I'll try the slurry runoff."

Max summoned the attention of the waiter hovering nearby. He was new — squat and toadlike — some member of the kitchen staff drafted in to replace Ugo, whose wife had been wounded in a strafing attack over the weekend while out strolling with friends near Rabat. Gratifyingly, the pilot of the Messerschmitt 109 had paid for this outrage with his life, a Spitfire from Ta' Qali dropping onto his tail moments later and bringing him down in the drink off the Dingli Cliffs.

"How's Ugo's wife?" Max inquired of the waiter.

"She dead."

"Oh."

In case there was any doubt, the waiter tilted his head to one side and let a fat tongue roll out of his mouth. The eyes remained open, staring.

"Two coffees, please."

"Two coffee."

"Yes. Thank you."

Max's eyes tracked the waiter as he waddled off, but his thoughts were elsewhere, with Ugo, and he wondered how long it would be before he smiled his crooked smile again.

He forced his attention back to the young man sitting across from him. Edward Pemberton was taking in his surroundings — the tall windows, the elaborately painted walls, and the high beamed ceiling — apparently immune to the mention of death.

"What a beautiful place."

"It's the old Auberge de Provence."

Once home to the Knights of Saint John, the grand baroque edifice now housed the Union Club, a welcome haven from the hard realities of war for the officer classes. The building seemed to bear a charmed life, standing remarkably unscathed among the ruins and rubble of Kingsway, Valetta's principal street. With its reassuring whiff of a Saint James's gentleman's club, there was no better place to break the news to young

Pemberton. It might help soften the blow.

"Who's Ugo?"

So he had been listening, after all.

"The head waiter."

"How did his wife die?"

Max hesitated, then told him the story. No point in pretending that things hadn't turned nasty of late. In fact, it might fire his sense of outrage, winning him over to the cause, although, when it came to it, Pemberton would have very little say in the matter. He wouldn't be leaving Malta anytime soon; he just didn't know that yet. Another bird of passage ensnared by the beleaguered garrison. Poor bastard.

Max spelled it out as gently as he could. The lieutenant governor's office had already been in touch with the brass in Gibraltar, who appreciated that Malta's back was up against the wall. If Pemberton's services were required on the island, then so be it. Needs must, and all that. Force majeure. First dibs to the downtrodden. You get the picture.

"I understand," said Pemberton.

"Really?"

"Absolutely, sir. No objections."

Max wanted to ask him if he had any notion of what lay in store for him: the breathless heat and the choking dust; the mosquitoes, sand flies, and man-eating fleas; the sleepless nights and the starvation rations. Oh, and the Luftwaffe, who, together with the Regia Aeronautica, were intent on wiping the island off the map, on bombing it into oblivion.

"I never wanted to go to Gib," Pemberton went on. "It never appealed . . . as a place, I mean."

*War as tourism,* thought Max. Well, that's one way of coming at it, and probably no better or worse than any other.

"Malta has a lot to offer," said Max. "When the history of the war comes to be written, this little lump of rock in the middle of the Med will figure large."

"If you're appealing to my vanity, it might just work."

Max gave a short loud laugh, which drew glances from a couple of artillery types at a nearby table. Pemberton was smiling coyly, faultless teeth flashing in his wide, strong mouth. Matinee idol looks *and* a sense of humor. *Perfect fodder for Rosamund,* Max mused. *She'll never forgive me if I don't offer her the right of first refusal.*

Pemberton explained (with a degree of candor he would soon learn to curb) that he was sick of being shunted from pillar to post under the protective tutelage of his

24

uncle, a bigwig in the War Office.

"I should warn you, he won't be best pleased."

"Then you can tell him that Malta has already saved your life," replied Max. "The seaplane you should have flown out on last night is missing."

"Missing?"

"Brought down near Pantelleria, we think. They have the radio direction finding and a squadron of 109s stationed there. We won't know for sure until we hear what Rome Radio has to say on the matter. They talk a lot of rubbish, of course, but we've grown pretty adept at panning for the small truths that matter to us."

Pemberton stared forlornly at his cup of coffee before looking up. "I had lunch with the pilot yesterday. Douglas. I knew him from Alex. Douglas Pitt."

Max had never heard of Pitt, but then the seaplane boys at Kalafrana Bay rarely mingled, not even with the other pilots. They were always on the go, running the two-thousand-mile gauntlet between Alexandria and Gibraltar at opposite ends of the Mediterranean, breaking the journey in Malta — the lone Allied outpost in a hostile Nazi-controlled sea.

"You'll get used to it."

Pemberton's eyes locked on to Max, demanding an explanation.

"Look, I'd be lying if I said casualty rates weren't running pretty high right now. People, they . . . well, they're here one day, gone the next."

When Pemberton spoke, there was a mild note of irritation in his tone. "That doesn't mean you have to stop remembering them."

*Well, actually it does,* thought Max. Because if you spent your time thinking about the ones who'd copped it, you wouldn't be able to function. In his first year he had written four heartfelt letters to the families of the three men and one woman he had known well enough to care for. He hadn't written any such letters in the past year.

"No, you're right, of course," he said.

Pemberton would find his own path through it, assuming he survived long enough to navigate one.

"So, tell me, what do you know about Malta?"

"I know about *Faith, Hope,* and *Charity.*"

Everyone knew about *Faith, Hope,* and *Charity;* the newspapers back home had made sure of that, enshrining the names of the three Gloster Gladiators in the popular imagination. The story had "courage in the face of adversity" written all over it, just what the home readership had required back in the summer of 1940. While Hitler had skipped across northern Europe as though it were his private playground, on a small island in the Mediterranean three obsolescent biplanes had been bravely pitting themselves against the full might of Italy's Regia Aeronautica, wrenched around the heavens by pilots barely qualified to fly them.

And so the myth was born. With a little assistance.

"Actually, there were six of them."

"Six?"

"Gloster Gladiators. And a bunch more held back for spares."

Pemberton frowned. "I don't understand."

"Three makes for a better story, and there were never more than three in the air at any one time, the others being unserviceable."

The names had been coined and then quietly disseminated by Max's predecessor, their biblical source designed to chime with the fervent Catholicism of the Maltese.

"It's part of what we do at the Information Office."

"You mean propaganda?"

"That's not a word we like to use."

"I was told you were independent."

"We are. Ostensibly."

Max detected a worrying flicker of youthful righteousness in the other man's gaze. Six months back, he might have retreated and allowed Pemberton to figure it out for himself, but with Malta's fortunes now hanging by a thread, there was no place for such luxuries. He needed Pemberton firmly in the saddle from day one.

"Look, none of us is in the business of dragging people's spirits down. The Huns and Eye-ties have cornered that market."

He manufactured a smile, which Pemberton politely mirrored.

"You're evidently a bright young man, so I'm going to save you some time and tell you the way it is."

He opened with a history lesson, partly because Pemberton's file made mention of a respectable second-class degree in that subject from Worcester College, Oxford.

It was best, Max explained, to take the stuff in the newspapers back home about "loyal little Malta" with a pinch of circumspection. At the outbreak of hostilities with Italy in June 1940, when that sawdust Caesar Mussolini threw his hand in with Hitler, Malta was a far more divided island than the British press had ever acknowledged. The Maltese might have offered themselves up to the British Empire back in

28

1800, but almost a century and a half on, there were many who wanted out of the relationship, their hearts set on independence from the mother country. Seated across the table from these nationalists in the Council of Government were the constitutionalists, defenders of the colonial cross. Not only were they superior in number, but they had the backing of the Strickland family, who effectively controlled the Maltese press, putting out two dailies: the *Times of Malta* and its vernacular sister paper, *Il-Berqa.*

The war had played into the hands of the Strickland loyalists. The first Italian bombs to rain down onto the island severely dented the affinity felt by many of the Maltese for their nearest neighbors, a short hop to the north across the blue waters of the Mediterranean. But neither were the Maltese fools — far from it. They could spot a lie at a hundred paces, and many were wary of the Strickland rags, which they knew to be slanted toward the British establishment.

Hence the Information Office, whose *Daily Situation Report* and *Weekly Bulletin* offered up for public consumption a cocktail of cold, factual, and apparently unbiased news. In essence, the *Daily Situation Report* was a scorecard. How many of their bombs had found their marks? And how many planes had both they and we lost in the course of that day's raids? There were gray areas, of course, not least of all the often-conflicting claims made by the RAF and the artillery. In the wild confusion of a heavy raid on Grand Harbour, who could say with absolute certainty that a diving Stuka had been brought down by ack-ack fire and not the Hurricane on its tail?

Mediating such disputes had ruined many a pleasant evening for Max, all thanks to the late situation report — an update to the five o'clock report — which he was expected to put out at ten forty-five P.M. He'd lost count of the number of times he'd been summoned to the phone in the middle of an enjoyable dinner party to listen to the tedious bleatings of HQ Royal Artillery and RAF Intelligence, each so eager to stake their claim to another precious scalp.

Max thought it best to hold this information back from Pemberton. He certainly didn't explain that the main reason he'd lobbied the lieutenant governor's office for an assistant to take over the editorship of the *Daily Situation Report* was so that his own evenings might remain uncluttered by such irritations.

Instead, he played up his own onerous

30

workload, spelling out in some detail the other activities of the Information Office: the monitoring of enemy radio stations in the Mediterranean; the translation of BBC broadcasts and speeches by the governor into Maltese; and the production of light entertainments, which, along with the relentless stream of news items, were put out over the island's Rediffusion system.

"Gilding the pill," said Pemberton distractedly, when Max was finished.

"Nicely put."

"But not propaganda."

"Perish the thought."

"Well, not ostensibly."

"Never ostensibly. Before the week's out, I'll be up in front of the finance committee fighting to justify the additional expense to the department of one Edward Pemberton."

No lie there. Max would have to make his case, then the Maltese representatives would haul him over the coals, and then they would agree to his demands. In its own small way, this predictable little theater, played out with tedious regularity, laid bare one of the grander themes of colonial administration: allow them a voice, then tell them what to say.

"I think I get the picture."

"Excellent. Now, where are you staying?"

"The Osbourne."

"We'll have to find you more permanent digs. There's a drinks party later. It would pay for you to show your face. We might be able to rustle up something for you."

"Sounds good."

"If you don't mind riding pillion, I can pick you up around five."

"You have a motorcycle?"

"Technically, it's three motorcycles, held together with wire and willpower."

Pemberton flashed his film-star smile.

*Yes*, thought Max, *Rosamund will be most pleased with her unexpected guest.*

She was.

Her hand even went to her hair when she greeted them at the door, something it had never done for Max.

The house sat near the top of Prince of Wales Road in Sliema, just shy of the police station. It was typical of many Maltese homes in that the unassuming façade gave no indication of the treasures that lay behind it. The wooden entrance door was flanked by two windows, with three more windows on the upper floor united by a stone balcony overhanging the street. Perfectly symmetrical, the front of the house was unadorned except for a brass nameplate set in the white stucco — *Villa Marija* — and a small glazed terra-cotta roundel above the entrance, which showed a disconsolate-looking Virgin clutching her child.

Rosamund was wearing an oyster-gray satin evening gown, and once her hand had tugged self-consciously at her auburn locks, Max made the introductions. Rosamund offered a slender hand, drawing Pemberton inside as they shook, which permitted her to fire an approving look over his shoulder at Max as she did so.

The entrance hall was cool and cavernous, impeccably decked out with antique furniture. A Persian rug sprawled at their feet, and a handful of colorful impressionistic paintings hung from the walls. Pemberton looked mildly stunned.

"Tell me, Edward, you aren't by any chance related to Adrian Pemberton, are you?"

"If he lives in Chepstow Crescent, then he's my cousin, I'm afraid."

"Why should you be afraid?"

"You obviously haven't heard."

"No, but I can't wait."

She hooked her arm through his, steering him across the drawing room toward the large walled garden at the rear of the house.

"Has he done something terribly wicked?

I do hope he's done something terribly wicked. It would bear out all my suspicions about him."

Max dumped his scuffed leather shoulder bag onto the divan and followed them outside.

Rosamund had three rules when it came to her "little get-togethers." The first was that she personally greeted everyone at the door. The second was that it was unforgivably rude to speculate about the source of the copious quantities of spirits on offer, when it was barely possible to locate a bottle of beer on the island. The third rule stated quite simply that there was to be no "talking shop" after the first hour, to which end she would ring a small handbell at the appointed time.

"All week I get nothing from Hugh but barrages and Bofors and Junker 88s. For a few small hours, I'd like to talk about something else, and I'm sure you all would too."

Hugh was her husband, a lieutenant colonel in the Royal Artillery. A mathematician of some standing before the war, Hugh had worked out the intricate calculations behind the coordinated box barrage over Grand Harbour — an impressive feat, and one that had seen him elevated to the position of senior staff officer at RA HQ. Though he was in his early forties, he looked considerably older, which played to his private passion — the theater — making him eligible for a host of more senior roles, which he scooped up uncontested every time the Malta Amateur Dramatic Club put on one of their plays. He was always trying to get Max to audition for some token part to make up the numbers: butler, chauffeur, monosyllabic house guest.

While Rosamund abandoned her first rule in order to parade her new catch around the garden, Max made for the drinks table in the grateful shade beneath one of the orange trees. True to form, there was no one to pour the drinks. It wouldn't be good for relations if the Maltese staff were to witness the excesses of their brothers in suffering. Max was concocting a whisky and soda when he heard a familiar voice behind him.

" 'Ah, thou honeysuckle villain.' "

*Henry the Fourth,*" Max responded, without turning.

"Not good enough, and you know it."

Max swiveled to face Hugh, whose forehead, as ever, was beaded with perspiration. It was an old and slightly tedious game of theirs. Hugh liked to toss quotations at him, usually Shakespeare, but not always.

*"King Henry the Fourth, Part II,"* said Max.

"Damn."

"Mistress Quickly to Falstaff. I studied it at school."

"Double damn. That makes three in a row."

"But only twenty-two out of thirty-eight."

Hugh gave a little chortle. "Glad to see I'm not the only one keeping score."

"Speaking of scores, congratulations on your century."

"Yes, quite a month. One hundred and two, all told."

"One hundred and one; 249 Squadron are claiming the Stuka over Ta' Qali yesterday afternoon."

"Bloody typical."

"Let them have it. Their heads are down right now."

"Not for much longer."

Max hesitated. "So the rumors are true."

"What's that, old man?"

"They're sending us another batch of Spitfires."

"Couldn't possibly say — it's top secret."

"Then I'll just have to ask Rosamund."

Hugh laughed. His wife had a reputation for being "genned up" on everything. No news, however trivial, slipped through

Rosamund's net. Given her connections across the services, it was quite possible that she knew near on as much as the governor himself. The fact that she had cultivated a close friendship with His Excellency — or "H.E.," as she insisted on referring to him — no doubt boosted her store of knowledge.

"I'll be right back," said Hugh, grabbing a bottle. "Damsel in distress over by the bougainvillea. Trevor Kimberley's better half. A bit on the short side, but easy on the eye. And thirsty."

"We like them thirsty."

" 'Thou honeyseed rogue.' "

*"King Henry the Fourth, Part II."*

"Doesn't count," said Hugh, disappearing with the bottle.

Max turned back to the drinks table and topped off his glass. Hugh was right; April had been quite a month — the darkest yet. The artillery might have knocked down more than a hundred enemy aircraft, but that was largely due to the more frequent and promiscuous raids. The figures were in, and the Luftwaffe had flown a staggering ninety-six hundred sorties against the island in April, almost double the number for March, which itself had shattered all previous records. The lack of any meaningful competition from the boys in blue had also

37

contributed to the artillery's impressive bag. There weren't many pilots who'd logged more than a few hours of operational flying time all month, thanks to the glaring lack of serviceable Spitfires and Hurricanes. Even when the airfields at Ta' Qali, Luqa, and Hal Far pooled their resources, you were still looking at less than ten planes. The pilots were used to taking to the air with the odds mightily stacked against them — things had never been any different on Malta, and you rarely heard the pilots complain — but what could a handful of patched-up, battle-scarred crates really hope to achieve against a massed raid of Junker 88s with a covering fighter force of sixty?

Things might have been less dispiriting if a large flock of spanking new Spits hadn't flown in just ten days before — forty-six in all, fresh from Greenock in Scotland by way of Gibraltar. The U.S. Navy's aircraft carrier USS *Wasp* had seen them safe as far as the waters off Algiers, and the fly-off had gone without a hitch, all but two of the batch making it to Malta on the long-range fuel tanks. It had seemed too good to be true. And it was. Field Marshal Kesselring, sitting safely in Sicily, was no fool. He had obviously got wind of the reinforcement flight and had figured it best to wait for the aircraft to land before making his move. Within three days of their arrival almost half of the new Spitfires had been destroyed, and the rest had been put out of action by the Luftwaffe's intensive carpet bombing of the airfields.

Kesselring had his man on the ropes and was going for the knockout. He knew it; they knew it. Because without fighter aircraft to challenge the Luftwaffe's aerial dominance, there was little hope of any supply convoys getting through. And if that didn't happen very soon, the guns would fall silent and the island would starve. Invasion, an imminent threat for months now, would inevitably follow.

Christ, it was unthinkable. *So, best not to think about it,* Max told himself, topping off his glass once more and turning to survey the garden.

He found himself face-to-face with Mitzi.

She had crept up on him unannounced and was regarding him with a curious and slightly concerned expression, her startling green eyes reaching for his, a stray ray of sunlight catching her blond hair. Not for the first time, he found himself silenced by her beauty.

"What were you thinking?" she asked.

"Nothing important."

"Your shoulders were sagging. You looked . . . deflated."

"Not anymore."

"Flatterer."

"It's true."

"If it's true, then why didn't you even look for me?"

"I did."

"I was watching you from the moment you arrived."

"You were talking to that bald chap from Defense Security over by the bench."

"Well, I must say, you have excellent peripheral vision."

"That's what my sports master used to say. It's why he stuck me in the center of the midfield."

"You don't really expect me to talk about football, do you?"

"When Rosamund rings her bell, we might have no choice."

A slow smile broke across her face. "My God, I've missed you," she said softly and quite unexpectedly.

The desire in her voice was palpable, almost painful to his ears.

"You're breaking the rules," said Max.

"Damn the rules."

"You're forgetting — you were the one who made the rules."

"Self-pity doesn't suit you, Max."

"It's the best I can come up with under the circumstances."

"Now you're being abstruse." She handed him her empty glass. "Mix me another, will you?"

"Remind me."

"Don't be ridiculous."

"Bandits at one o'clock," he said in a whisper.

He had spotted them approaching over her shoulder: Hugh with Trevor Kimberley's dark and pretty wife in tow.

"Oh, I don't know," Mitzi sighed volubly. "Another gin and French."

Max took her glass. "So where's Lionel? Out on patrol?"

Hugh was within earshot now. "Be careful, old chap. Asking questions like that can land a man in deep water."

"Hello, Margaret," said Max, ignoring him.

Margaret Kimberley nodded benignly and maybe a little drunkenly.

"I mean," Hugh persisted, "why would you want to know the details of what our noble submariners are up to?"

"Besides, I'm hardly the person to ask," said Mitzi. "Lionel doesn't tell me anything. One day he's gone, then one day he's back;

41

that's all I know."

"It's all any of us needs to know."

"Trevor tells me nothing," chipped in Margaret.

Hugh peered down at her. "That, my dear, is because your Trevor does next to nothing for most of the time. Take it from me as his commanding officer."

"Somehow, Hugh, I can't think of you as a commanding officer," Mitzi chimed, a playful glint in her eye. "A genial one, maybe, and slightly inept, but not a commanding one."

Margaret's hand shot to her mouth to stifle a laugh, which drew an affronted scowl from Hugh.

"Bang goes Trevor's promotion," said Max, to more laughter.

A little while later the ladies left together for the far end of the garden. Max fought to ignore the lazy sway of Mitzi's slender hips beneath her cotton print dress.

*"Entre nous,"* said Hugh, considerably less abashed about admiring the view, "all the subs will be gone for good within a week or so."

"Really?"

"Well, you've seen the pasting they've been taking down at Lazaretto Creek. And since Wanklyn came a cropper . . ."

The loss of the *Upholder* a couple of weeks back had rocked the whole garrison, right down to the man on the street. Subs had been lost before, subs driven by good men known to all, men who had once lit up the bar at the Union Club and whose bones were now resting somewhere on the seabed. "Wankers" Wanklyn was different, though. A tall, soft-spoken Scotsman with a biblical beard, he'd been modest in the way that only the truly great can afford to be. With well over one hundred thousand tons of enemy shipping under his belt and a Victoria Cross on his chest, he'd exuded a quiet invincibility that others had fed off, had drawn strength from. Not one of his peers had begrudged him his star status because he'd never once played to it; he'd just got on with the job. And now he was gone, sent to the bottom, a mere human being after all.

As the information officer, Max had been the first to learn of the *Upholder*'s fate. The announcement had been buried away in the transcript of an Italian broadcast — a brief mention of a nameless submarine destroyed in an engagement off Tripoli. Max had made some discreet inquiries, enough to narrow the field to the *Upholder,* and then he had sat on the news for a couple of days.

Yes, he had wanted Wanklyn to prove him wrong, he had wanted to see the Maltese packing the bastions again, cheering the *Upholder* home, straining to see if there were any new chevrons stitched to the Jolly Roger she was flying. But he had known in his bones that it wasn't going to happen. He had known that what he needed was a couple of days to figure out how to play it, how to soften the blow for his readers and listeners.

But that was then, and this was now, and while he understood that pulling the subs off the island might be the judicious thing to do, he wasn't thinking about his job and how he was going to break the news on the island. He was thinking about Mitzi. If the subs were really leaving, then she would be too; posted elsewhere with her husband. Where would they end up? Alexandria, probably. He wrestled with the notion — separated from Mitzi by nigh on a thousand miles of water — but it was too big and unwieldy to get a grip on.

Hugh misconstrued his silence as professionalism. "Mum's the word, but I thought I should tip you the wink."

"Thanks, Hugh. I appreciate it."

"You'll find a way to present it in a positive light; you always do." He rested a hand on Max's shoulder. "Now go and join the other renegades in the crow's nest. Freddie and Elliott are already up there. No Ralph, though — he called earlier to say he can't get away."

Max did as he was told, eager for the distraction of his two friends, the chance to throw a blanket over his confused feelings and put Mitzi out of his mind. Villa Marija had been occupied by a naval officer before the war, and its large flat roof, still referred to as the crow's nest, was where the younger crowd generally gathered to flap and caw. Anything under the age of thirty was deemed to be young, and you were never quite sure what you were going to find when you stepped from the stairwell into the glare.

There was usually a pleasing smattering of adolescent daughters in colorful home-stitched frocks, still coming to terms with their new breasts, which they wore with a kind of awkward pride. Circling them, inevitably, would be the younger pilots, barely more than boys but their speech already peppered with RAF slang. They were always taking a view on things — a good view, a dim view, an outside view, a ropy view — or accusing one another of "shooting a line." Enemy bombers were "big jobs," enemy fighters "little jobs." The cockpit was their "office," and they never landed, they "pancaked." The thing they feared most in a flap was being bounced by a gaggle of little jobs from up-sun.

Sure enough, the pilots were there, a bevy of slender young things with flushed complexions hanging on their every word. Others hovered nearby, one ear on the tales of doughty deeds. The airmen were the only ones in the garrison capable of carrying the battle to the enemy, and their stories offered a tonic against the daily round of passive resistance.

Freddie and Elliott were at the far end of the roof terrace. Freddie was making good use of a large pink gin, his face a picture of evident distaste at whatever it was that the tall American was telling him. Max pushed his way through the throng toward his friends.

"Gentlemen."

"Ah, Maximillian," said Elliott. "Just in time."

"For what?"

"A little conundrum I was posing to Freddie here."

"Is that what you call it?" Freddie grimaced.

"Well, it sure as hell is for their commanding officers."

"Sounds intriguing," said Max.

"It rapidly becomes disgusting," Freddie replied.

Elliott laughed. "I hadn't figured you for an old prude."

"It's got nothing to do with prudishness," Freddie said, bristling. "It's a question of . . . well, morality."

"Ah, morality . . ."

"To say nothing of the law."

"Ah, the law," Elliott parroted, with even more skepticism.

"You trained as a lawyer. You must have some respect for the law."

"Sure I do. You don't want to screw with an institution that can send an innocent man to the electric chair." Elliott turned to Max before Freddie's frustration could shape itself into a response. "You want to hear it?"

"Fire away."

"It's very simple. You're a wing commander taking a break from it all up at the pilots' rest camp on Saint Paul's Bay. You know it? Sure you do, from when Ralph was wounded."

"I do."

"Then you can picture it. It's late and, okay, you're a bit tight. But, hey, who wouldn't be, after all you've been through

47

these past months? Anyway, you're feeling good and you're looking for your room. And you find your room. Only it isn't your room. It's someone else's room. And that someone else is in what you think is your bed with someone else."

"You're losing me."

"Stay lost," was Freddie's advice.

"There are two guys in the bed, okay? And they're, well, I don't know how to put it. . . ."

"I think I get your meaning."

"Of course you do. You went to an English boarding school."

"As did you," said Freddie, "in case you'd forgotten."

"And a sorry dump it was too. Anyway, they're good men, officers, both of them. One's in your squadron. The other's not, but you know him. And he's a first-class pilot, reliable, what you Brits would call a 'press-on' type." Elliott paused. "What do you do?"

"What do I do?"

"What do you do?"

"Well, I order them to desist at once."

Elliott laughed. "I think you can assume they *desisted* the moment you opened the goddamn door. Do you report them?"

"Report them?"

"To the air officer commanding. It's not a question of morality, or the law, or even of taste. I mean, I've never felt the need to place my penis in another man's dung —"

"Oh Christ," Freddie blurted into his gin.

"But it doesn't stop me from being able to make a judgment on the situation."

Max thought on it. "I don't report them."

"Why not?"

"Morale. A squadron's like a family."

"You're ready to lie to your family?"

"No. Yes. I suppose. If the situation calls for it."

"Go on," said Elliott. "What else, aside from morale?"

"Well, the two individuals in question, of course. They'd be packed off home, and everyone would know why. It would leak out."

"An unfortunate turn of phrase, under the circumstances."

"Oh, for God's sake, Elliott!" exclaimed Freddie.

Elliott ignored him. "Interesting," he said. "Three differing views. Freddie said he'd report them, you're a no, and I'm for reporting them."

"I thought you said three."

"There's a difference between me and Freddie. He's a moralist. Me, I'm a pragmatist. I'd report them, but only cos if I didn't and word got out that I hadn't, then it'd be *my* head on the block."

"So what does that make me?" asked Max.

"That makes you a sentimentalist," was the American's sure-footed response.

"Oh, come on —"

"Relax. There are worse things to be than a sentimentalist."

"Yeah," said Freddie, "you should try being a moralist."

It was good to hear Freddie crack a joke. He had seemed strangely withdrawn, somehow not himself. Max was in a position to judge. They had been firm friends, the best of friends, for almost two years now, and in that time he'd learned to read Freddie's rare down moods: the faint clouding in the cobalt-blue eyes, the slight tightening of the impish grin. He still looked that way now, even after the laughter had died away and the conversation had turned to Ralph, the missing member of their gang. Ralph was a pilot with 249 Squadron at Ta' Qali, a burly and garrulous character who had taken the squadron's motto to heart one too many times: *Pugnis et calcibus* — "With Fists and Heels." Elliott had come late to the party, materializing as if from nowhere around Christmas, hot on the heels of Pearl Harbor and America's entry into the war, but in four short months he'd stitched himself into the fabric of their little brotherhood lorded over by Hugh. He'd even got them all playing poker.

Elliott had a natural ear for scandal and was recounting a lurid story he'd heard from Ralph involving a chief petty officer's wife and a Maltese gardener when the tinkle of Rosamund's bell rang around the rooftop.

"Most of you know what this means," she announced from the top of the steps. "Turn your minds and your talk to higher matters, to life and to art and, I don't know, past loves and future plans."

"But I was just hitting my stride."

"My dear Elliott, I doubt it was anything more than mere gossip."

"True, but of the most salacious kind."

"Then be sure to search me out before you leave."

This drew a few chuckles from the assembled company. These died suddenly as the plaintive wail of the air-raid siren broke the air.

They had all been expecting it. Breakfast, lunch, and cocktail hour — you could almost set your wristwatch by the Germans and their Teutonic timekeeping.

They turned as one toward Valetta. From the high ground of Sliema, Marsamxett Harbour was spread out beneath them like a map, its lazy arc broken by the panhandle causeway connecting Manoel Island, with its fort and submarine base, to the mainland. In the background, Valetta reared majestically from the water, standing proud on her long peninsula, thrusting toward the open sea. Beyond the city, out of sight, lay the ancient towns and deepwater creeks of Grand Harbour, home to the naval dockyards, or what remained of them.

One of the more eagle-eyed pilots was the first to make out the flag being raised above the Governor's Palace in Valetta.

"Big jobs," he announced.

"There's a surprise."

"Where do you think they're headed?"

"The airfields, probably Ta' Qali."

"The dockyards are due a dose."

It was a strange time, this lull before the inevitable storm, the seven or so minutes it took the enemy aircraft to make the trip from Sicily. All over the island people would be hurrying for the underground shelters they had hewn from the limestone rock, the same rock with which they had built their homes, soft enough for saws and planes when quarried, but which soon hardened in the Mediterranean sun.

Had Malta been blanketed with forests, had the Maltese chosen to build their homes of wood, then the island would surely have capitulated by now. Stone buildings might crumble and pulverize beneath bombs, but they didn't catch fire. And it was fire that did the real damage, spreading like quicksilver through densely populated districts, of which there were many on Malta. The island was small — seventeen miles from top to toe, and only nine at its widest point — but its teeming population numbered more than a quarter of a million. Towns and villages bled into one another to form sprawling conurbations ripe for ruin, and while they had suffered terribly, the devastation had always remained localized.

In the end, though, it was the underground shelters — some of them huge, as big as barracks — that had kept the casualty rates so low. The Maltese simply descended into the earth at the first sign of danger, taking their prayers and a few prized possessions with them. Max liked to think of it as an inborn urge. The island was honeycombed with grottoes, caves, and catacombs where their ancestors had sought refuge in much the same way long before Christ walked the earth or the Egyptians raised their pyramids. The threat might now be of a different nature, but the impulse remained the same.

He could remember running this theory past Mitzi on their first meeting. And he could remember her response.

"Once a troglodyte, always a troglodyte."

She had said it in that mildly mocking way of hers, which he had misread at the time as haughtiness.

"Have I offended you?" she asked.

"Not at all."

"I'm sorry. It's a lovely theory. I've always loved it."

The subtext was plain: don't think for a moment that you're the first person to whom it has occurred.

He knew now that she had been sparring with him, playfully batting his pretentiousness straight back at him to see how he reacted. He had failed that first test, lapsing into silence, obliging her to end his suffering.

"But to tell you the truth, I'd love it more if I didn't spring from a long line of Irish potato pickers."

The memory of her words brought a smile to his face.

"We're about to have seven kinds of shit knocked out of us, and you're smiling?"

Elliott remarked.

"I think we're safe."

Everyone else did too, judging from the number of people abandoning the garden for the grandstand view of the crow's nest. Max spotted young Pemberton among the stream of souls pouring onto the roof. Too polite to question the behavior of the other guests, he nevertheless looked very ill at ease. Who could blame him? Common sense dictated that they all seek shelter. A year back they would have done so, but somehow they were beyond that now. Exhaustion had blunted their fear, replacing it with a kind of resigned apathy, a weary fatalism that you were aware of only when you saw it reflected back at you in the shifty expression of a newcomer.

Max caught Pemberton's nervous eye and waved him over.

"Who's that?" Freddie inquired.

"Our latest recruit, bound for Gib when we snapped him up."

"Handsome bastard," said Elliott. "There'll be flutterings in the dovecote."

"Go easy on him. He's all right."

"Sure thing," said the American, not entirely convincingly.

Max made the introductions, with Pemberton saluting Freddie and Elliott in turn.

"So what's the gen, Captain?" Elliott demanded with exaggerated martial authority.

"The gen, sir?"

"On the raid, Captain, the goddamn air raid."

"I'm afraid I'm new here, sir."

"New! What the hell good is new with Jerry and Johnny Eye-tie on the warpath?"

"Ignore him," said Max. "He's having you on."

"Yank humor," chipped in Freddie.

"And that's the last time you salute him."

Elliott stabbed a finger at his rank tabs. "Hey, these are the real deal."

"Elliott's a liaison officer with the American military," Max explained. "Whatever that means."

"None of us has ever figured out quite what it means."

Tilting his head at Pemberton, Elliott said in a conspiratorial voice, "And if *you* do, be sure to let me know."

Max's laugh was laced with admiration, and maybe a touch of jealousy. Anyone who knew Elliott had felt the pull of his boisterous American charm. It was easy to think you'd been singled out for special attention, until you saw him work his effortless way into the affections of another.

"Freddie here's a medical officer," said Max.

"Never call him a doctor. He hates it when you call him a doctor," Elliott put in.

"He spends his time stitching people like us back together."

Freddie waggled his pink gin at Pemberton. "Well, not all my time."

"Don't be fooled by the handsome boyish looks. If you're ever in need of a quick amputation, this is your man." Elliott clamped a hand on Freddie's shoulder. "Lieutenant Colonel Frederick Lambert, a whiz with both saw and scalpel. His motto: What's an Arm or a Leg Between Friends?"

Freddie was used to Elliott presenting him as some medieval butcher, and he smiled indulgently, confident of his reputation, his renown.

Pemberton acquitted himself admirably during the brief interrogation that ensued. He judged his audience well, painting an amusing and self-deprecating portrait of his time in Alexandria, his meagre contribution to the war effort to date.

It was then that the first arms started to be raised, fingers pointing toward the north, toward Saint Julian's Bay, Saint George's Bay, and beyond.

An unnatural silence descended upon the

terrace, everyone's ears straining for the discordant drone of approaching aircraft.

"You're about to witness a very one-sided show," said Freddie. "Try not to let it get you down."

He wasn't joking. The artillery had just been rationed to fifteen rounds per gun per day. A Bofors could fire off its quota in all of seven seconds.

The enemy seemed to know this. There was something uncharacteristically loose about the first wave of fighters staining the sky, a lack of the usual German rigor when it came to formation flying. Like a boxer in his prime swaggering toward the ring, the adversary was confident.

A couple of the big guns barked an early defiance, and a few desultory puff-balls of flak appeared around the Me109Fs, which had already begun to break for their preordained targets. They swooped in flocks, birds of ill omen, the real danger following close behind them.

A great staircase of Junker 88 bombers came out of the north, fringed with a covering force of yet more fighters.

"Christ," muttered Freddie.

"Holy shit," said Elliott.

*Poor sods,* thought Max.

It was clear now that the airfields had been

singled out for attention: Ta' Qali, Luqa, Hal Far, maybe even the new strips at Safi and Qrendi. They all lay some way inland, beyond Valetta and the Three Cities, strung out in a broken line, their runways forming a twisted spine to the southern half of the island.

The 88s shaped up for their shallow bombing runs, and a token splatter of shell bursts smudged the sky. Arcing lines of tracer fire from a few Bofors joined the fray. From this distance the Bofors appeared to be doing little more than tickling the under-bellies of the bombers, but a shout suddenly went up.

"Look, a flamer!"

Sure enough, an 88 was deviating from its course, streaming black smoke. It climbed uncertainly toward the north, heading for home. This would normally have been the cue for a Spitfire to pounce on the stricken aircraft and finish it off, but the handful of fighters they had seen clawing for height just minutes before had probably been vectored away from the island for their own safety. It was easy to see why. The carpet bombing was well under way now, great pil-lars of smoke and dust rising into the sky, reaching for the lowering sun.

They all stared in silent sympathy at the

remote spectacle. Earlier in the year, Max had been caught in a raid at Ta' Qali, one of the mid-afternoon specials the Germans liked to throw in from time to time. He had spent twenty minutes lying as flat to the ground as nature would allow him in a ditch that bounded the airfield. There had been other close calls in the past couple of years — he still bore the odd scar to prove it — but nothing that even approached the deranging terror of his time in that ditch. His greatest fear at the time, strangely, had been of choking to death on the cloud of sickly yellow-gray dust, talcum-powder fine, that had enveloped everything, blotting out the sun, turning day into night. The ground beneath him had bucked like a living thing, and all around him the air had rung to the tune of flying splinters, a lethal symphony of rock and metal overlaid by more obvious notes: the whistle and shriek of falling bombs, the thump and crump of explosions, the staccato bark of the Bofors firing back blindly, and the screams of the diving Stukas.

His hearing had never fully recovered, and he suspected that something essential within him had been changed that day, almost as if he were a machine that had been rewired. It still functioned, though not quite as it had before.

He felt a light touch on his arm. It was Freddie.

"I need to talk to you," he said in a low, confidential voice. "Not here. Alone."

"Okay."

"How's tomorrow morning?"

Max nodded.

"Can you come to the Central Hospital?"

"What time?"

"Early. How does eight sound?"

"Barely acceptable."

"Meet me at the mortuary."

Max was obliged to curb his curiosity. Elliott had drifted toward the parapet for a better view of the raid, but he now turned to them and said, "Looks like old Zammit's got himself a new gun."

Vitorin Zammit lived in the house directly across the street. Well into his sixties, he was a slight and vaguely comical character who had been a regular dinner guest at Villa Marija until the death of his wife the year before. He had amassed a small fortune exporting lace, a business that had allowed him to travel the world widely, and he spoke impeccable English in the way that only a foreigner can. His wife's passing had hit him hard, and although she had been brought down by the same diabetes that had plagued her for years, he held the enemy unreservedly to blame. He now kept his own company, when he wasn't caught up in the activities of the Sliema Home Guard Volunteers, through whose ranks he had risen rapidly to become something of a leading light.

He owned a pistol, and when a raid was in progress, he was often to be found on his roof terrace taking potshots at the planes. Not only was this a futile gesture, it was in flagrant breach of the regulations. He should have known better, and he probably did, but no one begrudged him his bit of sport. If anyone took exception, Hugh invariably ensured that they came to see things differently.

Sometimes Zammit wore his uniform, sometimes a suit. He never went into battle in his shirtsleeves. Today he was wearing a black suit and a home guard armband, and he prowled around his roof terrace like some dark ghost, eyes on the skies, apparently oblivious to the large crowd gathered on the neighboring rooftop. Instead of his usual pistol, he carried a rifle in his hand.

"Is that a Lee-Enfield?" asked Freddie.

"Might just as well be a goddamn broomstick for all the good it's going to do him," replied Elliott.

The last of the bombers were making their runs now, dropping to four or five thousand feet before unloading over the airfields. Resistance was minimal, and they climbed safely away with a covey of fighters assigned to see them safely home. High above, all around, 109s blackened the sky like bees, keeping a wary guard. Their job done, the island's artillery all but spent, they would soon descend and begin picking over the carcass, making low-level attacks on targets of opportunity. If there was a time to be scared, now was it. Even a residential district like Sliema was fair game.

Knowing this, a few people started to drift below. Most stood their ground, though, eager to see how things would play out. Freddie made a drinks run downstairs. By the time he returned with their glasses, the dockyards in Grand Harbour were under attack, the enemy fighters rising into view behind Valetta like rocketing pheasants as they pulled up out of their dives. They couldn't hope to inflict much real damage with their cannon and machine-gun fire, but they were making a point. Max had heard from Ralph that a 109 had even made a touch-and-go landing at Ta' Qali the other day, rubbing their noses in it.

Today, pleasingly, this arrogance came at

a price. A 109 banking over Fort Saint Elmo appeared to stagger, then its starboard wing dipped sharply and it spun away. There was no question of the pilot baling out at that height, and the aircraft hit the water, throwing up a white feather of spume near the harbor entrance.

"Welcome to Malta, you sonofabitch," said Elliott darkly, as the cheers resounded around them.

Moments later, a couple of fighters swooped down onto Marsamxett Harbour from the direction of Floriana, flying tight down on the water, setting themselves for a strafing run at the submarine base on Manoel Island. There were no subs to be seen; they had recently taken to sitting out the daylight hours on the harbor bottom.

"Macchis," said one of the young pilots.

He was right, they were Italian planes, blue Macchi 202s. If there had been any doubt, the showman-like flourish with which they rolled away after releasing a couple of savage bursts of cannon fire settled the question of their nationality. The Italians were known, and mocked, for their aerobatic flair. Both aircraft made a second pass, their guns churning up the water in neat straight lines as they bore down on the base. They pulled away in a climbing turn to the left, making off to the north, skimming over the stepped rooftops of Sliema.

Their course brought them straight toward Villa Marija, the roar of their engines building quickly to a painful pitch, almost deafening, but not so loud that it drowned out the report of the first rifle shot. Or the second.

Max turned in time to see Vitorin Zammit fire off his third shot, in time to see a portion of the lead Macchi's engine cowling fall away.

"My God, I think he hit it!" someone called.

Old Zammit had not only hit it, he had actually done some damage. The Macchi's engine coughed, clearing its throat, then coughed again, and again, misfiring badly now, a ribbon of black smoke snaking out behind it as it climbed toward Saint Julian's.

"Well, holy shit," said Elliott.

The trickle of smoke soon became a raging torrent, and the Macchi started to lose height, falling well behind its companion.

"Is it possible?" Freddie asked incredulously.

"Oh yes," replied Max. A number of enemy fighters had been brought down over the airfields by rifle fire since the long-suffering ground crews had been issued with

Lee-Enfields — a gesture intended to boost their morale. No one had expected them to actually hit anything.

It came to Max quite suddenly what he had to do. He glanced over at Vitorin Zammit, who was staring in dumb disbelief at his handiwork. Then he turned and took Pemberton by the arm, leading him off through the crowd.

"Where are we going?" asked the Information Office's newest recruit.

"To work."

He lay stretched out on the mattress, naked, staring at the ceiling and the dancing shadows thrown by the small pepper-tin lamp.

He raised his arm and examined it in the flickering light, flexing his elbow, his wrist, his fingers, enjoying the silent articulation of the joints, the play of muscle and sinew beneath the skin.

He was proud of his hands. Men didn't notice hands. Women did. His mother had. She had always praised him for his hands. Then again, kind words had come easily to her, maybe too easily for the compliments to have had any real value. She had scattered them about her like a farmer spreading seed from a sack.

He saw her now as a young woman: the blue of her wide-set eyes; the arched eyebrows, dark and dense, which she'd refused to pluck as other women did because Father had liked them just the way they were. Or so he'd said.

*My, you're looking handsome today.*

*I think that's the best I've ever heard you play the piano.*

*The best day of my life? When I gave birth to you.*

*You're the best boy in the world.*

She'd come from parents with low intellectual horizons, and she'd used words such as "best" a lot.

Maybe that's what lay at the heart of everything. She had never felt worthy of the world in which she'd found herself, not worthy of the man who had taken her by the hand and led her into Eden. *See all this? This is my world, but now it is yours too.*

But Eden didn't come cheap — she must have learned that early on — and she had chosen to repay cruelty with kindness. She was known for her kindness. It was what defined her in the eyes of others. No one was unworthy of her selfless ministrations.

He suspected now that some baser urge had lain behind her behavior: an instinct for survival. How could her husband possibly harm such a kind and decent person, such a good wife?

It hadn't worked, but she had kept the faith. It was hard to respect her for it, but at least it had shown a certain determination.

*You're the best boy in the world.*

He saw her now, ruffling his hair, smiling warmly down at him, her prominent incisors, the small white scar on her lower lip from the time Father had struck her with a shoe. And he saw what she was doing: one person looking to provide the love of two. The intentions had been good, if ultimately counterproductive. The more she had smothered him with maternal affection, the more Father had felt the need to counteract her "damned pampering" of him.

It was strange that she had never stopped heaping praise upon all and sundry, even after the accident, when there was no longer any need to do so. He also found it strange that she had never taken tweezers to those unruly eyebrows when she must surely have wanted to, when at last she could.

That's what annoyed him most, he realized — that even after Father was gone, he had managed to live on in her.

He lowered his arm to the mattress and smiled at this thought, a smile of pleasant surprise. When was the last time he had cared enough about anything to be annoyed by it?

It made him feel almost human.

# DAY TWO

Freddie was almost an hour late for their meeting at the mortuary. When he finally appeared, reeking of iodine, from the bowels of the hospital building, he seemed surprised to find Max still waiting for him.

"I thought you'd be gone."

"I heard what happened — of course I waited."

"Yes, a nasty business."

It certainly was. A passing orderly had explained the situation to Max. A wayward bomb had fallen well short of the dockyards during the early-morning raid and exploded at the entrance to a shelter in Marsa. Everyone had been safely inside by then, but it would have been far better for all of them if they'd stayed at home. The steel doors of the shelter had been blown in, and the Maltese not torn apart by the hail of metal had found themselves consumed by the ensuing fireball.

Freddie had obviously made an effort to scrub up after his labors, but had missed a couple of spots of blood on his cheek. Max tried his best to ignore them.

"I don't know how you do it."

"It's what I trained for." Freddie shrugged.

"Really? This?"

Freddie smiled weakly. "Well, not quite this." He fished a lighter and a packet of Craven "A"s from his pocket. "Sometimes I wish they'd just invade. Then it would all stop."

"If it stops here, it just gets worse in a lot of other places."

"I suppose."

They all knew the reasoning; there was no point in going over it again.

"Do you want to get some air?" asked Max.

"No. Let's get it over with." Freddie held out the packet of cigarettes.

Max raised his hand, declining the offer. "I've just put one out."

"Take one," said Freddie. "For the smell."

Max had been in hospitals before, but only ever to visit wounded friends. Those airy, spotless wards with their ordered rows of beds and their gruff thick-ankled nurses had nothing in common with the mortuary of

71

the Central Hospital.

The mortuary occupied a run of vast and gloomy ground-floor rooms. The windows were partially shuttered, allowing in just enough light to make identification possible. Corpses carpeted the tiled floors. Some of the bodies were covered, others not, and some weren't bodies at all.

"We're out of blankets, I'm afraid," said Freddie as they picked their way through the first room. He might just as well have been apologizing to a house guest, and his matter-of-factness went some way toward calming Max's nerves. An orderly in what must once have been a white coat was mopping the floor. He was young — too young, you couldn't help thinking, to be exposed to such sights. His tin pail screeched in protest as he maneuvered it around the floor with the mop. It was the only sound. The stench was indescribable.

The second room was almost as large as the first, and the thing Max noticed immediately was a pile of limbs stacked up in the corner like so much firewood. The next thing he noticed was a Maltese man emptying the contents of his stomach onto the floor. He was being held around the shoulders by a ragged old fellow in a threadbare suit emitting deep and sonorous sobs. They had evidently just identified the body at their feet, and an orderly looked on awkwardly, clipboard poised to register the details.

It was a pathetic sight, upsetting — two broken men bent over a broken body — and Max was relieved when Freddie led him through double swing-doors out of the charnel house and into a long corridor.

"There are so many."

"It's been a bad week. And coffins are hard to come by, so they lie here for days, backing up."

"Some of them are, well, remarkably intact."

"Blast victims, snuffed out by the shock wave. Although it often scalps them."

Their destination was a small room at the far end of the corridor. Aside from a wooden desk in the corner, the room was empty. Max's relief was short-lived, though; he hadn't spotted the gurney pushed up against the wall behind the door. A body lay on it — a woman, judging from the bare feet poking out from beneath the piece of tarpaulin that covered her.

"This is what you wanted to show me?"

"She was found yesterday morning in Marsa, lying in the street." He reached for the tarpaulin.

"Freddie, I'm not sure I . . ." He trailed off.

"There are some wounds, but I've cleaned them up."

"What's this all about? I don't understand."

"You will."

"Try telling me now."

He was already steeling himself against the long walk back past the silent ranks of damaged and dismembered corpses; the thought of scrutinizing one of them up close filled him with alarm and horror.

Freddie didn't release the tarpaulin. "Max, you're my friend, and I don't know who else to tell."

They looked at each other in silence. Then Max nodded and Freddie folded back the tarpaulin.

The girl was young, maybe eighteen or nineteen, with an innocent beauty that even the cold pallor of death couldn't erase. Her hair was long, straight, black as bitumen, and it framed an oval face that descended to an elfin chin. Her lips were large and surprisingly red. Lipstick, he realized. Which was odd. It was in short supply, and not many Maltese girls wore it at the best of times.

Freddie tilted her head to the right and

74

gently drew back her hair. A raw and ragged gash ran from beneath her right ear toward her collar bone, widening as it went.

"Christ . . ."

Freddie's hand delved beneath the tarpaulin and produced a jagged shard of metal, twisted and razor-edged. "Ack-ack shrapnel. It was still in her when she was brought in."

It was a common cause of injuries and deaths, the lethal hail of metal dropping back to earth from exploding artillery shells. You could hear the splinters tinkling merrily in the streets and on the rooftops whenever a raid was on, a deceptively harmless sound.

"She bled to death?"

"It looks that way."

"So?"

Freddie hesitated. "I think it was made to look that way."

"What do you mean?"

"I mean these . . . and these." Freddie raised her wrists in turn. The marks were faint, easy to miss.

"Rope burns?"

"Her hands weren't bound when she was found. And look at her nails."

They were long, painted red, and several of them were cracked or broken.

"She fought back. There's also some

75

bruising around her shoulders and her thighs. Also her labia."

What a horrible word. It struck Max, enough to extinguish all thoughts of carnality. It was about all he could think as he struggled to take in what Freddie was telling him.

"You think she was violated?"

"I *know* she was violated. And probably by the same man who then killed her."

"Freddie, come on. That's a leap too far."

"She's not the first."

"What?"

"There have been others, two others I've seen since the beginning of the year. Not like this, not exactly. One had been crushed by falling masonry; the other one had drowned."

"Drowned?"

There were many ways to die on Malta, but drowning wasn't the first that sprang to mind, certainly not since the beaches had been wired off against invasion.

"She fell into a collapsed cistern while walking home in the dark. At least, that's the way it looked. Both were sherry queens from the Gut."

"Sherry queens" was service slang for the Maltese dance hostesses who worked the bars and bawdy music halls that infested

76

the lower end of Strait Street in Valetta, a disreputable quarter dubbed the Gut.

"Jesus Christ, Freddie. You should have told someone."

"What makes you think I didn't? Apparently the matter is now in the hands of the appropriate authorities."

"Sounds like lieutenant governor's office speak."

"You should know."

He certainly did. The Information Office answered directly to the lieutenant governor and his coterie of self-important lackeys.

"So why am I here?"

"Because she had something on her that changes everything. Something in her hand. I had to pry it out. Rigor mortis had set in."

Freddie reached into the hip pocket of his khaki shorts and handed something to Max. It was a piece of material — a cloth shoulder tab, torn where it had been ripped from a uniform. Enough of it remained, though.

"Oh Christ," said Max.

"That's one way of putting it."

Max's apartment was a short walk from the hospital through the streets of Floriana. He passed a long line of women queuing for paraffin. There was some kind of scuffle taking place that involved a lot of raised voices.

Spotting Max approach, a rangy young woman with fire in her eyes appealed to him in accented English, "Tell her she wait like all of us."

"You have to wait," said Max, without breaking his stride or even turning to identify the culprit.

His indifference was rewarded with a bank of baleful glares and a couple of mumbled curses in Maltese. He ignored them, too numb to care.

He was still trying to process the information sprung on him by Freddie in the mortuary. Whichever way he came at it, it spelled big trouble. Freddie had taken a certain amount of persuading to keep his latest findings to himself, at least for a couple of days. It would give Max time to think the matter through properly, make a few inquiries. What those might be exactly, he wasn't yet sure. Things would become clearer once they knew who the girl was. Her absence couldn't go unnoticed for long. She probably had family and friends who even now were discussing the dread prospect of doing the rounds of the mortuaries.

Her makeup, the livid nail polish, everything pointed to her occupation. It also pointed to a pattern: three dance hostesses from the Gut — more, for all they knew —

not unlucky victims of the war but of a man who had violated them before killing them. And not just any man, a British serviceman, a submariner. And not just any submarine, the *Upstanding* — commanded by Lionel Campion, Mitzi's husband.

He felt in his pocket for the torn shoulder tab Freddie had recovered from the dead girl's clenched fist. Instinct had told him to ask for it, and instinct now told him to dispose of it immediately. With the proof gone, it would be Freddie's word against his. Was he willing to trade their friendship for the alternative, the unthinkable?

The Maltese had not wanted this war; it had been called down upon their heads. And their almost childlike faith in the ability of the British to defend them, to ultimately prevail against the forces of evil, had been tested to its limits by the gathering hell of the past few months. After two long years of siege, they knew the truth about their predicament. How could they not know? The truth had been fed to them to shore up their morale — a badge of honor to be worn with pride.

They knew by heart the words of praise heaped on them by Winston Churchill in the House of Commons (and they joked that they'd be happy to swap those words for a few more Spitfires or a shipload of sausages). They knew that King George VI had awarded them, all of them, the George Cross earlier in the month (and they admired the king's advisers for their judicious timing). But the fact remained: they were still cut off from the world, alone, surrounded by an enemy intent on starving them into submission and annihilating them from the air. Twice the tonnage of bombs dropped on London during the worst twelve months of the Blitz had rained down on their heads in the last two months alone. It was an extraordinary statistic that conferred on their little island home the dubious honor of being the most bombed patch of earth on the planet. Ever.

Remarkably, in spite of all this, they had barely wavered, making light of their trials. But what would happen if they thought for a moment that they were also fighting an enemy within? How would they react to the news that a British serviceman was picking off their daughters, using the war as a cloak for his crimes? It was impossible to say, but it would change everything in a moment.

As Max turned into Pietro Floriani Street, he drew to a halt. The building at the northern end of the street had taken a direct hit at the beginning of April, collapsing completely, taking much of the adjacent apartment block with it, shearing rooms in half, exposing their contents to the elements and the voyeuristic gaze of passersby — a sideboard pressed up against a drawing room wall hung with framed photographs; a towel still draped over the edge of a cast-iron bathtub; an effigy of the Virgin, which, miraculously, had not been toppled from its perch on the mantelpiece by the sudden disappearance of the other half of the room.

It brought to mind the architectural cross sections he used to run off, slicing through buildings to reveal the guts of his designs. For a fleeting moment he glimpsed himself perched on the high wooden stool, hunched over his drawing board, feverishly applying himself to the task. He wondered what had become of that well-meaning young man dreaming of a bright future in a top firm of architects. It seemed impossible to him that he could have traveled from that to this in such a brief time, from an airy studio in the Architectural Association to a Mediterranean bomb site, from enthusiastic student to cynical military official.

They were dangerous thoughts, the kind that built swiftly to an overwhelming flood, and he pushed them from him before they could.

He gazed at the piece of material in his hand and told himself that his friendship with Freddie wasn't at stake. Freddie had offered no resistance to his suggestion that he take the shoulder tab with him. If anything, he had seemed eager to rid himself of it. *Take this,* he was saying, *and do with it what you will, because I don't know what to do with it.*

Shunting his conscience to one side, Max glanced around him to check that he was alone. Then he tossed the piece of material away. It was lost in the heaped rubble of what used to be 35 Pietro Floriani Street.

He set off at a brisk pace, not wishing to dwell on his actions. At the end of his street, he returned the salutes of the scruffy mob of Maltese boys at their flag station.

"No worries, Joe!" they called.

It was about all the English they possessed, that and "Speetfire."

*"Allura,"* Max replied. No worries.

Many of them had older brothers who had been conscripted into the Royal Malta Artillery or the King's Own Malta Regiment. Eager to emulate their heroes, they had rigged a flagstaff from a toppled telegraph pylon. The moment the red ensign appeared above the Castille in Valetta, the boys hoisted their own scarlet rag for the benefit of their little corner of Floriana. Amazingly, they never abandoned their post, even during an air raid, although they often strayed onto the pitted patch of earth near the bastion wall to play football against the crew of the Bofors gun site — Manchester men who liked the ball at their feet and who weren't afraid to send a small child sprawling in the dust.

Max's third-floor apartment at the end of Vilhena Terrace afforded a bird's-eye view of these contests, and in the evening he would sometimes sit and observe the antics from his balcony, Grand Harbour and the Three Cities providing the backdrop. It was a corner apartment, and the other view, from the bedroom window, was to the northeast, across the open area of ground that separated Floriana from Valetta. Both towns occupied the peninsula, and both were well protected from the water by a bewilderment of bastions, but the mighty ditch on the landward side of Valetta proclaimed Floriana's role as a first line of defense. The Knights of Saint John had engineered things this way against the possibility of another Turkish invasion of the island, and, four centuries on, the residents of Floriana were still left with the slightly uneasy feeling that they were disposable, that even in retreat the gates of Valetta, the all-important citadel, might not be thrown open to them. As things had turned out, the Turks never recovered from their first failed assault on Malta — a mere stepping-stone to mainland Europe, or so they had assumed — and the impressive fortifications built by the knights had never been put to the test. Not till now. Now they were useless. What good were soaring battlements against an enemy who assaulted you from the air with bombs? All you could do was cower and pray. The cowering had helped a little, saved a few lives, but the prayers had fallen on deaf ears.

In the past month, German bombs had laid waste to much of what mattered in Valetta, obliging the governor to flee his palace for his summer residence at Verdala, and causing extensive damage to the Auberge de Castille, the military and administrative hub of the island. The various departments had scattered like chaff before a stiff wind, seeking shelter wherever they could. Max no longer walked to work in Valetta. The Information Office had been relocated twice, from the museum in the Auberge d'Italie to the old audit offices at the top of the general post office building, and then to Saint Joseph's, an orphanage for boys in

Fleur-de-Lys, up on the hill beyond Ham-run. It was ten minutes inland by motor-cycle on a good day, considerably more when the carburetor was clogged with rust from the old gas tank he'd been forced to scavenge from another machine.

He missed the bustle and activity of Val-etta, the snatched lunches with friends at the Union Club or Monico's, but there were far worse places to work than Saint Joseph's. An ancient palace where, according to local lore, Napoléon had stayed during his brief dominion over the island, it had a spacious courtyard at its heart, planted with cypresses, which lent it the calm air of a convent or monastery. The rooms were large and light, the residents welcoming and unobtrusive. To ease their passage into the world, the orphan boys were taught a variety of skills and professions, one of which was printing, and a modern printing press filled a room on the ground floor of the south wing. This was the real reason the Information Office had been assigned to Saint Joseph's; it allowed them to run off their daily and weekly bulletins for distribution around the island. The close proximity of the lieutenant governor's office, which had been moved to the Vincenzo Bugeja Conservatory right next door, was an undeniable irritant — snooping and meddling came naturally to the penguins of the LGO. However, it was a small price to pay for personal safety. The Luftwaffe might have developed an uncanny knack for divining the exact whereabouts of key military departments, but for now at least, Saint Joseph's was anything but a first-strike target.

Max glanced at his watch. He should have been at his desk an hour ago, and he could see the papers already piling up in the wire basket on the desk. Maria, his long-suffering secretary, would be fielding the calls and making excuses for his absence. Both the papers and the calls would have to wait. There was something else he needed to do first.

His motorcycle was propped against the wall of his apartment building, the kickstand having rusted away during the hard, wet winter. She was in a temperamental mood this morning, but after much cajoling, the engine finally fired. Some of the sweat from his exertions dried off in the wind during the short ride up the hill into Valetta.

Lilian wasn't at the office. Or rather, she had come in early, and then she had gone out again, chasing up some story or other.

Rita couldn't be more specific, or didn't wish to be.

Rita manned the front desk at the newspaper offices. She didn't like Max. This wasn't paranoia on his part. Lilian, with characteristic candor, had told him that Rita didn't like him.

"Well, if you could tell her I dropped by . . ."

Rita leaned forward, placing her meaty forearms onto the desk. "Of course," she said.

But she didn't have to.

"Shouldn't you be at work?"

It was Lilian, entering from the street. Her long black hair was pinned up in an unruly mess, and she was rummaging for something in her shoulder bag.

"I just wanted to check that you got the film."

"She got the film," said Rita flatly.

Max had dropped the film off with Rita the previous evening, Lilian having already left for the day.

"How did the photos turn out?"

"Good," said Lilian. "You want to see them?"

"Have you got time?"

"Of course. Come."

When Lilian made for the staircase, Max

followed, glancing at Rita as he went. She peered back at him over the top of her spectacles with an impassive expression.

Max trailed Lilian up the narrow stone staircase to the newsroom. She was wearing a short linen skirt, fraying at the hem, which revealed the full glory of her legs. They had an aesthetic dimension, long and slender, tapering to ankles so narrow they looked as though they might break at any moment.

A sudden urge made him reach out a hand and run his fingertips down her left calf.

She gave a small yelp and spun round, glaring down at him.

"What do you expect if you insist on leading the way?"

"Then you go first," she said.

He squeezed past her. "You've changed your tune since last weekend."

"I was drunk last weekend."

"Oh, that's why you slurred your words when you said, 'Don't stop'?"

It had been their first kiss, and it had taken place under an orange tree in the garden of her aunt's palace in Mdina.

"Well, I hope you enjoyed it, because it was the last time."

As deputy editor of *Il-Berqa,* Lilian was entitled to her own office. It was a small box of a room, and it had somehow acquired a view of Grand Harbour since Max's last visit. It took him a moment to realize why. He wandered to the window and peered down at what remained of the church. The dome and the roof had collapsed into the nave, the pillars and arches of which were still standing, as was the greater part of the apse. Despite the destruction, the altar had been cleared of rubble and a priest was dressing it for Mass.

"Close," said Max.

"No one was killed."

"That's good to hear."

He turned back in time to see her unpin her hair and shake it out. It fell like silk around her shoulders.

"Better?" she asked.

"You could shave it all off and you'd still be beautiful."

She cocked her head at him, deciding whether to accept the compliment.

"It's true," he said.

It was. She could get away with it, with her large almond eyes, the sharp high-bridged nose, and full lips. She was of mixed parentage — half-Maltese, half-British — although her temperament owed considerably more to her Mediterranean blood. He still smarted when he remembered some of the words she'd directed at him, but he'd also shared many a full and proper belly laugh with her. He suspected that when it came to pure intellect there were few to match her on the island. He knew for a fact that he struggled to keep up.

"We don't have long," she said. "I have to be in Sliema at twelve o'clock and there are no buses."

"Sliema?"

"To talk to Vitorin Zammit."

"You're going to run the story?" he said hopefully.

"Felix isn't sure."

Felix was the editor, a plump and ponderous little character who didn't seem to do a whole lot around the place. It was common knowledge that Lilian effectively ran the show.

"What the old man did is not legal," Lilian went on. "We don't want half the island shooting at planes."

"I don't know. The artillery could do with all the help it can get right now."

She smiled. "True. But they'll shoot at everything, even our own planes."

"They'll have to find one first."

"But there are more Spitfires coming."

"Where did you hear that?"

"Is it true?" she asked.

"There are always more Spitfires coming.

When was the last time there weren't more Spitfires coming?"

Her eyes narrowed, seeing through his evasiveness, but she let it go unchallenged.

Max sat himself on the corner of her desk and lit a cigarette. "You have to run this story."

"I don't know, Max."

"Let's see the photos."

She pulled a folder from a pile of papers and spread a handful of black-and-white photos on the desk. They were almost identical. In a couple of them Vitorin Zammit was shaking the hand of the downed Italian pilot, whose parachute was piled up at his feet, and in all of them a ragtag band of grinning Maltese stood stiffly behind.

The young Italian was ridiculously handsome, and knew it; he had run his fingers through his thick hair to give his fringe some lift as Max had been preparing to take the first shot. Old Zammit's suit was powdered white with dust from their breakneck dash up into the hills. Wedged in between Max and Pemberton on the back of the motorcycle, he had complained all the way about his abduction, and had only ceased his moaning when they'd spotted the black smoke billowing from the wreck of the Macchi. It had piled into the base of a low escarpment just south of Gharghur, the pilot drifting to earth in a rock-strewn field nearby, where he had been promptly surrounded by a mob of blue-chinned and barefooted laborers brandishing sickles and hoes. His relief at the arrival of two uniformed officers on a motorcycle had been patent — although he must have known that the Maltese weren't the lynching kind — and when it had finally been conveyed to him through a series of gestures that the old man in the suit had shot him down, he'd put his pride in his pocket and laughed along heartily with everyone else.

"This is the best one," said Lilian.

She was right. Zammit's hand was resting on the Italian's shoulder — a protective, almost tender gesture — and the younger man's expression was an endearing picture of amused resignation. It was exactly the sort of image the Maltese would respond to — quietly triumphal and tinged with humor.

"Yes," Max concurred.

He could see from Lilian's face that she was still hesitating, and he knew why. She had crossed swords with the British authorities enough times in the past to have developed a reputation as something of a troublemaker. When the siege was in its infancy, she had fought for the rights of the islanders to dig their own shelters on public property, and she'd also unsuccessfully championed the cause of the Maltese internees — Italian sympathizers, or so it was claimed — who had been locked up like common criminals at the outbreak of hostilities and who had recently been shipped off to Uganda.

Running a story that might promote illegal behavior among the islanders could have consequences for her. She was thinking of her job.

"What he did might have contravened regulations, but look at it." Max handed her the photo. "This is what we all need right now. A hero. An improbable hero."

"*I* know that. *You* know that."

"Then I'll report it in the *Weekly Bulletin*, and you'll have your excuse to run it. The worst I'll get is a slapped wrist. Believe me, even the lieutenant governor will see the logic of putting it out there at a time like this."

Her eyes narrowed. "Why are you doing this?"

Mistrust, antagonism even, was part and parcel of their professional relationship, and they'd stopped pretending it wasn't. The Information Office and the only Maltese-language newspaper on the island might make for natural bedfellows, but Lilian's loyalties were to her own people, whose interests were not always best served by the British policy that Max was bound to promote. This made for an uneasy collaboration, a tentative trade of services. Lilian advised Max on how best to pitch the tone of his publications and broadcasts to appeal to a Maltese audience, and in return she received access to the kind of information she couldn't hope to get from anyone else. And both remained skeptical about the motives of the other.

Lilian was right to be wary in this instance. Max couldn't tell her the truth: that he knew a German invasion was imminent, and the signals from the summit were that they'd be fighting to the last man. If they were to stand any chance of turning back the Nazi tide, they needed the islanders at their side, willing and eager to take up arms. Vitorin Zammit in his dusty suit could do more to foster the necessary spirit of resistance than any number of pious speeches put out over the Rediffusion by the governor.

"Look, I'm just saying a story like this is good for everyone."

Lilian wasn't convinced. "There's something you're not telling me."

*If you only knew the half of it,* thought Max, images of the dead girl stretched out on the gurney in the mortuary suddenly crowding his thoughts, tightening his stomach.

He crushed out his cigarette against the sole of his shoe, anything to avoid her eyes. "There are a lot of things I don't tell you — *can't* tell you. You know that."

He kept grinding away at the dead cigarette.

"Max, look at me."

*I can't,* he thought. *Because if I do, I'll see her in you, you in her, and I won't be able to pretend that it doesn't matter. I won't be able to walk away from it.*

She waited for him to look up. "You're wrong," she said gently. "You *can* tell me. As a friend."

*Oh Christ . . .*

"You should get going," he suggested.

Now she was offended, and he tried to make amends.

"I'll give you a lift to Sliema on the motorcycle if you want."

"People will talk."

"And we can't have that, can we?"

"It's easy for you to say. When you are gone, they will still be talking."

They parted company in front of the building, though not before Lilian announced that he'd been invited to dinner again at her aunt's.

"Really?"

"She liked you."

"I can't think why. I ranted at her for most of the evening."

"I know. She said."

Lilian hurried for Saint Salvatore bastion in search of a *dghaisa* to row her across Marsamxett Harbour, and he watched her till the slope of the street had swallowed her up.

He didn't do too badly. Determined thoughts of the papers piling up on his desk successfully carried him all the way to the Porte des Bombes. But it was here that he found himself swinging the motorcycle around and doubling back into the gridlike streets of Floriana.

He located it almost instantly, which was a relief; he would have been hard-pushed to explain what he was doing scrabbling around in the ruins of a wrecked building. It was wedged in a crack between two bomb-spilled cubes of Malta rock. An inch or two to the left and it would have slipped away deep into the rubble, well beyond reach and any hope of recovery.

He dusted off the shoulder tab and stared at it, so light in his hand, so inconsequential.

It was hard to believe that a shred of cloth could have so much destructive power locked away in it.

High overhead, tall pencils of light stabbed and swept the night sky, sightless, searching for the drone of the lone bomber. Maybe it would drop an egg or two before returning to Sicily, or maybe it would hold back its high explosive for another day. Either way, a different aircraft would take up the baton before long, a relay designed to keep the defenders at their war stations and away from their beds, wearing them down.

Whatever you thought of the Germans — and he was still divided in his thinking — they approached the dirty business of war with a certain imaginative insolence that was hard not to admire.

He turned his eyes back to the pale thread of earth at his feet and set off once more up the slope.

He had always liked to walk, but alone, never in company. Walking was a time for contemplation, for introspection. The idea of tossing idle banter about at the same time had never appealed to him, even as a boy.

He had started going for walks when he was young — an excuse to get out of the house. The hours would fly by in his own company, whole afternoons sometimes, gone in moments, or so it had seemed at the time. He didn't much care for the countryside, although he probably knew more about its routine cycles than most. He could predict to the week when the buttercups would appear in the meadow, a yellow carpet reaching to the foot of the chalk hills. Or when the jackdaws would start to nest in the chimney pots, scavenging hair from the backs of supine heifers. Or when the Canada geese would abandon the lake in search of southern warmth.

He observed, and he registered these developments, but as a scientist might record the temperatures and quantities and colors of a chemistry experiment: dispassionately, at one remove. If he gathered up and carried home small trophies from his expeditions, it was only to lend some kind of credibility to his wanderings, to throw his parents off the scent.

He always made a point of returning with some keepsake — a fossil or a lump of fool's gold from the scree in the chalk quarry; the bone of an indeterminate animal, picked clean by predators and bleached white by the sun; the sloughed skin of an adder. To his parents' eyes, these tokens indicated a healthy interest in the natural world. To him, they were little more than meaningless debris. Until he discovered that they held the power to placate his father, to momentarily distract him from his strange and pressing need to mistreat his wife and his son.

On returning from his work in the city, his father would light his pipe and ask to see the latest addition to the collection, and they would wander to the hut at the end of the garden where he housed his cabinet of curiosities. There they would sit and talk together, wreathed in blue pipe smoke, and his father would tell him stories of his childhood, of the remote farm where he had grown up. He professed a love of nature, but it was a strange kind of love, one that led him to spend much of his free time shooting all manner of birds and animals with his friends. And when he wasn't slaughtering the local wildlife, he would be savagely pollarding trees or hacking back undergrowth. The truth was, his father viewed nature much as he viewed his family: as an unruly force, something to be tamed and mastered with a firm hand.

After the accident — his father dead and buried, truly at one with nature — he took up his private wanderings once more. They were the touchstone against which he was able to test the transformation that had occurred in him. He walked the same paths, clambered high into the canopy of the same ancient chestnut, lobbed stones into the lake to observe the play of intersecting ripples. He did what he had always done, and he felt nothing, nothing whatsoever, not even a dim glow of nostalgia.

This scared him at first, and he ascribed the vacuum inside him to guilt, to the secret he knew he could never share with anyone. He soon came to realize that he was wrong, though. It couldn't be guilt, because he felt no guilt for what he had done. He was able to play those last moments of his father's life over and over again in his head and they stirred nothing in him, neither shame nor satisfaction. In fact, he barely recognized himself in the small slice of cinema. It could just as well have been another fourteen-year-old boy sitting in the passenger seat of the swanky new roadster hurtling down the country lane.

His father was always buying new cars, fast cars. They fit with his "work hard, play hard" ethic, and he drove them hard, pushing them to their limits. When they disappointed him, which they invariably did, he simply replaced them. It had been a Saturday morning in early August and they'd been heading for a race meeting at Brooklands motor course. The events at Brooklands drew a rich crowd, an international crowd, and his father liked to gather there with his friends. Wives and daughters rarely showed their faces. Sons were permitted on the understanding that they were neither seen nor heard. This was fine by the sons, who congregated in front of the green-domed clubhouse before making for one of the circuit's massive banked curves, where they would spend the remainder of the day sneaking cigarettes in the long grass and silently praying for one of the drivers to misjudge the camber and go hurtling over the edge.

That's what should have happened that day, what would have happened if he hadn't reached out a hand and opened the glove compartment of his father's new car. He was used to his father's sudden jungle furies, used to being screamed at for some minor misdemeanor. He wasn't used to being slapped across the cheek. He knew that his father struck his mother, he had seen the bruises on her, but he had always been spared such treatment. Until now. He didn't cry — he knew that if he cried he was truly done for — but his father saw the tears moistening his eyes, and that was enough. The words cut deeper than they ever had before, and the shouts increased in volume, competing with the roar of the wind and the scream of the engine.

That's when he did it. Even now, he couldn't say what he had hoped to achieve. He certainly didn't pause to weigh the consequences. It was a purely instinctual reaction. He lunged for the steering wheel and yanked it toward him. The last thing he remembered before the world went black was his hand, pale and hairless beside his father's on the polished perfection of the wooden steering wheel.

His father died instantly when the roadster wrapped itself around the tree. Some curious law of physics chose to throw him clear at the moment of impact. All this he discovered some days later, when he came to in the hospital. His head was heavily bandaged, but everything else was intact — externally, at least, which was all the doctors cared about. They used the words "coma" and "miracle" a lot. His mother barely spoke. She did what she was supposed to do. She put on her widow's weeds and consoled her damaged son. But he knew what she was really thinking; he knew she was struggling to come to terms with her liberation. He saw her in a new light, clear and crisp and cold, a winter light. And it wasn't just her. He saw everything in this new and unfamiliar light.

Others must have detected something in him, because they started to remark on his behavior. His mother said it was grief. The doctors put it down to shock. One doctor, young and eager to please his superiors, prattled on about some recent case studies of frontal lobe trauma. Apparently there was evidence to suggest an association between a blow to the front of the head and a diminution in the subject's ability to feel emotion. Words such as "emotion" didn't sit happily with the consultants, and the young doctor learned a valuable lesson: it's only a good idea if your boss has had it first.

Enough science had accrued in the intervening years to bear out the theory, but he had known the truth of it at the time. He hadn't been in shock and he hadn't been grieving. He'd simply been unable to conjure up any feelings. It was as if he'd been observing the world through the viewfinder of a camera. Some invisible barrier stood between him and the subject of his attentions.

He learned this early on, and he quickly learned to compensate, to fabricate the required responses of a normal person. He must have done a good job, for one day the doctors suddenly announced that he had recovered his wits and was free to go. The bandage was gone by then, the scar on his forehead already healing to a fine fissure.

He sometimes wondered if his mother had seen through his act in those early days, while he was still finding his feet in the new world. He had made mistakes, he knew that. Taking her in his arms on the first anniversary of the crash and weeping on her shoulder was an ill-judged piece of overacting, but he had learned to refine his performance.

He took to rehearsing when he went for his walks, manufacturing a wide range of reactions: shock, delight, horror, amusement, curiosity, revulsion, wonderment — all the emotions that no longer came naturally to him. He learned to store away jokes and anecdotes for the entertainment of others. Judging which ones to pull out and when had taken longer. Reading your audience was no easy task when you felt no connection with them. It all came down to observation, he realized, and that's where he concentrated his efforts.

Again, the walking helped. He started to see things that previously his eyes had passed over, not birds and animals and plants, but human patterns. He noticed that the farmer on the other side of the wood, the burly widower, always did his washing on Saturday morning, irrespective of the weather, stringing the clothes up in the barn if it was raining. And the old couple who walked their two wirehaired terriers on the hill most evenings always stopped and kissed each other on the lips before negotiating the stile by the clump of gorse. He also noticed the mysterious black sedan parked in the driveway of the thatched house near the old meadow copse every Tuesday afternoon between the hours of two and four. At four, or thereabouts, he would see a young man, prematurely bald, hurry from the house to the car. And if he crept through the trees round to the back of the house, he could see a woman draw back the bedroom curtains the moment the car was gone.

Her name was Mrs. Beckett, he discovered, and Mr. Beckett sold engineering equipment around the country, spending much of his time on the road. They didn't have children. It took him a month or so to build up the courage to knock on the door. When he did, he was pleased with what he saw. Mrs. Beckett was more attractive up close, dark and petite and with a lively sparkle in her eye. When he asked if he could trouble her for a glass of water, she invited him inside.

The kitchen was large and light and spotlessly clean. He had caught her in the act of making jam, straining fruit through a piece of muslin slung between the legs of an upturned stool. He knew all about making jam but pretended he didn't, and an hour later he was still there, helping her.

She knew who he was, or rather, she had heard his story from someone in the area. He fed on her compassion, but picked his responses carefully, not wishing to overplay the role of tragic victim, which he judged would not appeal to her. He selected a couple of anecdotes to make her laugh, which she did, throwing back her head and emitting a throaty chuckle. When he finally left, she took his hand and shook it firmly and told him he was a brave and impressive young man. She also told him to stop by again if he was passing on one of his walks.

He left it a couple of weeks before doing so, during which time he toyed with his options, playing them through in his head in all their various permutations. Knowledge might equate to power, but the successful application of that power required meticulous preparation. He had a reputation to preserve, and he needed to be sure of Mrs. Beckett's silence.

He opted for a Thursday. It was a hot and sultry afternoon, a great cathedral of cumulus clouds stirring high overhead, threatening an electrical storm. She was in the garden, pulling weeds from the borders, and seemed delighted to see him. The perfect excuse to take a break, she joked. She poured them each a glass of lemonade from the jug she kept in the larder and suggested they drink it out of the heat, in the cool of the kitchen.

They sat facing each other across the scrubbed pine table, the sweat slowly drying on their skin. It wasn't a scene he had imagined, but it was close enough, so he set about his business. He told her he was going away for a month with his mother to Bad Reichenhall, a spa town in the Bavarian Alps, guests of some German friends of his father's. Herr Kettelmann was a regular at the Brooklands race meetings, and his eldest son, Lutz, had proved to be good company, bright and mischievous and fond of dirty jokes. He pretended to be under-whelmed by the idea of going abroad, dismissing the invitation as a gesture of pity toward a woman whom the Kettelmanns barely knew. She told him not to be so cynical, not to mistake kindness for pity. He lowered his eyes to the table, bowing to her superior wisdom and apologizing for his mean-spiritedness.

And so it continued, just as he had planned it: he, the troubled young soul in search of guidance; she, rising to the role of guide. She was less sure-footed when he turned the conversation to her, her life, her husband. He tried to show interest while listening to her tales of love and marriage and a happiness born in heaven — lies that invigorated him, entitling him to proceed.

When she rose to fill their glasses, he followed her to the larder and told her that he had never met anyone like her. She handed him his glass and told him not to be silly. When he took her hand and raised it to his lips, she snatched it away before he could kiss it. He was tall for his age, more man than boy, and she seemed to sense this now. Pushing past him out of the larder, she said that she had to get back to her weeding before the rain came, and suggested that he hurry home to avoid a drenching. He didn't reply; he just looked at her. When she asked him firmly to leave, he asked her about the bald man.

The color drained from her face, but she recovered quickly, pleading no knowledge of a bald man. When forced to concede that he did exist, she claimed that he was her brother. When he inquired if she thought it normal for a woman to spend two hours in a darkened bedroom with her brother every Tuesday afternoon, she began to grasp the hopelessness of her situation. She tried to wriggle off the hook a couple more times, first appealing to his conscience, then defiantly ordering him to go ahead and do his worst. But they both knew that they were edging inexorably toward a trade. She asked him what he wanted for his silence. Something I've never had before, he replied.

He might not have known what he was doing, but he was big, and he assumed that counted for something. He knew he was big because he had seen the other boys in the showers at school after games, as they had seen him, and they had remarked respectfully on his size.

It didn't seem to give Mrs. Beckett much pleasure. But he wasn't thinking of her; he was thinking of himself, watching himself moving in and out of her and wondering if this was what all the fuss was about. Looking to improve on the experience, he maneuvered her into a number of different positions, which helped a bit. Her passivity gave him no satisfaction, but neither did it hamper his performance. He did what he had come to do, then he got dressed and left. He turned at the bedroom door and reassured her that her secret was safe with him. He wanted her to know that he was a man of his word. She was sobbing quietly into a pillow and didn't look up.

The storm broke as he was crossing the meadow. Lightning scythed the sky, thunder echoed off the hills, and the rain sheeted down in warm torrents, soaking him to the skin. And yet he remained strangely immune to this assault on his senses, caught up in dark thoughts, wondering what he would have to do, just how far he would have to go before he finally felt something stir in him.

He wasn't to know it at the time, but the answer lay only a little way off, in Bad Reichenhall.

# DAY THREE

Max was at his desk, taking a red pen to a news item, when the phone rang. He snatched up the receiver distractedly, irritably.

"Yes?"

"I know the feeling."

"Freddie."

"Bad morning?"

"That new chap we took on, you met him at the party . . ."

"Pemberton."

"Turns out he thinks he's Shakespeare."

"He'll learn. You did."

"Thanks for that."

"Listen, Max, I know who she is."

Max's smile died on his lips. "The girl?"

"She has a name now. Carmela Cassar. Her father was here earlier and identified the body. It's as we thought, another sherry queen."

"You spoke to him?"

"Don't worry. I was very discreet."

"That's not what I meant."

"Yes, it is. Have you got a pen?"

Max scribbled down everything Freddie had gleaned, both from the official paperwork at the mortuary and from his conversation with the father. Carmela had lived with her parents in the family home on the hillside near Paola, just up the slope from Santa Maria Addolorata Cemetery. She always got back from work late, between one and two in the morning, but in the five months she had been working at the Blue Parrot she had never before failed to return.

Max knew the Blue Parrot, not intimately, and not of late. It was one of the few dance halls in the Gut reserved for officers, which meant that the establishment was slightly more spacious than most, the floor show moderately superior, and the drinks vastly more expensive. He'd been there several times soon after his arrival on the island, when the star attraction, the big draw — the very big draw — had been an act from Hungary.

Budapest Bessie hadn't been graced with either the build or the poise of a prima ballerina, but this hadn't prevented her from puffing her way through her version of "The Dying Swan" before the disbelieving eyes of

Britain's officer classes. For some reason, veils had been a feature of her routine, he remembered, angina the reason for her sudden retirement from the stage. Ammunition had been scarce even back then, but a couple of the shore batteries had been ordered to fire off a salute when the frigate bearing Bessie to a gentler life in Gibraltar had slipped out of Grand Harbour.

Max hadn't been back to the Blue Parrot since that time, but he could see the flaking gilt of the mirrors in the narrow dining room, the greasy velvet upholstery, and the tired palms dotted about the place.

"Did she work anywhere before?"

"I didn't ask. Should I have?"

"Anything else?"

"Yes. Something that doesn't make sense. She left for work on Thursday afternoon at five o'clock — she always allowed an hour for the walk, apparently — but she wasn't found till the Saturday morning."

"Where exactly was she found?"

"A backstreet in Marsa. Marsa was on her route home, but she can hardly have lain out there for a whole day without anyone seeing her."

Max weighed a range of explanations, rejecting each in turn. Only one withstood the test, and it didn't sit happily in the head.

"She was held somewhere for twenty-four hours."

"It looks that way."

"Or maybe she was already dead; he just couldn't dispose of the body for whatever reason, maybe it was too risky."

As explanations went, it wasn't quite as grim as the thought of her being held hostage for those missing hours, with the disturbing images that accompanied it.

"The rigor mortis suggests otherwise. It was well set in when I first saw her on Saturday around noon. It generally peaks somewhere between twelve and twenty-four hours after death, closer to twelve in this kind of heat."

Which suggested that her life was ended some time on Friday night. And probably not in Marsa. Marsa had simply been the dumping ground. As to where she was abducted, it could have been anywhere along her route home; a quiet spot, most likely. But where did he hold her captive during Friday? And how did he transport her there? The questions were coming in a torrent now.

"Max, I've been thinking. We have to go to someone with this."

"The lieutenant governor's office shut you out last time. What makes you think they won't do it again? We need evidence they can't ignore."

It was a disingenuous response, and he knew it: presenting himself as the champion of truth when all he really wanted was a bit more time to follow through on the consequences of a scandal of this scale breaking across the island.

"Freddie, I just need a day or two."

"I'm happy to give it to you. But is he?"

"What are you saying?"

"I'm saying I don't want another death on my conscience."

"You think I do?" Max paused. "I'm asking you to trust me on this. A couple of days to check some things out. I'll get straight onto it. I promise."

Freddie remained silent for a moment. "Okay, but you're on your own. They've got me working out of Mtarfa for the foreseeable."

It was a testimony to Freddie's skill as a surgeon that he spent much of his time being shunted among the island's hospitals, according to where his gifts were required. There was certainly no lack of call for them.

"When are you heading out there?"

"Ten minutes ago. A Beaufighter just pancaked at Luqa. The navigator is pretty chewed up, by all accounts."

"I'm going to need the exact dates when the other two girls were found."

"Then stay on the line. I'll be right back."

Max spent half an hour clearing his desk and briefing the members of his team. They were quite capable of holding the fort in his absence. He was on the point of leaving when the rising dirge of the air-raid siren stopped him in his tracks.

"Damn," he muttered, making for the staircase that led to the roof. Fleur-de-Lys occupied the high ground between Hamrun and Birkirkara, and the zinc-clad roof of Saint Joseph's offered one of the finest views on the island: a sweeping three-hundred-sixty-degree panorama that took in Rabat and the walled city of Mdina to the west, roosting on their spur of white rock, keeping watch over the parched southern plain, where towns and villages lay scattered like dice on a tabletop. To the east, beyond Valetta and her twin harbors, lay a seemingly endless expanse of viridian-green water. The corrugated hills that rolled off to the north beyond Mdina held little strategic importance for the enemy. Almost everything that was of interest to them — the airfields, the dockyards, and the submarine base — lay within the field of vision of a person standing on the roof of Saint Joseph's.

It was a biblical landscape — sun-bleached, shadeless, harsh to the eye — broken up into miniature fields by a dense lacework of stone walls. The walls were there to prevent the precious dusting of soil from being blown about by the hot summer winds from Africa. In the winter, the *gregale* blew in from the northwest, bringing the heavy rains that turned everything to mud.

Right now, though, a brassy sun was overhead, and the first white galleon clouds of the year were gathering over the island.

Max turned as the big guns up on Ta' Giorni ridge slammed a salvo into the air. Pale puff-balls of bursting ack-ack fire mottled the sky to the northeast, heralding the arrival of a vast and heavily escorted formation of 88s.

It soon became clear that the airfields were about to take another bad knock, and Max could feel his plans for the day slipping away from him. Traveling, like much of life on Malta, was something you did in between raids, and even then you kept one eye on the heavens for the lone marauders who slipped in under the radar screen. The scarcity of gasoline had stripped the streets of motor vehicles in the past couple of months, and a lone motorcycle throwing up a cloud of dust was more of an invitation than ever to an enemy pilot with an itchy trigger finger.

He had been strafed only once — on the old dirt road that switchbacked its way between Ghajn Tuffieha and Mdina — but the suddenness and ferocity of the attack were indelibly etched in his memory. One moment he was barreling along, the wind in his face; the next moment the road in front of him was erupting. The fighter was well past by the time Max registered it, and it was a further few seconds before his brain was able to make the connection between the dot twisting away into the distance and the strip of earth torn out of the ground across his path. He might have processed the information more rapidly if he hadn't been so joyously distracted at the moment when the attack occurred. Three dreamlike days by the sea at Ghajn Tuffieha had dulled his reactions.

He had earned the short break, his first in more than a year since arriving on the island and taking up his post as deputy to Charles Headley, the information officer at the time. Headley had also performed the function of deputy chief censor, which he had taken as an excuse to do neither job properly. Max was hardly industrious by nature, but he had never before witnessed anything approaching Headley's eagerness to shirk his duties (or, for that matter, Headley's curious desire to share with anyone who would listen that the art to skiving lay in cultivating a faintly embattled air).

Connections counted, though, and Headley's Oxford education might well have seen him through if he hadn't graduated from one of the more minor colleges. Few were surprised when Headley failed to return from one of his "recces" to Alexandria, and the attitude toward his "reassignment" was best summed up by Hugh, who had known him at university.

"Good chap, old Headers, but strictly front-of-house, if you know what I mean."

Max had never been quite sure if Hugh's observation had made a slight nod to the rumor doing the rounds that Headley had been caught in flagrante with a young Egyptian boy.

Either way, Max had found himself promoted, far beyond his years and experience, to run the department. Any pride in this meteoric rise was short-lived; he quickly realized what others had figured out long before him: that he had already been running the department. He had acquitted himself well in the top job — he knew that — but it was still strange to him that the task of manipulating minds came so naturally to him. He had always regarded himself as something of a loner. That had certainly been the picture presented to him by his family over the years, and one he had come to believe in. Yet here he was, deep in the minds of the masses, second-guessing their reactions to events, guiding and enlightening them, a high priest at the altar of the great god Morale.

It hadn't all been plain sailing. A month after his promotion he had been hit in the shoulder by shrapnel from a parachute mine, and it had looked for a moment as though he might be replaced. Then in early September the letter had arrived from Eleanor, requesting that he call off their engagement. It was dated May, and his first thought had been of all the letters, all the sweet words, he had written to her over the previous three months while her thoughts had been elsewhere, with the faceless and nameless Canadian pilot who had stolen her heart. It was telling, he now realized, that this should have been his first thought: pragmatic and self-pitying. Hardly the reaction of a man who has just lost the love of his life.

Word of his misfortune soon circulated, largely thanks to Rosamund and Hugh, who had long since set themselves up in his life as surrogate parents, psychiatrists, and general busybodies. He also sensed their hand behind the order that had come down from on high that he take a few days off from his duties to lick his wounds. Gozo had been an option. The fertile little island sat just off the north coast, a short ferry ride away, and was a popular destination for those looking to leave the war behind them for a bit. The Riviera Hotel at Ghajn Tuffieha had been Mitzi's recommendation, and she'd sold the place to him hard.

It didn't disappoint. The stone-built hotel was perched high above a shallow bay guarded by two towering headlands and backed by one of the few sandy beaches on the island. It was a remote and peaceful spot, a small oasis in the rugged stretch of coastline. The hotel was clean and comfortable, its kitchen offered a bewildering array of fresh fish and vegetables, and its bar was stocked to overflowing. On his arrival, Max ate his first full and proper meal in months, washing it down with a surprisingly good bottle of white wine. He then took to his bed for an afternoon nap and slept like a fallen statue for sixteen hours straight.

The same base need for rest and recovery was written on the faces of the other guests, and while the odd polite word was exchanged, they generally gave one another a wide berth. The enemy planes passing high overhead every so often were studiously ignored. Most of the guests adhered to the same regime: loafing about with lightweight novels on the beach in between bouts of swimming, eating, and drinking. The water in the bay was clear, warm, and inviting, even with summer slipping away. The fish, oblivious of the war, were abundant, as were the fishermen, who appeared from God-knew-where each morning, bobbing about in their colorful boats. Some sold straight to the Riviera, and every morning the stumpy little head chef would pick his way down the precipitous path to the beach, examine their catch, and feign disappointment — the standard prelude to a spell of noisy bartering.

The fishermen were keen to know when the Italian bombers would return. It was not a question Max could answer, or, for that matter, one that he properly understood, until it was explained to him that the Italians, unlike their fearless German allies, were inclined to jettison their bombs short of the island and turn tail at the first sign of resistance. When this occurred, a fisherman was no longer obliged to wring his living from the depths; he could pluck it willy-nilly from the surface. It was an impressive sight, apparently, the surface of the sea carpeted white with the bellies of stunned fish.

On his third day there, Max struck out south along the coastal path. It was a bright, windless morning, unnaturally still, and a millpond sea licked lazily at the base of the cliffs. A strange feeling crept over him as he walked, a sense of timelessness. Whose footsteps was he treading in? How many others had negotiated the same twisting path over the aeons? The same path, but different men, each carrying his own hopes, dreams, and regrets.

Malta's history was rich, romantic, and violent. How could it be anything else? The island stood at the crossroads of the Mediterranean, closer to Europe than Africa, though not by much. It also happened to possess one of the finest natural harbors in the world. No wonder that so many seafaring peoples had sought to make it their own. The Phoenicians, Greeks, Carthaginians, Romans, and Byzantines had all held sway over the island, only to be displaced. The Fatimid Arabs had gone the way of the others, although their language still lived on in the speech of the modern-day islanders. Since that time, Norman knights, Spanish grandees, and Napoleonic generals had all made their home here. How different was he, a commissioned officer of His Majesty's Army?

He tried to shrug off this fanciful notion, but it trailed him like his shadow. It was oddly comforting, the sense of connection coupled with the cyclical futility of it all. For a brief moment he could have died and it wouldn't have mattered to him one jot.

Set against this, his troubled saga with Eleanor took on a new complexion. He found himself feeling happy for her. She had no more wanted their marriage than he had. At least she had found the courage to do something about it. He sat on a rock, pulled the letter from his pocket, and read it again. This time he was proud of her, and he found himself hoping that they could remain friends. That's what they had always been — good friends, ever since they were young and he had played Joseph to her Mary in the church nativity play. That was long before they both began to sense that others expected something more of them. Well, his stepmother, to be more precise.

He was back at the Riviera in time for

lunch, and he entered the dining room in high spirits. They soared higher still when he spotted Mitzi at a corner table. She was alone, although as he approached, he noticed that the chair across from her had recently been vacated, if the full glass of wine and the cigarette smouldering away in the ashtray were anything to go by.

"Lionel back from patrol?"

"Not that I'm aware of," Mitzi replied sweetly, before tilting her head to peer past him. "Drusilla, look who's here."

Max turned to see Drusilla Gleeson bearing down on him. Secretary to the Naval Wives Association, she was a formidable creature known for wearing her husband's stripes. There was something of the overgrown Girl Guide about her, but she was redeemed by a certain gruff charm.

"Well, Major Chadwick. You look hot."

"I've been walking."

"Mad dogs and Englishmen, eh? We come here to walk — don't we, Mitzi? — but only at first light or last."

"I thought you had gone to Gozo," said Mitzi.

Max knew this to be a bald-faced lie, and while he struggled to make sense of it, he played along. "Someone persuaded me to give the Riviera a go."

"First time here?" snapped Drusilla. "Won't be your last."

"I've had a good time."

"Needed to, from what I hear. Fiancée slipped her moorings, eh?"

"Drusilla, a touch more tact wouldn't go amiss," Mitzi replied.

"No doubt, my dear, no doubt."

"Well, I won't keep you from your meal," said Max.

And he didn't. He ate lunch alone at his allotted table, then headed for the beach. He tried to lose himself in his book — *Wet and Windy,* a light romp by John Glyder — but his thoughts kept turning to Mitzi and her unexpected arrival and the lie she had laid on him in front of Drusilla. He was dozing facedown on his towel when she joined him, the citrus smell of her perfume invading his half dream, alerting him to her presence. By the time his filmy eyes had focused, she was settled on her towel beside him.

She was wearing dark glasses and a safari-print swimsuit with slender shoulder straps.

"Drusilla's sleeping."

"I'm happy for her."

"She can be a bit heavy-handed at times, but her heart's in the right place."

He felt her eyes straying over his body.

127

"You look well . . . if a little undernourished."

"Can't think why," he replied.

"We're all wasting away. I've had to take this in twice since I've been here." She tugged at the material of her swimsuit. "For the first time in my life I'm actually happy with the size of my derrière."

They were lying on their sides, facing each other across a respectable strip of sand. "I can't see it from here," said Max, "but I'm sure it's a very fine derrière."

A small smile played about the corners of her mouth, then she slowly turned to get her cigarettes from the straw bag on the sand behind her, twisting on her towel as she did so. It was done for his benefit.

"My God, you're right to be happy," said Max, more breathlessly than he would have liked. Like the rest of her, it was as close to perfection as anything he'd ever set eyes on.

She lit a cigarette, then tossed him the packet and the lighter. Thanks to Freddie, their mutual friend, he had got to know her well over the previous six months, well enough to come straight out with it.

"Why are you here, Mitzi?"

Exhaling, she replied, "I'll give you a clue — not to go walking with Drusilla."

He hoped she didn't notice the tremor in

128

his hand as he raised the lighter to his cigarette.

"Your hand's trembling."

"It does that when I'm nervous."

"If it's any consolation, you're not the only one who's out of their depth. I shouldn't be here. This is not me, not what I do." She lowered her eyes, tapping some ash onto the sand. "I'm sorry if I've embarrassed you."

"I'm not embarrassed. Shocked, yes. And flattered. And trying very hard not to crawl across the sand and kiss you."

"That would be a deviation from my plan."

"You have a plan?"

"Everyone knows you have to have a plan."

"When it comes to matters military, I'm not the real McCoy, I'm afraid."

"So I've heard." She stared off into the bay. "You're hairier than I imagined."

"I'm pleased to say you aren't."

Mitzi laughed. "You've always made me laugh. Maybe that's why I'm here."

"Not the rugged good looks?"

"Oh, those too. Eleanor's a damned fool."

"I'm not so sure anymore."

He told her about his little epiphany on the cliff top, and for the first time he shared with her the truth about the relationship, not the finished picture he had presented to her in the past — touched up, varnished, and framed — but the raw canvas.

Mitzi listened attentively, her eyes never leaving his. When he was done, she remained silent for a moment.

"I know all about the expectations of others, and I'm not just saying that."

She had been promised to Lionel pretty much at birth, she explained, a union intended to seal the bond between two navy families who had lived in the same village near Portsmouth for several generations. It was a good life, too good to question when young, impossible to question when a little wiser. She had never held Lionel responsible for his attitude toward her, although neither had she enjoyed the sense of entitlement instilled in him from an early age. It had colored their relationship. She had passed through life never knowing what it was like to be courted by a man, because the only man who had ever been allowed to have eyes for her happened to have believed she was already his by right.

"He has never once looked at me the way you are now."

"With desire?"

"As an equal."

"I've never considered myself your equal."

"Maybe that's the other reason I'm here — because you know your place."

He laughed and lay back on his towel, staring at the blue vault of the sky. "You do a very good job of hiding all this."

"I've had a lot of practice. I've also said too much. Let's talk about something else."

"Better still, let's go for a swim, and you can tell me about that plan of yours."

It was a simple plan, and they followed it to the letter. As soon as the sun dipped away and the heat dropped, Mitzi and Drusilla went for their walk along the coast. They returned in time for a late supper, just as Max was finishing up his meal. He stopped by their table, explaining that he would be leaving first thing in the morning and might not see them at breakfast. He wished them a pleasant stay, then walked to the ancient watchtower at the tip of the headland, where he smoked two cigarettes in the gathering gloom.

Drusilla's room lay on Max's corridor, just two doors down, so come midnight he was the one who found himself tiptoeing through the darkness, the tiles cold beneath his bare feet. Mitzi was waiting for him, naked under a cotton sheet. She had placed the mattress on the floor, presumably to avoid any undue noise. The curtains were open, the room awash with silver moonlight. They knew that silence was essential — they had even discussed it while swimming in the bay — but when Max joined her beneath the sheet, the first thing he did was say, "I'm afraid I'm not overburdened with experience."

Mitzi stroked his face. "There's no rush. I don't know about you, but I don't intend to sleep a wink tonight."

"I don't think anyone saw me."

"Good."

"And I locked the door."

"Ssshhh," she said, silencing him with a kiss.

The Maltese liked to rise early, and to be safe he left her room soon after four o'clock. He should have felt exhausted, drained, but there was a spring in his step, even a slight swagger. After reaching the safety of his room, he flopped onto the bed and tried to sleep, but his thoughts kept returning to the mattress on the floor, to the welcoming warmth of her body, its taut and slender beauty, her gift to him.

What had he done to deserve it? And how had he misread her so badly? The remote, imperious creature he had come to know was gone forever, laid to rest on that lumpy mattress. She had shown no signs of guilt at her betrayal of Lionel — far from it — just a hunger and urgency that had drawn the same from him. Apart from a few hushed words of encouragement, they had barely spoken, and the pauses between their love-making had been brief and breathless interludes. Even now he wanted more, and it was to prevent himself from doing something dangerously rash that he swung his legs off the bed and headed to the beach for a final swim.

An hour later, his bag was strapped to the back of the motorcycle and he was gone, tearing along the old dirt road that wound through the hills toward Mdina, his eyes screwed up against the wind and the low glare of the rising sun. He was a mile or so shy of Fort Bingemma when it happened, the enemy fighter swooping silently down on him and laying a trail of death across his path.

His first thought at the time had been of an avenging angel dispatched by Lionel to seek amends, and while this brush with his conscience hadn't persuaded him to leave Mitzi well alone, eight months on he was still incapable of mounting his motorcycle without thinking that the avenging angel was watching and waiting.

Standing there on the roof of Saint Joseph's, the skies over the airfields speckled with enemy planes, he certainly had no intention of making for Valetta before the siren had sounded its steady note of "Raiders Passed."

He tried to use the time constructively, planning how to proceed, formulating excuses for his inquiries so that they wouldn't arouse suspicion. But there was no ignoring the cruel coincidence of the thing, the eerie sense of predestination. All roads led to the *Upstanding,* the submarine driven by Lionel "Campers" Campion, lieutenant commander and cuckold.

It had been some months since he had visited the submarine base on Manoel Island, and the change was evident the moment he crossed the short causeway on his motorcycle. This time, he wasn't waved through by the guard detail. They stopped him and questioned him and almost turned him away. He recognized the look in their eyes, the hollow stare of men who have been on the receiving end for so long that they're itching to strike back at anything, even their own kind.

There were two of them, young and lean and mean-looking, members of the Special

Service Detachment assigned to the defense of HMS *Talbot,* as the submarine base was also known. They softened to his cause when he asked them if they'd heard about the Macchi brought down by Vitorin Zammit after its strafing run at the base. They had, and they were eager for details from an eyewitness. Their sense of camaraderie restored, they allowed Max to proceed. They even helped him bump-start the motorcycle.

The 10th Submarine Flotilla was housed in the Lazaretto, a run of old buildings that had once served as a quarantine center for the Knights of Saint John. They were strung out along the southern shore of Manoel Island, staring Valetta in the face, sandwiched between the water's edge and the soaring wall of rock on which Fort Manoel was perched. The Lazaretto had stood there unscathed for centuries but now wore a tired and decidedly sorry appearance.

The approach road was a patchwork of bomb craters, great gobbets of earth lay scattered about, and the small chapel had been gutted, although by some miracle its façade was still standing. The floating gangways where the subs berthed were deserted and damaged, reaching into Lazaretto Creek like the splayed fingers of an arthritic hand. The buildings themselves had fared far worse. At the western end, many of the roofs were gone, having taken the floors below with them.

When the base was viewed from this angle, the decision to pull what remained of the 10th Submarine Flotilla out of Malta made considerably more sense.

By some stroke of good fortune, the officers' quarters at the far end of the Lazaretto had not suffered to the same degree, and a surly rating directed Max to Tommy Ravilious's office. It lay off a sun-drenched loggia on the first floor, where a couple of officers, one of whom Max recognized from the Union Club, were lounging in wicker armchairs, smoking.

"I'm looking for Tommy Ravilious."

He was thumbed in the general direction. "His day cabin's three doors down on the left."

Max had picked up enough naval jargon to know that "day cabins" were offices, just as floors were "decks," and going out for lunch was "going ashore." It was the same at Fort Saint Angelo on the Grand Harbour side, a "stone frigate" renamed HMS *Saint Angelo* by the navy when they'd adopted it as their headquarters. The urge to scream *You're on dry land now, not a bloody ship* had never quite deserted Max.

One part of the corridor he picked his way down was open to the heavens, and the door to Tommy's office was hanging off its top hinge.

Tommy was at his desk, sharpening a pencil with a rusty scalpel.

"Well, well, well . . . ," he said cheerily when Max entered.

Others at Lazaretto might have lost some of their usual lustre, but Tommy's trademark brand of *Boy's Own Paper* enthusiasm appeared unscathed.

"To what do I owe this pleasure — nay, honor?"

"I was passing."

"Come now, my dear fellow, we're too old and too wise for that."

"So what are we doing *here?*"

Tommy exploded in laughter, casting a quick look around his dusty empire. "God only knows. Maybe we sinned in a previous life."

"I hadn't figured you for a reincarnationist."

"My grandmother's to blame. She loved all that nonsense. A committed naturist, too, right up until the day she died. 'I believe in the two sexes airing their differences,' she used to say. Drink?"

"What have you got?"

"Gin or gin."

"Have we earned it?"

"I know *I* have."

Max pulled up a chair. "Well, if only to dim the image of your grandmother airing her differences . . ."

It was Plymouth gin, favored by the navy men; Gordon's was strictly army.

Max raised his tumbler in a toast. "The fourth of May."

Tommy frowned, trying to figure the significance of the current day's date.

"One has to be celebrating something, or else one is simply a common drunk."

His impression of Hugh's sonorous bass voice must have been close enough, because Tommy laughed and asked, "How *is* old Hugh, and the lovely Rosamund?"

Tommy downed his gin as if making up for lost time, which in some respects he was. The enemy's recent fixation with the submarine base had kept him at his post and away from the clubs and dinners for the past month or more. As a senior member of the headquarters staff, he had barely any time for leisure when the heat was on. Max duly served up as much of the gossip as he could recall.

"Elliott was down here a couple of weeks

ago," said Tommy, topping off their tumblers.

"Elliott? What was he doing?"

"What he does best — snooping. I sometimes get the feeling he thinks we Brits are little more than a bunch of incompetents."

"Then he's not as stupid as he looks."

Tommy smiled. "Apparently not. Speaks a very passable Greek, according to some of our Hellenic friends who were here at the time. One of them thought he recognized him from Crete, just before it fell."

It seemed unlikely. Crete had fallen to the Germans almost exactly a year before, in May — a good many months before the Japanese raid on Pearl Harbor had persuaded the Americans to join the fray. But when it came to Elliott, you could never be quite sure. Despite the bonhomie and robust sense of humor, there was something of the dark horse about him. He seemed to have been everywhere, lived everywhere, including England, where he'd spent several years as a pupil at Charterhouse School in Surrey.

Max could recall one of their early conversations, not long after the tall American had materialized in Malta. While berating the British for their innate lack of hospitality, Elliott had remarked that they could learn a thing or two from the people of Kazakhstan.

"I'm telling you, in Kazakhstan when a stranger turns up at your place and asks for shelter, you house him and feed him, no questions asked — not who he is, where he comes from, or where he's going, not even how long he plans on staying. Nothing. Not a sausage. After three days, you're allowed to ask him where he's going, but that's it. Anything more is an insult to your guest."

"You've been to Kazakhstan?"

"There's oil in Kazakhstan," had been Elliott's typically elusive response.

Max sometimes sensed that these subtle deflections were designed to tantalize, that Elliott enjoyed the aura of mystery that hung around him. Everyone knew that he had access to the very highest echelons of Malta Command. More than once he had been seen leaving the offices of the mysterious Y Service and the even more secretive Special Liaison Unit, although, as Tommy said, for much of the time he seemed to just drift about, observing and absorbing.

But Max hadn't come to speculate about Elliott; he'd made the journey in search of information. With that mission in mind, he nudged the conversation back to the here and now.

"How are the Lazarene swine bearing up?"

"Surprisingly well, if a little jumpy."

No one begrudged the submariners their foibles — the dark and inhuman universe they inhabited while on patrol earned them the right to act pretty much as they wished when on terra firma — but their quasi-religious devotion to the herd of pigs they'd been rearing still raised a chuckle or two.

"What's going to happen to them?" Max inquired.

"Happen to them?"

"The pigs. When you've gone."

"Aaaahhh," drawled Tommy knowingly. "And I thought you'd come here to see how your old chum was getting on, but really it's bacon you're after."

Max smiled. "It's true, then."

Tommy leaned across the desk and stubbed out his cigarette in the aluminum casing of a spent German flare that now served as an ashtray.

"When?" Max asked.

Tommy looked up. "P34 left a few days ago. The others over the next week or so."

"That's all that's left?"

As the information officer, he might have felt stupid asking the question, but he knew the hard truth: that he was regarded as little more than a journalist, that privileged information was fed to him only when it was deemed expedient.

"Best not to shout it from the parapets."

"Of course not."

"Don't think for a moment we're happy about pulling out. We know how it'll look, what message it'll send to the Maltese."

"No one's going to blame you, Tommy. Everyone knows the pounding you've been taking. I mean, half the bloody island has watched it from their rooftops."

"The powers that be are calling it a 'tactical redeployment,' but the truth is we're bolting while we still can."

Tommy's dejection steered his hand once more toward the gin bottle.

"There's only one reason you've been targeted — because you've hurt them so badly. Rommel can't make headway in north Africa with you taking out his supply lines from Italy. Frankly, I'm amazed it's taken them so long to wake up to that fact."

"True. If they'd taken a serious pop at us a year ago, they'd have saved themselves seventy-five ships."

"That many?"

"Four hundred thousand tons of shipping."

"It's a hell of an achievement, Tommy. And there'll be more to come, wherever you end up."

Max was fishing now.

"Alexandria. But it still feels like a retreat."

"It isn't. And my job's to make people understand that."

"Time for a bit of buffing and polishing."

"Exactly, and it would help if I had a few more facts at my fingertips."

"What sort of thing?"

Max tried to sound as casual as possible. "I don't know. I imagine you have some kind of log that records the sorties of all the subs."

"That's confidential information."

"I'm not the enemy, Tommy, and I'm not an idiot. I wouldn't use anything that gave away operational practices. It's just to get a sense of what you've all been through . . . the scale of it, the relentlessness."

He didn't feel good lying to Tommy, but the prize was within his grasp now, and he tried to remain focused on it.

"I don't know, Max."

"It'll help bring your achievements to life."

Tommy scrutinized him for a moment before deciding. "Okay. But I'll tell you what you can and can't use."

He left the room, returning with a hefty leather-bound volume, which he dropped onto the desk in front of Max. Tommy pulled up his chair and they sat side by side, flicking through it.

Each submarine in the flotilla had a section devoted to it in which every detail of its time on Malta was noted chronologically in a neat cursive hand, everything from changes in personnel to maintenance and repair records to latitudes and longitudes of enemy sightings and engagements. The log would sometimes end with the ominous phrase "Last Known Position" or "Overdue, Presumed Lost," and when this was the case, Tommy was inclined to reminisce about the cold-drawn courage of the men of the "Fighting Tenth," many of whom had disappeared in circumstances that might never be entirely clear.

Max was impatient, eager to get to the relevant pages, but it was hard to remain immune to the tales of derring-do (and derring-don't). Subs slithered into foreign harbors under the cloak of darkness to wreak happy havoc, apparently oblivious to their own meagre chances of escape. Others braved minefields to head off enemy convoys that might otherwise have eluded them. Wanklyn in the *Upholder* once went it alone against nine heavily armed ships and, in spite of a faulty gyrocompass that forced him to fire by sight from a choppy surface at night, bagged three before slipping away. The *Porpoise,* well known on Malta for ferrying crucial supplies and personnel to the island, had once survived eighty-seven depth charges during one of her "magic carpet" runs.

The stories were coming thick and fast, and Max was so absorbed in the swan song that he almost missed his moment.

Staying Tommy's hand, he said, "Ah, the *Upstanding.* Lionel's sub."

"Hell of a man. Hell of a crew."

"Where are they now?"

"Well, if Lionel has any sense, he'll be lying in Mitzi's arms."

Max rose above the thought and even managed a small laugh. "And the crew?"

"Not here. We lost the mess decks last month to a parachute mine. They're in syndicate flats in Sliema when they're not on duty watch."

Max ran his finger slowly down the page, pausing at the details of an engagement off Tripoli, but his eyes were elsewhere, scanning ahead.

February 17 and March 8: the dates he'd got from Freddie, the dates that marked the discovery of the two other dance hostesses, the ones who had died in circumstances suspicious enough for Freddie to have alerted the lieutenant governor's office.

Max willed the *Upstanding* to have been on patrol, far away in the waters off Sardinia or some such place. But she'd been in port on both occasions, resting between sorties.

"Well?" said Tommy.

"Huh?"

He hadn't been listening.

"Mitzi . . . When we're gone . . . you'll see she's all right? Until she joins us in Alex, that is."

"I have the feeling she's quite capable of looking after herself."

"Oh, she likes to cut a certain figure, but she's not as tough as she makes out."

"You think?"

"I know."

Tommy seemed on the point of elaborating when the door creaked open behind them.

It was good to know that Lionel wasn't curled up somewhere with Mitzi. It wasn't quite so good to think of the flotilla's log spread open on the desk at the pages relating to the *Upstanding.* Max shifted in his chair to obstruct Lionel's view of it.

"Max, old man."

"Lionel."

Lionel turned his inquiring eyes to

146

Tommy. "Cat out of the bag?"

"He knows."

"Fair enough." Lionel shrugged. "Can't keep it secret forever, I suppose."

He was a handsome man, blue-eyed and flaxen-haired, although his mustache was of a slightly darker tinge (and a touch too bushy to be taken seriously). He was not as tall as he would have liked to be. It annoyed him that he had never quite reached six feet, but he knew he was well proportioned, and he was proud of his long legs and narrow hips, both of which he believed made him appear taller than he was.

These were just some of the facts Max had learned from Mitzi about her husband. Max also knew that Lionel only ever made love in the dark; that he'd been circumcised; and that when he snored, he sounded not unlike a bullfrog. Max derived no pleasure from these insights; he would have preferred not to know. Anything that rendered Lionel more human also made it harder to look him in the eye.

Getting to his feet, Max calmly closed the log before turning back. "I don't know what to say. It's a sad day indeed. Have you told Mitzi?"

"Last night."

"How did she take it?"

Tommy gave a dry little laugh. "What? Forced to leave a besieged island before it falls to the enemy?"

"Malta won't fall," Max found himself saying with a vehemence that surprised him.

Lionel ignored the statement. "Well, actually, she took it rather badly. What with her job and everything, she feels she's doing her bit for the war effort."

"I'm sure we can drum up some letter-writing for her in Alex."

"That's what I told her, though with slightly more tact."

Max knew he had to smile along with them — anything less would have been too revealing — but he wanted to scream at them. Were they really so blind? Was that really how they saw her: the little woman troubling her head with the affairs of men? He knew what she did, and he knew she did it well because he had sometimes helped her with it when Lionel was away on patrol.

By any standards, it was a grim job. Unable to attend to their own affairs, dead RAF personnel required others to do the business on their behalf, and that duty fell to the Standing Committee of Adjustment. From their ground-floor offices on Scot Street, they sifted through the personal effects of the victims. Small objects of sentimental value were dispatched free of charge to the next of kin; bulkier items were either shipped home at the expense of the families or sold for the benefit of the RAF Benevolent Fund.

Mitzi was in charge of the correspondence. She read all the letters the casualties had received during their time on Malta, judging which of them to hold back. It wouldn't do for a grieving widow to find a love note from another woman buried away in her dead husband's mail. When she wasn't preserving the memory of the dead, Mitzi was drafting the official letters that accompanied the personal effects back home. Most people would have dashed them off mechanically, but Mitzi worked hard to lend them a thoughtful and human touch, knowing that her words could make a difference.

"I've asked her to leave the flat in Valetta till she ships out to Alex. The Reynolds have said they'll have her in Saint Julian's."

"Good idea," said Tommy. "It's a far safer place to be right now."

"She's dead against it, won't listen to common sense." Lionel turned to Max. "A word in her ear would be appreciated, old man."

"Of course," said Max.

Tommy and Lionel accompanied him

back to his motorcycle, stopping to show him the stone wall on which Lord Byron had scratched his name while quarantined at the Lazaretto.

Tommy ran his finger over the sloping script.

"Adieu thou damnedst quarantine, / That gave me fever and the spleen," he intoned, presumably quoting from one of Byron's poems. "He didn't like Malta."

"And who can bloody blame him?" muttered Lionel.

Valetta was a welcome tonic after the desolation and destruction of the submarine base, which was saying something. In all its long history, the place had surely never looked worse. It had been almost a month since the opera house close by Kingsgate had received a direct hit, but its tumbled ruins still gave pause for thought. From here, it was a short walk down Kingsway to the shell of the Regent Theatre, where more than a hundred people had lost their lives on Carnival Sunday back in February during an afternoon showing of *North West Mounted Police.* Freddie, a devoted fan of Madeleine Carroll (and other ice-cool blondes in her mold) had dragged Max to see DeMille's curious and rather disappointing epic just the evening before. Several officers whom Max had known well enough to stand a drink for at the Union Club had not been so lucky with their timing.

Close brushes such as these brought to mind the grim words etched into one of the knights' tombs in Saint John's Co-Cathedral, remarkably undamaged still, a stone's throw from the Regent: *Hora Venit ejus, Veniet et tua.* "Death came for them, and it shall come for you." Maybe the Maltese had absorbed this stark truth with their mother's milk, for they had an impressive capacity for carrying on regardless. Even now, they were buzzing about their business, moving with purpose, and Max found himself falling into step with the jittery rhythms of the street, a welcome antidote to the weary defeatism of the submariners. He had to hurry if he was going to make his appointment. Iris had been very clear with him on the phone: she wouldn't hang around for him if he was late.

Iris was a civilian plotter with RAF Fighter Control in the Combined Operations Room. Sometimes referred to as "the Ops Room" but widely known as "the Hole," it lay deep within the rock below the Upper Barraka Gardens. A rough-hewn tunnel led to an unprepossessing run of musty and malodorous rooms, and it was from this poorly ventilated little warren that the defense of Malta was coordinated. Max knew the place well from his many meetings with the air officer commanding, and although it was undoubtedly the safest spot to be on the entire island, it still brought out a claustrophobic streak in him.

As ever, a gaggle of off-duty pilots hovered near the entrance, waiting for the girls to come off their shifts.

"Shouldn't you be up there mixing it with the enemy?" said Max as he pushed past them.

"Get us some bloody kites and we will," replied one who'd failed to clock the irony in his words.

"Why didn't you say? How many do you want?"

"A couple of hundred should see us good."

"Consider it done," Max replied, slipping inside.

"Bloody comedian," came an Australian voice as the door swung shut behind him.

One feature of the Hole was the permanent babble of voices echoing off the hard walls, the low urgent hum of men and women engrossed in serious business. Even if the navy plotting room was silent, the wireless signals receiving room next door would invariably be alive with activity, or the antiaircraft gun operations next door to that, or coastal defense. Max passed through each in turn, exchanging brief greetings as he went.

Fighter Control was alive with activity, and Max took up a discreet position on the gallery with a couple of Maltese girls waiting to go on duty. Down in the pit, Iris and her colleagues buzzed around the plotting table, shifting small markers around with long poles according to the instructions they were receiving from the filter room through their headphones. There seemed to be some kind of plot building just north of the island.

From his vantage point high on the shelf, Group Captain "Woody" Woodhall, the senior fight controller, peered down on the proceedings. It was good that he was on duty: good for the pilots in the air, and good for Max, who always enjoyed watching the master at work. Woody was known for his uncanny ability to anticipate the enemy's movements, and the pilots had developed a fanatical faith in his controlling. Max had often heard it said that even in a freezing cockpit at twenty-five thousand feet, you didn't feel alone if Woody was on the other end of the line.

"Hello, Pinto Red Leader. This party is about ten miles north of you now, coming south."

The voice helped: deep, measured, always reassuring.

"Thank you, Woody."

"Keep your present angels and save your gravy."

Woody exchanged a few words with the gunnery liaison officer seated beside him on the shelf. Down in the pit, Iris caught sight of Max and sketched a small wave in the air. The tense seconds ticked by. Then voices started to come over the public-address system.

"There they are!"

"Can't see them."

"Two o'clock below. Big jobs and a swarm of little boys."

"Jeez." Probably an American pilot.

"Still can't see them. You lead, you lead."

"Happy hunting, fellers." Definitely an American.

"Do us a favor, Woody, and tell them to put the kettle on."

"Milk and two sugars, right, Harry?"

"Just the one sugar. I'm watching my waistline."

Woody laughed. "Well, don't forget to watch your back too."

An unsettling silence followed. Anxious glances were exchanged. There was nothing to do now other than sit back and wait. It wouldn't take long. The nature of aerial combat in Malta didn't allow for drawn-out dogfights, not when you were so heavily outnumbered. The handful of Hurricanes and Spitfires would swoop from high above, out of the sun, ignoring the covering force of 109s, each singling out a bomber. It was the bombs that did the damage, and the aim was to prevent the Junker 88s from reaching their targets. Ripping through the German formation with the throttle through the gate, the pilots would be happy if they got off a couple of squirts before racing for home. To linger any longer would be suicide.

The silence stretched out ominously; the atmosphere in the Ops Room grew more expectant. Then the PA crackled into life.

"I got one! I got one!"

"Good show," said Woody.

"He's going down over Saint Paul's."

"Don't hang around and gloat."

"Yes, I can see him. He's for it."

"And stop burning up the R/T."

"Sorry, Woody."

"Okay, Woody, out of ammo. Think I damaged one." It was the American.

"Good show, Mac. All Pinto aircraft,

pancake as quickly as you can."

"Emergency, emergency. I'm losing glycol, and my oil's gone from ninety to twenty. Little yellow bugger jumped me!"

"Harry —"

"I may have to step outside. Transmitting for a fix, transmitting for a fix." And after a worrying interval: "Yes, I'm going down in the drink off Saint George's. Here goes. Hope my brolly works."

"Good luck, Harry. Transport's on the way."

It was extraordinary to hear it played out live, this drama of planes and men going down. With luck, Harry's parachute would open and the high-speed launch would find him bobbing in the ocean in his Mae West, but it was no longer a concern for those in the Ops Room. They were dealing with an ever-evolving situation. Already, Woody was warning the other pilots of a couple of 109s in the circuit at Ta' Qali, waiting to jump them when they came back in to land. Only when the raid had played itself out would they all stop and reflect on the skirmish.

This occurred some twenty minutes later, by which time the airfield at Luqa had taken another pitiless pounding and news had come in of the downed pilot's successful rescue from the water. The new girls went on their shift, and Iris joined Max up on the gallery.

"Sorry about that."

"You're a dab hand with that pole of yours."

Iris checked herself in her vanity mirror. "I've had a year of practice."

On went the lipstick. Some girls ground rice into dust for face powder, but Iris was never short of the real thing, receiving a steady supply of cosmetics from her steady supply of admirers.

"Is it really that long?" Max asked. But looking at her he could believe it. The skin around her eyes appeared looser, her lips less full, and there were dark roots showing in her wavy blond mane.

"I know, I look dreadful."

"I was about to say quite the opposite."

Iris capped her lipstick. "You're a sweetheart. You always were."

"What do you say to a late lunch at Monico's? Hot pork sandwiches and John Collinses."

"I say lead the way."

Monico's had been an old haunt of theirs during Iris's brief stint at the Information Office, and a brace of John Collinses brought out a nostalgic streak in her. She insisted on retracing their history, starting with their first meeting at a dance at the Engine Room Artificer's Club in Floriana. It had been a rowdy affair, and Iris and her two flatmates had been right in the thick of it.

High-kicking his way across a crowded room while singing "Knees Up, Mother Brown" at the top of his lungs would never be Max's idea of fun, but Freddie had announced to everyone present that he wouldn't be banging out any more tunes on the piano until Max joined in. It was Iris who had dragged him from his chair into the fray, Iris who had hooked her arm through his and refused to release him until Freddie turned his gifted hands to some Cole Porter numbers.

At the time, Iris was still a member of the Arabian Knights, a concert party made up of six girls and two young men who walked from the hips down. They were one of the more popular outfits on the island, if only because their routines verged on the downright bawdy. What was it about the English that allowed them to find so much humor in men dressing up as women, and vice versa? Hugh would have said that Shakespeare was to blame.

Max had only once seen the Arabian

Knights in action; they'd been mostly on the road in an old Scammell truck provided by the Navy, Army and Air Force Institutes (NAAFI), performing at airfields and forts and remote gun sites. The arrival of the Luftwaffe in Sicily in early '41 spelled the end of the troupe, the Germans taking over from their Italian allies and teaching them the true meaning of a bombing campaign. Malta shook to a holocaust that left little place for frivolous entertainments, and the Arabian Knights were forced to disband.

Crueler tongues than Max's had speculated about Charles Headley's decision to employ Iris at the Information Office. What did Max care if Headley was getting his oil changed in return for offering her a job? She was a performer, fun to have around, and competent enough when it came to reading out the news bulletins for the Rediffusion. Moreover, she hadn't fled the island when the opportunity to do so had still existed, which suggested a certain commitment to the cause.

Admittedly, there had been something slightly self-serving about this commitment. At the first opportunity, she had left the Information Office for the giddy heights of Fighter Control, but Max had never begrudged her her resourcefulness and ambition. She was a young woman from a tough neighborhood of south London who had pulled herself up by the boot straps, exchanging a sequin-encrusted brassiere for a key job at the heart of the military machine. He knew that the wives of the high-ranking officers with whom she now rubbed shoulders despised her for her pretensions, her efforts to dress more like them and improve her accent — and maybe there was something of the same thinking in their husbands — but as someone who had suffered at the hands of knee-jerk prejudice, Max knew whose side he was on.

His easy companionship with Iris had never been haunted by the spectre of physical attraction. On that score, Max did nothing for her. She had told him as much the day he'd accompanied her and her mangy dog to the blessing of the animals at the church of Santa Maria Vittoriosa.

"I don't know why. You're tall and dark and very handsome, and you have perfectly lovely green eyes, but I'm not in the least bit attracted to you."

"That's okay, Iris."

"It's just the same with Freddie. Something about him leaves me cold."

"I'm sure he can live with it too."

Sitting there in Monico's, Iris ran him

through an impressively long list of other men who *had* managed to stir something in her since they'd last caught up on each other's news. Her current weakness was a Free French pilot named Henri who had purloined a Latécoère torpedo bomber in north Africa and flown to Malta to join the fight. As ever, she was in love, and this time it was the real thing.

Max waited for her to talk herself to a standstill before making his move.

"Iris, I need your help."

"My help?"

"It's a sensitive matter, for your ears only."

It occurred to him only then just how difficult this might become. For a person bent on reinventing herself, she wasn't necessarily going to appreciate being reminded of her seamy past.

"What was the name of that place you worked when you first came to Malta?"

He knew the name. And he knew the place. It was still there: an apology for a dance hall just off Strait Street where it dipped away toward Fort Saint Elmo. Like many other girls with a London show or two under their belts, Iris had been lured to Malta before the war with the promise of fame and fortune, only to find herself prancing around a postage-stamp stage for a bay-ing mob of drunk and hormone-fueled sailors.

"Why?" she asked warily.

"I know it's a world you've left behind — and good riddance to it."

"It wasn't such a bad life."

He had heard enough stories from others to know she was stretching the truth.

"Well, maybe it's got worse. Or maybe it hasn't. Maybe it's nothing."

"And maybe you should spit it out."

"As I say, it's probably nothing . . ."

This was a phrase he kept returning to over the next few minutes. He tried to remain as vague as possible, making out that he was only doing someone else a favor by approaching her. This person — he couldn't say who exactly, they had asked him not to — was of the feeling that casualty rates were running unnaturally high among the sherry queens of the Gut. He was fumbling his way toward the request when she preempted him.

"You want me to ask around."

"A few discreet inquiries to some of the people you know — knew. See if there's any truth in it. As I say, it's probably nothing."

"Let me get this straight. You think someone's killing sherry queens, and you want me to go in there and be discreet?" She seemed amused by the idea, and probably with good reason.

"I don't think anything."

"No, that's right, this 'person' thinks someone's killing sherry queens." She made no attempt to conceal the heavy irony.

"Iris, look, he doesn't know anything. He's just doing his job, making sure. Forget I ever mentioned it, okay?"

He meant it. He should never have approached her with it.

Iris pulled a cigarette from the packet and waited for him to light it for her.

"I'm sorry. I shouldn't have asked you."

"Of course I'll do it," she said.

It wasn't a diary. He had always disliked the idea of diaries. They smacked of vainglory. What drove people to record the mundane drift of their ordinary lives for posterity's sake? Did they really think that posterity didn't have better things to concern itself with?

His scribblings were of an altogether different kind, a loose assemblage of thoughts and impressions and memories laid down for his own benefit. Not to mention the deeds. The deeds were anything but mundane.

He kept only one notebook, and the moment its pages were filled, he destroyed it, ritually, always with fire. He felt no sense of loss at the notebooks' annihilation. Quite the reverse. He set about despoiling the virgin pages of a fresh notebook with renewed vigor, starting again, telling the story from scratch, reaching back to the very first days.

The years lent a proper perspective. He was continually evolving, and so should the record be.

What did the blinkered musings of some former self — some lesser self — have to offer him? Why revisit the youthful confusion of that long walk home through the rain from Mrs. Beckett's house? Far better to see it in its proper context, as part of the overarching pattern, a necessary step in his metamorphosis.

If it hadn't been for Mrs. Beckett, Bad Reichenhall would never have happened. That was the truth of it, the undeniable logic.

Her name was Constanze, and she was a first cousin of Lutz Kettelmann. Blond and voluble, she was also keen to point out that she was a couple of years older than the two boys, although this didn't stop her from searching out their company at every opportunity. Her haughtiness irritated Lutz, whereas it washed over him. Whenever she talked down to them, which was often, he would simply smile and think of Mrs. Beckett facedown on the bed, her naked rump in the air.

Constanze wasn't the only reason he looked back on his time at Bad Reichenhall with fondness. He appreciated the routine, the Teutonic order of the place, the almost comical devotion to saltwater cures and vigorous exercise. At that time, Germany was still suffering, but the winds of change were blowing through it, bringing good things to the Kettelmanns and their kind. Breakfast in their hotel was at eight o'clock sharp, and while the brisk and efficient staff buzzed around their long table under the awning on the terrace, Herr Kettelmann would draw up the day's timetable, marshaling his troops, getting them to repeat their orders so that there would be no unfortunate slipups. Since children were not generally afflicted by the sort of ailments that drew the adults to the waters of Bad Reichenhall every summer, they were spared the morning session in the spa baths. There was to be no idling, though. The surrounding countryside offered any number of opportunities for building up a healthy appetite for lunch. It was an impressive landscape, a landscape of extremes, of soaring pine-clad mountains and deep emerald-green lakes.

Constanze loved to walk, but she loved bathing more, and the three of them spent much of their time at the Thumsee, a lake to the west of town. He had shared many moments with Lutz at Brooklands, but their friendship was forged on the shores of that lake, lazing in the sun and swimming in the crystal-clear waters. Maybe friendship was overstating it, even now, but he could remember feeling anchored by the company, no longer adrift on a boundless sea.

Constanze never once made mention of his father's death, almost as if she knew that it had left no gaping hole in his life. Once, when Lutz was skimming stones at the water's edge and he was alone with Constanze on the grassy bank of the lake, she claimed that she could read his thoughts, which he interpreted as meaning that she had felt his eyes on her. He wasn't embarrassed. Embarrassment was an emotion he no longer experienced. Besides, she was right. It was hard to ignore her, parading about in her costume with her long pale limbs and her high firm breasts. He asked her if she had ever kissed a boy. Of course not, came her indignant reply; she had only ever kissed men. The intended snub fell on deaf ears, and her eyes almost popped out of her head when he told her about Mrs. Beckett. He left out the stuff about blackmailing her into bed, but told it pretty much as it had been. He also asked her not to say anything to Lutz. It was to be their secret.

The ploy worked. The secret festered away over the following days. Constanze was as puffed-up as ever, maybe more so, but he caught the conspiratorial looks she threw his way, and sometimes she brushed against him unnecessarily. Then came the urgent, whispered questions whenever they found themselves alone for a moment. Had he really done it with Mrs. Beckett? Was it really like he had said?

The evening before they were all due to leave Bad Reichenhall, she took him aside and suggested they meet up later after everyone was in bed. She billed it as a last walk to the Thumsee, a final farewell to their lake. Her excuse for not including Lutz in the expedition was that his bedroom adjoined that of his parents, and he was liable to give the game away if he joined them.

It was a warm, balmy night, and a crescent moon lit their path to the lake. They stripped off and swam to the big rock and back. Then they kissed in the shallows and her hand closed uncertainly around him. She gave a small squeal of pain as his hand returned the favor, fingers probing, delving. She released him immediately and made off out of the water, long and lean and ivory-white in the moonlight. He knew that his crude fumblings had killed the moment, but he was damned if he was going to take all the blame. After all, it was she who had lured him there with the promise of greater things.

She was too preoccupied with pulling on her clothes to see him coming. He grabbed her and spun her around and forced his tongue into her mouth. She resisted, of course, even when he told her that he would hurt her if she didn't stop. Seizing her hair seemed the sensible thing to do, as it would leave no mark. It certainly subdued her enough for him to have his way with her, right there on the grassy rise beside the lake. And while he did it, he told her why he was doing it. After a month of her stuck-up ways, he was not lost for words. The more she tried to twist free of him, the more pleasure he derived from her struggles, a dark and deeply satisfying pleasure he had not felt with Mrs. Beckett. And when it was over, he didn't thank her and promise his eternal silence, as he had done with Mrs. Beckett. He threatened her with a fate far worse than the one she'd just endured if she ever breathed a word of it.

While they were getting dressed, he took a more reasoned tack, pointing out that it would be her word against his. Even if she persuaded people of the truth, her reputation would still be in tatters. "I understand," she said. And she seemed to.

The following morning she was at breakfast at eight o'clock sharp, composed, if somewhat more subdued than usual. This was put down to the prospect of returning to Bremen after a glorious month in the Alps.

She had gone on to marry a wealthy corn merchant. He knew this because over the years he had asked after her, and Lutz had filled him in on the dreary details of her life: another child, a new holiday house by the sea, her charity work for the unemployed. Unsurprisingly, the war had restricted these updates, but he still thought of her with something approaching affection. She might not have been the very first, but it was she who had triggered the first stirrings of life in him, she who had set him on the road. He had taken wrong turns, dangerous deviations that had almost proved to be his undoing, but he was wiser now — more cautious, more patient, and far better at covering his tracks.

# DAY FOUR

Max had been hopelessly awake for hours, wrestling with the sheet, when the building wail of the siren cut through his thoughts. The windows were shuttered, but a pale dawn light leaked into the bedroom through the crack in the wall. He'd tracked the progress of this jagged fissure over the past month with a mixture of curiosity and alarm. It had set off on its journey from the floor beside the chest of drawers, traveling in fits and starts on a diagonal path toward the ceiling, widening to a hand's width as it went. At a certain moment it had disappeared behind the only picture in the room — a naïve watercolor of some unidentifiable fruit in a bowl — only to reemerge a week or so later from behind the shell and coral frame and carry on its way.

There was no stopping it. What it would do when it reached the ceiling was anyone's guess; structural engineering had never been his forte at college. Diagonal was bad, though; he knew that much. So was the fact that the doors in the apartment no longer closed properly.

His neighbors had long since fled, part of the great exodus that had all but emptied Valetta, Floriana, and the Three Cities, stuffing the surrounding towns and villages to bursting point. His refusal to budge had both puzzled and pleased them; at least someone was left to deter looters. But there was nothing noble and defiant in his decision to remain. From his bedroom window he had a direct view of Mitzi and Lionel's flat in Valetta, and that kind of proximity was not something he'd been ready to give up. Well, not until now.

Theirs was a third-floor flat, large and light, overlooking Hastings Gardens. Max knew it well. He still had a key to the entrance door downstairs. The key was tucked away in the drawer of his bedside table, redundant for more than two months, ever since Mitzi's abrupt termination of their relationship.

It had been hard to fault her logic.

"Everyone reaches for a crutch in war. That's what we've done. We're like two cripples leaning on each other. It can't continue, Max. I'm a married woman. It has to stop."

He knew her well enough by then not to argue. She rarely spoke in haste. She had thought the matter through and drawn her conclusion. Nothing he said or did would dissuade her.

"Okay."

"I knew you'd understand."

"I didn't say I understood."

They had been naked at the time. Five minutes later, he was fully dressed and heading home on foot, sticking to the shadows, as he always did. That's when he remembered the key in his hip pocket. The black void beyond the bastion wall called out for it, but he kept it clutched tightly in his fist. He had always prided himself on his ability to cope with rejection, and he was happy to be able to ascribe the tears pricking his eyes to the dust carried on the stiff wind whipping through the streets.

His attitude had hardened considerably over the following days and weeks, especially when it became clear there was to be no change of heart on Mitzi's part. Numb resignation slowly gave way to indignation, then to morose self-absorption.

Tellingly, Lilian was the first to note the change in him.

"What's wrong?" she had asked as they

were winding up one of their weekly meetings. "You're not yourself."

"Who of us is?"

She cocked her head at him as if to say, *You'll have to do better than that.*

"I mean it. Life here . . . it's like another incarnation. I can't remember who I was."

"So tell me."

"What?"

"Tell me. It might help you remember."

He spoke mostly about architecture, the curious and inexplicable passion that had nibbled at the fringes of his consciousness during childhood, and that he had finally acknowledged, just in time, a week shy of taking up the post he'd been offered by the Foreign Office while still a student at Oxford.

His university friends, taking the first teetering steps in their respective careers, were baffled by his decision to start over from scratch, dismissing it as the whimsy of someone who was an eternal student at heart, which probably wasn't so far from the truth. His father, on the other hand, had embraced the idea. He'd even embraced Max — something he hadn't done in years — congratulating him on his courage and offering to cover the cost of a small apartment in London for the duration of his studies.

His time at the Architectural Association had been a revelation, both thrilling and humbling after the dilettante posturing of Oxford, the endless round of dining clubs and debating societies. No one cared if he thought Ezra Pound or T. S. Eliot was the daddy of contemporary poetry. He felt stripped bare, naked, exhilarated. The work came first, *their* work, not someone else's. He even learned to find beauty in the tedium of a technical drawing class, the utter silence of people doing rather than discussing. Yes, they talked about architecture — as he did now to Lilian — about its power to make the human spirit soar, and about the green shoots of the exciting new aesthetic pushing through the establishment soil. If he bored her, she didn't show it.

That one conversation had marked a notable shift in their relationship. She might have been the instigator, but they both played their part in it. Almost imperceptibly, their weekly get-together became a twice-weekly get-together, and he found himself manufacturing further excuses to drop by the offices in Saint Paul's Street whenever he was in town. The first time he invited her for a drink at the Union Club, it was on some doubtful professional pretext.

Perched on a chair in the ladies' bar — amusingly nicknamed the snake pit, which didn't amuse her — she told him the story of her father, a captain in the Yorkshire Light Infantry who had spent a year of his life on Malta, recuperating from injuries sustained in the Salonika campaign. Malta had catered to well over one hundred thousand sick and wounded during the Great War, and had come to be known as "the nurse of the Mediterranean." Lilian's mother, like so many other Maltese girls at the time, had been a volunteer nurse, and she'd lost her heart to the lanky Yorkshireman in her care, marrying him a few months before he was sent back to the front. George Flint wasn't killed by a Bulgar bullet or bomb; he died from malaria in September 1918, a few days before the war in Salonika ended.

Her mother had never remarried, unable to square the concept with her faith, although it hadn't stopped her from disappearing off to Italy a couple of years before the outbreak of war, on the arm of a visiting professor of archaeology from the University of Padua. This was the reason Lilian now lived with her aunt's family in Mdina. The invitation to dinner there had followed a few weeks later.

With its walls and ramparts and sweeping views, Mdina reminded him of a number of hilltop towns he had visited in France with his father before the war, and while it lacked a cathedral to match those of Laon or Vézelay, it more than made up for this in other ways. As the seat of the Maltese nobility, its streets and squares were lined with stately palaces, mostly built in a restrained baroque style. The same graceful architecture was evident in the churches, convents, and seminaries that accounted for almost all the other buildings in the compact citadel. The effect was ordered, aristocratic, ecclesiastical; and an ancient peace seemed to hang over the place, a silence broken every so often by the slap and scuff of leather sandals on stone as friars and nuns shuffled about their business.

Lilian's aunt, her mother's younger sister, had married into one of the more ancient families, acquiring a convoluted title in the process, although she insisted on being addressed simply as Teresa. Her husband, the twentieth baron of something or other unpronounceable, was an officer in the Royal Malta Artillery. He commanded an antiaircraft battery near the fuel reservoirs at Birzebbuga in the south of the island,

and he was rarely around, which left his wife, his niece, and his two young daughters free run of the palace on Bastion Square.

At dinner, Max had been a little put out to find himself seated next to Teresa at one end of the long table, while a handsome and amusing young captain with the 2nd Battalion Cheshire Regiment monopolized Lilian at the other end. He drew some consolation from the fact that Teresa appeared to know a fair amount about him already, although this didn't stop her from quizzing him further. She was an attractive woman with a ready laugh and large eyes made for drawing confidences from strangers, especially ones who had consumed too much fine red wine.

He told her about his life back home in England, about the big house in Oxfordshire where he had grown up, the farm that came with it, and the fields and woods and lakes that had served as his playground when he was a boy. She wanted more, though. What was his father like? A modest, soft-spoken man. Kindhearted, if slightly remote. And his mother? She was dead. How? In childbirth. Giving birth to him.

Silence. The same awkward silence that always followed this revelation, as if people were weighing in their minds the exact extent of his culpability. But Teresa was different.

"How terrible that you did not know your mother."

"I couldn't say. I've nothing to compare it with."

"Are her family still in your life?"

"They're French. *She* was French."

"And her name?"

It didn't come readily to his lips. In fact, he couldn't remember the last time he'd uttered it.

"Camille."

He was too far in by now to extract himself, so he told her the story, in so much as it had been handed down to him. His father, the youngest of three sons, had always harbored dreams of being a painter, dreams that had carried him to Paris against the wishes of his parents. The advent of war, along with a creeping recognition of his own creative limitations, conspired to foul his plans, and in 1914 he returned to England with his French bride — the daughter of a notary who had lived in the same apartment building in Paris. Both of his brothers were dead within a year. Miraculously, he survived the Western Front to find himself first in line, the sole heir, to a small estate north of Oxford.

It was the kind of life Max's father had never wanted or imagined for himself, but Camille's death in childbirth a short while later sealed his fate. A number of local ladies pounced on him, and he was too disorientated and weak — yes, weak — to repel the pushiest candidate.

"Your stepmother?"

"Sylvia."

"How old were you?"

"Too young to remember."

This was a lie. Strange and mildly unsettling memories still came to him from time to time, static images, snapshots, cold and stark and remote: the high shine of his father's shoes on the day of the wedding . . . a faceless woman dressed all in white and framed in a doorway . . . his nanny holding him at the nursery window, watching the wedding party return from the church. Whether or not they were reliable memories, he couldn't say. It was quite possible that his brain had assembled them from photographs and hearsay. He knew for a fact, however, that Sylvia had insisted he shouldn't attend the ceremony.

"Did they have children?"

"I have a half brother and sister, not much younger than me. Roland and Elizabeth. Elizabeth's a fine woman."

"And Roland?"

Max hesitated, reaching for his wineglass. Idle. Overweight. Overbearing. Cruel.

"Roland's all right."

Any pretense of a relationship had disappeared long ago, when Roland — not for the first time — had referred to Max's mother as "that French whore." Dr. Tomkins, the local GP, had done a good job of resetting Roland's nose, although it still veered a little to the left when viewed in certain lights.

Even as he had landed that punch, Max had known that Roland hadn't been wholly to blame, that he had only been parroting the words of his mother. Sylvia had worked tirelessly over the years to drive a wedge between Max and her own son. Everyone knew the reason why. Everyone knew what was at stake.

Max had toyed with the idea of forgoing his birthright, of stepping aside and allowing the estate to pass to Roland — and maybe he still would — but prolonging their distress offered some small satisfaction for their hostile treatment of him over the years, the injustice of which still filled him with impotent and uncomprehending anger in his darker moments.

He labored under no illusions — he'd had

a privileged upbringing, and to complain about it seemed somehow perverse — but he had always felt himself very much alone in the world, and he held Sylvia and Roland largely to blame for this. His father was exonerated on the grounds that he had never given Max cause to doubt their special bond. They shared many of the same interests. Whether it was facing each other across a chessboard or fiddling with the guts of some motorcycle or casting flies for trout on the river, they both knew that those private moments were more about reinforcing their silent alliance than about the activity itself. They discussed literature and art and films, and all the other things that Sylvia deemed too trivial to be aired at the dinner table, such as the book his father had been working on for the past ten years or more.

It was a biography of the young Frenchman Jean-François Champollion, who, in spite of his lowly origins, had won the race to decipher the Egyptian hieroglyphs, beating the most eminent orientalists in Europe to the coveted prize. It was a story well worth telling, but why his father should have devoted so many years of his life to the subject was anyone's guess. Max suspected it was something to do with the idea of a young man setting his sights on a goal and persevering in the face of insuperable odds — something his father had failed to do. He also suspected that the book would never be completed, because if it ever were, his father would no longer have an excuse to potter off to the London Library or the British Museum on the train.

Max had had no intention of sharing any of this with Teresa, but the words had just tumbled from his lips, almost as if he were under the spell of some sorceress, which he began to think he might be.

"Maybe he has a lover in London," Teresa remarked.

"That's . . . well, an unexpected observation."

"Why?"

"From a Catholic."

"Say what you like about us Catholics, but we understand human weakness." She gave a knowing smile. "And I see from your face that the idea is not such a bad one for you."

No, it wasn't: his father stealing a few moments of happiness in the arms of a lady friend. He just felt a little foolish that it hadn't occurred to him before.

Meanwhile, down at the other end of the table, the captain from the Cheshires was evidently doing a good job of entertaining Lilian, judging from her laughter. A few weeks before, it wouldn't have mattered to him. Now it did. So much so that when the evening finally broke up, he was quite ready to leave, to be gone. That impulse vanished the moment Lilian asked him to stay on a while longer. There was a work matter she needed to discuss with him.

It was a chilly, clear night, and she held her woolen cardigan tight around her shoulders as they strolled in the palace garden, their feet crunching softly on the gravel pathway.

"You looked like you were enjoying yourself with the blond Adonis from the Cheshires."

"Tristran."

"Of course. How could I forget?"

"He's very brave."

"Really?"

"Yes, he told me."

In the darkness he could just make out the gleam of her teeth.

"You know what? He probably is. The Cheshires have had the dirty end of the stick for quite a while."

"You're defending him?" she asked.

"Yes. No. I hate him."

They both knew there was another message buried in the words — an admission on his part — and he quickly filled the awkward silence with a question.

"So, what did you want to talk about?"

She had a couple of questions about some material sent by the Ministry of Information to the *Times of Malta* that had found its way through to her at *Il-Berqa*.

"Ignore it," was Max's advice. "Most of what we get from them is complete rubbish or out of date — usually both."

"That's no way to talk about your superiors."

"I can only imagine it's done on purpose."

"On purpose?"

"To confuse the Germans, should they ever intercept a dispatch."

Lilian laughed before drawing to a halt on the pathway.

"Over here," she said quietly, setting off across the grass.

"Why?"

"My cousins."

"What about them?" he asked, falling into step with her.

Felicia and Ena were two leggy creatures in their early teens.

"I know what they're like. They'll be watching from their bedroom."

She led him beneath the boughs of a large

orange tree. It was so dark that he sensed rather than saw her take a step toward him.

They kissed briefly, almost cursorily, their lips barely touching.

There was nothing cursory about their second kiss. She pressed her body against his, and the warm tip of her tongue forced its way between his lips.

"Don't stop," she said, when they broke off briefly.

And when they finally separated, he bent to recover her cardigan from the ground and replaced it around her shoulders.

"Oh dear," she said. "Now I'll have to lie to them at breakfast."

"Oh well. In for a penny, in for a pound." He slipped an arm around her waist and pulled her toward him. She avoided his lips.

"And then I'll have to tell Father Tabone in confession that I lied to them, and he will want to know why."

"And when you tell him, he'll say, 'Lilian, Lilian, not the soldier under the orange tree story again.' "

She gave a horrified gasp and playfully pinched his arm. "You think I am like that, do you?"

"I think I want to kiss you again."

She didn't resist, and this time her hands roamed beneath his shirt and up his back.

No thoughts of Mitzi had intruded at the time. Only later, during the long ride back to Floriana on the motorcycle, the searchlights roving the heavens high above his head, did he weigh those first tentative embraces against the urgent abandon that had always marked his lovemaking with Mitzi.

Mitzi had unleashed something in him, presented him with a side of himself that he'd never known existed — a dark and sometimes unsavory side. Maybe it was her guilt, but there were occasions when she had required him to dominate, even demean her. And he had duly obliged, warily at first, like an observer hovering above the bed, then more willingly.

He had since abandoned his theory of an errant wife's unconscious desire for castigation, partly because it was insulting to her. Did errant husbands feel obliged to act out their guilt with their lovers? Somehow he doubted it. And besides, who was he to pass judgment? An embarrassingly brief encounter with a girl named Felicity after a May Ball at Oxford and a bit of awkward fumbling with Eleanor had represented the entire scope of his sexual experience. Who was he to say what people got up to in the privacy of their bedrooms?

Moreover, since terminating their affair, Mitzi had shown no signs of guilt or regret for what had passed between them. He had fully expected her to withdraw from him, to avoid him whenever possible, but their public relationship had suffered no such reverse. If anything, it had flourished under the unsuspecting eyes of their friends and acquaintances. He still found it strange to spend time with her in company — knowing every inch of the lean body beneath the cotton frock, as well as its most intimate requirements — but her ability to carry on with life regardless had allowed him to package up and parcel off the memories.

That had all changed at Hugh and Rosamund's drinks party.

*My God, I've missed you.*

A voice straight from their private past, from the flat overlooking Hastings Gardens.

*Me too,* he had wanted to shout. *Me too.*

This was the reason he'd been unable to sleep, his brain in open rebellion, deaf to the dictates of his weary body, thoughts of Lilian and Mitzi swirling endlessly, aimlessly, around and around in his head, overlapping, intertwining. And as if that hadn't been bad enough already, the dead dance hostesses had somehow entered the mix, the pale, lifeless features of Carmela Cassar rising to the surface every so often like some ghoulish phantasm clamoring to be heard. She was unhappy with him, and she had every right to be. What had he done for her? What had he *really* done for her? No more than the bare minimum, hoping that the affair would somehow resolve itself, or simply go away.

He knew of a number of individuals, men as well as women, who had cracked up and been carted off — one had even tried to end it all with a tube of Veronal — but until now it had never occurred to him to feel much sympathy toward them.

Outside, the first bombs were beginning to fall on Grand Harbour, and a couple of the big guns were barking back. The Bofors wouldn't open up until the Stukas showed, which they would after the 88s had had their sport, if the pattern of the past week was anything to go by.

Flakes of plaster showered from the ceiling as he wandered through to the living room. Strangely, the prospect of observing a bombing raid on his doorstep almost seemed like light relief after the mental inquests of the past few hours. He pushed open the shutters and stepped out onto the balcony.

He just had time to register the pall of dust hanging over the dockyards and Senglea before a column of water erupted from French Creek. It stood tall and upright, frozen in motion, before collapsing in on itself. Down below, by the bastion wall, the boys in the Bofors gun pit were scanning the skies. If anyone had a right to crack, it was them, especially since the Germans had started targeting the gun emplacements. They didn't appear too perturbed, though. A couple of them were even laughing.

A few minutes later, they weren't.

The Stukas came in waves, a cascade of dropping planes, plunging almost vertically through the barrage, shrugging aside the few puffs of pale smoke writhing in the sky. Gone were the days when the Grand Harbour barrage had looked like a giant chestnut tree in full flower, and admiration for the gallantry of the enemy pilots had been at its height. This ack-ack was small beer by comparison, little more than a thin splatter.

He spotted a bare section of four Spitfires following the Stukas in, looking to get among them, waiting for them to come out of their dives. This was the moment when the Stuka was at its most vulnerable, when its bombs had been released and the German pilot flicked the gizmo that pulled the aircraft up on its tail and for a few brief seconds both he and the rear gunner blacked out from the rapid climb. Easy meat for a Spitfire pilot who knew how to time his attack.

So it proved. Max saw two rising Stukas shredded by cannon fire, spinning away and dropping into the harbor. Their ammo exhausted, the Spitfires headed for home, running the gauntlet of 109s waiting for them over Hamrun. Meanwhile, the Stukas kept coming, sharp-angled birds of prey swooping from out of the blue.

Down on the bastion wall, the Bofors crew had yet to fire their gun. The long barrel swept the sky, searching for targets that warranted the precious ammunition. It found one as the raid was petering out: a lone Stuka whose dive didn't seem to be directed at the dockyards. It wasn't. The aircraft was bearing straight down on the gun pit.

"Traverse left . . . Down two . . . Lateral zero."

Max was close enough to hear the bombardier's shouts even above the scream of the diving Stuka.

"On!" yelled the layers almost simultaneously.

"Engage."

"Fire!"

*Pom-pom-pom-pom* . . .
*Pom-pom-pom-pom* . . .

The stream of shells ascended toward the plane, bursting in its path, but not hitting it. A moment later, the pilot unloaded his twin bombs.

Max watched, mesmerized, as the two dark objects fell earthward, his brain processing their trajectory and struggling to make the calculation. Bang on target? Or a touch too short?

The gunners appeared oblivious to the menace, their minds on other matters. The Bofors's barrel swung round to pick up the Stuka as it came out of its dive.

"Engage. . . ."

Max didn't hear the command to fire. It was drowned out by a mighty explosion that shook the balcony beneath his feet and sent him reaching for the rail to steady himself.

The bombs had fallen short, slamming into the sheer bastion wall below the gun pit.

*Pom-pom-pom-pom* . . .
*Pom-pom-pom-pom* . . .

Max raised his eyes toward the Stuka, guided by the red phosphorescence of the tracers, and saw the tail section part company with the main body of the aircraft, cleaved clean away as if by a knife. He glimpsed the pilot and the rear gunner, strangely inert in the high Perspex hood, unconscious still because of the g-forces. The Stuka spiraled away over the rooftops. He hoped for their sakes that they wouldn't regain consciousness before the end, but it was a good few seconds before a distant *crump* was heard — time enough for them to have come to and seen death rushing up at them.

The "Raiders Passed" siren sounded as Max was running a razor over his chin. He dressed quickly and headed downstairs, out into the unearthly silence that always followed a raid. The stench of cordite sat heavily in the chill morning air, and the flocks of pigeons were once more settling warily onto the rooftops, having spent the past half hour whirling around in agitated flight. A crowd of admirers was gathered around the Bofors gun pit. The Maltese boys had abandoned their nearby flag station and were reenacting the final moments of the doomed Stuka. The gunners were smoking and laughing and looking justifiably pleased with themselves. It had been a fine piece of shooting, each of them playing their part, a true team effort.

"Congratulations," said Max.

"Thank you, sir," replied the bombardier,

the oldest of the bunch, a skinny fellow with jug ears and tombstone teeth.

"I saw it all from up there." Max nodded toward his balcony.

"Wish I had too, sir," said one of the layers, to a round of laughter.

"There's only one thing troubling me." Max threw in a brief pause for effect. "I was watching closely, and the way I saw it, you fired off four clips at four rounds apiece."

One round more than their daily allowance of fifteen. They quickly figured Max was joking, and the bombardier spun round to the No. 4, the man who worked the pedal that fired the gun. "Oi, Bennett, you plonker. You hear that?" Bennett was the best footballer of the bunch, a sturdy little left-footer who could send an opponent the wrong way with the merest dip of a shoulder. "You're in for it when the battery commander gets wind."

"Go easy on him, sir."

"Yeah. Bennett can't count for nowt."

"Don't know the difference between fifteen and sixteen."

"Just like his sister, sir. She told me she was sixteen."

More laughter, and more cigarettes, and a promise from Max that they'd get a special mention in the Information Office's *Weekly Bulletin,* something to show the folks back home.

He meant it. He was impressed, not only by the accuracy of their shooting, but by their sheer bloody doggedness. Even as the Stuka's bombs had been dropping toward them, they had stayed focused on the task of bringing their gun to bear on the enemy. Max knew that he would have frozen; he knew that he would have suffered some quaint metaphysical moment, rooting him to the spot. And it took only one to freeze for the whole team to fall apart.

A chain is only as strong as its weakest link.

This was the tired expression he toyed with as he headed for Paola, dodging the craters in the road. He wouldn't use it, but he could take its essence, extrapolating the courage of a single gun crew to the bigger picture of the besieged garrison. Better still, he could give it to young Pemberton to play with. The fellow was itching to flex his literary muscles.

The Cassars lived in a long, squat farmhouse on the hillside above Paola, just off the Luqa road. It was an ugly building, notable only for the large beds of brightly colored flowers that hemmed it in on all sides.

Max heard the wailing before he reached the front door. It was loud enough to justify entering the house without knocking.

A dozen or so women were gathered in the drawing room, dressed entirely in black, some sporting *faldettas,* the ugly, yawning black head-dresses favored by the more elderly. The door on the far side of the room was ajar, and through the crack he could just make out the bare feet, poking from beneath a white robe, of someone laid out on a table.

The urge to spin on his heel was sudden and overwhelming, but he had been spotted.

She caught up with him as he stepped outside into the sunlight.

"Excuse me . . ."

She was young, twenty or so, and she spoke English with barely any accent.

"May I help you?"

The syntax suggested that she worked in some kind of official capacity — a nurse or a teacher, maybe, or an employee at one of the regional Protection Offices. Her name was Nina and she was Carmela's cousin.

Max had formulated a story that wouldn't arouse too much suspicion, and she seemed to fall for it, suggesting that it was probably best right now if he spoke to Carmela's father. News had just reached them that the coffin intended for Carmela had been destroyed by a wayward bomb while en route from Rabat, along with the cart, the horse, and the driver.

"Victor speaks English, but I am here if you need me."

Victor Cassar was younger than Max had imagined, although his stooped shoulders suggested a man well into old age. He was at the back of the house, watering the flowers with his son, Joe. They moved mechanically, in silent tandem, Joe charging his father's watering can with buckets of water hauled from below by hand.

It had been a miserable winter, one of the wettest in memory, but at least the wells were full.

Max introduced himself, explaining that he'd known Carmela from the Blue Parrot and had come to express his condolences at her death. Victor visibly perked up, touched by the gesture, which made Max feel worse for lying. He had no choice. The only other excuse for the visit he'd been able to think of — that it was part of a new policy of following up on civilian casualties — would have rung alarm bells with any Maltese worth their salt.

This story, though, was swallowed whole, even if it didn't endear Max to Joe, who scrutinized him with a sullen scowl. When Joe was sent in search of refreshments, Victor explained that his son, like his wife, had never approved of Carmela's line of work. He, on the other hand, knowing she was a good girl who would never have allowed herself to be drawn into bad ways, had sanctioned her decision.

Max offered up the words Victor was seeking.

"She was a great girl, fun and intelligent and very . . . proper."

"Proper?"

He evidently didn't know the word.

"Moral. Not like some of the other girls."

Victor beamed, his conscience clear, the memory of his dead daughter secure.

Refreshments arrived in the form of two tumblers of *ambeet,* a winelike drink still in circulation. Max took a small sip of the poisonous liquid and smiled as best he could. When Joe retired, the two men sat themselves down on a sun-bleached plank of wood set in a low stone wall.

In the valley below them, Santa Maria Addolorata Cemetery lay spread out like a map, some sprawling city of the dead, with its high perimeter walls and tree-lined avenues, a soaring Gothic cathedral at its heart. The Cassars, Max discovered, were intimately connected with the cemetery. For three generations they had sold flowers at its main gates. Carmela had learned the trade at her father's knee, excelling at it, effortlessly attracting customers — a gift that, presumably, she had carried over to the Blue Parrot.

Mention of Carmela's name permitted Max to steer the conversation back to her. Feigning ignorance, he asked what exactly had happened on the night in question. It soon became clear that the family wasn't aware of the exact date and time when Carmela's body had turned up in the streets of Marsa. In the confusion and upset of identifying the corpse, that information had evidently not found its way through to them. This was good. It meant they had no unanswered questions about the missing day between her disappearance and her discovery. It meant that the situation could be contained.

Having satisfied himself on this score, Max moved on to the other reason for his visit. This was a more delicate subject to broach because it threatened to make him sound like some jealous or neglected admirer. He wanted to know if Carmela had ever mentioned anyone in particular from the Blue Parrot, any of the customers.

Victor sweetly confessed that he couldn't recall her ever speaking of Max, but that meant little — he had a terrible head for names. However, his memory clearly wasn't as bad as he thought, judging from the list of other individuals he was able to reel off.

Max was making a mental note of the names when he sensed the disturbance. They both turned to see a tide of black advancing toward them from the house. At the front strode a dumpy but pretty woman. This was clearly Carmela's mother, and her eyes burned with a fierce grievance.

Max rose to his feet to face the onslaught, the tumbling babble of Maltese. She reserved the rough side of her tongue for her husband, but her hand flicked dismissively, disdainfully, toward Max every so often.

The sight of Joe smugly observing from a safe distance confirmed that it was time to be going. Max was clearly persona non grata for everyone other than Victor, and maybe Carmela's cousin, Nina, whose expression hovered somewhere between embarrassment and pity.

Max mumbled an excuse, leaving poor Victor to his fate. An ancient woman with a gnarled and knotted face refused to move out of his way, raising her cane as if to strike him. He stared into her milky eyes, waiting for the blow to fall, almost willing it — just punishment for the lies he'd told.

Maybe she read something of this in his face, but she lowered the cane and let him pass.

The ride to Saint Joseph's from Paola passed in a daze, Max's brain struggling to process the encounter, the open display of hostility. In all his time on Malta, he'd experienced nothing even approaching it.

His secretary, Maria, was already at her desk, sifting through the mail. A few years older than Max, she was an attractively bookish woman who had worked in the Education Department before the war. Her contacts on the island were invaluable, her cheery disposition a daily tonic. She greeted him with one of her ready smiles and the news that the lieutenant governor had just called in person. He wished to see Max in his office at eleven o'clock sharp.

"Did he say why?"

"He didn't sound happy."

That meant nothing; he was a solemn soul at the best of times. The calling in person was worrying, though. The lieutenant governor rarely soiled his own hands with matters relating to the Information Office, not when he had a whole team of cronies to do the dirty work for him. It had to be something important, and top of the agenda right then was the dread prospect of the estimates.

In a week's time they would all be up in front of the council of the Malta government with their begging bowls, justifying the expenditures of their various departments. It was irritating enough that the Maltese held the purse strings on funds that came straight from the pockets of British taxpayers; it was downright absurd that they should have to haggle over money while being bombed and starved to the brink of extinction.

That was the way of it, though. If anything, the bureaucratic behemoth that ruled their lives had actually prospered since the beginning of the year, as if feeding off the downpour of bombs, bogging them down in pointless paperwork and futile committee meetings. There were clearly some who sought comfort from the trials of war in the machinery of administration, but Max didn't number himself among them.

They would get their money — they always did — but they would have to rehearse their performances first, which meant sitting down with the lieutenant governor. Hence the summons.

Max knew his lines pretty well already — Vincent Falzon in accounts had been busy during the past couple of weeks, juggling the books and padding out certain costs so that the Information Office had something to concede on the big day — but Max thought it best to reacquaint himself with the finer details. He just had time to brief Pemberton on the Bofors gun crew and dictate two quite pointless letters — one to the postmaster general, the other to the provost marshal — before heading next door for his meeting.

The Vincenzo Bugeja Conservatory had started life as an orphanage for girls, and judging from its palatial proportions, it had not lacked for wealthy benefactors in those early days. Set some distance back from the road beyond iron railings and an imposing stone gateway, the building soared majestically around a vast open courtyard. There was another courtyard, out of sight beyond the domed chapel, that stood at the center of the complex.

Saint Joseph's Institute felt like a poor cousin in comparison, cramped and huddled in the conservatory's shadow. But what Saint Joseph's lacked in stature it more than made up for with rough-and-ready charm. At least its corridors thronged with bright-eyed and mischievous orphan boys, not puffed-up paper-pushers who seemed to have become infected by the grandiosity of their new home.

Max had had cause to visit the lieutenant governor's office only once since they'd all been relocated from Valetta, and now he lost his way in the labyrinth of corridors.

"Second floor, then ask again."

This curt response was delivered in passing by a tall rake of a man hurrying along a hallway with a bunch of files under his arm. He didn't even deign to glance at Max as he carried on by.

He did, though, when Max called after him, "Your shirt's hanging out."

The man groped behind him with his free hand, discovering only that he'd been duped.

"My mistake," said Max.

It was a juvenile triumph, but strangely satisfying, and he was still smiling when he entered the suite of rooms occupied by the lieutenant governor and his team.

Hodges, the department's bespectacled gatekeeper, was seated at his desk, poring over a pile of papers.

"Ah, Major Chadwick."

Hodges checked his wristwatch, clearly disappointed that he couldn't berate Max for being late. It was eleven o'clock on the dot.

"I know how much it means to you," said Max. "That's why I make the effort."

Hodges was a remarkable character, a dour, taciturn little man, always scrubbed and pristine. He was utterly without a sense of humor, which somehow compelled one to take up humor as a weapon against him.

"Please," said Hodges, gesturing to the corner. "Take a seat."

It was the one corner of the room Max had not surveyed on entering, and it was a moment before he registered that the man on the low divan was Freddie.

"What are you doing here?" asked Max, settling down beside him.

"I wasn't sure till you walked in."

"Oh Christ . . ."

"That's what I thought when they showed up at the hospital. I would have called, but they had a car waiting for me."

"No talking, please," called Hodges flatly.

"Excuse me?"

"No talking, please."

"Why not?"

"I wasn't aware that I needed a reason,

205

Major Chadwick." His features shaped themselves into a pinched and condescending smile. "Besides, from what I hear, the two of you have been doing quite enough of that already."

They knew. And there was no other way that they could know, not unless Freddie had let it slip, which seemed unlikely, given the inquiring and mildly accusatory look in the eyes that were now fastened on Max.

It had to be Iris. It could only be Iris. He was a fool to have trusted her with the confidence in the first place. He was twice the fool for having believed her when she had sworn her eternal silence on the matter.

"We'll be okay," said Freddie in a whisper. "Just take your lead from me, and with any luck we'll get to keep our jobs on this god-forsaken island."

Max tried to stifle the laugh. Hodges's head snapped up, but before he could spit out a reprimand, a door swung open and a man whom Max had never seen before said, "Gentlemen . . ."

Max found himself transported back to prep school: he and Freddie like two schoolboys being summoned into the headmaster's study for a thrashing, denounced by matron for talking after lights-out.

It soon became clear that the deputy head

would be dishing out the punishment today. Colonel Gifford was at the lieutenant governor's desk, warming his master's seat.

"Congratulations, sir," said Freddie, after they had saluted. "I had no idea."

*Bad lead,* thought Max. So did Colonel Gifford.

"Under the circumstances, Lieutenant Colonel Lambert, do you think it's wise to take that tone with me?"

"No tone intended, sir. And I'm not sure I know what circumstances you're referring to."

"Sit down," said Gifford wearily. He made no attempt to introduce the other three men present. One was short, stocky, and dark; the second long-limbed and flame-haired. The third required no introductions. It was Elliott, the American, sitting off to one side near the window. His lean face gave nothing away.

"The lieutenant governor has been called away on urgent business, I'm afraid," Colonel Gifford said.

Already distancing himself from a dirty business, it occurred to Max. And why not? He knew he had a devoted servant happy to fall on his sword if the affair turned sour.

"I suggest we drop the pretense," Colonel

Gifford continued. "We all know why you're here."

But what exactly did they know? Max had mentioned nothing to Iris about the discovery of the shoulder tab pointing to the involvement of a British submariner in the deaths.

"We were going to tell you," said Freddie.

"It's the 'we' that I find interesting." Colonel Gifford placed his palms flat on the surface of the desk. "What made you think the two of you were equipped to tackle something like this on your own?"

"It's my fault," said Freddie. "I involved Major Chadwick."

"How very noble of you to take the blame."

"It's true."

"And what exactly were you going to tell us?" inquired Elliott, leaning forward in his chair.

Colonel Gifford wasn't happy about losing the floor to him, but Elliott wasn't to be deterred. "I may be wrong, Colonel, but it's possible that some new evidence has come to light."

All eyes in the room settled on Max and Freddie.

"Well, has it?" demanded Colonel Gifford, snatching the reins back from Elliott.

"It has," said Freddie.

He told them everything, holding back till the very end the revelation about the shoulder tab he'd found in Carmela Cassar's clenched fist.

A number of looks were traded around the room in the silence following this bombshell.

"You have it?" asked Colonel Gifford, his studied composure faltering.

Max fished the tab from the breast pocket of his shirt. Getting to his feet, he approached the desk and handed it over. Colonel Gifford scrutinized the scrap of cloth.

"There's not very much of it."

"There's enough of it," said Max.

"May I?" asked Elliott.

The tab was passed to him. It then passed through the hands of the other two men before being returned to Colonel Gifford.

"Why didn't you come to us with this?" the colonel asked.

Freddie shifted in his seat. "Maybe because I didn't see a whole lot of progress the last time I came to you."

Colonel Gifford flicked through a file in front of him. "I have your original statement here, along with a note suggesting that your suspicions be brought to the attention of the police."

"And were they? No one came to speak to me."

"The police were alerted."

"And will you alert them this time? Or do you want me to do it on my way out?"

Police headquarters in Valetta had recently been relocated from the Sacra Infermeria in Valetta to the conservatory.

"What I would like you to do," said Gifford starchly, "is give us a moment alone."

A moment proved to be about fifteen minutes, during which time Max and Freddie sat in strained silence in the entrance room under the watchful glare of Hodges, who grudgingly permitted them to smoke a cigarette. Freddie was summoned back into the office alone. He reappeared a short while later with one of the nameless men — the small, dark one of the pair.

"You can go in now, Major Chadwick," the man said, escorting Freddie toward the door. Freddie managed to slip Max a reassuring look that said: *It'll be okay.*

And it was, but only just.

Colonel Gifford fired off his opening salvo as Max lowered himself into the chair.

"You're a bloody fool, Chadwick. What in God's name possessed you to turn detective? If I had my way, I'd sling you out on

210

your ear — I would — but Major Pace here has argued convincingly in your defense." Max glanced at Elliott. "The last thing we need right now is any disruption to the Information Office. But let me be quite clear: I was against your appointment in the first place, and I want you to think of this as a reprieve rather than a pardon."

Max was to put the matter from his mind and talk to no one about it, on pain of court-martial. Gifford wound up his speech with a peculiar flourish.

*"Non omnia possumus omnes."*

"We can't all do everything," or something like that.

"I'm sorry, sir, my Italian's a little rusty."

Max saw a whisper of a smile appear on Elliott's lips.

"It's Latin. Virgil. From the Eclogues."

"It means, just stick to your bloody job, Chadwick." This from the fourth man in the room, the one with ginger hair and lobster-pink skin. They were the first words he'd spoken, and his accent screamed high birth, summoning up images of Henley Royal Regatta and riding to hounds and tea on the lawn at the family pile in the country. His pale blue eyes were the color of thick ice, and possibly just as hard.

"Tell me about Lilian Flint," he drawled,

with an air of cold command.

Max was momentarily thrown by the question. "What's there to tell? She's the deputy editor of *Il-Berqa*. She's also very good at her job."

"Well, you would know, given the amount of time you spend liaising with her."

Max ignored the thinly veiled insinuation. "Yes, I suppose I'm better placed than most to make that judgment."

"Her mother is in Italy, if I'm not mistaken."

"That's right. She was in Padua when Italy declared war. She was unable to make it home."

"Home? I would have thought home was at her husband's side."

It wasn't just the cold blue eyes, it was their steady, piercing scrutiny that was so unsettling.

"She's not married."

"As good as, though, wouldn't you say?"

"I have no idea."

"I believe he's a professor of archaeology at the University of Padua."

"I believe so."

"And do you also believe it's possible for a man to hold such a post at an Italian university if he isn't in some way sympathetic to the regime?"

"I wouldn't know."

"Hazard a guess."

Max generally burned a long fuse, but was struggling now to hold himself in check. He could see what was being done to him. He had boxed at Oxford; he had been on the receiving end of the irritating jabs designed to make you drop your guard and risk it all on a roundhouse.

"For what it's worth," he said icily, "I would stake my job, my reputation — my life, even — on Lilian's loyalty."

The ginger one seemed almost amused. "There's really no need for such grandiloquence. Do you think for a moment she would be the deputy editor of *Il-Berqa* if we weren't of the same mind?"

"So what, with respect, is your point?"

"My point, Major Chadwick, is this: we like her, we like what she does, we like the fact that the two of you work so well together. She's inclined to sail a little close to the wind at times, but her readers value her forthright opinions, and it's important that they're permitted a vent for their frustrations. You seem to temper her more extreme tendencies." He paused. "So you see, we're quite content with the way things are, and it would be unfortunate if — how shall I put it? — those of a more prejudiced disposition were allowed to prevail on the question of her current employment."

Diplomatic doublespeak, but the threat was plain and simple: back off or we pack her off.

Lilian's job meant everything to her. She had dreamed of it since childhood; she had fought for it against the wishes of her family. It was her life, the one fixed point in her universe.

"I think I get your meaning."

"Then you may go now."

Max noted that Colonel Gifford wasn't aggrieved by this man subverting his authority, as he had been with Elliott. In fact, he seemed almost in awe of him.

"I'll see Major Chadwick out," said Elliott, levering himself to his feet.

"There's no need for that," said the colonel.

"I'd like to."

Colonel Gifford was about to object, but something in copper-top's expression silenced him.

Max made a point of ignoring Hodges on the way out.

"That went well, don't you think?" Elliott declared chirpily when they were alone in the corridor.

Max wasn't in the mood for lightheartedness. "For God's sake, Elliott, what the hell were you doing there?"

"They thought I might be in on it, knowing the two of you as I do. And I've got to say, I'm a little insulted I wasn't in the loop."

Max ignored the comment.

"They're not going to do anything, are they?"

"I doubt it. Not with *Upstanding* about to leave the island."

"And what happens when dead girls start showing up in Alexandria?"

Elliott hesitated. "I see you've been doing your research."

"What happens?"

"Not our jurisdiction, old man." He stretched out the vowels in a convincing parody of the ginger-haired chap.

"Who is he?"

"You know, under different circumstances I can see the two of you hitting it off."

"Christ, Elliott, can't you ever give a straight answer to a question?"

Elliott looked affronted. "It doesn't matter who he is. What do you want to know? He's part of the stuff that goes on behind the scenes."

"Behind the scenes?"

"You think war is all bombs and bullets, aircraft and subs?"

"Yes. I think if you can hurt your enemy more than he hurts you, then you win."

Elliott weighed his words. "You're right, of course. But you're also wrong. An enemy can be persuaded to squander its assets. Take the Battle of Hastings. A lot of crap's been written about the Battle of Hastings — believe me, I read most of it at West Point. You want to know the long and short of it? Harold holds the high ground; William has to attack uphill. William fakes a retreat. Harold forsakes the high ground. Harold loses. Yes, horses and men and spears and arrows helped determine the outcome, but that's a battle Harold should have won. He gave up his advantage."

"Thanks for the history lesson."

"Simple deception — that's why he lost it."

Max stopped at the top of the staircase. "And is that what you do, Elliott?"

"I wouldn't have the first clue about faking a retreat."

"You know what I mean."

"Put it this way: I don't fly planes and I don't fire guns."

"Yet again, I've learned nothing new about you whatsoever."

Descending the staircase in stony silence, they passed the gangling fellow, no longer with files under his arm, coming in the op-posite direction. "Your shirt's hanging out," he said curtly to Max.

"No it isn't," Max fired back.

Elliott cast a puzzled glance behind him as they carried on down the stone steps. "What is that, code or something?"

Max let him stew in his ignorance.

"Jeez, there are some things about you Brits I'll never understand."

They emerged from the building into the dancing heat and the cyclopean glare of the sun. Elliott put on his sunglasses — he was very proud of his Polaroid sunglasses.

"Look, if you want to talk truth, come and see me tonight."

"I can't," said Max. "I'm dining with Ralph at the mess in Mdina."

"You call Maconochies stew and tack biscuits dining?"

"I'm hoping corned beef's on the menu tonight."

"How does grilled fish and a chilled bottle of Chassagne-Montrachet sound?"

"Chassagne-Montrachet?"

"You just have to know where to look." Elliott grinned.

A shot of truth was an undeniable temptation. So was a glass or two of white burgundy.

"I can't. I promised Ralph, and I haven't seen him in a while."

"Maybe I'll join you."

"I'm sure you'd be welcome."

"I'm detecting a lack of enthusiasm."

"That's because I'm sulking."

Elliott smiled. "I'll call you later, when you're over it."

"Yes, do that."

Elliott made off across the courtyard before stopping and turning back.

"Don't let them get you down," he called. "Like my granddaddy used to say: 'There's more horses' asses in the world than there is horses.'"

The very first thing Max did on returning to the Information Office was snatch up one of the phones on his desk. He twirled the handle and asked the operator to put him through to the 90th General Hospital at Mtarfa.

Freddie wasn't back yet. The car had probably been held up by the raid developing over Ta' Qali.

Max replaced the receiver and stared at the papers that Maria had laid out in prioritized piles for his perusal. There was no point in even trying to work his way through them. He was too distracted, his thoughts turning to the ordeal of the past hour, skipping among Iris's betrayal, his roasting in the lieutenant governor's office, and Elliott's promise of some answers.

It was a while before he was able to bring any order to bear in his head. Something about the meeting had struck a false note at the time, and he now realized what it was. Assuming that they'd learned of Max's interest in the deaths from Iris, then there was no way they could have known about the shoulder tab. But if that was the case, then what were the two mystery men doing at the meeting? They had the distinct whiff of military intelligence about them — hardly the types to get involved in such an affair, not unless they knew there was more at stake than just a couple of local girls dying in what might or might not be suspicious circumstances.

Colonel Gifford, on the other hand, had appeared genuinely shocked when presented with the shoulder tab. His face had betrayed all the signs of someone coming to terms with the dire ramifications of such a discovery.

So what was going on? Colonel Gifford was in the dark while the others knew more than they were letting on? And where did Elliott fit? In one or other of the camps, or somewhere in between?

The questions kept proliferating, and Max was beginning to wish he'd taken Elliott up on his offer of barbecued fish, burgundy, and a heart-to-heart, when the steady wail of the "Raiders Passed" siren sounded outside.

He took himself up to the roof, where he smoked a cigarette and watched the dense pall of dust hanging over Ta' Qali slowly disperse on the breeze.

Down below in the courtyard a fretful Father Bilocca was doing his best to marshal a bunch of boys into an ordered line, oblivious to the obscene gestures and the faces being pulled whenever his back was turned.

"Is everything okay, sir?"

Max hadn't heard Pemberton join him.

"Fine. Just dandy. Smoke?"

Pemberton took a cigarette, and Max lit it for him.

"I hear Rosamund came up trumps."

"She certainly did. I even have my own bathroom, not that there's any water in the pipes."

Rosamund had found him digs in Saint Julian's, living with the Copnalls. Their eighteen-year-old daughter, Elizabeth, was a pale and pretty creature prone to blushing who worked in the naval cipher department at Fort Saint Angelo. Max could picture her state of agitation at having Pemberton living under the same roof. The same thought must surely have occurred to Rosamund.

"How's Elizabeth?"

"She's a fine pianist."

It all sounded very Jane Austen: the daughter tickling the ivories for the benefit of the handsome house guest. Rosamund was definitely up to something, but he couldn't see it yet.

"I had a shot at that piece for the *Weekly Bulletin*."

Max took the sheet of typed text. "That was quick."

"It probably shows."

He was clearly eager for Max to cast an eye over it there and then.

"The length looks good. I'll let you know."

For want of anything better to do, he started to read the moment Pemberton had disappeared back down the stairwell.

He read it twice, trying to find fault with it, something, anything. The tone was spot on, muscular and defiant yet not too triumphalist. He didn't play to the heroism of the Manchester boys working the Bofors gun — that spoke for itself — rather, he presented the young gunners as workers at the coal face, grinding out a slow but inexorable victory. The mining metaphor was a small stroke of genius. It resonated with danger and hardship and collective enterprise, and it carried with it the shared experience of a people who daily descended into the earth. The theme also permitted him to round off the piece with a comic touch. There were no coal mines on Malta, a detail that seemed to have escaped the notice of the Italians, who in the early days of the conflict had proudly announced the destruction of a Maltese coal mine by the Regia Aeronautica — still the cause of much hilarity across the island.

Pemberton had done well, more than well; the article was pitch-perfect. So why, then, did it leave Max cold? A few hours before, it would have had him racing downstairs to congratulate the author.

Pemberton would get his pat on the back, and the piece would go out in the *Weekly Bulletin,* but Max would know it for what it was: another lie peddled to the masses. They weren't one happy family pulling together in adversity. His experience at the Cassars' house had made that starkly clear to him.

He remembered something that Charles Headley, his former boss and mentor, had said to him soon after his arrival at the Information Office.

"You know what the great thing about our line of work is, old man? I'll tell you, it's very simple. A lie can make its way halfway round the world before the truth has a chance to put its boots on."

There was probably no less truth in those words now than there had been at the time, but for once Max found himself calling into question the words' central assumption — that the power of a lie was something to be admired and cherished.

How much angrier would those grieving women at the Cassars' have been with him had they known the truth about Carmela's death? The answer, he suspected, was that they would have been less angry.

Thanks to Lilian, he knew the Maltese well enough by now to say that they would at least have respected him for his honesty. They were an ancient people, a wise people. They had seen civilizations come and go around their island home, and yet they were still there, as they would always be, with their wry humor, their rough savoir faire, and their burning faith. Max and his kind were simply passing through. Maybe their hosts deserved a little more credit, a little more respect.

He could see where he was going with this, and he knew the reason why. He had just been insulted, intimidated, threatened with court-martial, even blackmailed. More than anything, it was the blackmail that angered him. Exploiting his friendship with Lilian to keep him in line was about as low as it got. So much for the happy family.

Feeling his hackles rising again, he lit another cigarette and did something he hadn't done in a long while when caught in a quandary: he asked himself what his father's advice would be to him.

The sun was at its zenith, and the heat rising in waves from the zinc roof was almost unbearable, but a small chill ran the length of Max's spine when the answer came to him.

The town of Mtarfa lay scattered along the ridge just north of Mdina, its skyline dominated by the austere military architecture of the 90th General Hospital. The sprawling complex of wards and accommodation blocks had consumed the army barracks nearby to offer more than a thousand beds to the sick and wounded.

An attractive Maltese VAD eventually tracked Freddie down to the burns ward. Infection was a problem, apparently, and she asked Max to wait outside. He was quite happy to oblige. The few glimpses he got through the swing-doors as nurses came and went were enough of a trial. Some of the patients were so swaddled in bandages that they looked like Egyptian mummies laid out in state. Others were having their fresh burns scrubbed and sprayed, their eyes irrigated, or old dressings changed. There seemed to be so much activity, all of it centered on flesh that was either red raw or black and encrusted. The sweet smell of ether carried through the doors, along with a low murmur of morphine-dulled pain.

When Freddie finally appeared, they made for the long terrace at the back of the building. It had a grandstand view of the hills to the north and would normally have been thronging with invalids of all varieties making the most of the low, late sunshine, but people had grown more wary since the targeted raid on the 39th General Hospital at Saint Andrew's.

It was the first chance Max and Freddie had had to talk openly about the meeting that morning, and Freddie didn't hang about.

"I should just have gone to them again. I shouldn't have involved you."

"They're not going to do anything,

225

Freddie. They're going to bury it."

"I suppose."

"You suppose?"

"It's what they do."

"And you're happy with that?"

Freddie drew hard on his cigarette and exhaled. "No, Max," he said with a slight stiffening of tone, "I'm not happy with it. But what do you want me to say? I followed my conscience. I came to you first. It didn't work out." After a brief pause, he added, "Someone messed up, and I know it wasn't me."

Fair point. There was no getting away from it.

"It was Iris," admitted Max.

"Iris?"

"It couldn't have been anyone else. I didn't tell anyone else."

"Forgive me," said Freddie, "I'm tired, not thinking straight, but what on God's earth possessed you to tell Iris, of all people!"

Max did his best to explain his thinking at the time, the logic of his argument failing miserably to translate itself into words.

"Okay," he conceded, "I was naïve."

"It's not the first word that springs to mind. The most ambitious girl in Christendom? You'd have done better to take out a page in the *Times*."

"Maybe we should have."

It sounded glib, but it was a serious statement, intended to test Freddie's mettle.

"Listen, Max, this is way beyond us now. It's a dirty business. This whole damn thing is a dirty business. You know what I was doing in there when you showed up? There's a man, I couldn't tell you how old exactly because his face is gone. I know he's German, though, and that he bailed out of a burning 88. He should have stayed in that plane, gone down with it. He has no lips, no eyelids, no eyes, and his nose is all but gone. I'm hoping for his sake that a bug gets him. This is what we do to one another. After God knows how many millennia of human evolution, this is how we choose to treat one another still."

"That's your excuse? People do bad things? We're talking about murder. There's a principle at stake."

Freddie dropped his cigarette on the tiled terrace and crushed it underfoot. When he finally looked up, he said a little shamefacedly, "They scared me in there today. They threatened to take it all away, everything I've worked for, everything I do. I don't know how to do anything else."

"For God's sake, Freddie, you're young.

This war will end, life will return to normal, people like that won't be running the show when this mess is over."

"You really believe that?"

"I know it."

"I think you underestimate them. Our cards are marked and there's nothing we can do about it."

*You're wrong,* thought Max. *There is.*

He wanted to tell Freddie the what and the how of it, but there was no point. Freddie's mind was made up and it was an undeniable disappointment. The two of them had always stood apart from the others. Ralph and Hugh were career servicemen trained and primed for combat. Max and Freddie were mere guests at the table of war, competent amateurs shipped in to make up the numbers after a big chunk of Czechoslovakia had failed to appease Hitler. Yes, they'd both learned the ropes in the Officers' Training Corps at their respective schools, but the experience had fired neither of them with enthusiasm. They knew this because they'd discussed it one night when there were no "real soldiers" within earshot.

Max had been packed off to Wellington College at the age of thirteen at his stepmother's insistence, on the grounds that the men in her family had always gone there —

a perplexing line of reasoning, given the assortment of disagreeable uncles and male cousins Sylvia had brought with her into their lives. Wellington was reputed to be Britain's most military of schools, and Max had done just enough to get by without insulting that tradition, learning to march and fire a gun and bumble around with a blackened face up on the heathland toward Broadmoor during field day.

His failure to become commander of the Picton platoon had been taken by Sylvia as further evidence of his utter fecklessness. All the men in her family had commanded their house platoons. This was a lie that, after some cursory research in the school records, he'd felt obliged to point out to her over Christmas dinner one year — his first public challenge to her authority, and a declaration of open warfare as far as Sylvia was concerned.

Maybe he was doing her an injustice, but he sometimes suspected that she'd waited years to exact a suitable revenge. The family strings she'd pulled, supposedly on his behalf, had seen him carried first to Egypt and then to Malta, and although she couldn't possibly have known at the time what horrors lay in store for the little island, he wouldn't have put it past her.

Perversely, surviving the war had become as much about denying Sylvia the pleasure of his extinction as anything else. And maybe, just as perversely, standing up to the Colonel Giffords of the world, refusing to be cowed by the sort of high-handed military types whom he associated with Sylvia, had its roots in the same ancient animosity.

The reasons didn't matter. He had picked his path and was set in his resolve. Yes, it would have been good to have a companion on the road, but Freddie wasn't essential to the plan taking shape in his head. The real issue now was one of time, or rather the lack of it. With the *Upstanding* set to leave for Alexandria in less than a week, the clock was ticking.

Freddie and Max quietly shunted the topic into the shadows and talked of other things, such as dinner with Ralph at the officers' mess in Mdina. Freddie wasn't on duty again until the following morning and asked to tag along.

"If you'll have me, that is," he said a little sheepishly.

"After this morning, I think we could both do with a dose of Ralph."

They also got a dose of Hugh.

Apparently he'd become something of a regular at the Xara Palace in the past few weeks, ever since Royal Artillery HQ had relocated to Saint Agatha's Convent in Rabat following the bombing of the Castille. Rabat and Mdina stood cheek by jowl on the ridge, almost one and the same, and Hugh had taken to stopping off for a "swift sundowner" with Ralph on his way home to Sliema.

The Xara Palace — a grand fifteenth-century building close by the main gate in Mdina — had been requisitioned by the RAF as an officers' mess for the Ta' Qali squadrons, although Ralph treated the place as if it were his private residence. As ever with Ralph, this was done with playful insouciance, his tongue firmly in his cheek.

Ralph was tall, with a shock of sand-colored hair that the sun bleached to a startling white in summer. He wore it longer than regulations permitted, but regulations didn't figure large in his thinking. He set store by the adage that "rules are made for the guidance of wise men and the obedience of fools" — a line he was quite happy to quote to his superiors.

The brass tolerated his idiosyncratic ways because they knew he had qualities far above the general run. He also served a useful purpose. The Xara Palace was a beautiful building, but ghosts stalked its wide corridors: the ghosts of dead pilots. Beds fell free at an alarming rate, and the young replacements shipped in to fill them knew they stood a fair chance of going the same way as the previous occupants. At twenty-nine, Ralph wasn't the oldest member of 249 Squadron, but he'd been around the longest, and his presence offered some hope of survival to the new arrivals.

Ralph's lack of respect for "the machine," as he called it, was a product of hard experience reaching back to his very first day on the island. Of the reinforcement flight of twelve Hurricanes that took off from the aircraft carrier *Argus,* Ralph's was one of only four to make land. The others were lost to the unforgiving waters of the Mediterranean because someone, somewhere, had miscalculated the amount of aviation spirit required to see them safely as far as Malta. Ralph had crossed the Dingli Cliffs on vapors, gliding in to Luqa on a dead propeller. He had lost his best friend that day, and he'd lost many more friends since, thanks to the "sheer bloody incompetence of the machine operators."

Bovine compliance didn't come naturally to him; his trust had to be earned. He would have cut his hair if the order had come from someone he respected, but the few people he esteemed tended to rate him highly in return and were happy to let him operate with a certain latitude. His reputation helped. With ten "destroyed" and six "probables" to his name, he was one of the few aces on the island, albeit one who had badly blotted his copybook.

The incident had occurred the summer before while Ralph was convalescing at the pilots' rest camp on Saint Paul's Bay following his accident. Jumped by a gaggle of 109s over Qormi, he'd been forced to crash-land in a field — a nearly impossible thing to do on Malta without hitting a stone wall. Unconscious, he only survived the burning wreckage because a couple of Maltese women working nearby heaped earth on the flames (after struggling and failing to haul his inert six-foot-something frame from the crumpled cockpit). Patched up by Freddie, he had spent two months in traction at Mtarfa Hospital, successfully resisting all efforts to have him posted home "noneffective sick." The air battle for Malta was one fight he intended to see through to its bitter conclusion, and he'd managed to secure for himself a further period of convalescence at the pilots' rest camp on Saint Paul's Bay.

"Camp" was something of a misnomer. It was a villa with a sloping lawn and honeysuckle arbors and a winding pathway leading down through a shaded avenue of trees to the water's edge, where a couple of rowboats and an offshore swimming platform bobbed lazily on the swell. At the mouth of the bay lay the flat little island where Saint Paul had been shipwrecked in a storm some two thousand years before. Struggling ashore, Paul had been welcomed in Mdina by Publius, the chief man of the island, whose father had been gravely ill at the time. When Paul healed him, Publius promptly converted to the new religion, carrying his people with him and building the first ever Christian church in Mdina. With a heritage like that, it was hardly surprising that the Christian faith remained the mainspring of Maltese life.

The proximity of Saint Paul's Island with its solitary statue of the healer saint lent a certain logic to the location of the rest camp: a peaceful spot where men came to repair themselves, a haven amidst all the suffering and destruction. Max had grown to know the place well during Ralph's stay, riding out there on his motorcycle whenever he could snatch a moment. It was the day after one such visit when Ralph overstepped the mark.

He and some others had been lazing in the garden, listening to gramophone records, when a dogfight broke out high over their heads. They strained to make sense of the specks darting around the heavens, but as the aircraft lost altitude in a bid to gain speed, it became clear that two Hurricanes were taking a pasting from a covey of determined 109s.

One of the Hurricanes broke for home with a German on his tail; the other Hurricane didn't fare so well. Streaming a white plume of glycol, it spun away earthward and piled into the hillside at the back of Saint Paul's with a sickening crump.

By the time Ralph and the others made their way to the crash site, the army was already on the scene and a wallet had been recovered. It revealed that the pulped mess amidst the smouldering wreckage had once been Greg Dyer, a young Canadian based at Hal Far. Ralph knew him — not well, but well enough to take issue with the army major who ordered his men to dig the body in. The fellow had come halfway round the world to join the fight, Ralph protested, and he deserved a decent burial, just as his family deserved the right to come and stand at a white cross in a cemetery and pay their tributes when the war was over. The family could have their white cross, was the major's reply, and if Ralph wanted to bag up some bits of flesh and bone to bury at the foot of it, then he had five minutes to do so.

Opinions were divided as to which of them threw the first punch — the witnesses were split along predictable army/RAF lines — but there was no doubt about who came off worst. The major's jaw was broken in two places, and he was still eating through a straw when he flew out of Malta a few weeks later.

Fortunately for Ralph, the air officer commanding was one of his fans, and Ralph was spared the punishment he probably deserved. Other pilots had been sent packing for far more minor misdemeanors, such as drunken behavior in the bars of Valetta. However, the RAF had to be seen to be taking some form of action against him, and he found himself grounded until further notice. This might have sounded like a godsend, but not for a man itching to get back up there and have another crack at the enemy. His only consolation was that it gave him time to fully recover from injuries that might well have affected his performance in the air and cost him his life. When it came to working the rudder pedals, multiple fractures of the lower legs didn't help. They were considerably less of a hindrance to the duties of the squadron's chief intelligence officer, a position Ralph filled for several months before being eased back into action with the Photographic Reconnaissance Unit. This was a compromise that satisfied the army and annoyed the hell out of Ralph, although it beat sitting at a desk all day.

The PRU had a couple of unarmed Spitfires with long-range tanks for snooping on enemy convoys, but Ralph flew a Martin Maryland — in his own words, "a big bugger of a kite." He'd grown strangely fond of the twin-engine bomber. It was surprisingly nippy and maneuverable, and it was well armed, which allowed him to have a pop at the enemy if the opportunity presented itself (which it seemed to do with far more regularity than was the case with the other Maryland pilots).

Since joining the PRU Ralph had added two to his tally: an Italian Cant seaplane in Taranto harbor and, just a few weeks ago, a 109 over Sicily, one of six fighters that had jumped him while he'd been making a study of the Catania plain. The Germans' determination to bring down the Maryland made sense only the following day, when the photos taken on that sortie were developed.

They showed new ground strips being built near Gerbini airfield — glider takeoff areas — confirmation that an airborne assault on Malta was imminent.

This grim news sat like a dark cloud over those in the know, but it failed to dampen Ralph's spirits; he certainly wasn't going to let it mess with his social calendar. He still traveled into Valetta to bend his elbow at the bar in the Union Club (or one of the city's less salubrious establishments), and the invitations to dinner at the Xara Palace kept coming.

Rationing had reduced the quality of the food on offer there to the purely functional role of soaking up the booze, of which there was always plenty, thanks to Ralph's deep pockets. His father had died when he was a boy, and a small fortune had been settled on him when he was twenty-one: "enough to keep me in snuff and absinthe," he had once joked to Max. It was money he seemed quite happy to fritter away on his colleagues and friends.

That evening, he had somehow managed to get his hands on two cases of Chianti and six bottles of Johnnie Walker whisky. God only knew where he'd got them from (or what he'd paid for them) — contrary to official pronouncements, the black market was thriving — but the first toast of the evening, as always, was to the good health of his great-aunt Enid, for her generosity with the liquid refreshments.

"Enid," the whole room bellowed before dropping back into their chairs, everyone except the Maltese orderlies, who returned to the kitchen clutching their tumblers of red wine and "a bottle of the brown stuff for the chef."

Heavy drinking was just about the fastest route to an early grave for a fighter pilot, but given the shortage of serviceable aircraft on the island, almost everyone present could guarantee that they wouldn't be flying the following day. And if by some miracle they did find themselves called to readiness, then a few minutes of raw oxygen through the mask while waiting to take off worked wonders when it came to clearing away the cobwebs.

The usual smattering of teetotalers and cautious newcomers abstained, but Hugh was happy to take up the slack.

"Rosamund's arranged one of her women-only whist drives, so I'm good for a glass or five."

Max and Freddie were happy to match him. For reasons that soon became clear, Ralph took longer to warm up. He was a painter — a watercolorist, primarily — and not a bad one, and he wasn't going to let the minor inconvenience of a war keep him from his craft. That morning he had set off on his bicycle, as he often did, to record some little corner of the island. Chiaroscuro was his thing, light and shade, and he had found a subject that played to his strong suit: a small chapel in a sun-dappled glade near Verdala Palace. The proximity to the governor's summer residence may well have played a part in what then happened.

Someone denounced him to the local police for suspicious behavior, and a small crowd of Maltese was present at the confiscation of his artist's pad by two local constables. Not one of the grinning natives rose to his defense, even though a few of them knew him by sight. Almost tearful with frustration, he had watched some of his best work carried off.

"Toilet paper *is* running extremely scarce," said Hugh.

Somehow, this set the tone for the evening. Serious subjects weren't ignored, but they were treated with a light hand, which made a change from the synthetic gaiety that usually prevailed in the mess.

A South African flight lieutenant at their table mentioned that he'd also detected a shift in the attitude of the Maltese toward them, a souring of the relationship. The fighter pilots had always been regarded as the heroes of the garrison and were accustomed to being mobbed and cheered by young boys wherever they went. Lately, though, there had been something sneering in the cries of "Speetfire."

Hugh was horrified to hear this. Ralph, on the other hand, was sympathetic to the Maltese.

"They've every bloody right to be browned off, in my book. They saw the new Spits fly in a few weeks ago, and what do they get? More planes in the sky? No. More pilots mooching around Valetta. Meanwhile, they're dying in droves."

He had nothing but praise for the gunners and the "poor bloody infantry." The navy was beyond reproach, and the merchant seamen, well, they were the real heroes of the piece as far as he was concerned, gambling their lives away to feed, fuel, and arm the island. No, his own service — the RAF — was the one at fault. Air superiority was the key to Malta's survival, but how could they hope to achieve it if the imbeciles back home continued to view Malta as a lost cause, little more than a convenient dumping ground for their shabbiest aircraft and least promising pilots?

"No offense intended, I'm sure," said Max to a couple of ruddy-cheeked flight lieutenants listening in — new boys from 603 Squadron.

"But best to face the hard truth," added Ralph. "You'll last longer if you do. That's why you're here. That's why *I'm* here. My squadron CO at North Weald couldn't wait to see the back of me. 'Tindle,' he said, 'I've got just the thing for you. . . .' "

"Ralph, you're scaring them," said Freddie.

"They're already scared. And they're right to be. They're up against Hitler's best. Those boys earned their spurs on the Russian front. They say Werner Mölders has bagged more than a hundred. What do you two have in your lockers? A couple of massed sweeps over France?"

At most, judging from their expressions.

Freddie raised his glass to the dejected pair. "Well, here's hoping the new Spitfires never arrive."

"They're coming," said the youngest of them. "They've got us building new blast pens like there's no tomorrow."

Ralph drained his glass. "And Kesselring knows it. He has his eyes and ears on this island."

"You and your bloody fifth columnists," said Hugh. "You see enemy agents under every rock."

"Oh, they're here, all right. For all I know, one of you is one of them." His eyes made the tour of the table. "Well, are you?"

*"Nein,"* said Freddie, which set everyone off.

After dinner, the four friends retired upstairs to the terrace with a bottle of Johnnie Walker. Night was falling fast, and as they sat there in the gloaming, Ralph announced, "I didn't want to say before, but they'll be here on the ninth."

"The Spitfires . . . ?"

"Mark Vs is the word. Sixty or so this time. Enough to tip the scales in our favor."

"Where did you hear this?" asked Hugh, who liked to think he had a jungle telephone attached to every brass hat.

"Elliott."

"Elliott!"

"Don't underestimate Elliott. He may be a bloody Yank, but he sees the big picture. And he's got clout where it counts, which is more than can be said for the congenital idiots running our show."

Ralph didn't know for certain, but rumor had it that Elliott had played a significant role behind the scenes in the last reinforcement flight to reach the island. The Spitfires had been delivered deep into the Mediterranean by the U.S. aircraft carrier *Wasp* — a commitment that, in Ralph's view, Britain's new ally wouldn't have made without the sanction of their man on the spot.

"I wish I could be somebody's man on the spot," said Hugh. "It sounds like fun."

"Not when it all goes wrong. The last fly-in was a complete bloody disaster. And sixty more Spits count for nothing unless we can get them armed, fueled, and back in the air before Kesselring pounces."

"Elliott should be here," said Hugh. "When was the last time all five of us were together?"

They calculated that it had been back in late March at the Union Club.

"It would have been the other day if you'd bothered to show up at our drinks party," Hugh remarked to Ralph.

"Sorry about that. Prior engagement in Naples."

"How's the old girl looking?"

"Not too bad from twenty-five thousand feet."

It seemed unlikely. Ralph was known for flying in foolishly low in search of the perfect picture.

They sat out on the terrace for a good

long while, trading stories and other inanities, the darkness coiling around them, the whisky working its silent way through their systems. At a certain point, Ralph declared that he would henceforth be referring to Freddie as "Mr. Ten Degrees," this being the angle at which Ralph estimated his right foot now stuck out to the side since Freddie had bolted his lower leg back together.

"Believe me," said Freddie, "others would have saved themselves the trouble and lopped it off at the knee."

"Well, it's shoddy work all the same."

"Ten degrees doesn't sound like much," said Hugh.

"Yes," said Max, turning the screw. "I hardly even notice anymore."

"Although it looks more like twenty to me," Hugh said.

"Anything under twenty is deemed acceptable," said Freddie.

Ralph was looking aghast, raising his lower leg to examine it in the candlelight.

"Come on, old man. You're lucky to be alive."

"Yes, Freddie saved your life."

Freddie spread his hands to Ralph. "That's what I'm telling everyone, and they seem to be listening."

"Well, it's the first I've heard of it."

"That's because we know how you don't like to feel beholden to others."

"Yes," said Max, concurring with Hugh. "We knew it would wrong-foot you."

After the laughter had died away, it was Max's turn to be victimized. That was the way things generally went when they were together: everyone would have the sights turned on them at one time or another. Hugh kicked it off.

"So, Odysseus, how is the fair Calypso?"

"Excuse me?"

"You don't know the story? It's from Homer."

"Pray tell," said Ralph, eager for revenge.

Legend held that the island of Gozo, just off the north coast, was Ogygia, home to the sea nymph Calypso, who ensnared Odysseus in her web of feminine wiles, holding him hostage for seven years.

It was the first time Max had been ribbed about Lilian, and he wasn't quite sure how to react. He decided to adopt an air of amused tolerance while they went at him.

"She's certainly got her claws into him," said Ralph. "I saw her aunt in the street the other day, and she wanted the lowdown on our friend here."

"What did you tell her?"

"That he's an upstanding young man with

a fine future ahead of him."

"It can't be right to lie to the natives."

"No, I hear the definite clangor of wedding bells."

"It'll mean converting to the Roman Church."

"Absolutely. They have no truck with our watered-down faith."

"Well, he could do far worse," said Freddie. "She's a beauty."

"That's the truth. I'd happily play hide the sausage with her."

"Ah, but we all know what happens to these Maltese girls when middle age sets in. Suddenly they're sidestepping through doorways."

"Less sea nymph than sea cow."

They talked around him, over him, anything but to him. And as he listened to the imaginary life they were mapping out for him — the meddlesome Maltese relatives, the early-morning masses, his olive-skinned progeny — it dawned on him that Freddie was right: he could do far worse for himself. After all, he almost had.

His thoughts strayed to Lilian, probably in bed by now, just a few streets away, a hop, skip, and jump across the rooftops. He saw her jet-black hair spread across the pillow, and the rise and fall of her breasts beneath the sheet.

Strangely, he had never stopped to think what she really thought of him. What did a kiss in a darkened garden mean to her? Was it loaded with significance? Maybe all she wanted was a pleasing flirtation, a little diversion from the grim realities of life. If so, it was no more than many girls of her social class were looking for. Mdina was home to a number of noble families whose daughters weren't averse to the odd romantic dalliance. Maybe Lilian was no different. This, after all, was the world she inhabited.

Somehow, he couldn't see it, though. She was older, too much of her own person to follow the flock simply for the sake of it. He knew immediately that this conclusion flattered him by lending weight to her feelings. It came to him more slowly that they were feelings he was quite happy for her to have.

Or maybe it was the whisky speaking. He had a tendency to turn dewy-eyed under its influence.

Hugh, meanwhile, was growing downright maudlin. He could just as well have been speaking about the burning of the Great Library of Alexandria, so stirring was his account of the destruction by an enemy bomb of the premises of the Malta Amateur Dramatic Club.

No one had been in the building on South Street at the time, but Hugh had been there since and had picked over the rubble, pulling out props and costumes from the plays they'd put on over the years, each one unleashing a memory, many of which he now felt obliged to share with his friends.

The friends, meanwhile, did their best not to laugh. This wasn't easy, especially when Hugh started to recite lines.

"Do you remember *Return to Sender?*"

Ralph leaned forward in his chair. "How could we forget, old man?"

This was said for Max and Freddie's benefit, Hugh being too caught up in the moment to detect the irony.

" 'I say, Margaret, wasn't that the doorbell? Or could it be that my ears are still ringing from our little contretemps earlier?' "

He gave a smile that said, *Step aside, Shakespeare. You've had your day.*

"Didn't Olive Bratby play Margaret?" said Freddie.

"She certainly did. And with great authority. Margaret's not an easy character to play. Remember when her poodle goes missing? That requires a deft touch."

"Oooo," said Max, "that's a horrible moment."

"It is, it is, and an actress of lesser ability would have over-egged the pudding. Far better, though, that Margaret is seen *not* to react. She buries the pain away. It's what she does, you see? As with the poodle, so with life."

This last line was a tough one to hold out against. They all managed it, though, rising to the challenge of the unspoken game: which one of them would crack first? Freddie, annoyingly, was the master of the poker face and the little glances designed to send you over the edge. Max's only real chance lay in lighting Ralph's fuse.

"Maybe I'm wrong, but didn't I hear that Lord Mountbatten once attended one of your shows?"

"Absolutely. Just before my time, sadly. It was *On Approval* by Frederick Lonsdale, and he was extremely complimentary."

Max already knew the story because he had heard it from Ralph, who had heard it from Hugh, who could, apparently, quote by heart from the letter Mountbatten subsequently wrote to the MADC.

He most certainly could. Verbatim.

Ralph had his mouth buried in his glass to hide his smile when Hugh leaned back, staring at the stars, and declared wistfully, "Lord Louis loved us."

The whisky went everywhere, much of it up Ralph's nose. The dam then burst for Freddie and Max.

Hugh's bewildered expression took on a steely edge of realization before softening to one of grudging amusement.

"Bloody Philistines."

Max was fairly accomplished at riding his motorcycle when drunk, and he knew from his little jaunt with Pemberton and Vitorin Zammit that it was just possible to squeeze three grown men onto the machine. He had never attempted to do both things at the same time.

Fortunately, it was a short trip across the valley to Mtarfa Hospital, where Freddie dismounted and stumbled off in search of his digs. Unfortunately, Hugh was growing more voluble by the minute. As they came down off the ridge onto the plain, he started to recite lines from Tennyson at the top of his lungs while slapping Max on the thigh and exhorting him to go faster.

" 'Forward, the Light Brigade! / Charge for the guns!' . . . Faster, faster! . . . 'Storm'd at with shot and shell, / Boldly they rode and well, / Into the jaws of Death, / Into the mouth of Hell / Rode the six hundred.' "

"Shut up, Hugh."

" 'Theirs not to make reply, / Theirs not to reason why, / Theirs but to do and die.' "

They didn't die, although a gaping bomb crater on the outskirts of Attard tried its best to oblige, swallowing them up before spitting them out again.

"Now *that's* more like it!" trumpeted Hugh, clinging on for dear life.

On the outskirts of Floriana, they bore left through Pieta and Msida, taking the road that wound its way around Marsamxett Harbour, but as they approached Sliema, Hugh suggested that they carry on past to Fort Tigne'.

"No point in going home just yet," he called into Max's ear. "The coven will still be at their cards."

Fort Tigne' felt like the end of the known world, stuck out on its promontory at the harbor mouth. To the east lay almost a thousand miles of clear water and the low horizon where the sun rose every morning. It was a wild and lonely spot, and the gun emplacements there had taken a beating in the past few weeks, targeted attacks intended to annihilate them. A visit by a high-ranking officer from Royal Artillery HQ, albeit at such a late hour, was a timely and welcome thing.

Maybe it was the actor in him, but Hugh

did a fine job of concealing his waterlogged state from the battery commander, seemingly sobering up at will. His handling of the gunners when he insisted on making a tour of the gun pits was even more impressive. There was nothing remote or routine about his handling of the men. He was relaxed, familiar, and amusing.

In one of the pits, a jug-eared young corporal was playing a mournful tune on a harmonica for his downcast comrades. A backfire had blown out the breech the day before and killed two men.

Taking the harmonica from the corporal, Hugh tapped it against his hand to clear it.

"There goes tomorrow's water ration," he joked, which got a big laugh.

Max experienced a flush of pride in his friend as Hugh proceeded to play a heartfelt rendition of Vera Lynn's "We'll Meet Again." He then shook the hand of every man present, wishing them well in the fight ahead and assuring them that victory would be theirs.

Max and he wandered down to the slender strip of sand at the water's edge for a smoke.

"I didn't know you played the harmonica."

"Don't tell Rosamund. She thinks it's an uncouth instrument."

They stood in silence for a moment, the

dark Mediterranean stretching out before them.

" 'What from the cape can you discern at sea?' "

"You're going to have to give me a little more than that," said Max.

"Nothing at all: it is a highwrought flood;
I cannot, 'twixt the heaven and the main,
Descry a sail."

"You've got me there."

"*Othello*. Montano is searching for the Turkish fleet with some gentlemen of Cyprus. It turns out the fleet's gone down in a storm."

"We should be so lucky."

Hugh shrugged. "We don't need luck; we need determination. History's on our side."

Hugh had always been taken with the idea that the siege in which they were caught up was not so very different from that endured by Malta in 1565, when Suleiman the Magnificent had dispatched forty thousand men to take the island. Malta had held out against the Ottomans on that occasion, saving Europe in the process, and the little sea-girt sentinel of the Mediterranean was now engaged in a similar showdown against the Nazi scourge.

It was a romantic notion, and one that Max was quite happy to go along with in his capacity as the information officer. Hugh, on the other hand, embraced it with an almost mystical fervor, latching on to the parallels and ignoring the differences. It was true that in both instances there was much more at stake than a dust-blown lump of limestone in the middle of the Mediterranean. It was also true that in 1565 the defense of the island had been coordinated by outsiders, men from the north of Europe.

Hugh revered the Knights of Saint John and knew their story intimately. They were a relic from the crusading era, when the order had provided lodging and security to pilgrims visiting the Holy Land. When forced to repair to Rhodes, they effectively ruled that island for two centuries before being driven out by Suleiman. Malta became their next home — a grant from the Emperor Charles V — but it wasn't long before Suleiman pursued them there and the stage was set for one of the bloodiest and most brutal sieges in history.

At one point, soon after Fort Saint Elmo had fallen to the Ottomans, the defenders began using the severed heads of their prisoners as cannonballs. This wasn't because they lacked for ammunition. It was a ghoulish gesture of defiance by the knights, a response to the sight of their headless comrades from Fort Saint Elmo floating toward them across Grand Harbour, lashed to wooden crosses.

Against impossible odds, the besieged towns of Senglea and Birgu (now known as Vittoriosa) held out against the Ottoman Turks for a further two months. Continuously bombarded day and night from the heights around Grand Harbour, their defensive walls breached on numerous occasions, they stood firm under the resolute leadership of Jean de Valette, Grand Master of the order, a man more than willing to snatch up a pike and step into the fray like a common foot soldier.

Many thousands died on both sides in any number of gruesome ways before the Ottoman army finally withdrew from the island, taking to their galleys, their tails between their legs. It was a setback from which their territorial ambitions never fully recovered. Malta had stemmed the Turkish tide; Europe could rest easy once more.

"How bad do you think things will get if they invade?"

"Not as bad as last time," quipped Hugh. "But you might actually have to get that service revolver out of its holster."

"I'm a hopeless shot. Always was. The pheasants' friend."

" 'The pheasants' friend'?"

"It's what my stepmother used to call me."

Hugh laughed. "Then I'll make damn sure I'm standing behind you."

Maybe it was the fatherly hand that settled onto his shoulder, but Max experienced a sudden impulse to unburden himself, to seek approval for the hazardous course he'd settled on in his head. Hugh liked to play the buffoon, but it was a colorful cloak. Beneath it lurked a serious and somewhat high-minded soul. Hugh would understand. He might even be willing to help.

"Hugh . . ."

"Yes?"

Max dropped his cigarette onto the sand and ground it out beneath his boot.

"I'd better run you home."

The message was short and straightforward, the means of delivering it considerably more complex.

To an uneducated eye, the apparatus in question might well have passed for a typewriter, but the keyboard belied the sophisticated mechanics buried away inside. First, the rotors had to be selected and inserted in the correct order, the alphabet ring set relative to them, and the plug board wired. These were easy enough tasks to perform. All you needed was the codebook listing the daily key settings. This being one of the naval machines with the extra rotors, it required a naval codebook, and the numbers were printed in red water-soluble ink.

It gave him pleasure to think that out there, somewhere, there were people listening, waiting attentively for his next transmission. For some of the eavesdroppers, the message would read as gobbledygook and forever remain that way. Field Marshal Kesselring, on the other hand, would have the correct text on his desk within the hour:

Everything progressing according to plan. Virgil.

His German was up to the task of sending the message in the language of his paymasters — they'd asked him to do so for reasons of security — but the idea of bucking their instructions appealed to the contrary streak in him. Besides, the devilish piece of equipment in front of him was too good at its job. He could just as well have signed off using his own name; the Allied signals operators would have been none the wiser. The chances of them ever deciphering the text were so remote that they could be ignored.

As for the message, well, it didn't tell the whole story. The submarines were such a feature of life on Malta that he hadn't even considered the possibility of their withdrawal from the island. This unexpected turn of events had repercussions for his plans, but there seemed little point in worrying those up the line with the details. He would have to rise to the challenge, adapt his strategy to the new time constraints.

Last night, he had flirted with the idea that another girl might have to die, only to dismiss it as too much of a risk. Today, it seemed like a risk worth taking. If he had been burdened with a conscience, he might have tried to convince himself that it was a necessary move, that it served the plan, but he had long since given up lying to himself. He knew that he had probably done enough already. He had lit the touch paper and disappeared safely into the night. Common sense dictated that he lie low and allow the affair to play itself out.

But where was the fun in that? This is what Malta had taught him: that he enjoyed the killing.

It hadn't always been that way. The first, the very first, before the war — Elsie, the theater usherette with the crooked front tooth — had brought him little pleasure that he could recall now. He hadn't set out to take her life, but she had recognized him, and silencing her for good had been the only sensible option.

A very observant girl, that one. He had made three visits to the theater in the course of a year, and on all three occasions had carefully avoided showing any interest in her, let alone talking to her. And yet, on a

moonless night in a dense patch of woodland she had recognized him. An observant
girl. And a foolish one. If she'd kept her
mouth shut, she'd still be alive, not molder-
ing in a coffin beneath a cheap headstone
bearing the hopeful epitaph *Now Flying with
the Angels.*

He had left it a good long while before
visiting her grave, curious to know how it
would feel. Standing over her, he had
experienced no emotions of any real note
— no guilt, no self-loathing, no regrets —
just a mild puzzlement when he recalled the
last moments of her life. Unlike the ones
who had gone before her (and survived to
tell the tale), she had not fought him; she
had almost given herself to him. Why had
she been so biddable, so unresisting, so ac-
cepting of the inevitable?

"Not my face. Don't hurt my face," she
had said.

The voice of experience? Was her father to
blame? Or an uncle? Had she spent her
childhood submitting to the unnatural
advances of some man in her life? It seemed
quite likely. The thought had occurred to
him at the time, and he had struggled to
enter her, although once inside, he had soon
hardened. And when it was over, she had
wiped herself with the hem of her skirt and

calmly announced that she had seen him before. She was even able to list two of the three productions he'd attended at the theater. She was searching for the name of the third — "No, don't tell me" — when he closed his hands around her throat.

She resisted then, but succumbed so quickly that he thought she might be faking. She wasn't, so he got to his feet and brushed himself down. He left her handbag in the narrow lane that led to her parents' house, at the spot where he'd snatched her into the trees, so that she wouldn't lie there undiscovered for too long. It was a small gesture to her. She had asked him not to harm her face, and he wanted the world to know that he hadn't, before she became so much carrion for the animals and insects. And maybe her father, or whoever he was, would see his own sin reflected back at him in her unblemished features.

The car he had borrowed from a friend had been parked well off the beaten track, beyond the wood and over a hill. He drove through the night, passing through sleeping towns and villages, making good time, and was back in his bed before first light. Not one of the two hundred or so miles he'd covered in the round-trip was registered on the car's odometer because he'd disconnected the cable.

Over the next few months he had grown sullen and depressed, disappointed by the experience. He had broken the ultimate taboo, and it had stirred almost nothing in him. He had tried to analyze why this might be, concluding that the answer lay in the fact that the situation had been forced on him. He had not set out to do it. He had simply responded to a pragmatic need, that of protecting his identity. He had not been in control of the situation, and control was where much of the pleasure lay. Control and anticipation. On both these scores, the incident with Elsie had been a disappointment.

Looking back, it was clear to him that he was always going to test this analysis. At the time, he had felt no overwhelming urge to do so. Well, not immediately. As always, the compulsion to strike again built up slowly, invading his thoughts by small but insistent degrees, taking them over until nothing else mattered.

He opted for a prostitute, a small and undernourished girl, birdlike in her brittleness. He had never been with a prostitute before, but something in the clinical character of the services on offer chimed with the experimental nature of what he was about to do. She was more than happy to drive off with him to a remote corner of the countryside; somewhat less happy when he produced the rope.

The promise of a substantial bonus and the fact that he was clearly a gentleman — A gentleman! That still brought a smile to his lips — persuaded her to play along. He gagged her as soon as her wrists and ankles were tied. It was a warm evening in June, and in the late, long twilight he could see hope in her eyes: the hope that she hadn't just made the biggest mistake of her life.

Control, he discovered over the following few hours, was indeed the key, and the taking of a life because you wanted to, because you could — not because it was forced on you — was the quintessence of that control.

Peggy, the name she had given him, proved to be her nom de guerre. The sandstone tablet placed flush in the turf at her grave revealed that one Cybil Hughes had spent eighteen years on earth and was now *In God's Keeping.*

Her gaunt, pinched face had been added to the gallery of other girls in his head. It was a place he visited every night before falling asleep, an imaginary space, yet somehow as real to him as any room. Its tall windows reached almost to the parquet floor and were swathed in loose blinds so diaphanous they barely muted the light bleeding into the room. It was always sunny outside, and the old wooden floor would creak beneath his feet as he made the rounds of the gilt-framed portraits, lingering every so often to recall the details, beginning with Mrs. Beckett before moving on to Constanze Kettelmann. . . .

Chronology was important; it allowed him to trace his evolution, the slow mastery of those early impulses into some kind of method. Lying in bed at night, he would make his leisurely, unhurried rounds before selecting one of them, according to his mood, to help ease him into sleep, the memories melding seamlessly with his dreams.

The Maltese girls lent an exotic touch to his collection. With their honeyed complexions and deep, dark eyes, they exuded the easy sensuality of Gauguin's native creatures, and he had rehung the gallery to give them their own wall. They marked a new departure, a union of business and pleasure.

The proposal had come from him. Lutz Kettelmann had then dangled it in front of his superiors, not expecting them to bite. But they had. Anything that undermined the faith of the Maltese in the British could only favor the Germans when they finally invaded the island. The order to proceed with caution had come on New Year's Day, and he had done just that: five victims carefully selected from the lower reaches of society, dance hall hostesses, their deaths tainted with just enough ambiguity to arouse suspicion and get Maltese tongues wagging.

He hadn't foreseen the ruthlessness of the British in burying the crimes. Malta Command had simply suppressed the matter, quite content, it seemed, for local girls to keep on dying. The shoulder tab in Carmela Cassar's hand had been his way of forcing the affair into the open, and although it hadn't been discovered by a Maltese, as he'd intended, at least the wheels were finally turning. He would have to keep the momentum up, but he had a few ideas up his sleeve on that score.

No, the thing was narrowing down to the fine point, not quite as rapidly as he'd planned, but the *Upstanding*'s imminent departure, far from being a setback, would see things accelerate now. His only mild cause for concern was Carmela Cassar. His baser instincts had got the better of him. Something about her had obliged him to spend time with her — a full twenty-four hours that were not going to go unnoticed. With hindsight, a foolish indulgence. At the time it had made complete, all-consuming sense to him. He would make no such mistakes next time round.

He was repeating this vow to himself when the transmitter suddenly squawked into life. He snatched up the pencil and scribbled down the Morse code. It was a brief message, a meaningless jumble of enciphered letters. He keyed them into the Enigma machine, the decoded text showing up on the lamp board letter by letter.

The message was in German:

Herkules delayed. Dinner is off until further notice. Tacitus.

He sat very still, absorbing the information, trying to control his anger.

They had pulled the plug — on the invasion, on him.

Ten minutes later, he was still sitting there, motionless, and his decision had been made.

The plan was his. He had brought it into the world. It was not for them to snuff it out. What did he care for them? He felt no loyalty. How could he? Loyalty was a notion beyond his grasp. The money meant little to him. It was the sweetener, not the spur. He had offered his services to prove a point to himself: that others were not so very different from him, that they were happy to be complicit if it served their own ends.

Did they really think they could brush him off with a single line of enciphered text?

All the key pieces were in play and the endgame was approaching. For that's what it was: a game. He would close up the Enigma machine in its nondescript wooden box and tuck it safely away, and with it would go one part of him.

The other parts he could perform at will. He covered the full range of moods and emotions now, effortlessly passing for one of the crowd.

Sometimes he even convinced himself.

# DAY FIVE

For the first time in many days, Max was not shaken awake by the wailing of a siren. Rather, it was the unnatural silence that stirred him — the curse of existing in a permanent state of vacant alertness, even when asleep.

He checked his watch, dismissing the idea that the Germans were running late. It just wasn't the sort of thing they did. They were probably holding themselves back for a big midday blitz.

He felt surprisingly alert, even invigorated. His head hurt, but the throbbing at his temples brought with it good memories of the night before. He couldn't recall the last time he'd passed such an enjoyable evening in the company of his friends. It seemed somehow to have stiffened his resolve overnight. He felt alive, refreshed, eager to get out there and at it. He would set up a meeting with Lilian. After that, there would be no turning back.

He was right not to have involved Hugh.

He was heading for the door when the phone rang. It was an unfamiliar sound. The line to his flat was down for so much of the time that he'd dismissed its trill from his life.

"Chadwick."

"Max, it's me."

"Hi."

"Hi," said Mitzi. "No raid this morning."

"Doesn't look like it."

"I called last night. Several times."

"I got back late."

"I know. I just spoke to Hugh. He sounded a little the worse for wear."

He wanted to ask her what she was doing calling Hugh at this hour of the morning, but before he could, she said, "I need to see you."

"I was just on my way to work."

"I'm working too. Later. This evening."

"Where's Lionel?"

"Out. He won't be back." There was a short silence. "I need to see you, Max."

They had spoken many times on the phone, but always in a vague sort of code in case one of the girls at the exchange were listening in. "I need to see you, Max" wasn't code; it was a bald and brazen statement.

"I'm meeting Elliott this evening."

"I'm sure you can rearrange it," she said.

Under other circumstances, maybe.

"It's not a moveable feast, I'm afraid."

"My, it must be important."

She was annoyed now, unaccustomed as she was to him calling the tune. He could picture the obstinate tightening of her jaw at the other end of the line.

"Just one of those things, I'm afraid."

"Well, this is more than just one of those things," she replied flatly. "So if you could find a moment in your busy schedule . . ."

He knew what she was like; she wasn't going to give up.

"How late tonight?"

"I'm not going anywhere, and I believe you still have a key."

If the girls at the exchange were listening in, there'd be a flurry of speculation. It was Mitzi's way of saying she didn't care.

"Okay."

"I'm honored," said Mitzi tersely before hanging up.

The key was where he had always kept it — in the drawer of his bedside table, along with the letters from home. There had been no mail in months, and the bundle of envelopes with their out-of-date news seemed only to deepen his sense of isola-

271

tion. For all he knew, his father had finally seen sense and separated from his step-mother; Elizabeth was bearing the child of the stockman's son; and Roland, well, there were any number of things he could wish upon Roland, syphilis springing readily to mind, but the irritating truth was that Roland would probably be kicking his heels with his regiment somewhere in southern England and sneaking as much leave as was humanly possible.

He spread the letters on the bed, searching for the one from his good friend Lucinda. There was no address, no stamp, only his Christian name, because she had handed it to him in person just a week before he'd gone abroad. He had taken the train to Lewes, where, in her own words, she was now living in sin with a painter old enough to be her father. If that was sin, then the devil really did have all the best tunes.

The painter was named Roger and the house was a large brick-and-flint-built affair on the edge of a hamlet at the foot of the South Downs. The garden was wild and unkempt, not unlike Roger's hair.

They ate lunch outside on the terrace beneath a cotton awning slung between wooden posts. Roger's son was away at boarding school, but his daughter, Clare, was there, with her sulky pout and downcast gaze, as befitted a thirteen-year-old. She attended the school in Lewes where Lucinda taught French.

"I was also Max's teacher," Lucinda explained. "Many, many moons ago."

*"La femme de Monsieur Dupont a les yeux bleus."*

"Excellent, Chadwick — give yourself a gold star."

"We used to ascribe a whole load of other attributes to Madame Dupont when you weren't listening. There's nothing I don't know about Madame Dupont."

Roger had erupted in laughter, and even Clare had smiled.

Whenever Max was feeling down and desolate, he would think of the house and its garden bursting with blossom and lime-green loveliness on that warm day in early May. He could see it now as he pulled the four pages of paper from the envelope.

He hadn't read Lucinda's letter in a while, probably because he knew he had failed to live up to her kind and flattering words.

It started with a simple statement, barely legible. Her handwriting had always been atrocious, like a doctor's scrawl.

Our friendship began with a letter, and

this letter is all you shall have to sustain it over the coming months or, God forbid, years.

Well, God hadn't been listening; it had been almost two years since she had handed him the letter on the platform at Lewes station as he'd been boarding the train back to London. He had waited till Haywards Heath before opening it, and he had still been pondering its contents when the train drew into Victoria station a good while later.

In the letter, she went on to say that she would not be writing to him again while he was away at war. Anything she had to report would only appear trite and commonplace when set alongside his own experiences. Also, there was a strong likelihood that her letters would not reach him, and as strong a likelihood that any reply of his would not reach her. These silences would only fuel her fear that he had been killed.

Rather, she preferred to trust entirely to Providence that he would return safely — as she knew he would — and she looked forward to that moment. Meanwhile, these words would have to suffice. He could carry them with him wherever he went, dip into them at will. They were not limited by time or place. They were eternal and infinite.

He knew that there had always been a special bond between them — even when he was a ten-year-old schoolboy and she his twenty-one-year-old French teacher — but it was strange to see it spelled out in her hieroglyphic scrawl. Hunched on a bed in a crumbling room in a bombed and besieged city, her words, paradoxically, now made more sense to him than they ever had.

In many ways, the letter was a declaration of love — not a physical love (although she confessed that not long after he had graduated from Oxford there had been a moment when she had wanted to carry him off to bed with her, and had even come within a hairs-breadth of putting the proposition to him).

The love she spoke of was something else. It was to do with a man having many fathers in his life, and sometimes more than one mother. She wasn't looking to set herself up as a replacement, but she couldn't deny that she had sometimes felt and acted as such. She listed the qualities in him that had stirred those feelings in her.

Rounding off the letter, she wrote:

I don't know what you made of what you saw today, but if the house under the Downs is still my home when you return, then it is also your home. And if I have moved on, then I will have packed your bags and carried them with me. This is as much as I have ever promised anyone, but it is far less than you deserve.

"Deserve" was a big word. It suggested that he had earned the right to her feelings, and he could find little in his behavior of late to justify this exchange. The brass door key in his hand was evidence enough of that.

He felt the tears brimming in his eyes and he willed them to disappear. When that failed, he wiped them away on the back of his arm.

He didn't know what he was weeping for.

For Lucinda? Her kind words? England on a May day? The person he used to be? The person he had become? The lack of sleep? The pinch of hunger? The remorseless hail of bombs? The death of his friends? The faceless German pilot in the burns ward? Carmela Cassar?

Maybe he wept for all of these things.

Or maybe just one: his mother, Camille.

The morning limped by, hot and humid. Max spent much of it editing copy for the *Weekly Bulletin* and waiting impatiently for Lilian to call him back. By noon, everyone was remarking on the fact that an air raid had not yet materialized.

Neither had Lilian.

There was still no sign of her at the office, and no one was answering the phone at her aunt's palace in Mdina. There was nothing in the reports to worry about; two bombs had fallen on Rabat at about three A.M., but that was it.

An hour later, Maria put the call through to his office.

"Good of you to show up at work," he joked.

"I'm not at work; I'm at home."

She sounded tired, drained, downcast. And with good cause, it turned out. A childhood friend of hers, Caterina Gasan, had been killed by one of the two bombs that had fallen on Rabat, her family home receiving a direct hit that had made a mockery of the concrete shelter in the basement. Caterina's mother and her younger brother had also perished in the ruins. Her father and her elder brother, the two men who had laid the concrete with such confidence, had both survived almost entirely unscathed.

Max had met Caterina only once, back in March, but he could see her clearly: short, voluptuous, full-lipped, and feisty. He could see her rapt expression, lit by the screen,

277

while Dennis O'Keefe and Helen Parrish warbled their way through *I'm Nobody's Sweetheart Now* at the Rabat Plaza. They hadn't agreed on the merits of the film, but he had enjoyed her efforts to persuade him of the error of his ways.

"God . . . ," he said, pathetically.

"What God?" Lilian replied.

"You don't mean that."

"Don't I? It doesn't make sense, not Caterina."

"It's not meant to make sense."

There was a short silence before she spoke. "I want to see you."

"That's lucky. I want to see you too."

"Can you come to Mdina?"

"I'll be there in twenty minutes — Luftwaffe permitting."

Ena, the younger of Lilian's two cousins, answered the door to Max. He could see from her eyes that she'd been crying.

"They're in the garden," she said simply, taking him by the hand and leading him there in silence.

They were seated at a tin table in the shade of an orange tree: Lilian, her aunt Teresa, and Ralph. It was a surprise to see Ralph there, and Max experienced a momentary twinge of jealousy.

"I saw Squadron Leader Tindle in the street and told him about Caterina," Teresa explained. Like Lilian, she was dressed in black.

"I was just leaving," said Ralph, stubbing out his cigarette and getting to his feet. "My sincere condolences again." He graced both women with something between a nod and a bow.

"Lilian . . . ," Teresa prompted.

"No, stay," said Ralph. "I'm sure Max will see me out."

The tall glazed doors at the back of the palace were crisscrossed with tape, and as two men entered the building, Ralph said, "Bad blow for them. Caterina was a great girl."

"You knew her?"

"Only to ogle. She used to come to the Point de Vue every now and then."

The Point de Vue Hotel stood on the south side of the Saqqajja, the leafy square separating Mdina and Rabat. Like the Xara Palace, the hotel had been requisitioned by the RAF as a billet for pilots stationed at Ta' Qali. The hotel barman was known for his John Collinses, the bar itself for the local girls who were drawn there come nightfall, like moths to a candle flame. For some reason the pilots called these flirtatious encounters "poodle-faking." Well, that had all stopped the month before, when the Point de Vue had taken a direct hit during an afternoon raid, killing six.

"That place is cursed. When I think of the times we had there, and those who are gone . . ."

It wasn't like Ralph to come over all maudlin — breeziness was his stock-in-trade — and Max wasn't sure how to respond.

"Thanks for last night" was the best he could come up with.

"Might be a while before we get to do it again. Had a summons from the CO this morning, and the fly-in's definitely set for the ninth."

"Three days . . ."

"Believe me, I'm counting. He passed me fit to fly Spits again."

"Congratulations."

"It's going to be one hell of a scrap. That bastard Kesselring's going to throw everything he's got at us."

"But this time you're ready. I saw the new blast pens when I passed by Ta' Qali."

"What counts is up there," said Ralph, nodding heavenward. "If the new Spits really do have four cannons and are faster in the climb, we stand a chance. Who knows, we might even bloody their noses.

We'd better, or it's all over."

"You think?"

"I know. This is it — the last roll of the dice."

Max paused in the hallway at the front door.

"When we're old and sitting in a pub somewhere, I'm going to remind you of this conversation."

Ralph smiled weakly. "Tell me more about the pub."

"It's at the end of a long track, and there's a river, with trout, and a garden running down to the water. It's summer and the sun is shining, and there's a weeping willow near the jetty where our grandchildren are playing. They're naked, jumping off the jetty, flapping around in the river, splashing the people drifting past in punts."

Ralph gave a sudden loud laugh. "Damn your detractors. Now I know why you got the job."

"What detractors?"

"Come on, you're at least ten years too young for the post."

"I forgot to mention . . . at the pub, you're in a wheelchair. You lost both legs when you got shot down over Malta in May 1942."

Ralph laughed some more as he pulled open the front door. After the cool of the palace and its shaded garden the heat in Bastion Square hit them like a hammer.

"She's a great girl, Max, war or no war. She's the real thing."

"She's just a friend."

"Then you're a bloody fool."

"If you say so."

"Hugh says so too."

"Hugh?"

"And Freddie."

He knew Freddie was a fan of Lilian's. The three of them had spent a raucous evening together at Captain Caruana's bar in Valetta a few weeks back. He struggled to recall when Hugh had ever set eyes on her.

"Now go in there and look after her. She needs it."

Lilian didn't appear particularly needy. She sat there silent and grim-faced while he made the right noises, and the moment Teresa withdrew, leaving them alone together, she suggested that they head for Boschetto Gardens. Actually, it was more of a command than a suggestion, and there was something wild and reckless in her eyes when she issued it.

"On the motorcycle?"

Until now, she had always refused to be seen with him on the motorcycle.

"Well, I'm not walking there in this heat."

■ ■ ■ ■

It was a short trip, a few miles at most along the ridge toward the coast. He took it slowly, savoring the experience.

Lilian rode sidesaddle because of her skirt, and as Rabat fell away behind them, she shifted closer on the seat, holding him around the waist just that little bit tighter.

She was a good pillion passenger, not fighting the curves in the road, leaning with him.

"You've done this before," he called over his shoulder.

"I've never done what I'm about to do."

"And what's that?" he asked, turning to look her in the eye.

"I think it's a goat," she replied calmly.

They missed the emaciated creature by a matter of inches.

It would have been a pity to kill it, a survivor like that. Most had gone the way of the pot long before now.

Boschetto Gardens offered the only genuine patch of woodland on Malta — a rare glimpse of what the island must have looked like long ago, before it was stripped of trees by early shipbuilders. Max had walked its weaving pathways a handful of times, often with Ralph, who loved to go there to paint. It was a tranquil, sun-dappled world where dark pines towered over groves of lemon, orange, and olive trees. There was an ancient atmosphere about the place, a whiff of dusty fables by classical authors you'd heard of but never read.

"I half expect a unicorn to come trotting round the corner any moment."

They were making their way along a shaded path lined with ivy-threaded walls.

"Or Pan," replied Lilian.

"I've never liked Pan."

"Why not?"

"I'm sorry, he's too creepy."

"But he's the god of music and nature and love."

"Exactly, so why's he got goat legs?"

He told her about *The Wind in the Willows,* and the bizarre chapter in the book where Pan helps Rat and Mole locate Otter's lost son.

She liked the sound of the book, especially Toad, and he promised to send her a copy of it when he got home.

Maybe it was the mention of home, but she grew silent before asking, "It is going to end, isn't it?"

"Of course it is. And one day Germans

will come here in peace and walk this path and admire this view." He spread his hands before him.

"I hate them."

It was said in a calm, low voice, and was all the more menacing for it.

"They're only doing their job. It doesn't mean they enjoy it, or even that they agree with it."

"How can you be so reasonable? You've lost friends too."

She sounded almost angry with him, and maybe she was, but he also sensed she was searching for answers she hoped he might hold. He didn't have any to offer her, though. What could he say? Ivor, Wilf, Delia, Dicky . . . they had all died defending a cause in which they believed, for which they'd been ready to fight. That was his consolation. Caterina, on the other hand, had been obliterated while watching from the sidelines — an innocent bystander caught in the cross fire.

"I don't know," he said. "I really don't." He stopped on the pathway, staring down at his dusty desert boots before looking up into her lambent brown eyes. "But I know that being unreasonable doesn't help. It doesn't do justice to those who have died. It doesn't honor them. They're the ones who matter, not the man — the *boy,* most likely — who pulled the lever or pressed the button or did whatever he was ordered to do. I doubt he's so very different from the rest of us, just happy to be alive and eager for it all to end."

She weighed his words awhile.

"So who do I blame? I have to blame someone."

"Try the politicians — the idiots who dragged us into this mess in the first place. I find that works best."

Not long after, she led him off the path, through the trees, until they found themselves in a small glade. When she sat herself down at the base of a gnarled old olive tree, he followed suit, remembering what she had said on the motorcycle about doing something she'd never done before.

"Can I have a cigarette?" she asked.

"You don't smoke."

"But I want to try."

He lit two cigarettes and handed her one, amused by his presumption.

She didn't cough and she didn't complain about the taste; she just smoked the cigarette, then stubbed it out in the sandy soil.

"Verdict?"

"Not so special. I feel a bit dizzy."

She sat back against the trunk and closed

her eyes. There was nothing awkward about the silence that now enveloped them. It gave him the opportunity to think about how he was going to broach the subject. It was hardly the time to do it, not while she was still reeling from the death of her friend, but time was a luxury he couldn't afford right then.

Over the tops of the trees he could make out Verdala Palace, the governor's summer residence, rising foursquare on the ridge above, lording over the gardens. With its corner towers and crenellations, it resembled a medieval castle, although the pale stonework lent it an exotic and less forbidding air. He could picture the vast barrel-vaulted hall with its frescoes, where he had dined soon after his promotion. Being a Plymouth Brother, Governor Dobbie was a teetotaler, but he had nevertheless kept the wine waiter on his toes that night, ensuring that his guests' glasses had been properly charged.

"What are you thinking?" Lilian asked. She still had her head resting against the trunk, but her eyes were open now, locked on to him. "It looks serious," she added lightheartedly.

He placed his hand over hers and gave it a small squeeze. "It is, I'm afraid."

He told her everything, from the moment when Freddie had first summoned him to the Central Hospital to show him Carmela Cassar's corpse. First, though, he made her swear on all she held dear that she wouldn't share a word of what he was about to tell her with any living soul.

She was on her feet before he had finished his account, and only when he was done did she speak.

"The lieutenant governor tried to stop you?"

"He wasn't present."

"But he was still in the room."

"I suppose they must have been acting with his authority."

"I can't believe it."

She was angry now, pacing around.

"It's true. They threatened us both in no uncertain terms."

"But they're doing something about it. They must be."

"I wouldn't bank on it. They don't want to have the drains up at a time like this. It's like Elliott said — when the *Upstanding* leaves, the problem goes with her."

"The problem?" she fired back crisply. "Is that what you call murderers in your country?"

He raised his hands in placatory gesture.

"Don't get angry with *me.*"

"But I *am* angry with you. I'm angry with all of you — the way you treat us, the way you think of us, the way you *talk* about us. *'The natives are getting restless'* — I heard that yesterday in the Union Club. And I saw the looks and the smiles. They all thought it was very funny, until they saw me listening. Then they were embarrassed. Good. I'm glad the little native embarrassed them."

"Lilian —"

"It's true. You know it is."

"Not everyone thinks like that, or talks like that."

"Oh, you're innocent, are you? I read what you write, and I see the same thing in your words. What was it last week? 'Malta Can Take It'? Well, good old Malta."

"That was a line from a BBC broadcast," he bleated in his defense.

"Yes, Malta can take it, because Malta has got to take it. But we're not doing it for you; we're doing it for us." She slapped her palm against her chest to make her point. "It's our island. It's not yours, and it's not theirs. It's ours."

Technically, the island was a British crown colony, but it probably wasn't the best moment to point out this detail.

"If it wasn't for us, you'd be under German occupation by now."

"Well, at least they wouldn't be dropping their bombs on us."

"No, we would be."

The words popped out of his mouth unbidden, illuminating Malta's grim and perennial predicament, a toothless lump of limestone prey to the whims of mightier nations.

"Don't you see? People have always come here because they can. But they always leave. If the Germans invade, one day they will go." She paused. "And one day you will go too."

Her republican rant had strayed into dangerous territory with that last comment. They both knew it.

"I'm not the only one to think it," she said defensively.

"I don't doubt it. But keep it under your hat unless you fancy a holiday in Uganda."

"And that says it all, doesn't it?"

He wasn't going to argue the point, because at heart he agreed with her about the "pro-Italians" and the other "subversive elements" who had been shipped out to Uganda earlier in the year. They'd had a number of heated discussions on this thorny issue, with Max trotting out the official platitude: "Extraordinary times call for extraordinary measures." When it came down to it, though, there was something chillingly draconian about the stretch of power that allowed the British to intern and deport Maltese citizens at will, without due process. They came from all walks of life — dockyard workers to priests, pensioners to university professors — and not one of them had ever been formally charged with a crime.

It was an injustice that had touched Lilian on a personal level. A friend of hers, the daughter of the chief justice, had spent two years under house arrest with her family before opting to board the *Breconshire* and follow her father into exile. Sixteen years of loyal service to the crown had, apparently, not been enough to place the family's loyalty beyond doubt.

"You're probably right," conceded Max. "I'm no better than the rest of them. But maybe I've learned something. Maybe that's why I'm here, why I told you."

"Yes, you tell me, but first you make me swear my silence. I can't stay silent."

"You must. They'll shut you down in a moment."

"They can't."

"They told me they would. That's what they threatened me with."

She cast him a curious glance. "They think you care what happens to me?" She seemed almost amused by the idea.

"They're right. I do."

She stared down at him, her body now still, the agitation gone. He reached up, took her hand, and drew her back onto the ground beside him.

"You have to trust me. You have to let me do this my way. I need your help — a small favor — but that's as far as your involvement goes."

She stared off through the trees.

"What do you want me to do?" she asked eventually, without turning.

At three o'clock, when Max returned to the Information Office, an enemy air raid had yet to materialize over the island, and this had shaped itself into the hopeful speculation that the Luftwaffe had been pulled out of Sicily, summoned back to the Russian front. It had happened before, but never at this time of year, and Max remained skeptical.

At four o'clock, Elliott called from the Combined Operations Room.

"Is there anything on the table?" Max asked.

"Nothing. *Niente*. Nada. Dead as a dodo."

"Maybe it's Hitler's birthday."

"That was a couple of weeks back."

Max laughed.

"It's true. April twentieth. The sonofabitch just turned fifty-three. You've got to hand it to the guy: it takes a special gift to fuck up a planet in fifty-three years."

"He's had a little help."

"True, but I doubt we'd be frying our asses in Malta if young Adolf had been hit by a streetcar on his way to school forty-odd years ago."

Elliott was calling to confirm their dinner plans and to give Max directions.

"Elliott, I know where you live."

He'd spent any number of enjoyable evenings on the roof terrace at Elliott's apartment in Gzira.

"I'm talking about my country residence."

"Your country residence?"

"You mean you don't have one? Now grab a pen; it's a little off the beaten track."

This was putting it mildly. Wayside shrines, stone gateposts, and oddly shaped trees figured large in the directions.

"Shall we say seven o'clock?"

"With directions like these it might be nearer ten."

Elliott chuckled. "Well, don't expect to find any of the Chassagne-Montrachet left."

■ ■ ■ ■

The last town of any note before Elliott's directions degenerated into obscure landmarks was Siggiewi. The road there ran through Qormi and Zebbug, bisecting the low southern plain, passing between the airfields at Luqa and Ta' Qali. The men had had a whole day to lick their wounds from the previous day's pasting, and Max could picture the scene: the ground crews and infantry busily filling bomb craters and repairing blast pens, one wary eye on the heavens. The early evening raid was due any moment. The unnatural silence that had hung over the island all day surely had to end soon.

It hadn't by the time Max had reached Siggiewi. The inhabitants were milling around the main square, moving tentatively, unaccustomed to being aboveground at that hour. Max stopped at a bar near the church and begged a glass of water, not to slake his thirst so much as wash the dust from his mouth. An old man asked him hopefully if the war was over, and when he got back on his motorcycle, a gaggle of barefoot boys chased him through the narrow streets, falling away in dribs and drabs as he opened the throttle.

The rutted road south of Siggiewi wound its way toward the sea and one of the few corners of the island he had never explored. He knew the coastline to the east because that's where the megalithic temples of Hagar Qim and Mnajdra were to be found, standing like two mini-Stonehenges atop the cliffs. Lilian had insisted he visit them, delivering a lecture on their unique place in the panoply of ancient European sites. She was biased. The professor of archaeology who had whisked her mother off to Italy was a leading expert on Hagar Qim. That's how the couple had met, some years before the war, during one of the professor's many visits to his precious temple.

To the west lay the Dingli Cliffs, mile upon mile of sheer limestone rock face rising two hundred feet from the water. The Dingli Cliffs were home to another kind of temple, one that celebrated the new technology, for it was there that the island's primary radio direction finding station was located. In between, though, lay a stretch of coast Max hadn't even known existed. There seemed to be only one dirt track in and out, and without Elliot's directions he would hardly have noticed the junction.

The track elbowed its way up a hillside of

stunted trees and rock-strewn fields. It then dipped away sharply toward the cliffs, before veering to the right and hugging the coast-line. To his left the ground descended in narrow cultivated terraces until the slope became too steep to hold them. On his right rose a rocky escarpment. True to form, the Maltese had responded by pouncing on this meagre scrap that nature had tossed them, this precarious step of land at the edge of the world. Judging from the age of the few farmhouses he passed, people had been there for centuries, scratching a living from the powdery soil.

He was on the point of turning back when he saw the isolated chapel with the faded blue doors that Elliott had mentioned. A few hundred yards farther on he came across the sorry-looking cypress where the track bifurcated. The lower route petered out at a cluster of whitewashed farm build-ings arranged around an open courtyard and towered over by two Aleppo pines. It was just as Elliott had described it, although he hadn't mentioned the short wireless mast on the roof of the farmhouse.

Beyond the compound, the ground fell away in stone-trimmed terraces toward the cliff edge, and it was here that Max saw a tall figure silhouetted against the lowering sun. Elliott appeared to be scything grass, but as Max drew closer, it became clear that he was swinging a golf club.

Max propped the motorcycle against one of the pines and made his way over.

"Do you play?" asked Elliott.

"Badly."

"Then you're in excellent company."

The tin pail at Elliott's feet was brimming with golf balls.

"From the Marsa Golf Club," he explained. "They've got no use for them anymore." Not since the club's fairways and greens had been plowed up and turned into allotments.

"There's a whole load more in the barn, so don't hold back," he added, making for the farmhouse. He returned a little while later with the promised bottle of white burgundy, two wineglasses, and a Maltese man carrying a folding side table.

"Pawlu helps me out from time to time."

Pawlu was the sort of fellow you'd want on your side in a fight — not tall, but thickset and bull-necked. When they shook hands, Max's felt like a child's in a bear's paw.

"I am pleased to meet you."

"Pawlu speaks good English. He used to work down at the docks as a stevedore but now has a farm up on the ridge there, as well as a beautiful wife and two young sons who make a good living picking up the golf balls that don't go over the cliff."

"Which is most of them."

"He's also extremely insolent, and I'm thinking of dispensing with his services."

Pawlu gave a disarmingly warm smile, then excused himself. He was expected home for dinner.

Max and Elliott spent the next half hour quaffing the excellent wine and driving golf balls out to sea, toward the setting sun. Anything clearing the cliff (which required a perfectly struck three iron) scored one point; anything less scored no points, even if the ball bounced over the edge. Elliott liked to play dirty: "You're forcing it with your shoulders" . . . "Stop lifting your head" . . . "Let the club do the work" . . . "You're getting a bit wristy, must be the wine" — irritating observations intended to throw Max off his game.

They were level at a far-from-impressive four points apiece when the contest was brought to a halt by the building roar of an aircraft engine.

"Here," said Elliott, thrusting a seven iron into Max's hand. "You're going to need more loft."

"What?"

"On my word, okay?"

They both set themselves, ready to swing.

Max saw them now: four fighters coming at them from the west in wide line abreast, hugging the cliff top. They were enemy aircraft, new Me109Fs with their distinctive yellow noses.

"Now!"

They swung their clubs in unison. In his eagerness, Max topped his ball, but Elliott's sailed high into the air with just the right amount of lead on it. For a moment it seemed that the impossible was about to be achieved, and if the ball had carried another fifty yards or so, it might well have been.

The four fighters thundered past unscathed. It was probably just a trick of the light, but Max could have sworn that he saw one of the pilots wave.

"He waved," said Max. "One of them waved."

"That's because they know me."

They were regulars, apparently, marauders who often appeared at this hour.

"They turn inland just down from here, coming at Safi and Luqa out of the low sun. Didn't think they'd show today, though — nothing else has."

The remote crackle of light antiaircraft

fire carried up the coast to their ears.

"There they go. First action of the day."

It also proved to be the last. By eight o'clock, there was still no sign of any bombers, and the last slither of the sun was sinking into the sea.

The warm orange light suffusing the courtyard gave way by almost imperceptible degrees to the distinctive purples and blues of a Maltese twilight. Elliott had got a fire going in an upturned dustbin lid that served as his barbecue, and a second bottle of Burgundy had appeared from the cellar. He had another white wine in mind for when the fish hit the table.

There were two of them, big and fresh and in need of gutting.

"Pawlu gets them for me."

"I thought the fishermen had stopped going out."

There had been a number of fatal strafing attacks on fishing boats in the last month — all part of the new policy of deliberately targeting the locals.

"These two beauties would suggest otherwise," Elliott said, grinning.

He sat himself down across from Max at the rough lumber table in the courtyard and began to prepare the fish, working the knife with an expert hand.

"You look like you know what you're doing."

"Don't be fooled. Pawlu showed me how." He glanced up at Max. "It's not in my blood, if that's what you're asking. I'm from mountain stock."

It was near enough the first information Elliott had ever volunteered about himself, and it didn't stop there.

He had grown up in the Berkshire Hills in western Massachusetts. Writers such as Nathaniel Hawthorne and Herman Melville had lived there and waxed lyrical about its stubborn and stony beauty, its soaring peaks and plunging valleys, but such romantic considerations had probably not figured very large in the minds of Elliott's forebears on his mother's side when they had chopped their farm out of the wilderness.

Winters there were long and harsh. Elliott could remember milk freezing in a pail left by an open door, and his mother thawing out the buttonholes on his jacket with a hot flatiron. He could also recall his grandfather getting caught in a blizzard and being carried home in the back of a cart, closer to death than life, not long for the world.

Elliott had been twelve at the time, and when it had finally been his turn to say his farewells, he had gone upstairs to the bed where his grandfather lay. Drawing him close by the hand, the old man had whispered weakly into his ear: "It is appointed unto man once to die."

"I can tell you," Elliott went on, "I was pretty glum when I woke the next morning. And you know what? The first thing I saw when I went down to breakfast was that hard-shelled old bastard moaning to my grandma that she'd overcooked the bacon again."

His father's side of the family was an altogether different story, one of New Yorkers drawn to the forest-clad slopes of the Berkshires by the fortunes to be made from paper. The Berkshire mills manufactured the paper from which United States currency was made, and this near enough amounted to a license to print their own money.

It was paper that carried the family to England when Elliott was a teenager, his father taking up a post with Wiggins Teape in Basingstoke.

"Do you know Basingstoke?"

"Only to pass through."

"That's the best way to know it. It's like Hawthorne said of Liverpool: 'a most convenient and admirable point to get away from.'"

Max laughed. Elliott placed the fish on the grille over the glowing embers and continued with his account.

He hadn't enjoyed his time in England, although his few years at Charterhouse School had been pleasant enough. His Calvinist boarding school back in the Berkshires had prepared him well for the vagaries of life in a prewar English public school: several hundred young men paying fearful homage to a handful of slightly older young men while a bunch of rather bewildered old men looked on.

Being a foreigner with a funny accent, he'd found himself the subject of ridicule, which had taught him a valuable lesson: to keep his mouth shut. Also, to bide his time; opportunities for revenge would present themselves sooner or later.

"I was the 'lanky Yankee,' a figure of fun." He smiled as a thought came into his head. "Which is pretty much how people look at me here."

"And are you plotting your revenge on us?"

Elliott's voice took on a sinister edge. "Don't worry. *You* get off light."

Max smiled. "Why are you here, Elliott?"

"Because we're allies."

"I mean, why are you really here?"

"Because we're allies."

"You promised me some answers."

"It's an honest answer. We're allies, and allies don't always see eye to eye."

"That's a half answer."

"We've been watching things over here for a good long while. It gives us a different perspective, and of course we're going to take a view on what we see."

"What's the view?"

"The only one there is: that the two-bit upstart with the smudge on his upper lip has taken the first few rounds without breaking a sweat."

"And . . . what? Now that you're in the ring, he's punching above his weight?"

Elliott gave a little shrug. "You wrote us out of your history of the last war, and you'll do the same with this one. But the truth is, without us you're screwed; with us, you stand a chance. A bold statement, I know."

"And some might say an arrogant one."

"Now, that's one area where you beat us hands down. You're the only people in the world who could turn Dunkirk into a victory — a mass retreat, for Christ's sake!"

"I suppose."

"What is it about you Brits and your constant refusal to know when you're beaten? Don't get me wrong, I admire you for it. I mean, last month, when the *Penelope* was in port for repairs, you remember?"

How could anyone forget? The Germans had hurled everything they'd had at the damaged cruiser. Day after day the Stukas had come to finish her off, reducing the dockside to a mesh of craters. The ship's quarterdeck became known as the "rock garden," and when she finally slipped away under darkness to Alexandria, there were more than two thousand wooden pegs in her, stopping up the shrapnel holes and earning her the nickname HMS *Porcupine.*

"I got caught down there one morning during a raid. It was bedlam, like nothing I'd ever seen, and right in the middle of it the ship's company started singing. Singing, for Christ's sake, to keep the spirits of the gunners up! I don't get you guys, I really don't."

"So why did they pick you for the job?"

"I asked for the posting."

"Regretting it yet?" Max inquired with a faint smile.

"Things are a bit hotter than I'd hoped, but hey, look around you. . . ." He spread his hands. "Nine miles below hell, it ain't."

Elliott flipped the fish on the grille.

"Why Malta?" Max asked.

"Because we're making history here."

305

"Not that they don't have enough of it already."

"This will be right up there with the best of it. The war can turn on what happens here."

"You've been speaking to Hugh."

"Hugh's a romantic, but he also happens to be right. Malta saved Europe once before, and it might just do it again. You won't know this, but Mandalay fell to the Japs a couple of days back. Burma's as good as gone, and they're coming at India through Ceylon. If Egypt falls to Rommel, there's nothing to stop the enemy linking up. They'll cut the world in half and lay their hands on all that oil in the Middle East. If that happens, well, I know which horse *my* money's on. Egypt has to hold out, and that's where we fit in — this dot of an island in the middle of nowhere, so easy to ignore."

"You call this being ignored? Every day for the past God-knows-how-many months they've dropped the same tonnage of bombs on us as they did on Coventry."

"Field Marshal Kesselring's no fool. Far from it," conceded Elliott. "He knows the importance of Malta. But does he have Hitler's ear? Because in the end, that's what counts."

"None of it's going to matter when they

invade."

"They're not going to invade."

"I'm so glad you told me," Max replied, with casual sarcasm.

"I mean it. The invasion's off."

"Off?"

"Put back. But that's enough. Once the new Spitfires get here, it's dead and done for. This was their one chance, and it looks like Hitler's made the same mistake again. He should have invaded you guys two years ago. July 1940. That was his moment, and he missed it. This time, his big mistake was listening to Rommel. Rommel thinks he can get to Cairo, Malta or no Malta. But Rommel's not an administrator; he's a tactician — and a good one, if only because he's unorthodox and therefore hard to read. Logistics like supply lines are beneath his dignity; it's quartermaster stuff. He takes for granted he'll get whatever he needs, and right now he is getting it. But if we gain air superiority over this island, then the Wellingtons and Blenheims will start flying again from Luqa, and he'll know what it's like to feel the pinch. Maybe he'll take Tobruk — odds are he will, in my book — but Cairo's a step too far."

"Anything else I should know while you're at it?"

Max intended the question as a joke.

"Depends if you can keep a secret or not," replied Elliott, lighting a cigarette. "The governor's about to be relieved."

"Dobbie?"

"That's impressive — the information officer knows the name of his commander in chief."

Max was genuinely shocked. Dobbie was — well, he wasn't just part of the furniture, he was Malta itself.

"Why?"

"He's lost the confidence of his service chiefs, and they've started sneaking to teacher. Personally, I blame the command structure you've put in place. It's a goddamn shambles. You've got a governor who's answerable to the colonial secretary *and* to the War Office, and a general officer commanding who can't coordinate the defense of the island because your naval and air force commanders report directly to their C-in-Cs in Cairo."

"When you put it like that . . ."

"It *is* like that, and Dobbie's taking the fall for it. I'd play the 'poor health' ticket if I were you, if only because there's some truth in it. Oh, and better get drafting your piece. It's going to happen soon, any day now."

"In the middle of all this?"

"No point in hanging about once the decision's been made. Thanks for everything, amigo, and adios."

"Who's replacing him?"

Elliott smiled. "You don't expect me to hand you everything on a plate, do you?"

"No, although a piece of fish would be nice, before it's cooked to buggery."

They ate the fish with a simple salad of tomatoes so sweet that it suddenly made sense why they were classified as a fruit rather than a vegetable.

"I've been doing all the talking," said Elliott. "Time for a bit of quid pro quo."

"You really think I have anything up my sleeve to match what I've just heard?"

"I was talking about you. Tell me something about Max Chadwick that I don't already know."

"There's a whole load of stuff you don't know."

"Don't be so sure; I've read your file."

"There's a file on me?"

"You're the information officer in a key theater of war. What do *you* think? I even know the name of your housemaster at Wellington."

"Old Arsebreath?"

Elliott laughed. "That's a level of detail it

doesn't go into."

It came pretty close, though. Apparently Max had been described as "coming from a good family."

"Well, that's rubbish, for a start," he protested. "My great-grandfather made a lot of money sending coal miners to their deaths. His son was a drunk, a bully, and a bigamist who never did an honest day's work in his life."

"A bigamist?"

"Well, maybe not technically, but he led a double life with another woman and other children."

"And his son?"

"My father? He's proof that the apple doesn't always fall close to the tree."

"Good on him," said Elliott. "And that's from a man who also had a bully for a father."

Elliott already knew that Max's mother had died when he was young. He didn't know that she'd died in labor, giving birth to Max.

"There — something you didn't know about me."

"Doesn't make the grade. I want something more personal."

Max thought on it. Then he told Elliott about the letter his mother had written him.

It was a common enough practice, certainly for women like his mother, whose
narrow hips weren't best suited for bringing
babies into the world. The doctor had
warned her that it would be a difficult birth,
that she might have to choose between
herself and the child. She had chosen Max,
and she had survived long enough to hold
him in her arms before the loss of blood
had killed her. Sometimes he saw himself
spread-eagled on her chest, worn out from
all the effort, as she slowly slipped away into
oblivion. That's how it had been, apparently; his father had told him so.

His father hadn't told him about the letter
she'd written to him, her unborn child —
well, not until Max was sixteen. He'd found
it long before then, though, hidden in his
father's desk, biding its time. The desk had
always held a deep fascination for him, with
its inlaid mother-of-pearl decoration and its
drawers and pigeonholes stuffed with detri-
tus from the world of adults. It was an ir-
resistible Aladdin's cave for a young boy,
and whenever the coast was clear, he would
go and poke around in it.

He found the letter tucked away with
some other correspondence in a leather
portfolio. It wasn't sealed, and at first he
was unsure what he was reading. Not long

after, when he was packed off to boarding school near Oxford, he took the letter with him, a guard against loneliness. It had worked. The disembodied voice of his mother — recorded in her distinctive handwriting, with its looping p's and g's and y's — had blunted his sense of isolation. She'd been with him, watching over him.

It was a long letter, and in it she spelled out the story of her life, everything from her childhood in the countryside near Versailles to the comical first encounter with his father in the lobby of the apartment building in Paris. She went to great pains to say that he (although she used the neutral "you" throughout) was the product of a fine and fulsome love affair, and she signed off with a line of French that made no sense to him whatsoever.

Had his French teacher been some creaky old chap in a tweed jacket, he probably wouldn't have sought him out and asked for a translation. Mademoiselle Leckford, as Lucinda was known, had offered an altogether different prospect. She was young and pretty, and all the boys were a little in love with her. Max copied out the line on a piece of paper, which he presented to her after a class:

She scrutinized it a moment before asking, "Where does it come from?" Seeing that the question unsettled him, she quickly added, "You don't have to say."

But he told her anyway. It was good to have the excuse to tell someone about his mother and the letter she had written him, especially someone like Mademoiselle Leckford.

"It means . . . ," she said softly, peering down at him with a strange look in her eyes. "It means, 'You would have been my life.' "

"Oh."

She turned away, staring out the window. "Now run along, Chadwick."

Only later did he learn that she had turned her back on him because she hadn't wanted him to see the tears building in her eyes.

Of course, the pity felt by an adult for a ten-year-old boy could hardly be dignified with the name of friendship, but it had nonetheless been the start of something enduring and important for both of them.

"I still see her," said Max, speaking of Lucinda. "And maybe I'm still a bit in love with her."

"That'll do me," Elliott replied. "I like that. It's a good story. Very revealing."

313

"If you say so."

"Oh, I do."

Only when the plates were cleared away did they broach the subject they both knew they'd been avoiding, and it was Elliott who took the initiative.

"Recovered from the meeting yesterday?"

"Oh, that's what it was. Seemed more like a court-martial to me."

"From where I was sitting too."

"Where exactly *were* you sitting?"

Elliott leaned back in his chair. "Put it this way: I can see both sides."

"You think I can't? You know what I did when Freddie first showed me the shoulder tab?"

"No, but I can guess. You thought about getting rid of it."

Max was momentarily thrown by the response. "And what would you have done?"

"Same as you, probably — thought about it, changed my mind, snooped around a bit. The only difference is, I wouldn't have got caught."

"Well, bully for you."

Elliott shrugged the comment aside. "I'm trained for that kind of thing. You're an architect with a gift for writing the kind of upbeat bullshit that people want to hear at times like this."

"If you're trying to put me in my place, you're doing a pretty good job — better than Colonel Gifford, even."

"Gifford's about as subtle as an anvil. I told him you couldn't be strong-armed."

"Well, he proved you wrong."

"Did he? I doubt it. My guess is you've thought about nothing else since then . . . and what you're going to do about it now."

"What do you care?" said Max warily.

"You think I'm completely without principles?"

It was a typical play from Elliott, answering a question with a question. Nevertheless, Max reached into his hip pocket and pulled out a folded piece of paper. Elliott took it from him, angling it at the light from the candles.

Max had scribbled three questions on it: *Where does he find them? Where did he take Carmela Cassar? Why does he do it?* He had put a line through the last of these.

"Interesting," said Elliott. "But why cross out the last one?"

"Because it's imponderable. Who knows why he does it? Some sick urge buried away deep inside him."

"Him?" asked Elliott. "Why not them?"

The thought hadn't occurred to Max. "I just assumed . . ."

"Well, don't. Wethern's Law of Suspended Judgment: assumption is the mother of all screwups." Elliott pointed to the third item on Max's list. "For all you know, this is the key to it all. Don't dismiss it."

"I don't understand."

"Jeez, your ignorance is refreshing. I'm saying, what if he's doing it for reasons other than self-gratification? What if he's looking to destabilize the situation here? What if he's working for the enemy and the whole thing is one big setup, all part of a plan to turn the Maltese against you, to break the special relationship?"

"Now you're sounding like Ralph. He sees spies and fifth columnists everywhere."

"Ralph is right to be on his guard. They *are* here. I can tell you that for nothing."

It was a big statement, and one that raised more questions, but Max tried to remain focused on the issue.

"Freddie said there was evidence of sexual interference."

"Ah . . ."

"So either this person — or persons — takes his job very seriously, or he's getting some kind of pleasure from it."

"Maybe both."

"Now you're reaching."

"It's possible, though."

316

"Anything's possible under what's-his-name's rule. It's okay to make assumptions if they're based on evidence."

"What evidence? One trip to the sub base?" Elliott paused to allow his words to sink in. "I called Tommy Ravilious this afternoon. Don't worry, I played my cards close. He still thinks the sun shines out of your skinny fundament."

"Thank God for that. I can sleep easy tonight."

"I don't know," said Elliott, glancing up at the cloudless sky. "That's a 'bomber's moon.' I wouldn't bank on any of us sleeping easy tonight." Looking back at Max, he asked, "So? Do the dates match with when the *Upstanding* was in port?"

"Of course. That's not the sort of slip an enemy agent would make."

Elliott regarded him with a look that hovered on the fringes of disappointment. "I've got to say, I'm surprised at your skepticism."

"I don't like to leap to assumptions."

"Touché," said Elliott with a little nod. "But maybe they're more than just assumptions. Maybe I know more than I'm letting on."

Max swirled the wine in his glass, staring at it, pensive.

"I think I can see what you're doing," Max said eventually.

"Enlighten me."

"It's complicated."

"So boil it down."

Colonel Gifford's threats might not have worked, but if Max could be made to believe there were other factors at play, things far beyond his understanding, then maybe that would persuade him to back off, especially if he thought that by taking the matter further he would only be playing into the enemy's hands, serving their nefarious cause. Elliott was simply finishing the job that Gifford had started.

Elliott listened attentively to the theory before announcing, "You're wrong. As far as I'm concerned, what you get up to is your own business. But this" — he wagged the sheet of paper at Max — "is taking you nowhere fast. I mean, look at it. Where did he take Carmela Cassar? It's the wrong question. Valetta's a ghost town, so are the Three Cities, even Sliema and Gzira. Most of the people have left. He's got options coming out of his ears. The question should be: *How* did he take her there?"

It was a good point. Gasoline was so scarce that motor vehicles had become a rare sight on the roads in the past month or more. Most servicemen were reduced to getting around on foot or on bicycle or in the horse-drawn gharries favored by the Maltese. These were open-sided carriages on four large sprung wheels — hardly an ideal mode of transport for moving a victim about.

"Okay," said Max, "I'll add it to the list."

"You're really set on seeing this through?"

"You think it's a bad idea?"

"Yes, because they'll be watching you closely."

"Then you can stop me. All it takes is a quick word in the ear of your ginger-haired friend."

"He's not my friend. And I'd never do that to you."

"I wouldn't put it past you."

"Hey, now I'm insulted."

"Something tells me you'll get over it."

Elliott smiled. "Coffee?"

"Really?"

"Colombian or Sumatran?"

"Now I know you're joking."

But he wasn't. The pantry off the bare stone kitchen was stocked with both. It also housed a range of other rarities: tinned fruits, several varieties of tea, a bowl of hens' eggs, bottles of olive oil. There were even a couple of cured hams hanging from hooks.

"Bloody hell, Elliott, where did this lot come from?"

"I'll show you."

The pantry had been impressive, but it was nothing compared to the barn. Small wonder the doors were secured with a hefty padlock.

"Promise not to tell?" asked Elliott as he led Max inside. The light from the hurricane lamp cast wild shadows around the interior, revealing a storehouse of goods piled high in boxes. In one corner stood a stack of gleaming ten-gallon fuel canisters.

"Impressive, huh?"

"I'm not sure the military police would see it the same way."

"We don't get a lot of Red Caps out in these parts."

Max strolled through the cases.

"I'm not a profiteer, if that's what you're thinking," Elliott said.

"Just a hoarder?"

"Not even. This is work. I'm the sole representative of the United States government on the island, and sometimes I need to get things done. This lot counts for more than money right now."

"Ah, ambassadorial privilege."

"Nicely put. I like that."

"Well, let's hope you don't ever have to

plead it."

"Is that a threat?"

"Nothing that a small bribe can't rectify."

Max was joking, of course, but when he set off back to Valetta after two cups of very fine coffee, it was with a full tank of gasoline sloshing between his legs and half a dozen eggs secreted about his person.

He usually wrote with a fountain pen. However, ink had grown scarce on the island, obliging him to fall back on a pencil. The words lacked their usual authority on the page, but they still spoke clearly to him.

The witless Germans might have lost their nerve, but he wasn't ready to hang up his boots, not quite yet. It would be like abandoning a game of chess just when the board was set for a perfect endgame. Risks had been taken, sacrifices made, in order to maneuver the pieces into position. There was no question of walking away. The question, rather, was one of how exactly to proceed.

He had listed his options neatly on the page, and by the light of the guttering candle he pondered them in turn, playing each of the little dramas through to its conclusion.

Caution dictated that he be extremely

thorough, more so than ever. Released from his contract with the Germans, he was a free agent, and a whole new range of possibilities presented themselves for wrapping up the affair in his own fashion. He knew what he was like, though; he knew he was liable to leap at the most ambitious of these, ignoring the added dangers for the sake of the greater satisfaction it would bring. He needed to keep his instincts in check, to keep his perspective.

Malta marked a new stage of his journey, but that's all it was — a stage. There was far more to come. He couldn't say what exactly, he couldn't perceive the pattern yet, but he'd be a fool to wager it all on one roll of the dice.

His eyes strayed to the top of the list, the first entry: *Do nothing. Vanish away.*

It was too easy. And too hard. How could he not go and stand at Carmela Cassar's grave? She was freshly buried and waiting for his visit. It would be wrong to break the tradition. It might even bring bad luck. He sat and saw all the things that wouldn't come to pass, and he wrote them down. As ever, on the page, things became clearer. The words bristled with undeniable truths.

He didn't put a line through the first entry on the list; he didn't believe in crossing things out. Everything served a purpose, momentary doubts included. Even now, he could feel a new idea taking shape, triggered by a phrase he'd just written: *The next girl?*

There were three he had in mind. Two were bar tarts. The third was a slim wand of a girl who worked in the garrison library. Her name was Rosaria Galdes, and she planned to become a schoolteacher when the war was over. She had a small gap between her front teeth that lent her an air of sensuality, although nothing in her bearing suggested the same. In movement and speech she was brisk to the point of awkwardness.

He had always been intrigued by this apparent contradiction in her, and was tempted to put it to the test. Maybe that time had finally come. She was the obvious candidate, and yet something was holding him back. But what?

He laid the pencil aside and lit a cigarette. He closed his eyes and emptied his mind, waiting for the answer to present itself to him. It was there, lurking at the periphery of his vision, like some wild animal patrolling the circle of light thrown by a campfire — a palpable presence, yet indistinct. He didn't encourage it forward for fear of startling it, and when it finally stepped from the shadows, he smiled, more than satisfied with what he saw, amazed that the idea hadn't occurred to him before.

It was perfect. *She* was perfect.

He spared a thought for gap-toothed Rosaria Galdes and her dream of becoming a teacher, an ambition she would now live to fulfill. He wasn't going to stand in her way, not anymore. A new and far more satisfactory candidate had just presented herself for the post of last victim.

Taking up the pencil, he began to write, drawing up a balance sheet, weighing the beauty of the idea against the inevitable risks.

# DAY SIX

It was past midnight by the time Max reached the Porte des Bombes on the outskirts of Floriana. The journey seemed to have passed in a flash, eaten up by memories of his conversation with Elliott.

The fellow was unfathomable, impossible to gauge. For a master of irritating circumlocutions, the revelations had come surprisingly thick and fast: the Germans' aborted invasion plans, the governor's imminent departure, Field Marshal Kesselring's standing with Hitler, Rommel's gifts and failings as a general. Was there nothing Elliott wasn't privy to? And as for the intimation that the killings were the work of an enemy agent intent on sowing seeds of discord, what was to be made of that? Admittedly, the relationship between the British garrison and the Maltese was more strained than it had ever been, but would the enemy really have hatched such a heinous plan in order to destabilize it further? Rumors abounded of atrocities committed in the name of Hitler's Reich — and no doubt the British had a few skeletons of their own tucked away in the same closet — but would they really go that far in the name of victory?

Quite possibly. War did that to men. Whether it forced such behavior on them or whether it offered a convenient release for some dark impulse deep within them was a debate he'd shared with Freddie on more than one occasion. Freddie subscribed to the dualist school of thought, that men were essentially good and evil at the same time. It was a view rooted in his experiences as a medical officer. He claimed to have observed it at work in the wards.

It was known that a number of Allied pilots had plummeted to their deaths after baling out, thanks to an enemy fighter making a low pass over their parachutes, collapsing the canopies with the downdraft. By the same token, it was known (though rarely spoken of) that enemy seaplanes clearly marked with red crosses had been shot to pieces while going about their business of recovering downed colleagues from the sea off Malta.

And yet, despite these aberrations, an

almost innocent camaraderie prevailed in the hospitals. Injured enemy pilots and crew occupied beds in the same wards as their Allied counterparts. Not only that, they were liable to receive a string of visitors intent on plying them with cigarettes and other creature comforts.

It was true that not all the pilots condoned this practice. To Ralph's mind, the enemy was the enemy and not to be fraternized with, although he bore the Italians slightly less rancor than he did the Germans. As a keen fan of motor racing, he felt that any nation that had produced Enzo Ferrari and Tazio Nuvolari couldn't be all bad. He ascribed both the wariness of their bombers and the flamboyant aerobatics of their fighter pilots to the inferior nature of their aircraft. They were simply reacting to circumstances, making the best of a bad thing, as anyone in their right mind would.

He was far more wary of the Germans. This prejudice had first lodged itself in him just before the war, when he'd visited the country as part of a rowing eight cobbled together from a number of Cambridge college crews. He had found their German co-competitors at the regatta cold and high-handed and — sin of sins — obsessed with calisthenics. To cap it all, when the British eight's engagingly amateurish approach to competition rowing had brought them victory, the home crews had proved remarkably ungracious in defeat. This unfortunate experience had flicked a switch in Ralph's head. He now saw evidence of the German master plan wherever he looked.

Wagner's belief in the *Gesamtkunstwerk*, the total work of art, and Hegel's concept of the "Absolute Idea," which amounted to a total philosophy of human culture, were two examples of a Teutonic propensity to extremism. A more plausible prop to Ralph's theory, maybe, was General Erich Ludendorff's book, published a few years before the outbreak of hostilities, entitled *Total War*.

Max had always found Ralph's ideas as dangerously extreme as those he purported to despise. But maybe Ralph's instincts were sound. In the grand scheme of things, what did the lives of a few innocent Maltese girls matter to the enemy if they served a greater purpose? The indiscriminate targeting of the islanders had seen a surge in civilian casualties over the past month, but it had also succeeded in stiffening the resolve of the people. So much better for the Germans to be selective about who they killed, and actually achieve something in the process.

Max could see the logic in the thinking. It made sense. But it also raised as many questions as it answered, not least of all: Why had Elliott chosen to share the theory with him when there had been no call to do so? It just wasn't in Elliott's nature to let slip something like that.

Max was no closer to determining some invisible agenda by the time he reached the Porte des Bombes, at which point questions of a more immediate kind began jostling for his attention. Would Mitzi still be expecting him to show up, even at this late hour? What if Lionel's plans had changed and he was now happily tucked up in bed with his wife? It had happened once before, and on that occasion Mitzi had been unable to get word to Max of Lionel's unexpected return from patrol. Letting himself into the building with the key, Max had crept silently up the staircase to the third floor only to find the door to the flat firmly locked. Thank God he'd conquered the temptation to knock. No excuse, however inspired, could have convincingly explained just what he was doing there in the dead of night.

On this occasion, common sense dictated that he leave the motorcycle outside his flat and walk the rest of the way, but somehow it wasn't an option. He drove straight to

Hastings Gardens, tucking the machine out of sight in a narrow alleyway, leaning it against a wall daubed with the words "BOMB ROME."

As ever, the lock downstairs resisted the initial advances of the key. And, as ever, he paused to catch his breath on the third-floor landing before placing his palm against the door to the apartment. It was unlocked and swung open without resistance.

A ghostlike apparition stood before him. It was Mitzi, her naked limbs rendered more pale by the dark negligee.

She drew him silently inside, easing the door shut behind him. "I was beginning to think you wouldn't come."

They stood close, the way they used to stand. And in the deep darkness of the entrance hall he could feel the heat coming off her.

"Where's Lionel?"

"Gzira. He's spending the night in one of the officers' rest flats."

Gzira sat on the slope right across from the sub base, and ever since the transport infrastructure on the island had all but collapsed, the navy had taken on a number of flats there where officers could overnight.

Max reached into his hip pocket, then placed his hand in hers.

"An egg? I'm lost for words."

"There are more where that one came from, if you play your cards right."

"Well, let's see, shall we?"

He hadn't meant it that way, and when she dropped to her knees in front of him, her fingers groping for the buttons of his shorts, he protested.

"Mitzi, don't . . ."

He heard the egg rolling away across the tiled floor, discarded.

"Mitzi . . . ," he pleaded.

"Ssshhh . . ."

"I can't."

"If memory serves, you most certainly can."

The shorts dropped to his ankles, and her long fingers closed around him.

"This isn't right."

"Of course it isn't. That's the point. It never has been."

"Mitzi . . ." He took her by her bare shoulders and raised her to her feet, proud of his resolve. "I don't want to."

"So why are you getting harder in my hand?"

Did she really think him so powerless in the face of her desire?

He was on the point of posing the question when she dropped once more to her knees, and all thoughts of resistance were swept aside by the warm embrace of her mouth. His hands went instinctively to her head, his fingers entwining themselves in her soft hair.

It always surprised him that she appeared to derive so much enjoyment from having him in her mouth. Her pleasure seemed almost to equal his own, if the low moans she emitted every so often were anything to go by.

Breaking off, she peered up at him. "You see, that wasn't so bad, was it?" Rising slowly to her feet, she added, "You don't have to follow me. I'll quite understand if you let yourself out."

With that, she made off down the corridor, a dim form fading into the gloom.

His thoughts turned to Lilian. He imagined her standing there in the darkness beside him, observing him, waiting to see what he did, and yet he still stepped out of the shorts gathered around his ankles, leaving them where they lay.

Mitzi was waiting for him on the bed. He couldn't see her, but he could hear the faint squeak of the springs as she adjusted her position. He removed his shirt and laid it carefully on the floor, aware of the eggs, two in each of the breast pockets.

"I should warn you, I'm very wet."

He shed his desert boots and his socks and lay down beside her, naked.

"I've been wet for hours, thinking about you."

She liked to talk, and she liked to take her time, he knew that, just as he knew that her lovemaking with Lionel had always been a rushed and entirely silent affair.

"Are you sure you didn't start without me?"

"I might have, just a bit," she admitted coquettishly. Reaching for his wrist, she drew his hand down her body, guiding his fingers between her legs. She could have raised the hem of the negligee, but chose not to, preferring that he first feel her through the material.

"You see? I wasn't lying."

He slowly worked a finger inside of her, as far as the restraining tension of the moist satin would permit. Her mouth reached for his, her tongue edging between his lips, mimicking the movement of his finger.

Apart from the first time, when he had gone to her room at the Riviera Hotel and found her naked beneath the sheet on the mattress on the floor, underwear of some kind or another had always played a role in their lovemaking. Underwear lent an illicit frisson to their trysts, a whiff of the forbidden, its flimsy barrier a token gesture to Victorian prudishness.

Max didn't mind; it cost him nothing to play along. It was also an excuse to draw out their few precious moments alone.

On this occasion, though, Mitzi's characteristic restraint seemed to desert her suddenly. Straddling him in one swift movement, she guided him into her.

"I'm sorry, I need to feel you inside me. Just for a moment. Just for a moment . . ."

The moment was heralded by the eldritch scream of the air-raid siren, its sickening cadence somehow all the more ominous for the fact that it had gone unheard for so long.

"Oh God . . . ," Max breathed.

It wasn't the siren. For all he cared, two hundred German bombers could have been closing in on Malta with instructions to obliterate Number 18 Windmill Street. They were nothing when set alongside the sensation of Mitzi lowering herself onto him.

"I'll stop if you want," she teased. "We probably should."

He placed his hands on her hips and drew her down the rest of the way. She winced, adjusting her position to accommodate him.

"My God, you're a good fit. Any more would be too much."

His hands climbed to her small firm breasts, the nipples hard beneath the satin. She placed her hands over his, holding them there.

"We've still got time to make the shelter," she said, almost drunkenly.

"Oh, I think I've already found safe harbor."

It was a terrible joke, a childish *jeu de mots,* but she laughed, recognizing it for what it was — a cheap swipe at Lionel and his submariner chums. He already knew from her how they liked to talk in such terms when it came to women. Expressions such as "raising the periscope" and "arming the torpedo" figured large in their schoolboy innuendo.

"Well, as long as you don't blow the tanks too early."

That was one he hadn't heard before, and they giggled like two naughty schoolchildren.

"I can feel it when you laugh," said Max.

"And when I do this . . . ?"

She started to move, a slow, rhythmic roll of the hips, a reminder that they weren't in fact welded together, one being.

The distant bark of a heavy battery suggested that the searchlights had picked out the first of the raiders.

"There's no hurry," she whispered.

"Tell that to our German friends."

"Let them do their worst. We're untouchable."

"I mean it."

"So do I. If I'm going to die, I want it to be like this, with you inside me."

And that's where he stayed. Long after it had become clear that Valetta was the target, long after the whistle and crump of the first bombs had drowned out the dirge of the siren, he was still there, inside her. And as the heavens outside pitched and rolled in one vast, undying thunderclap of sound, they twisted and turned together on the bed, at one with the holocaust, somehow a part of it, immune to it. Terrific concussions tossed the building, but the tremors seemed only to resonate with the febrile tension of their bodies. And as the raid built in ferocity, so did their own exertions, rising to a crescendo, almost in defiance now, looking to drive back the deadly storm, to outlast it.

This they did, their wild cries of release rending the air as the last of the bombers headed for home, chased back to Sicily by a few hopeful shell bursts.

They lay damp and spent in each other's arms for a long while, lacquered together in the eerie silence, the acrid smell of cordite leaking into the room through the shutters.

"That was . . . well, like nothing else I've ever known," said Max.

"Did the earth move for you too?"

They laughed weakly and kissed and held each other tighter.

"I told you they couldn't touch us."

"They came pretty damned close."

An enormous explosion had shaken the building to its foundations during the height of the raid — *Brr-ummmph!* — probably a parachute mine, picked off by one of the Bofors crews before it could land.

Outside, the "Raiders Passed" siren sounded its single note.

"They'll be back," said Max.

They all knew the pattern by now. Kesselring would keep the planes coming, varying his targets throughout the night. It was unlikely that Valetta would suffer another assault, but you couldn't bank on it.

"Maybe you should go now," said Mitzi.

"Maybe I don't want to. Maybe I want to know why you summoned me here."

"You know the reason. I know you know, because Lionel told me this afternoon. Apparently he bumped into you at the submarine base the other day."

"That's right."

"And was a jolly time had by all?"

"What's that supposed to mean?"

"How long have you known? Three days? Four? A week? Longer?"

"Hugh told me at the party."

"And you didn't think to share it with me?"

"He only mentioned it later, after you and I had talked."

Mitzi lay silent for a moment. "I'm sorry. It just seems like I'm the last person to hear that I'm leaving the island."

"You should be glad. Things aren't going to get any better here for a long while."

"Alexandria sounds ghastly."

"Well, it isn't."

He had rather enjoyed his time in Alexandria, although his appreciation of the place might well have had something to do with the fact that he'd arrived there directly from Atbara, a desolate, flyblown corner of the Sudan, where he'd spent a miserable couple of months on an intelligence course.

"The bar at the Windsor Palace is worth a visit," said Max. "Their cocktails are second to none."

"My God, a bright future beckons with Baedeker's."

"I'm just saying there are worse places to be. At least you won't be pounded to pieces on a daily basis."

"Lionel's convinced Alexandria will fall."

"Then he should have a word with Elliott."

"Elliott? What does Elliott know about anything?"

"Considerably more than he likes to let on."

She kissed him tenderly on the lips. "You're so sweet and trusting."

A part of him bristled at her condescending tone, and normally he would have reacted. He didn't because he wanted to steer the conversation back to the question of her imminent departure, and for reasons that showed him to be neither sweet nor trusting.

"Did Lionel say exactly when he's leaving?"

"Monday. They're still making repairs to the *Upstanding*. She'll be the last sub to leave."

Four days was nothing. He was going to have to move fast, push things along.

"He said you'll be staying on for a bit, maybe moving in with the Reynolds in Saint Julian's."

"Not anymore. The sea transport officer has booked me on a seaplane from Kalafrana the next day."

"So what's this, then? Goodbye?"

"I suppose. And I couldn't leave without telling you."

"Sounds intriguing."

"Oh, it's more than that."

She lapsed into an unnerving silence.

"Mitzi . . . ?"

She took his hand and placed it gently on her belly. The negligee had long since been discarded, and his palm was rough against the soft skin around her navel.

He was about to speak when it dawned on him.

"I'm thinking something." He twisted onto his side to face her. "Am I wrong?"

"No. It's yours."

"Are you sure?"

"It can't be his."

"He was away on patrol?"

"Even if he'd been here."

"I don't understand."

"It's very simple."

They had tried and tried to have a child, Mitzi explained, but it hadn't worked. Leaping to the assumption that she must be to blame for their fruitless efforts, Lionel had dispatched her to a doctor in London just before the war, unaware that she'd already visited two Harley Street specialists, both of whom had given her a clean bill of health. The third was of exactly the same opinion:

341

that everything was in fine working order, and that the fault most likely lay with her husband. She still wasn't sure why she had lied to Lionel, presumably to protect his over-heightened sense of masculinity, but that's what she had done, casting herself as the barren wife to spare him the shame.

Conveniently, the war had come along soon after, allowing them to ignore the issue. Neither of them wished to bring a child into a turbulent world. But that, it seemed, was exactly what was about to happen.

"It's early days still, but it's the real thing. I know it is."

Max struggled to find the words. "What do you want to do?"

"I want to have a child, Max."

"My child? Or any child?"

"It's probably my only chance."

"Not if you take another lover."

"That's not fair. I didn't set out to get pregnant by you."

"An unfortunate slip, then?"

"Rationing."

"Rationing?" he scoffed.

"Malnutrition. It messes with our menstrual cycles. If you don't believe me, ask Lilian."

He had never heard Mitzi mention Lilian's name before. In fact, he'd had no idea she was even aware of Lilian's existence.

"From what I hear, you know her well enough to ask," Mitzi added archly.

"What's that supposed to mean?"

"It means please don't play the saint with me. For all I know, you were seeing her at the same time as me."

"Well, I wasn't. And I'm not 'seeing her.' "

"Call it what you will, I don't blame you, not after the way I treated you. I hurt you, I know that, but I was confused."

"And now?" he asked.

"Now? Now I'm wishing I hadn't told you."

"Why not?"

"Because you didn't need to know."

He lay beside her in silence, absorbing the meaning of her words.

"I'm not ready to throw my family, my friends, and my reputation to the wind."

"You might find you have no choice."

"That depends on you."

"Mitzi, it's going to look like me."

"Not if it's lucky."

"I'm being serious. I'm dark. Lionel's fair, and so are you. Two blonds can only produce a blond child — remember your biology lessons?"

"Yes, I remember my biology lessons."

"So what happens when it pops out with

a mop of black hair?"

"Your father's fair-haired."

"My father?"

"You showed me a photo of him once. If he's fair-haired, then the child can be too."

It was a moment before he responded. "My God, you've really thought this through, haven't you?"

"Of course I've thought it through. It's not the sort of thing to be taken lightly."

She was getting angry now, and so was he.

"What happened to dying with me inside you?" he asked.

"You know how I talk when I'm aroused."

"Don't I have any say in this whatsoever?"

"You do now, but only because I told you when I didn't have to. And if you have any respect for me, you'll go along with my wishes. When you've thought on it, you may find they're your wishes too."

"Don't count on it," he said, swinging his legs off the bed.

His shorts were still in the hallway, but he remembered his shirt on the floor only after feeling the soft crunch of eggs underfoot.

"Bloody hell!" he snapped.

Mitzi misinterpreted the expletive. "Okay. I'll ask Lionel for a divorce and marry you. Is that what you want to hear? Because I don't think it is."

He groped around for his socks and desert boots.

"Tell me I'm wrong," she insisted.

He couldn't, so he didn't. He just left the bedroom with his clothes bundled beneath his arm.

Sleep was out of the question. All he could manage was a kind of limbo, a restless tug-of-war between exhaustion and wide-eyed wakefulness, a contest punctuated every half hour or so by another cigarette. He thought back to his student days and the cramped ground-floor flat in Waterloo, when anything less than nine hours of full and proper slumber would have had him snoozing happily on his drawing board come three o'clock in the afternoon.

How simple life had been back then. A morning lecture on Piranesi; half a day given over to tweaking a floor plan or an elevation; the Northern Line home from Tottenham Court Road station; three pints and a slice of pie in the King's Arms on Roupell Street, followed by a short stagger to his front door. What had his concerns been at the time? They must have existed, but he struggled now to recall them. They certainly couldn't hold a candle to his current predicament, he ruminated wearily.

The news that he had fathered a child — the very fact that he was capable of doing so — had touched him at some deep, primordial level that defied words. It was as if the lens through which he viewed the world had been shattered and then hastily repaired. He could make out the rough shape of things, but it was a fragmented picture, one of refractions and reflections and unexpected associations — an alien landscape where past, present, and future somehow coexisted.

He saw himself screaming at the top of his newborn lungs in the arms of his dying mother, and for the first time he saw the logic of her sacrifice. He watched it playing out before his eyes, with Mitzi standing in for his mother and the ending rewritten. Try as he might, though, he couldn't write himself into the scene.

He wasn't wanted at the bedside, where his father had once stood. Mitzi had made her feelings clear on that score, and he couldn't see her changing her mind. It was easy to resent her, and more than a little unfair. There was no denying the sudden clutch of fear he'd experienced when she had tested him, confident of his reaction, proposing that she seek a divorce from Lionel and marry him. It just didn't fit with the future he'd envisaged for himself: the architect, the man about town, looking to leave his mark on the world. He couldn't find a place for the young child and the disgraced ex–navy wife in his dream. And he thought less of himself for it.

He tried to console himself with the alternatives. He would be the mysterious gentleman watching the Colts' football match against the rival school, stifling his cheers as his son broke free in the dying seconds of the game to score the winning goal. That didn't work. Lionel barged his way into the fantasy, sidling toward him along the touchline.

"Hello, old boy. What brings you here?"

"Oh, nothing much. That fine figure of a young man you have always assumed to be your son is in fact the product of a brief but passionate affair I conducted with your dear lady wife during our time on Malta."

"Well, I say. I didn't see that one coming."

"Doubtless, dear fellow, but who can blame you? We were very discreet."

Somehow all the scenarios he came up with collapsed into absurdity, leaving him lost and floundering in a future world of his own creation.

The past and present offered more of a

refuge. He found himself drawing a strange kind of strength from the prospect of fatherhood. Just as his own father was the touchstone by which he tested himself, so it now fell to him to set an example, to light the path for the next generation — a mawkish sentiment, he knew, but at least it gave some small degree of comfort.

It had just passed five o'clock when he heard the knock. His first thought was of Mitzi, but she didn't have a key to the downstairs door. His second thought was of his neighbor, the young sculptor on the floor below, the one who used to teach at the art school on Old Bakery Street and who now made a living running off devotional plaster models of the Virgin (much in demand), the neighbor who was always cadging a scrap of bread or a smear of jam. Then he remembered that the sculptor was long gone, off to stay with relatives near Zejtun, where the bombs didn't rain down with such deadly persistence.

He dragged on his shorts and shuffled to the front door.

"Who is it?" he called.

"Busuttil."

The name meant nothing to him until the low grumble of a voice added, "From Lilian."

He slipped the latch and opened the door. In the darkness it was hard to make out much of Mr. Busuttil other than that he was short, was rounded in the shoulder, and appeared to have something odd on his head.

It was a straw hat, but only just. Stained and crumpled, it looked like it had been pulled from the rubble of a bombed building. This became clear once they were in the kitchen and Max had lit a candle.

Busuttil glanced around the bare room. It was hard to guess his age, hard to say whether the hat concealed a bald pate or a thick head of hair. His face had a lean hangdog look to it, as if someone had let the air out of it. His eyes, in contrast, were bright, alert, and restless.

"She said no phone, so I come instead."

"You're a friend of Lilian's?" Somehow Max couldn't see it.

"I know the brother of the cousin of her uncle."

"And you're a policeman?"

Max had been very clear about that with Lilian: it had to be someone who knew the ropes, someone with authority. The man in front of him didn't appear to score highly in either department. He could hardly be held to blame for the large carbuncle on his neck, but there was something essentially dishev-

349

eled about the fellow that didn't scream "dependable upholder of the law."

Busuttil pulled back his dusty jacket and flashed the pistol at his waist. "CID. Inspector for five years."

Max tried to look suitably impressed.

"Do you have tea?"

"It's the only thing I do have."

This wasn't entirely true. He also had a three-penny bar of chocolate he'd been holding back for a special occasion. He wasn't sure that this qualified but produced it nonetheless. Busuttil eagerly devoured it all before the water had even come to a boil.

Max had his own contacts within the police department, men with whom he communicated every day over casualty figures, and he was beginning to wish he'd taken the risk and gone with one of them. He started to feel more comfortable only when the tea had brewed and they were sitting at the table.

"I see your eyes," said Busuttil. "I see you are not happy. So before I ask questions, I tell you about Busuttil." He paused to take a sip of tea. "I was born 1901 in a small house near Siggiewi. My father, he was a farmer of corn. There were also goats, six goats . . ."

*Oh Christ,* thought Max, *he's going to tell*

350

*me their names.*

Without warning, Busuttil erupted in laughter, gripping Max's forearm as he did so. The laughter accounted for the long furrows flanking his mouth.

"Your face!" Busuttil gasped. Once he'd recovered enough to risk another sip of tea, he added, "It is good for my work that people see me like you see me."

His work, it turned out, was pretty eye-popping stuff. It was hardly surprising that in a garrison of twenty-six thousand British servicemen there were a few bad apples, but Max was taken aback by the true extent of the rot. Busuttil wasn't talking about men banged up in the guardroom for "conduct prejudicial to good order and discipline"; he was talking about the genuine article: racketeers, extortionists, rapists, and murderers. He claimed to have cracked a ring of NAAFI men responsible for the theft of five hundred cases of whisky from a convoy back in September. He had also arrested a corporal in the West Kents who'd slit the throat of another soldier in a quarrel over a girl. He reeled off a grim catalogue of other crimes perpetrated by British servicemen that he'd investigated, though not always with success.

On the one hand, Max felt ridiculously

naïve, a victim of the sort of propaganda he peddled; on the other, he drew comfort from his ignorance. The fact that he hadn't got wind of such matters suggested that men such as Busuttil were accustomed to bringing a certain discretion to bear on their work. And that's exactly what Max required of him.

"Is it possible there's already an investigation under way?"

Busuttil shook his head. "I would know."

"Unless Defense Security's handling it."

"I would know."

Lilian had briefed Busuttil thoroughly, but he wanted details, specifics, all of which he recorded meticulously in a scuffed notebook.

He was intrigued by the idea that the killings might be the work of an enemy agent, but was more curious about the mechanics of the meeting in the lieutenant governor's office. He asked for physical descriptions of all the men present.

His most reassuring question, though, related to the torn shoulder tab discovered in Carmela Cassar's hand. He wanted to know where someone would go for such a thing if he needed a replacement. Max was able to give him the name of the military outfitters in Valetta favored by the submariners, because Lionel was forever moaning about Griscti's. Unforgivably, Lionel's second bar had been on order there since the beginning of the year, as if shipping in his medal to the besieged island were more of a priority than fuel, arms, and essential foodstuffs.

Busuttil made it clear to Max that time was against them and that the chances of success were low.

"You should have come to Busuttil before."

"There are a lot of things I should have done differently," said Max. "Look, I don't know if Lilian said, but I can't pay you."

A shade of disappointment darkened Busuttil's solemn countenance. "And you?" he asked. "Are *you* doing it for money?"

Max wouldn't hear from him for twenty-four hours, Busuttil explained. Until then, he was to go about his business as normal. He advised against any contact with Lilian but didn't forbid it.

As he was leaving, he turned at the door. "There *is* one thing you can do for me. The Spitfires, are they coming soon?"

"The Spitfires?"

"You are the information officer, no?"

"Believe me, that doesn't count for much."

Busuttil accepted the brush-off with a

gracious nod and made off down the stair-well.

"Two days," Max found himself calling into the darkness.

"Two days?"

"The ninth. Lots of them. More than sixty."

"Ohhhhh," cooed Busuttil from below. "Ohhhh, that is good."

"We'll see."

"No, *they* will see. In two days *they* will see."

There seemed to be a new lightness to the footfalls as they carried on down the stone steps.

Max took Busuttil at his word, throwing himself into his work, losing himself in a fog of intra-departmental meetings. Generally, he regarded these as an almost complete waste of time. The deadwood had long since been cut out of the rotting ship he'd inher-ited. His staff was faultless to a man (and woman), their proficiency and dedication beyond reproach. They also worked de-manding schedules that left little room for lunch, let alone a series of ultimately point-less get-togethers called by their boss. They didn't need the distraction. He, however, did. Anything to keep his mind off Mitzi and the revelation she'd sprung on him.

Shortly before midday he returned to his office and was surprised to find Freddie seated in an overstuffed chair near the window, nursing a mug of tea.

"Very good," he said, raising the mug.

"Maria holds the best stuff back for visitors. We don't get many."

"I thought it best to tell you face-to-face. Your face, for what it's worth, has looked better."

"I didn't sleep a wink last night."

"He's left-handed."

It came from nowhere, and Max wasn't sure if he'd heard right. "He's what?"

"Left-handed." Freddie leaned forward in the chair. "I should have realized it before. It occurred to me only when I was in surgery yesterday. The wound in Carmela Cassar's neck, it was on the right-hand side, her right, which means he used his left hand."

Max could still picture the long gash, the one inflicted by the bomb splinter that had sliced through her carotid artery. It was an image, he suspected, that would haunt his thoughts for a good long while.

"Unless he was standing behind her."

"True," conceded Freddie. "But unlikely."

Getting to his feet, he took up the ebony

letter opener on Max's desk to demonstrate his point. The carotid artery was set deep in the neck. To penetrate to the required depth demanded considerable thrust, to say nothing of accuracy, neither of which was afforded by taking up a position behind the victim. It was a convincing demonstration, if a little unnerving.

"So, he's left-handed," said Max, taking the letter opener back.

"How many left-handers do you know?"

"Not many. We're a significant minority."

"Exactly. It narrows the field considerably."

Max lit a cigarette. "I thought you didn't want to have anything more to do with this."

"So did I. It seems I was wrong."

Freddie moved to the window, peering outside briefly before turning. "I've done a lot of thinking since the other day. Maybe it's the way they treated us, but I don't care anymore what they do to me. It'll be their loss if they send me packing." He hesitated, a flicker of uncertainty clouding his gaze. "Or maybe I've just had enough of it all and I'm hoping that's exactly what they'll do."

"You know that's not true."

"Isn't it? I'm tired, Max. I've been here too long, seen too much — enough for a lifetime. You have no idea how I spend my days."

"I can imagine."

"No you can't. We ran out of morphine yesterday. It was only for a few hours till they sent some over from Saint Patrick's, but it was long enough. You wouldn't believe the screaming — like they were being fed thistles." He paused briefly. "I learned something new, though. The power of the mind. You can inject a man with saline solution, and if you tell him it's morphine, his body will believe you."

"Placebo."

"I'm impressed."

Max shrugged. "It's what I do too — tell them it's all okay and hope they'll believe me."

Freddie gave a weak smile. "Yes, I suppose it is."

Max had seen Freddie low before, but he'd never heard him admit to it. His quiet and uncomplaining resilience had always marked him out from the rest of them. While Ralph kicked against the incompetence of his superiors and Hugh moaned on ceaselessly about the lack of recognition afforded to the artillery, Freddie had always just got on with the grim business of putting people back together.

"Maybe Elliott was right. Maybe I *am* a moralist at heart."

Under other circumstances Max would have sought to buoy up his friend, to make him see sense. Selfishly, the prospect of an accomplice prevailed. It was good to have Freddie back on board. He reached for one of the phones on his desk and asked Maria to hold his calls.

Freddie seemed genuinely shocked by the speed of developments, and not nearly as skeptical as Max had been about Elliott's hypothesis that the murders might be the work of someone looking to frame the British for the crimes, some spy within their own ranks, or a Maltese fifth columnist.

"It's possible, I suppose. I can see it. He could have planted the shoulder tab in her hand."

"Or they. That was another of Elliott's suggestions."

"Why's he being so helpful?"

"I don't know."

"Did you tell him about this detective . . . ?"

"Busuttil? No, and I don't plan to until we know which side of the fence Elliott's really sitting on."

Not for the first time that day, Josef Busuttil

found himself running for shelter. As if the running weren't bad enough already — a stark reminder of just how rapidly his body was betraying him with age — all that the finish line had to offer was some gloomy ill-ventilated tunnel hacked out of the rock. He hated confined spaces. He hated them more when you had to share them with a swarming mass of humanity.

Fortunately, this shelter was considerably larger than most. At least he wouldn't have to spend the next hour or so upright, pressed tight with a bunch of strangers, like anchovies in a tin. The tunnel was wide, and judging from the run of paraffin lamps suspended from the vaulted ceiling, it stretched far beneath Valetta. The walls on either side of the central gangway bristled with iron bedsteads and wooden bunks. Here and there, niches had been hollowed out of the walls, some small, some large enough to accommodate a whole tribe of relations. Wherever possible, curtains had been rigged up to offer some degree of privacy.

The smell, as always, hit Josef with the force of a blow, clutching at his throat — a fetid cocktail of paraffin fumes, garlic, sweat, and other human excretions.

For those who had been bombed out of

their homes, this was now their permanent residence. They were easy to spot; they were the ones already in place, staring at the plug of newcomers crowding the entrance. Some waved them deeper into the tunnel, welcoming them. Others were more mistrustful, or simply too weary to care. Outside, the bombs started to fall. The noise was met by a low murmur of prayers.

Josef made his way to the far end of the tunnel, closing his mind to the musty pressure of the walls, challenging the fear he had always carried in him. Small children darted about, lost in their games. Old women, beads in hand, said the rosary before ramshackle shrines to the Virgin. Mothers poked at pans on sputtering Primus stoves. *This is what we have become,* he thought. *This is what they have turned us into: a race of cowering cave dwellers.*

He found himself staring at a pretty and petite young woman perched on a bed, reading from a book to her two children. The girl was curled up on the lean mattress, head in her mother's lap. The boy was seated on the hard floor, looking bored, eager to be elsewhere. Josef wondered what their story was, wondered if they would all live to tell it. The woman caught his eye and gestured him over, into their world. He hesitated. What kind of woman would make such an overture to a stranger when her husband was absent? A woman who had lost her husband, it occurred to him. But she was gesturing at the other bed now, and the prospect of taking the weight off his feet won through.

"You look tired."

"I *am* tired."

"Then rest."

The boy glowered up at him mistrustfully.

"Thank you."

He removed his shoes and lay down on the bed. There was nothing more he could achieve outside while the raid was on. Why not rest awhile? Besides, things had moved fast that morning and it was an opportunity to stop and take stock of the situation.

His first port of call had been the Blue Parrot. It had a reputation as one of the more upmarket dance halls, although in the harsh light of day it was hard to imagine why. The place looked tired and cramped and dirty, its owner not much better. The owner's startled reaction to a visit by an inspector from the CID suggested that he was guilty, though not necessarily of murder. Most places were running on black market booze by now.

The man had clearly been suspicious of

the questions put to him about Carmela, but he'd known better than to say so. Her tragic death had shocked them all. She had been a great girl, a little on the quiet side at first, but bright and eager to learn. Her earnings had improved steadily in the five months she'd worked there, and she'd twice pocketed half a crown in commission for persuading clients to buy bottles of champagne.

Josef didn't push it. He knew he'd be back later, after nightfall, when the place came to life. The real questions could wait till then, till the other hostesses were at work. They were the ones he needed to speak to, because his instinct told him that the killer had targeted Carmela right there in the dance hall, which meant that someone had seen him. Before leaving, Josef asked if the "officers only" door policy was strictly enforced. It was.

Major Chadwick had been able to provide him only with the names of the other two girls who had died suspiciously, but within the narrow world of the Gut, it didn't take Josef long to find out where the girls had worked. Dirty Dick's and the John Bull were both down at the far end of the Gut, where the narrow street fell away sharply toward the nether regions of Valetta. Their location was significant. It marked them out for what they were: low-grade establishments that catered to "other rankers." According to the wooden sign nailed to its barred and pad-locked doors, Dirty Dick's was *Closed for Renovation* — an amusing understatement; the top three floors of the building were missing, reduced to a tumble of rock and rubble and splintered beams.

The John Bull, almost directly opposite, had been spared. It was a cellar bar, with steps leading down from the street to a recessed door set in a carved stone gateway. From here, more steps descended into the gloom. The place was far larger than it appeared from the street, a vaulted labyrinth of passageways and deep alcoves that incorporated the cellars of the two flanking buildings. The bar and the dance floor were at the back, where even at this hour of the day the only light came from a handful of paraffin lamps scattered about the place.

It took Josef's eye a few moments to adjust to the spectacle. The barman was busying himself with some glasses, feigning disinterest in the couple seated at the counter. The girls huddled at a nearby table were making no such pretence. They watched and whispered among themselves.

The man at the counter was a British

serviceman. He sat slumped on his stool, head bowed, sobbing quietly. His companion, a Maltese girl with bleached blond hair, had an arm around his shoulder. She was whispering to him, sweet words of comfort, but every so often she rolled her eyes with boredom for the amusement of her colleagues gathered at the table. They, in turn, struggled to stifle their giggles.

Josef's instinct was to take the soldier by the arm and lead him out of this den of harpies, but that didn't fit with his mission. The table of girls eyed him with undisguised indifference as he wandered over to them. Even the lowliest British serviceman had twenty or so shillings a week to spend, which was far more than the average Maltese could muster.

They perked up a little when he asked, "Thirsty?"

He knew better than to order the drinks himself; their commission was what mattered to them. The youngest was dispatched to bring the refreshments, and Josef found a chair pulled up for him. He immediately turned his attention to the oldest, a baggy-eyed specimen in a grubby white frock. Win over the mother hen, and the others would follow.

"What's the story?" he asked her, nodding

at the sobbing man.

"He misses his wife."

It was a voice coarsened by drink and cigarettes.

"You don't say? Me too."

"So why aren't you crying?"

"You haven't seen my wife."

He knew he had them when they laughed.

"Where's your wedding band?" asked mother hen, more practiced at such matters.

"Sold, so that the poor orphan boys of Saint Joseph's might eat."

This set them off again, although they sobered up fast when he raised the subject of Mary Farrugia. A few of them crossed themselves at the mention of their dead colleague. Josef made his play. He said he was Mary's uncle, and he was there on a sensitive matter. It involved a pair of silver earrings, a gift to Mary from one of her customers just before her death. The family felt that the earrings should be returned to the British serviceman in question, the only trouble being that they had no idea who he was.

This triggered a flurry of speculation around the table. Judging from the number of names bandied about, Mary Farrugia had been a popular girl with the clientele of the

John Bull.

"I think he might have been a submariner," offered Josef, which was met with shrugs and blank faces. "Possibly an officer, unless she was lying."

"Well, they're not supposed to come here, but they do."

"They dress down on purpose."

"They know where to come for a good time."

"A *much* better time."

"We can show you, if you like," said one of the younger girls, a frail-looking creature who must once have been pretty.

They were teasing him now, losing interest in his quest. He made one last effort to draw a name from them. When this failed, he made his excuses and left them to their drinks.

Mother hen caught up with him near the entrance.

"Tell me something — if you're Mary's uncle, then why weren't you at her funeral?"

She had him cold.

"Are you a cop?"

"Yes."

"What's this about?"

"Nothing that concerns you."

"It might."

"You know something?"

"I know I have a nephew in prison."

Oh, so that was it.

"What's he in for?"

"Looting."

Josef despised looters.

"Some would say prison's the right place for a looter to be."

"Some would say it's no place for an eighteen-year-old boy who fell in with the wrong crowd and who's learned his lesson."

Josef let the silence linger awhile. "It depends on what you've got."

"Will a name do?"

"Maybe," he said, trying to contain himself.

She gave a quick glance over her shoulder. "There *was* a man. I never met him. That lot don't even know. Mary asked me not to tell. Her 'special friend,' that's what she called him. She also said he was an officer with the submarines."

Josef could feel his pulse quickening. "Go on."

"That's it."

"His name?"

"Ken."

"Ken?"

"That's what she said."

"No surname?"

"Just Ken."

It was possible she was lying. At the table he had asked for the name of a submarine officer, and now she had just given him one. He stared into her bloodshot eyes. He prided himself on his ability to ferret out a fiction from a person's eyes. Bombarding the person with rapid-fire questions also helped.

"She never described him to you?"

"Only that he was tall and handsome."

"If they didn't meet here, where did they meet?"

"In the street, I think, out and about."

"What sort of relationship did they have?"

"What sort . . . ?"

"You know what I mean. Did it demand privacy? Did they go somewhere?"

"She mentioned a flat. She didn't say where. Gzira maybe, or Sliema."

"Which? Gzira or Sliema?"

"I can't remember."

"Was it his flat?"

"She didn't say."

She was growing agitated now, regretting her decision to speak to him.

"Okay," he said, more gently. "Thanks."

"And my nephew?"

"If it checks out, I'll come back and see you."

"He's a baby. He shouldn't be in that place."

"No, he should be. But that doesn't mean I can't help."

When Lilian had come to his house in Naxxar and told him her tale of dead girls and cover-ups, Josef had agreed to meet Major Chadwick only out of courtesy to her and their mutual acquaintances. As he had seen it, the whole thing was either too preposterous for words or too hot to touch. The major had made Josef see things differently. It wasn't what he had said so much as how he had carried himself. The quiet conviction of the man had touched Josef. If anyone was playing with fire, it was Major Chadwick. That an officer of his standing was prepared to throw everything away on a point of principle was more than just intriguing; it obliged you to take a long hard look at yourself.

He had decided to help on an impulse, not believing he'd make any real progress in a few short days. And yet, he already had a name: Ken. He ran it over and over in his head, testing it to see if it rang true. Was it too much to ask that the killer had given his real name to Mary Farrugia? Probably. *Best to remain skeptical,* he told himself, as he lay there on the mattress, the mother reading aloud to her two children the story of Little Red Riding Hood. She read well, fluently and with feeling. . . .

He woke with a start, seizing the hand on his shoulder. The woman didn't struggle or recoil, allowing him to orientate himself in the half-light, his filmy eyes slowly focusing.

"I'm sorry," said Josef, releasing her wrist.

He saw that his jacket had fallen open while he was asleep, revealing the gun at his hip.

"I hope it didn't scare them off."

He meant her children, who were no longer there.

"Why do you have a gun?"

"I'm a policeman."

"Where's your uniform?"

"A detective."

He swung his legs off the bed and pulled on his shoes. "How long have I been asleep?"

"Two hours, maybe a bit more. It's easy to lose track of time down here. The all clear's only just sounded."

"Some life," he said.

"It won't last forever. There are more Spitfires coming."

She had large, knowing eyes and a level stare.

"Can you keep a secret?" he asked.

"Most of the time," she replied with a ghost of a grin.

"They'll be here the day after tomorrow. More than the last time, more than sixty this time."

Her teeth showed, white and even, when she smiled. "I don't believe you."

Josef extended his hand. "I'll bet you a shilling."

"I don't have a shilling."

"Then I'll allow you to pay your debt in installments."

"Okay," she said after a moment, "but I can't promise to offer you such generous terms."

She took his hand, sealing the bet, providing them with the excuse to see each other again.

As he was leaving, she said, "You should put some baking soda on that thing. It'll bring it to a head."

She was referring to the carbuncle on his neck.

"Baking soda? I didn't know that."

"Well, now you do."

"Where can I find baking soda?"

"You can't. It's all gone, months ago."

"Well, thanks for the tip anyway."

"Don't mention it."

Outside in the blinding sunshine, Josef paused to fill his lungs with fresh air and get his bearings. He felt invigorated by the sleep, or was it something else, something he hadn't felt in a long while? He hadn't even asked her name. That's how hopeless he had become in his dealings with women.

He rarely stopped to think about how it had crept up on him, this solitary life of his: the small house in Naxxar inherited from his father, the house that would have gone to his older brother, if Karlu hadn't given himself to God, turning his back on all worldly possessions. Karlu with his undying faith in man's ability to rise to the challenge set him by the Almighty; he, Josef, the one with the biblical name, mercilessly hunting down those who failed to measure up.

He used to care about the job, he used to think he was serving a purpose, but now he wasn't so sure. There would always be others to fill his boots, and yet he couldn't give it up. It was his excuse for the half-life he'd landed himself with.

Strange that a chance encounter in an air-raid shelter could challenge his weary resignation. He smiled at the memory of her words, playfully defiant: *I can't promise to offer you such generous terms.*

*A pretty woman, and a funny one too,* he

mused as he pushed open the door to Griscti's military outfitters.

The wooden counter ran the full width of the shop, and on the felt panels covering the wall behind it were pinned a dizzying array of caps, berets, badges, and buttons. The cabinets lining the side walls had lost their glass and now stood empty. Behind the counter a dapper-looking man with a goatee beard and pince-nez spectacles was berating a shopgirl for something or other to do with a reel of gold braid. He schooled his features into an unconvincing smile as Josef approached.

"May I help you?"

Josef produced his badge and demanded to see the shop ledger. The manager grudgingly handed it over.

There was no record of a sale of a submariner's shoulder tab in the past ten days, not since Carmela Cassar had been found dead in the street with the remnants of one in her hand. In fact, the ledger recorded barely any sales since the beginning of the month. This wasn't so surprising; the soldiers, sailors, and airmen on the island had better things to think about right then than the trim of their battle dress. Ken, assuming that was his name, assuming that he had killed Mary Farrugia before going on to murder two more girls, assuming that he existed at all and that mother hen hadn't been trying to pull a fast one for the sake of her nephew —

"Have you finished?" demanded the manager.

Josef silenced him with a look, irritated by the distraction, irritated by the number of assumptions driving the case. Facts and evidence were what counted.

He flicked back through the ledger — April, March, February, January . . .

"Do you have a ruler?" asked Josef.

"A ruler?"

Unprompted, the shopgirl pulled one from a drawer and handed it over.

"Thanks," said Josef with a smile, taking it from her and using it to tear off the relevant pages of the ledger.

The manager looked stunned by this act of desecration.

"Don't worry. You'll get them back."

Tacitus contacted him at the usual time.

He had made a point over the past days of neither broadcasting nor receiving, choosing instead to leave the machine tucked well away in its wooden box. He could imagine Tacitus's frustration, but he couldn't picture the man behind the code name. He vacillated between an unassuming character, easily underestimated, and a more obvious type in the Lutz Kettelmann mold: tall, officious, blandly handsome. His tastes ran naturally to the former. He liked a dark horse, being something of one himself.

The message brought a smile to his lips. It was the first time that Tacitus had addressed him in English.

Silence is not always golden. Tacitus.

He punched his reply into the machine,

noting down the enciphered text before transmitting it.

And talk is not always cheap. Virgil.

It was a satisfying riposte: a play on the same proverb while at the same time implying that they would have to pay dearly for any more information. He was over his little sulk, now that his plans were back on track, but that didn't mean he couldn't punish them for throwing those plans into disarray in the first place.

It was a while before he heard back from them, time to read a couple of chapters of his book. Their request, when it finally came through, was predictable enough. They wanted to know everything he'd learned about the reinforcement flight of Spitfires heading for the island. Did he have an exact date? An idea of the numbers involved? What preparations were under way at the airfields? How did they plan to disperse the aircraft? In short, had they learned from their mistakes last time round, and if so, what new measures were they adopting?

He thought about lying; the idea amused him. One hundred and twenty Mark V Spitfires due at first light tomorrow morning. That would certainly have had Tacitus tearing his hair out, or what was left of it. His preferred incarnation of Tacitus was thin on top.

In the end, he was a good boy, and answered the questions as precisely as possible. He even threw in a bonus, advising that it would be worth keeping an eye on the seaplane base in Kalafrana Bay that evening. A well-timed raid might just kill two birds with one stone — the outgoing governor *and* his replacement.

When he was done, he packed the machine away and wandered through to the living room. He poured himself a large whisky and wound up the gramophone. Sitting there with a glass in one hand, a cigarette in the other, his thoughts turned to Max — handsome, hopeless Max, torn between two such different women.

Was he even aware of the true scale of the cliché? It was a corny conundrum straight from the pages of *Ivanhoe* or *Daniel Deronda:* the young man whose heart is divided between the blond embodiment of his own kind and a creature altogether more dark and exotic. Sir Walter Scott and George Eliot had each chosen to throw a Jewess in the path of their hero. Max, it seemed, had fallen hard for a Maltese of mixed ancestry. He knew that Max had fallen hard because he'd watched them up close and he'd watched them from afar, and the body language was unmistakable.

Max had proved himself a far more capable dissimulator with Mitzi. Even when observing the dumb play of their moving lips across a crowded room, when they'd thought they were alone, he'd been able to detect little of their private history. Almost nothing in their behavior betrayed them. You really had to know what had been going on in order to see it.

He poured himself another whisky and recovered his notebook from its hiding place. If he were any different, he might have been able to sustain his natural sympathy for Max. A part of him even wished it were possible. It wasn't, though. That became evident as soon as he began to write.

The characters lost their lustre, like wet clay hardening in the sun. Baked, cracked, and flawed, the tiny effigies were hard to care for. He shunted them about, choreographing the final act as best he could. The days ahead would be turbulent and unpredictable. He couldn't foretell the exact hour when the new Spitfires would fly in, or when the *Upstanding* would slip away to Alexandria, or where exactly the official duties of the various players, himself included, would carry them during the inevitable chaos.

His meditations were interrupted by the building wail of the siren. Yet another raid, the third of the night. He lit a cigarette, annoyed by the distraction that had caused him to lose his train of thought. Extinguishing the candle, he crossed to the window and pushed open the shutters.

The blue-white fingers of the searchlights groped around the heavens, their efforts thwarted by a low blanket of clouds that played in the Germans' favor. Before long, he heard the grumbling roar of unseen Junkers approaching. There weren't many of them, a mere handful by the sound of it. The reason for that became clear a few moments later.

They dropped through the clouds in the hundreds, sputtering into life — bright white, falling silently to earth, dripping phosphorescence, illuminating the underbelly of the clouds. And still they kept coming, hundreds of them, thousands of them, like swarming fireflies, turning night into day, lighting up the whole island now, laying bare the undulating mosaic of the Maltese landscape.

It was a spectacle he'd witnessed before,

but never quite on this scale, and it was impressive, almost moving, until you remembered that it was the harmless prelude to a far more devastating display of pyrotechnics. The other bombers, the ones carrying death in their bellies, were already approaching, the air throbbing with the menacing beat of their engines.

The revelation came to him as the searchlights converged on the first wave of planes to break cloud cover: a new ending, a bold and unexpected finale, one at which Max and Lilian would both be present.

# Day Seven

Unfortunately, Busuttil was a man of his word.

He reappeared at Max's flat at five A.M., exactly twenty-fours after his first visit. He seemed surprisingly perky given that he hadn't made it home to his own bed, opting instead to pass the night in a shelter in Valetta.

"You're welcome to stay here, you know."

"Thank you, but the shelter is okay."

Max had raided Maria's secret store of quality tea for the occasion, sneaking home just enough for a small pot.

"She'll kill me for it."

"I might do the same," said Busuttil, the taste sending him into a worrying trance. Once he'd recovered, he got straight to the point, bringing Max up to speed on his findings.

"Ken?"

"That's what she said. Maybe it's his real

381

name. Maybe it isn't. Maybe she was lying. I found nothing at Griscti's. I'll try the other outfitters today."

"Maybe I can help?"

"Of course you can. But be careful who you speak to."

Busuttil had paid two visits to the Blue Parrot, neither of which had revealed anything of note regarding Carmela Cassar. The other girls she'd worked with had painted a picture of a scrupulously moral young woman who had never associated with clients outside the confines of the club. This didn't mean there wasn't more to discover on that front; he'd ascertained that the club was popular with officers from the submarine flotilla. He also intended to pay a visit to Carmela's parents. He stood a better chance of extracting something from them, which, given the hopeless failure of Max's visit, wasn't saying much.

Max had nothing much to offer Busuttil in return besides Freddie's theory that the killer was left-handed.

"Interesting," said Busuttil, before adding, "Tell me about Freddie."

"Freddie?"

"Tell me about him."

"Why?"

"Because everything starts with him. He

tells you. You tell Lilian. She tells me. The story grows. Maybe that's what he wants. Who do *I* tell?"

"No one, I hope, until you know exactly what's going on," replied Max firmly.

"You never know exactly. What makes a man kill? I don't know. Do you?"

"I know you're barking up the wrong tree with Freddie."

Busuttil shrugged. "I'm very suspicious. I have even asked myself if it is you."

"Well, it isn't me."

It was a slightly sour note on which to end. Busuttil suggested that they meet again at ten o'clock that night to pool their findings, and then he disappeared into the new day.

Pemberton was waiting for Max when he got to work, bursting with barely concealed excitement, although he waited till they were alone before spilling the beans.

"The governor's gone."

"Gone?"

"Last night. From Kalafrana. Left in a seaplane."

It was good to know that Elliott wasn't a total fraud.

"Why are you whispering?" whispered Max.

Pemberton looked crestfallen. "You knew?"

"I got a whiff of it."

Keep it cryptic, keep the new boy in his place, then find out how the hell the new boy got the jump on him.

"Who did *you* hear it from?"

"Rosamund, who heard it from Hugh. Apparently he's known for a couple of days. She was very upset."

Rosamund had shown up at breakfast at the Copnalls' house in Saint Julian's, where Pemberton was lodging. If she was to be believed, the governor of Gibraltar, Lord Gort, was now the governor of Malta, having flown in to Kalafrana on the same seaplane that had then carried the Dobbies off.

Gort was a good man, by all accounts — a tough no-nonsense type — and Rosamund would get over it once she'd secured a place for herself at the new court.

It wasn't long before the call came through from the lieutenant governor's office, as Max knew it would. He wandered next door to the Vincenzo Bugeja Conservatory, pushing aside memories of his last visit.

The sight of Hodges perched self-importantly behind his desk brought them flooding back.

"It's good to see you again, Major Chadwick."

A pointed comment intended to go over
the heads of the other men already gathered
there, waiting to be called through. They
were standing in a loose huddle, smoking
and talking in hushed tones. Max nosed his
way among them. There were representatives from Defense Security and Censor-
ship, along with a couple of faces he recognized from the Union Club.

"Heard the news, old man?"

"About Dobbie?"

"Damn shame, if you ask me."

"Straight out of left field. Didn't even say
goodbye."

"He's been poorly for a while."

"Yes, a bad case of *'Et tu, Brute?'* from
what I hear."

"Really?"

"Methinks Mabel has been up to her old
tricks."

Mabel Strickland was the editor of the
*Times of Malta,* and a force to be reckoned
with. It was well known that her influence
extended far beyond the shores of Malta to
the corridors of Whitehall.

"Oh goody, a scandal. We haven't had one
of those for a while."

*If you only knew,* thought Max.

385

He stayed well out of the was-he-pushed-or-did-he-jump speculation that followed, which was soon interrupted by the appearance of Colonel Gifford, who summoned them through.

The lieutenant governor rose from his desk to greet them. Despite the suntan, his face appeared drawn and careworn. He didn't hang about, confirming that Lord Gort was indeed the new governor and commander in chief. In the fullness of time they would all have a chance to meet him, but right then he had his head down with the service chiefs, poring over the preparations for the forthcoming battle. The fly-in of Spitfires would meet with fierce resistance from the Germans, as would the arrival of HMS *Welshman* the following day. The fast minelayer was going to be making a lone dash from Gibraltar loaded to the gunwales with ammunition, aircraft parts, and food. They were calling it Operation Bowery, and Lord Gort was firmly of the view that nothing should be allowed to distract the islanders during this time. News of his appointment should therefore be kept under wraps for a couple of days, and it was the responsibility of the men in the room to see that his wishes were fulfilled.

The lieutenant governor assured the men

that they wouldn't be disappointed with the new governor, and even shared an anecdote to bear out his point. As luck would have it, the seaplane base at Kalafrana had suffered a heavy air raid soon after Lord Gort's arrival, the first bombs raining down right in the middle of the swearing-in ceremony. A very large egg, possibly a two-thousand-pounder, had narrowly missed the base commander's house where they were all gathered, sending everyone diving for cover — everyone other than Lord Gort, who had barely flinched.

*He'll learn,* thought Max.

"Something for you to use, Major Chadwick, when the time's right."

"Absolutely, sir. Stirring stuff."

He saw Colonel Gifford's nostrils twitch, sniffing for sarcasm.

The meeting over, the men filed out of the office, past Hodges, and into the corridor. Colonel Gifford followed close on their heels.

"Major Chadwick . . ."

He evidently wanted a word in private, so Max hung back. Gifford waited for the others to drift out of earshot before speaking.

"No hard feelings about the other day, I hope?"

"No, just suitably chastened." He threw in

387

a coy and contrite little look. "I was a bloody fool. I don't know what I was thinking."

Gifford appeared to swallow it. "That's war for you. It messes with our perspective on things."

"Not yours."

"No, even mine."

This admission of fallibility was accompanied by an almost beatific expression.

*Just think of Busuttil,* Max told himself, *out there at this very moment, digging for the truth.*

"Well, we're all going to have to stay focused over the next few days," said Gifford. "The time of reckoning is here."

"Let's hope," replied Max.

Mother hen was seated at the counter, talking to the barman, and her lined face lit up when she saw him.

Josef dumped himself at a table well away from the other girls and waited for her to join him. She made her way over with a small glass of something brown.

"On the house."

Josef sneaked a sip. It was whisky, and it hadn't been watered down. He flattened a larger sip against his palate, savoring it.

"I need to know if you were lying."

"Lying?"

"About Ken."

"Why would I lie to you?"

"Because of your nephew."

"I told you what Mary told me."

"She definitely said he was with the submarines?"

"Yes."

"Anything else? Dark, fair? Thin, fat?"

"How many fat people do you know on Malta?"

"True."

"Gozo, maybe. I hear they still eat like kings on Gozo."

She reached for one of his cigarettes, and he lit it for her.

"I see him as having a mustache, but I don't know if that's because of something Mary said."

"Can you think of anyone else she might have talked to about him? Maybe someone from her family?"

"She wasn't close to her family. She wasn't close to many people. She lived alone in Hamrun."

He didn't bother asking for the address. He had enough on his plate already without a trip to Hamrun.

"Are you going to tell me what this is about?"

"No," replied Josef. "But you're going to

tell me the name of your nephew and I'm going to see what I can do for him."

"There's no need to take it so personally. We've all been through it."

Pemberton shifted in his chair. "You're asking me to lie?"

"To exercise a certain discretion. The press correspondents are out to make a name for themselves. Good news, bad news, it's all fair game to them."

Pemberton had made the mistake of being honest with one of the correspondents about a couple of Beaufighters that had failed to return to Luqa after a mission. It was the sort of news you didn't want going off the island.

"All I'm saying is, be a bit more guarded in your responses to them."

"Guarded?"

"Gray. Until you've spoken to me."

Pemberton fumbled for a cigarette. *Poor boy,* thought Max, *he's probably never put a foot wrong.* It was written all over him: top of the class, captain of sports, *victor ludorum,* head boy, handsome as hell, and now this — a small blunder that had tarnished his perfect record.

"Rosamund says no one reads the *Daily Situation Report,*" Pemberton moaned.

"Does she?"

"She says it's a joke."

"Not for the men whose deaths you're recording."

Max was beginning to lose his patience, but Pemberton didn't appear to notice.

"She says no one reads it and the Maltese don't believe a word of it."

True enough; he knew that from Lilian.

"Surely they have to read it in order not to believe a word of it."

"That's semantics."

"Semantics is our business. The sooner you understand that, the better it'll be for you."

This time, Max invested his voice with a firm touch of authority that startled Pemberton into silence.

"Look," sighed Max, "whatever you think, whatever you've heard, they'll all be reading it over the next few days. It's my guess you're about to chronicle one of the great moments of this war."

"You think so?"

"I do. I think we're going to show the Germans a thing or two tomorrow. I think they won't know what's hit them. I think we're going to be standing on the beach when the tide turns."

It was hardly Churchill, but it seemed to

lift Pemberton's spirits.

"I like that image of the tide turning. I was brought up by the sea, you know?"

*Probably swims like a fish, too,* thought Max.

The moment Pemberton was gone, Max lit a cigarette and reflected on the exchange. He felt bad for having raised his voice. He knew he had only been taking out his own frustrations on his young charge, the most recent conversation with Tommy Ravilious still fresh in his mind.

Max had thought about heading over to the submarine base in person. Remembering Busuttil's warning to tread carefully, he had picked up the phone instead.

"Tommy, it's Max."

"Ahhhh, Max . . ." There was something strange in his tone.

"A quick question —"

"I should stop you there, old man. I'm under orders not to speak to you."

"What?"

"Apparently you've become persona non grata. I told them you always were."

"Who's them?"

"Does it matter? The powers that be."

"Tommy, this is important."

"So's my pension, old man."

"Ken."

392

"Come again?"

"I'm trying to find a chap called Ken. He's one of yours, probably an officer."

"They said you weren't to be trusted and I was to let them know if you tried to make contact."

"You can't do that."

"I most certainly can, but I'm not going to. I'm going to hang up."

"Is he one of yours? Yes or no?"

"Sorry, no ken do."

"That's not funny."

"It's code, you idiot. We don't have a Ken — not now, not ever."

"Thanks, Tommy."

"What for? We never spoke."

A dead end. There was nothing more he could do to move matters along. The waiting game was messing with his head, and young Pemberton had paid the price for it.

He was thinking about taking another turn on the roof when the phone rang. It was Maria, and she had Hugh on the line.

"Your presence is requested for dinner at ours this evening, seven for seven-thirty. You won't guess what we're eating."

"I'm so hungry that dog would do."

"Try duck."

"Duck? Not Laurel and Hardy!"

Laurel and Hardy were two plump mallards who'd inhabited the pond at the end of Hugh and Rosamund's garden. They were part of the family, like surrogate children. Max had spent many an hour gathering snails to feed them.

"Think of it as a noble act of self-sacrifice. And if that doesn't work, think of the taste."

"Hugh, you can't."

"Lady Macbeth already has, I'm afraid. It's a special occasion — farewell to Mitzi and Lionel."

"They're going to be there?"

"Bit of an odd farewell bash if they weren't, don't you think?"

Max suggested they meet at the Union Club beforehand. He was going to need a couple of drinks to set himself up.

"I wish," said Hugh. "The CRA has got us jumping through hoops. I'll be lucky to get away by seven as it is."

Busuttil made his way beneath Victoria Gate and down to the customhouse at the water's edge. He had a particular fondness for the elegant old building from his days on port control and was saddened to see that it had taken a couple of bad knocks since he'd last been there.

It was while waiting for a *dghaisa* to take him across Grand Harbour that the feeling first came to him: a distinct sensation of being watched.

He removed his hat and fanned his face with it, resisting the urge to turn around, trusting his instincts. They rarely played him false, and it cost him nothing to indulge them now. He had a long walk ahead of him once he'd crossed the harbor. There would be plenty of better opportunities for testing his intuition. Even when he boarded the *dghaisa,* he made a point of sitting with his back to Valetta.

It was a short run across the water to Vittoriosa, the colorful little craft skimming effortlessly along, propelled by the expert oars of the two boatmen. The persistent raids in the past few weeks had reduced Dockyard Creek to a shocking picture of devastation. Most of the buildings fronting the water were gutted or simply gone altogether, and it looked like some monstrous creature of the deep had chewed large chunks out of the quaysides. Vittoriosa and Senglea, rising proudly on their long promontories either side of the creek, had also taken a battering, their ancient skylines redrawn for all of time by German bombs.

"Santa Maria . . . ," whispered Josef.

"You think this is bad, you should see French Creek."

The boatmen eased the *dghaisa* alongside the rubble-strewn quay beneath the walls of Fort Saint Angelo. Disembarking, Josef lingered with them awhile in conversation, allowing the other *dghaisas* now threading their way across the harbor from Valetta to draw nearer. When he set off, it was at a leisurely pace along the waterfront, out in the open, an easy target to track.

The narrow, winding streets of Cospicua at the head of Dockyard Creek were heaped with ruins, slowing his progress, which was just fine by him if it allowed his tail to gain on him. Once clear of the old defensive walls on the landward side, he was out in the open again, making his way up the slopes toward Tarxien.

He was sweating now, and the feeling of being followed was more acute than ever. So was the temptation to spin round and confirm it. Trees and huts were few and far between on the hillside, and the lacework of low stone walls offered minimal cover. He would know in a moment, but so would the other man, and that would be that. It would come down to a foot chase, and he was in no physical condition to even contemplate one of those. Better to just carry on his way for now. At most, he was maybe fifteen minutes from the Cassars' place.

Once there, he would figure out a way to turn the tables on his shadow.

Max made a point of turning up at the offices of *Il-Berqa* with a couple of files under his arm even though work was the furthest thing from his mind.

"You're late," said Rita from behind her desk.

"I know I'm late. There was a raid on Ta' Qali. No doubt you would have risked it."

Paradoxically, Rita didn't bristle at his rudeness. She seemed almost to appreciate it. Maybe that's what he'd been doing wrong all this time — trying too hard to please and appease her.

"Well, she's waiting for you."

"Thank you."

"It's my pleasure."

"Mine too. I cherish our little moments together."

"Don't push it," said Rita.

He hadn't been lying about the raid, but he would have been less late if he hadn't stopped by the Ops Room on his way there and done something he'd been wanting to do for days: tear a strip off Iris for her treachery toward him. The actress in her had squeezed out some crocodile tears, prompting the gunnery liaison officer on duty to intercede on her behalf and shepherd Max away. He'd probably made a fool of himself, but for now the sweet taste of retribution more than made up for it.

Lilian was still wearing black out of respect to Caterina.

"When's the funeral?" he asked, the moment she had closed the door of her office.

"Monday. Why?"

"So long as it's not tomorrow. The new Spitfires are flying in."

She breathed in the news, her relief evident. "When?"

"Midmorning. Tell your aunt to keep Felicia and Ena indoors."

"I will."

"In fact, tell anyone you like. Kesselring probably knows their ETA already."

Ten days before he wouldn't have dared to divulge such information to her in case of possible reprisals. Her expression said as much.

"Thank you."

He shrugged.

"I mean it. Thank you. Not just for this. For everything. For what you're doing."

"Busuttil's the one doing all the hard work. He's quite a character."

"They say he's the best on the island."

"He'd better be. He's got only two more

days before the *Upstanding* leaves."

She wanted details of the investigation, which he refused to give her. The less she knew, the better — for now, at least. Instead, they talked at length about the change of governor and how they both planned to break the news when finally allowed to do so.

As he was leaving her office, she placed her palm against the door to prevent him from opening it.

"What?"

"What do you think?" she replied.

"I have to guess the password?"

She smiled. "Hold me."

"I haven't washed properly in days."

"You think *I* have?"

He drew her into his arms, and for the first time he felt the soft pressure of her breasts against his chest. Her hair was powdered with dust, the omnipresent Maltese dust.

She raised her head to peer up at him. "You weren't lying."

"Oh God . . ."

"I like it," she said, holding him tighter to prove her point.

"The first thing I'm going to do when I get home is have a bath. Not just any bath. The bath to end all baths. I'm going to sit there and soak for hours. With a good book. And a big glass of pure malt whisky. And I'll use my foot to top it up with piping hot water from time to time."

"Your foot?"

"On the tap."

"Oh."

"You've never done that?" he asked.

"No."

"It's not so hard. The hardest part is using your other foot to remove the plug so the tepid water can drain away."

"I can see you," she said.

"Can you?"

"Like I was standing there."

Max hesitated. "You can come in, if you want."

"You'll have to put your book down."

"As long as I don't have to let go of the whisky."

"Okay," she conceded with a small smile. "Now kiss me."

It was a long and languorous kiss, neither of them wishing it to end.

It was growing dark, and Busuttil had spent more than enough time with the Cassars. He knew pretty much everything there was to know about their dead daughter — how as a young girl Carmela had hated having her hair braided for church; how she had loved having her back stroked in the bath; how she had won the art prize at school with her drawing of the Tarxien Temples. She had always been strong-willed, good with animals, tough on bullies, and indifferent to boys.

Josef searched for lies in their words, but was left with a picture of a model daughter, proud, principled, and kindhearted. So eager were they to bring her back to life with their reminiscences that only once did they ask him why he had come visiting. He palmed them off with the usual line about it being standard police procedure.

Carmela had been laid to rest in Santa Maria Addolorata Cemetery just a few days before, and before the light faded, her father was able to point out the spot from the house — a quiet corner near the western wall that apparently caught the early-morning sun. Carmela had always said that she wanted to be buried there.

Well, now she was. And only a stone's throw away, Josef suspected, from the place where she'd been abducted. He knew from her parents the route she'd taken home from work every night, and he had played it through in his mind, walking the streets with her back from the Blue Parrot: Valetta,

Floriana, down past the Porte des Bombes to Marsa, skirting the end of Grand Harbour, leaving the racetrack on her right. Until this point she'd have been on main roads. Better to wait till she took the shortcut, up the valley and through Santa Maria Addolorata Cemetery. That's what he would have done. That's what anyone who knew her movements would have done — waited till she was on the home stretch, well off the beaten track. Josef knew it in his bones, just as he knew that out there somewhere, someone was watching and waiting.

Who they were, and just where they'd picked up his trail, he didn't know. But he would know soon enough. That's why he had lingered so long with the Cassars, allowing the sun to set and darkness to descend. The night was his time, his friend. It was when he had always done his best work, even as a student at the university. The Cassars were keen that he stay and eat with them, but he made his excuses and left.

There was a waning moon overhead, only half-full, yet bright enough to illuminate his path down the hill. It was ideal. Any less light, and it would have been too dark to see what he was doing; any more, and the hunter might have realized that he had become the hunted.

The iron gate set in the south wall of the cemetery offered an added bonus. Its dry and dusty hinges groaned in protest as Josef slipped the latch and eased it open. After closing it behind him, he quickened his pace, stepping lightly down the central avenue for fifty yards or so before breaking left, weaving through the gravestones, and taking up a position behind a run of large family tombs.

There he waited and listened, filtering out the sounds of the night. He started to feel foolish after several minutes had passed, and was about to break cover when he heard it, buried away in the drone of cicadas: the sound of the gate being opened.

His hand went instinctively to his waist, closing around the stock of his pistol.

From where he was hidden it was hard to judge the height of the man because the avenue was shaded from the moonlight by a screen of cypress trees. From the sound of his footfalls, he was moving stealthily but with purpose, looking to narrow the lead.

Josef kicked off his shoes and set off along the narrow pathway behind him. It ran parallel to the main avenue, and he hurried in a low crouch to get ahead of the man. He was familiar enough with the cemetery to know that the main avenue divided at the back of the cathedral, skirting it on both sides. It was as good a spot as any for Josef to make his move.

He was in position, hunched behind a gravestone, when the man reached the junction and stopped. If he headed left, Josef would strike, leaping from the shadows and delivering a quick pistol whip. He couldn't afford to take any chances. It was a case of act first, ask questions later. If the man gave him the slip, there would be little hope of finding him in the labyrinth of tombs.

The man set off again, his footsteps receding. Josef peered out from his hiding place in time to see the shadowy figure disappear from view along the right-hand fork. He gave a silent curse at the prospect of yet more running, then padded off around the other side of the cathedral.

He was heaving for breath by the time he reached the point where the two pathways converged once more. It was a darkened spot, perfect for his purposes: a circular patch of ground fringed with trees at the foot of the low plateau on which the cathedral was perched. A double stone staircase set in a sheer bank of rock marked the beginning of the long climb up to the main entrance of the building, and it was here, in the deep shadows to one side of the staircase, that he placed himself.

The blood was beating in his ears after his exertions, and he strained to hear the man approaching. When he did, he sneaked a quick look. The man was no more than twenty yards away and approaching at a brisk rate down the pathway. Josef's fingers tightened around the pistol. *Go for the side of the head and hit him again if he tries to get up. . . .*

His muscles were tensed, poised to spring into action. If they hadn't been, he might have reacted to the sound more quickly. It came from behind him, and by the time he had registered it, by the time he had turned, it was too late.

His last impression before his world went black was of a tall figure looming over him. His last thought was of the air-raid shelter and the young woman whose name he now knew.

"Anyone for seconds?" asked Rosamund.

"That's a question I haven't heard in a while," said Max.

Lionel gave a hearty laugh. "Too right, old man."

"A bit more of Hardy, if there's any going," said Freddie.

"Freddie!" chided Mitzi.

"Well, he's more tender than Laurel."

"Stop it!"

*"She,"* corrected Rosamund. "Hardy was a girl."

"Really? How can you tell?" asked Lionel.

Mitzi rolled her eyes. "The plumage, for one."

"And Hardy always peed sitting down."

This earned Max a big laugh around the table. Lionel even slapped his thigh. Mitzi took the opportunity to fire Max a look that only he could interpret. It said, *I know what you're doing, and I don't care.*

But she *did* care, which was why he intended to carry on doing it.

"Shouldn't we hold the rest back for the others?" he suggested.

"They don't deserve it," said Rosamund.

Elliott had failed to show, and Hugh was supposed to have been back from Rabat almost two hours before, having scooped up Ralph in Mdina en route.

"I'm sure it's not their fault they're late."

"Oh, it's never Hugh's fault."

This was uncharacteristic of Rosamund, who generally liked to present a united front. Realizing her transgression, she tried to make light of it.

"I keep a list of Hugh's excuses. He must

too, because he's never used the same one twice."

His excuse, when he showed up a short while later with Ralph, was difficult to fault. He'd spent the afternoon touring gun emplacements ahead of the big day, geeing up his men. The whole thing had overrun because of the afternoon raids.

"You could have phoned."

"I tried, my darling. The lines were down."

"Not when I called HQ and they told me they had no idea where you were."

"That's as it should be. We'd all be in terrible trouble if HQ actually knew what was going on."

The laughter put an end to the matter, and attention shifted back to the guests of honor. Freddie proposed a toast to Lionel and Mitzi, following it up with a small speech he'd prepared. It was a touching tribute, heavy on the humor, which brought some tears from Mitzi. Even Lionel's eyes misted over a little.

His response to Freddie's kind words was a predictable mix of awkward affability and pomposity: friendships smelted in the furnace of battle . . . memories to last a lifetime . . . the eternal struggle of good versus evil . . . not "goodbye" so much as "au revoir." He made no mention of Mitzi and the fact that she had chosen to stay at his side throughout it all, whereas most of the wives had long since bolted for home. Max knew that he should keep his mouth shut, that to speak would only draw attention to Lionel's oversight, but when the smattering of applause had died down, he raised his glass.

"To Mitzi and all her good work at the Standing Committee of Adjustment."

Mitzi tilted her head at him in gratitude.

"Hear, hear," said Rosamund emphatically. "If it wasn't for women like you, women like me wouldn't get to sit around all day playing gin rummy and moaning about the scarcity of zip fasteners."

The final toast of the evening was to Ralph, and in many ways it was the most poignant. None of them around the table was facing a trial like his, and they all knew it was one he might not survive. The next morning, when the replacement Spitfires flew in, he would be waiting at Ta' Qali, ready to take to the air in one of the new machines. No one doubted that the ensuing air battle would be the fiercest yet, and Ralph was going to be in the thick of it.

"Are you sure you remember how to fly the bloody things?" asked Freddie.

"Stick, rudder pedals, firing button —

how hard can it be?" scoffed Max.

Lionel gave a loud snort. "Well, I must say, that's pretty rich coming from you, old man."

"He was joking," Mitzi sighed.

"Oh."

When they all moved outside for coffee, Max and Freddie snatched a moment alone on the back terrace. It was the first chance they'd had to talk in private, and Max filled him in on Busuttil's discoveries, including the name he'd turned up.

"Ken?"

"I checked with Tommy Ravilious at the sub base. Nothing."

"An assumed name?"

"Maybe. Busuttil's chasing it down."

"I hope so. Mitzi says the *Upstanding*'s due to leave on Sunday."

"I thought it was Monday."

"It's been brought forward a day. They want her gone before things really heat up around here."

"Christ."

Only one more day for Busuttil to crack it. He wasn't going to appreciate this new development when Max saw him later.

Freddie wanted to know if there was anything he could do to help. He had just been assigned to the naval hospital at Bighi, on the Grand Harbour side of Valetta, but was more than happy to shirk his duties if the situation called for it.

"You can't do that."

"It's not like I'm stuck out at Mtarfa anymore. I'm right here on the doorstep and ready to do whatever — hang the consequences."

"I'll mention it to Busuttil, see what he says."

Freddie glanced toward the house. Lionel was still seated at the dining table, pontificating to Hugh and Ralph about something or other.

"Have you ever wondered if it's him?"

"Lionel? For all of five seconds. Why?"

"I hadn't noticed before tonight. . . . He's left-handed."

As if on cue, Lionel raised his wineglass to his lips with his left hand.

Max didn't have a chance to respond.

"What are you two looking so furtive about?"

The voice came from high above them. It was Mitzi, peering down from the crow's nest, barely discernible in the darkness.

"What are you doing up there?" called Freddie.

"Having a last look."

"Don't pretend you'll miss it."

"Oh, but I shall."

"And us?"

"I've already packed some extra hankies."

"You'll latch on to another pair of handsome, witty young men within a week of landing in Alexandria."

"Is that what I did: latch on to you?"

"Brazenly. It was almost embarrassing, wasn't it, Max?"

"Absolutely. I still shudder when I think about it."

Freddie laughed. Mitzi didn't.

Max was still thinking about Lionel.

It was perfect, maybe more perfect than it had ever been in the past.

Preparations had been made, contingencies planned for, but it wasn't the logistics that accounted for his deep sense of satisfaction. That came from the beauty of the stratagem, its plain and simple trigonometry.

There had been moments when he had feared he'd taken on too much. He could admit to that now, now that he was so close and could see it all unfolding before his eyes.

He loved this moment, and he tried to record his almost dizzying sense of anticipation.

Reading back the words, he realized that some things lay well beyond the scope of language.

# DAY EIGHT

Max woke with a start, unsure why at first, the reason slowly dawning on him.

He struggled to read the luminous dial of his wristwatch — just after five — which meant Busuttil was running more than seven hours late.

Max had been the first to leave the dinner, racing home to make the ten o'clock appointment and managing to stay awake until after midnight before nodding off. He had left the door downstairs unlocked and the one to his flat ajar. It still was.

Maybe Busuttil had been caught in one of the night raids, injured even. It seemed unlikely. The 88s had concentrated all their efforts on the airfields, wave after wave, suggesting that Kesselring had full knowledge of the fly-in and was doing everything in his power to hamper the operation, chewing up the runways and scattering what remained of them with delayed-action bombs.

By seven o'clock, there was still no sign of the detective.

Max left the flat, pinning a note to the door that said he'd gone to work, and giving the phone number. Outside, he ran an apologetic hand over the motorcycle. He had thrashed her on the way home, hurling her around the looping bends of Marsamxett Harbour. He gave her a little shake to check the contents of the tank. Running low on gasoline yet again, but the coil of tubing was tucked away under the seat, ready for some surreptitious siphoning. She started the first time.

There was an air of expectancy in the office. Everyone knew what was coming, but not when exactly. They congregated on the roof of Saint Joseph's, eyes fixed on the distant ridge where Rabat and Mdina stood shoulder to shoulder. That's where the Spitfires would come from, out of the west. High overhead, 109s stooged about the skies, keeping watch, biding their time.

By nine o'clock there was still no word from Busuttil, so Max put a call through to the offices of *Il-Berqa*. Lilian hadn't shown up at work yet, which was strange. She was usually at her desk by eight at the latest. His next call was to her aunt in Mdina.

"Teresa, it's me, Max."

"How nice to hear your voice."

"Is Lilian there?"

"No, she's at work."

She had left early, grabbing a ride down the hill to Ta' Qali on the pilots' bus, as she usually did.

"She's not at work."

"She must be there by now."

"Well, she isn't. No one has seen her."

"Max, what are you saying?"

He could hear the anxiety creeping into her voice.

"She probably couldn't get a lift from the airfield into Valetta. I'm sure it's nothing."

But he wasn't sure. Even if she'd been forced to walk all the way — which simply never happened to women with her kind of looks — she would have arrived by now.

He waited half an hour before calling *Il-Berqa* again and drawing another blank. He could feel the seed of fear germinating in his chest. First Busuttil disappears, and now Lilian. Coincidence? Not if they really were missing. That suggested something far more sinister. He remembered Elliott's warning: *They'll be watching you closely.* Maybe he should have heeded those words of caution more closely. Maybe Colonel Gifford —

No, that theory didn't hold up. If Busuttil had been pulled in by the authorities and had coughed up Lilian's name under questioning, why hadn't there been a knock at his door by now? Why hadn't his name also come out in the wash?

He heard footsteps outside in the corridor, approaching his office. He hoped that they belonged to Colonel Gifford, or the ginger-haired fellow. He was happy to be dragged off and hauled over the coals if it settled the question of Lilian's whereabouts.

The footsteps carried on past his door.

He sat there, rigid in his chair, breathless. There was no ignoring the unthinkable: that Lilian and Busuttil had somehow fallen into the hands of the killer.

The phone rang. He snatched at it.

"Yes."

It was Luke Rogers from the deputy censor's office with some thoughts on the rewording of a BBC broadcast.

"I can't talk now, Luke. I'm expecting an important call."

"I hope you're not implying that this isn't," joked Luke.

Max felt bad about cutting him off without replying, but he was panicking now, struggling to think straight.

Freddie. Maybe Freddie had been hauled in. A call to the naval hospital at Bighi established that he hadn't been; he was in surgery. Elliott. Elliott would know if they'd been taken into custody. But Elliott was nowhere to be found. He wasn't at the Ops Room or the Y Service offices, and no one picked up at the Special Liaison Unit. In desperation, Max tried the Union Club. When that failed, he headed for the roof.

The whole office was gathered there by now, and he took Maria to one side.

"I don't care who it is, but someone has to stay downstairs to man the phones. If anyone calls for me, anyone, tell them to try the Intelligence Office at Ta' Qali."

"Ta' Qali?"

"That's where I'll be."

She looked at him as if he were mad. "You think Ta' Qali is a good place to be now?"

"With any luck I'm in and out before the party starts."

Ta' Qali lay just shy of Mdina, down on the sunbaked plain. He covered the eight miles or so from Saint Joseph's in about as many minutes.

It had been a while since he'd visited the airfield, and he was shocked by what he saw. Most of the familiar structures had been reduced to jumbled masses of masonry, and charred and twisted heaps of metal lay scattered about the place, barely identifiable as aircraft. It was hard to believe that the place still functioned, and yet hordes of men moved like ants through the shimmering heat. Out on the runways, battle-dressed soldiers bent their backs alongside bronzed and shirtless airmen, filling bomb craters and clearing rubble. Ground crews were putting the finishing touches on the new blast pens that fringed the airfield like some gleaming necklace. They'd been constructed from old gasoline canisters filled with earth, and the bare metal building blocks flashed silver-white in the sunlight, clamoring to be targeted. Out there, somewhere, was Ralph, waiting at his designated pen to relieve one of the incoming pilots of his Spitfire.

The Intelligence Office hadn't been relocated, even though the small stone building that housed it had lost its roof and most of its walls in the past month. A sheet of tarpaulin had been rigged above the ruins to provide protection from the sun, and a slit trench with a corrugated iron roof had been dug into the ground nearby for cover during a raid.

Harry Crighton was at his desk in his alfresco office, a cigarette glued to his lower lip. He was a rambunctious and foul-mouthed Australian flight lieutenant who had taken on the duties of intelligence officer after breaking his neck in a forced landing earlier in the year. He was known for his dogged tenacity when it came to following up fighter claims.

"Holy shit, what the bloody hell are you doing here?" he called, seeing Max approach.

" 'To swear is neither brave, polite, nor wise.' "

"Who said that?"

"My headmaster, but I think he got it from Alexander Pope."

"Well, I never claimed to be any of those things," Harry replied with a grin, "so fuck 'em both."

"Has anyone called for me?"

"What do you think this is, a bloody message service? No, no one's called for you. And do you have any idea what's about to happen here?"

"A vague inkling."

"Pull up a pew and tell me what's going on, why don't you?"

Max pulled up a chair and told him almost nothing of what was going on. All he wanted to know was if Lilian had indeed hitched a lift down from Mdina on the pilots' bus that morning.

"Yes, and a fine old sight she is too at that hour of the morning, I can tell you. Brings a little color to the caravan."

"Where did you drop her?"

"Where we usually do — by the perimeter track. There's a small chapel, more of a shrine, I suppose."

"Did you see anything?"

"What do you mean?"

"I don't know — a person, a vehicle, anything?"

"Can't say I was paying attention. Why?"

"She's gone missing somewhere between here and Valetta."

"Are you sure?"

"As good as. She should have been at work more than two hours ago."

Before Harry could respond, there was a low, building roar of engines from out of the west. This was met with wild cheers from around the airfield as a flock of shapely planes swept into view over the ridge just south of Rabat. They were in formation, four sections of four flying in line astern, wingtip to wingtip, nose to tail.

"Bloody fools," muttered Harry. "They're way too tight. Did no one tell them?"

He was right. Tight formations were the kiss of death on Malta. So was line astern. Fortunately, the Spitfires fanned out, entering the circuit, before the first Messerschmitts swooped on them. The 109s came low and fast out of the sun from the direction of Valetta, ripping through a smattering of ack-ack. A handful of Hurricanes from Luqa or Hal Far did a fine job of heading off the attackers. The Hurriboys were an experienced bunch. Battle-hardened (and usually bearded), they prided themselves on the superior maneuverability of their otherwise inferior aircraft, and this advantage served them well in the tussles that now developed over Ta' Qali. A lunatic chatter of light artillery fire accompanied the spectacle as the Bofors and twin Lewis guns opened up on the enemy.

"Here comes the first," shouted Harry above the din.

The pilot was struggling to keep his aircraft from lurching about in the eddies of rising heat. The Spitfire hit the ground hard, bouncing and bumping along the pitted strip. A large number eight was emblazoned on its fuselage. A motorcyclist flashing a card with the same number raced to meet it, leading it off toward one of the new blast pens at the southern end of the airfield.

Harry was jumping around like an excited child. "It's a Mark Vc, with four cannons! Look! So's the next!"

All sixteen Spitfires touched down without mishap, and all were guided to their pens.

The cloud of white dust stirred up by their propellers rolled toward the Intelligence Office, engulfing it, filling Max's eyes and mouth with grit.

"Which number is Ralph?" Max yelled above the din.

"He came down with a dose of the Malta Dog last night. The CO won't let him fly. He's pretty browned off . . . so to speak."

Ralph had been more subdued than usual over dinner the night before, only picking at his food, but Max had put it down to nerves, not the pernicious strain of dysentery that plagued the island.

Overhead, through the breaks in the billowing dust, he glimpsed fighter planes wheeling and twisting against the blue. He was trapped. To run for it now would be madness — a 109 could pick him off before he even reached the perimeter track — but the prospect of staying put filled him with a cold and creeping dread. Memories of the last time he'd been caught in a bombing raid at Ta' Qali blew into his mind. He wasn't sure he could go through that again and emerge with all his mental faculties intact. How on earth the gunners and the ground crews put up with it — day after day, night after night, month after month — was anyone's guess.

Harry called in the safe arrival of the sixteen Spits to Fighter Control. Hanging up the phone, he turned to Max, face alight.

"Ops don't have anything on the table."

"So what's that?" said Max as a 109 rocketed by overhead.

"No big jobs. Nothing between here and Sicily."

"That doesn't mean they're not coming."

"No, but it means they're already too bloody late. We've been working on our turnaround times."

They certainly had been. The first of the new Spits was back in the air within ten minutes — armed, refueled, and with an old Malta hand in the cockpit.

"Go, you bastard!" yelled Harry as its wheels left the ground. The others weren't far behind.

Max watched in amazement. At the last fly-in back in April, Kesselring had obliterated most of the reinforcements on the ground soon after their arrival. On that occasion, "soon" had meant anything from an hour to two hours, while the aircraft were in their pens being made ready for combat. Ten minutes was a whole world apart; it was almost beyond comprehension. That's why Kesselring, their nemesis, the master tactician they all grudgingly respected, had failed to allow for it in his calculations. For once, he had been outmaneuvered. It was good to witness this reversal firsthand. It also offered Max a small window of opportunity.

Even if swarms of 88s were taking off from Sicilian airfields at that very moment, he still had time to make it to Mdina before the bombs started to rain down. The 109s were the problem. Or were they? They seemed to be drifting south, away from Ta' Qali. And now he saw why. A fresh formation of new Spitfires was flying in from the west, making for the airfield at Luqa.

It was as good a moment as any. If he didn't risk it now, he was liable to spend the rest of the day cowering in a slit trench.

He seized Harry's hand and shook it. "Good luck, Harry."

"You too. Hope you find her."

It was a terrifying ride, a blind, choking, headlong dash; he was half expecting to be torn apart by cannon fire at any moment. Only when he started to climb toward Mdina did he rise above the dust and the din and allow himself to glance over his shoulder. Max spat the dirt from his mouth and blinked his streaming eyes, cursing himself for leaving his goggles behind at the office in his haste.

Despite his best efforts to turn himself into something vaguely presentable, the maid still recoiled when she opened the front door to him. Teresa had ignored his words of warning relayed by Lilian. A steep stone staircase led from the palace garden up to the bastion wall, and it was here that he found her, out in the open with her daughters, watching events unfold on the plain below. Felicia and Ena scampered up to him. They had seen a motorcyclist tearing up the hill from Ta' Qali. Had that really been him? What had he been thinking? Was he mad? He could have been killed.

Teresa shepherded the girls back down the steps and across the garden, ordering them to remain indoors from now on. Max was led through to the drawing room. He remained standing, not wishing to soil the antique sofa.

"She's still not at work."

"I know. I also know that she went to visit someone in Naxxar a few nights ago. She wouldn't tell me who." Teresa raised her hand, silencing him before he could reply. "If you lie to me now, Max, I shall never forgive you. Never."

"Look, I don't know who she visited in Naxxar, but there's a good chance it was a man named Busuttil."

"Busuttil?"

"He's a detective with the CID." He hesitated. "He's also missing."

Teresa stared at him. "What have you done?" she said quietly.

"I haven't *done* anything. I'm just as confused as you are."

"Oh, I doubt that." She wagged her hand irritably at the sofa. "For goodness' sake, sit down. And give me one of your cigarettes. I think I'm going to need it."

He spared her the unnecessary details, and she sat in silence, listening attentively to his account.

"It's still possible the authorities are holding them both."

"You think? I don't. I think you were very wrong to involve her."

"It wasn't like that. She was keen to help."

"You stupid boy!" she spat. "Of course she was. Don't you understand? She would do anything you asked her. She loves you."

Three simple words spiked with bitter truth. He knew what he had become, but now he saw himself as if through Teresa's eyes, perched pathetically on the sofa, already groping for excuses: *if only Lilian had told me earlier, it would all be different.* But there were no excuses, and there was no one else to blame. He had been blind, not just to her feelings, but to his own too. He had made a terrible mistake, and it was one that would plague him for the remainder of his life if he couldn't rectify it.

"You find her," said Teresa. "You find her and you bring her back to me."

His decision to make straight for the Xara Palace at the other end of Mdina was one of expediency. The public phone lines might be out of action because of the raids, but the central phone in the mess would still be functioning.

The palace appeared to be deserted at first, swept clean of all human life. That was because the terrace at the back of the building was jammed thick with spectators — the sick, the injured, Maltese orderlies, and fresh-faced flight lieutenants. There was an exultant edge to the babble of voices passing comment on the dogfights unfolding high overhead.

Max pushed his way through the distracted throng toward the intelligence room at the end of the terrace. It was empty, and he pulled the door closed behind him. Picking up the phone, he spun the handle.

"General staff, please."

The door swung open while he was waiting. Max didn't recognize the young man.

"Excuse me, what are you doing?"

"What does it look like?"

"I have orders to keep that line clear."

"And if you'd been at your post, it might still be."

He was obviously one of the new boys, low on combat experience, tasked with manning the phones to keep him from smashing up one of the new Spits.

"Look, you can't just come in here —"

"Don't make me pull rank on you."

"My orders came from the AOC himself, *Major.*" The schoolboy smirked. "That's who you'll be pulling rank on."

Max wasn't in the mood to drag out the conversation.

"Just bugger off. Better still, bugger off and find Ralph for me."

Ralph's name was what did it. Ralph was royalty.

For Max, though, Elliott was the one who mattered right then. It was time to call his hand, find out just what he knew, because it was certainly more than he'd been willing to reveal up until now.

Elliott, however, seemed to have disappeared from the face of the earth. There had still been no sign of him at the Ops Room, or anywhere else for that matter. It was possible that the man who'd answered the phone at the Y Service offices had been lying, but there was no way of knowing. Even if Max took himself off to Valetta, he'd never gain entry to the offices. Access was strictly limited to a select few.

He had just settled on his only course of action when the young flight lieutenant returned.

"Ralph isn't here."

"Well, he's not down at Ta' Qali, because I was just there."

"He took himself off to the hospital this morning. No one's seen him since."

The Dog could do that to a man, if it bit him hard.

Outside, the heavy artillery opened up, which meant that Kesselring had finally got round to sending his bombers. They were too late to take out the Spitfires on the ground, but just in time to mess up Max's plans.

"Damn," he said, pushing past the young pilot onto the terrace.

They came from the northeast and they came in numbers, darkening the sky over Naxxar. The big guns scored a couple of early successes, one of the 88s vaporizing in a ball of fire, another spiraling earthward. A swarm of new Spitfires raced to greet the attackers, engaging with the covering force of 109s. For the past month or more the RAF had effectively been spent as a defensive force, yet here they were, back in action, wreaking havoc. It was a remarkable sight, captivating, although someone still had the presence of mind to call, "Tin hats, gentlemen, if you're staying out." Moments later, the first shell splinters started to rain down on Mdina.

Max remained indoors during the raids, pacing with frustration, desperate to be gone. But the planes kept coming, and precious hours ticked agonizingly by. He might have risked it if there'd been less at stake, but if he didn't survive, what chance did Lilian have? The sporadic whoops and cheers from the terrace suggested that the Germans were receiving a battering, but somehow it didn't matter. Nothing else mattered.

The last wave of bombers was still droning off to the southwest when he finally mounted his motorcycle. The light was beginning to fade, and he drove carefully through Rabat, eyes scanning the road surface for shrapnel. If he shredded a tire now, well, it didn't bear thinking about.

He left Rabat by the same road he'd taken with Lilian just a couple of days before, the

430

one that led to Boschetto Gardens. This time, though, he carried on past, following his nose. His sense of direction was notoriously poor — something he'd inherited from his father — but even *he* knew that Elliott's cliff-top house lay to the south. He also knew that the only route in and out was somewhere to the east, so if he could just pick up the road he'd taken there from Valetta . . .

He never got a chance. The motorcycle coughed, sputtered a few times, offered one last burst of speed, and then died on him. He knew the symptoms well enough by now and cursed himself for not having checked the gas tank before setting off from Mdina. He wheeled the machine out of sight behind a stone wall. There were few landmarks of any note to guide him back to the spot, so he snapped off the branch of a carob tree and laid it on the wall. When he was done, he struck out cross-country.

The terrain was as bleak and barren as any he'd come across on the island. It was also treacherous, pitted with abandoned stone quarries, deep and sheer-sided, where a man could easily fall to his death and go undiscovered till all that remained of him were his bleached and broken bones.

The ground rose by slow degrees toward

the coast, crisscrossed by ancient cart tracks that had worn neat furrows into the limestone rock beneath the thin coating of soil. He hurried as best he could, racing to beat the failing light. The sun had dropped into the western sea, and twilight was fast giving way to night.

A line of low trees, gnarled and stooped by the wind, stood guard along the narrow ridge where the ground leveled off briefly before plunging sharply away to the sea. Max paused to catch his breath and get his bearings. He had hit the coast just south of the Dingli Cliffs. This was good. It meant that Elliott's place lay somewhere below him and to his left.

He lost his footing several times during the descent, sliding away on a stream of scree, snatching at bushes to stop himself. Fear numbed the pain of the cuts and grazes. He knew he was close when he hit a band of thick vegetation. Edging his way through the spiny shrubs, he found himself on level ground once more, a rutted trail beneath his feet. He headed left through the gloom and was pleasantly surprised some ten minutes later when he came upon the twisted cypress tree and the narrow track leading down to Elliott's farmhouse.

He paused to collect his thoughts. There

was nothing to be gained, he decided, by storming right in there, and nothing to be lost by having a quick look around before announcing himself.

It appeared at first that the place was empty, closed up, but as he crept across the courtyard, he heard noises from inside the farmhouse, coming from the kitchen: the scrape of a chair against a stone floor, the clatter of cutlery on crockery. And a voice. Not Elliott's. It was low and gruff and speaking Maltese.

Through a crack in the shutters he saw Pawlu, the stocky fellow he'd met on his previous visit, the one who helped out around the place. He was at the kitchen table, eating by candlelight. Max couldn't make out who he was speaking to, but that became clear when a deep growl exploded into a chorus of barks.

Max fought the instinct to run. "Hello," he called. "Anyone at home?"

Pawlu appeared at the kitchen door, gripping the dog by its collar. He held a shotgun in his other hand. The barrels came up momentarily, then lowered again as Max approached.

"Pawlu, it's me, Major Chadwick. We met before."

The dog was big and black and of dubi-

433

ous parentage. Pawlu silenced it with a sharp reprimand.

"Is Elliott around?"

"No."

"Do you know where he is?"

"No."

"Nice-looking dog," he lied. "What's his name?"

"Why are you here?"

"I ran out of gas near Boschetto Gardens. I know Elliott's got some cans of the stuff in the barn because he filled me up last time."

"He's not here."

"I'm sure he won't mind me helping myself. I'm in a bit of a fix."

Max started edging toward the barn. Pawlu moved to block his way.

"It is locked."

"The key's under that rock there," said Max, pointing.

"No. Elliott has the key and he is not here. I'm sorry I cannot help you."

He wasn't sorry, and he was probably lying about the key, but he had a gun and a mean-looking dog, and Max was in no position to push the point, not unless he came up with some way of turning the tables. He didn't care about the gasoline anymore, but he wasn't going to leave without taking a look inside that barn. Pawlu's suspicious behavior demanded it.

"Do you at least have a flashlight? I'll never find my way back in the dark."

When Pawlu headed back inside the farmhouse, Max loitered at the kitchen door. Pawlu snapped a command to the dog, and it curled up dutifully near the fireplace. That was good. Pawlu then laid the shotgun on the kitchen table, which was even better, before returning to the door with a hurricane lamp.

"Thanks," said Max.

Reaching for the lamp, he seized Pawlu's wrist, yanking him with all his force into the courtyard. Almost in the same movement, he pulled the door shut on the charging, snarling dog.

Pawlu had stumbled and fallen to the ground, dropping the hurricane lamp, but he was on his feet quickly.

"What's in the barn, Pawlu?"

Pawlu didn't reply. He dropped his head and charged, a bull-necked battering ram, sending Max sprawling back onto the ground. Pawlu was on him in an instant, astride him, pummeling him with both fists, going for the head, working his little arms like windmills. It might have been comical if the fists hadn't been granite-hard.

Pawlu should have pressed home his advantage; it was a mistake to go for the service revolver at Max's hip. Max seized the moment, unleashing a scything right that caught Pawlu on the side of his head, knocking him clean off. The revolver skittered away into the darkness.

Max had never been a violent man by nature, but he knew how to box and he was fighting for a good cause. When Pawlu came at him again, he was ready, and he was angry, and he didn't stop till Pawlu was on his knees, flailing blindly, weakly, like some automaton running down. Max finished him off with an uppercut that laid him out cold.

The dog was going wild inside the kitchen, scrabbling at the base of the door. Max recovered the revolver and stripped Pawlu of his belt, using it to lash Pawlu's hands behind his back. The key to the barn was in his pocket.

Max lit the hurricane lamp before entering.

"Lilian . . . ," he called hopefully, working his way through the jumble of hoarded goods.

She wasn't there.

Busuttil was.

He was laid out on the floor behind a heap

of boxes. His hands and feet were bound, he was gagged, and dried blood masked one half of his face. He lay utterly still.

Max stared in abject horror at the spectacle, until he registered the slight rise and fall of the detective's chest.

Dropping to his knees, Max untied Busuttil. Then he hurried outside and used the same ropes to truss up Pawlu good and proper before dragging him by the heels across the courtyard to the door of the barn. Busuttil was finally stirring, but was in no state to stand, so Max carried him to the entrance and sat him against a pile of boxes.

"Have you seen Lilian?" Max asked.

Busuttil shook his head groggily. He was fighting and failing to come to his senses, as if he'd been drugged.

The interrogation of Pawlu didn't go much better, even after Max had emptied half a canister of gasoline over him to bring him round.

"Where is she?"

"Who?"

Max lit a match. "You think I care what happens to you? I don't."

Pawlu writhed like a maggot on the ground, trying to distance himself from the flame. He claimed to know nothing about a girl. All he knew was that Elliott had asked him to guard the barn, to let no one in there.

If it was a lie, it was a convincing one. Three more matches failed to shake the truth from him, and he was almost weeping when Max tossed the last one away.

"There were two men," slurred Busuttil.

"You saw them?"

Busuttil shook his head.

"I have to go now," said Max. "I'll send help." He pressed the revolver into Busuttil's hand. "Try not to shoot them when they get here."

Busuttil mumbled something that Max didn't catch.

"What?"

"Ken . . ."

"What about him?"

"I think he has a mustache."

Max lost most of the skin off his knees slogging back up the escarpment. It didn't help, having a hurricane lamp in one hand and a gas canister in the other. He almost discarded the lamp once he was clear of the quarries, which would have been a mistake. He might have been able to find the motorcycle again without it, but he couldn't have stripped the carburetor down by the light of the moon alone. It was clogged with rust, the tank having run dry. The gods, it seemed, were set on having a good laugh at his expense, and he cursed them at the top of his lungs.

It was a fiddly operation, time-consuming, and it gave him a chance to think things through. Busuttil had mentioned two men. One had to be Elliott, but who was the second? The mysterious Ken who now, it seemed, had a mustache? Max knew only one submariner with a mustache, and that was Lionel. But it was a preposterous notion: Elliott and Lionel in cahoots, a team, killing off girls together. He even laughed at the thought of it.

He strained to find another explanation, anything that would exonerate his friend, but there was no escaping the fact that Elliott had abducted Busuttil, thwarting the investigation, which meant that he sat at the heart of the affair, and had probably done so all along. If anyone knew where Lilian was, then it was Elliott. Finding him, and finding him fast, was the obvious — the *only* — course of action open to Max.

He was finally able to kick the motorcycle into life. He knew where he was going, and he knew what he was going to do when he got there. He wouldn't involve the lieutenant governor's office; they weren't to be trusted. No, he would go straight to his own kind, to the Combined Operations Room in Valetta. At a time like this, brass hats from all the services would be gathered in the underground HQ. There would be no ignoring his story. How long could Elliott hope to remain hidden once the news had been spread that wide?

Max had passed through Zebbug and was making good time when the German bombers began to unload over the Luqa airfield. It was a heavy and systematic raid, and it lay almost directly in his path. He pulled to a halt, buffeted by the concussions, the bomb bursts ripping red holes in the darkness, blanketing the airfield. He decided to chance it. The road to Valetta skirted the airfield to the north — the direction from which the bombers were making their runs. It was well known that bombs tended to overshoot their targets, and that certainly seemed to be the case now. The southern end of the airfield was suffering badly.

He had the throttle wide open when he saw it — a rogue line of bomb bursts coming at him out of the darkness to his left — and he realized almost instantly that he was done for. The geometry was against him, the leaping trail of destruction destined to converge with his own trajectory a short way down the road, any moment.

He braked hard, the back wheel sliding away from under him. He was aware of a strange feeling of weightlessness, of flying, before a blinding white light snuffed out his senses.

Carmela Cassar had sobbed and squirmed and struggled the moment the sedative had worn off. Lilian, on the other hand, just lay there on the table, inert, denying him any satisfaction. Or so she thought. She wasn't to know that it didn't matter to him either way. If anything, her self-possession was a welcome challenge. It gave him something to work with.

He rose from the chair and approached the table.

She was spread-eagled on her back, her wrists and ankles lashed to the four legs. The gag and the blindfold were the same ones he had used on Carmela.

She flinched when he placed his hand on her chest, assuming that he was feeling for her breast.

"Don't worry," he said. "Not yet."

He was feeling for her heart. Again, he was impressed. It wasn't thumping away beneath her rib cage, betraying her apparent composure.

"I'm beginning to understand what Max sees in you."

She didn't like the mention of Max. The thought of him upset her. It showed in her face.

He smiled, sensing an opening. She might be able to close down her body, but she couldn't shut off her ears.

"He has a certain quality about him, doesn't he? Oh, I'm not talking about the good looks — those will fade with time. It's something else, something more lasting. Men feel it too. He's not a threat to men. Maybe that's what it is. He doesn't try to impose himself on people. He's not looking to prove anything."

He lit a cigarette. Rather than blowing out the match, he held it close to her thigh — absently, almost without thinking — the flame licking at the skin just below the hem of her black skirt. Her leg jerked, twisting away from the heat. He dropped the match onto the floor.

"You have great legs, you know? They're not quite as long as Mitzi's, but your breasts are larger. Oh, I'm sorry, I'm forgetting, you don't know about Mitzi, do you? I can't imagine Max has told you about her. Why would he?"

All the while, he was searching her body for signs.

"I'm not sure you would like her. She's very different from you. Not unintelligent, but frivolous, unreliable. Flighty — that's the word I'm looking for."

Still no reaction.

"Why he needs her in his life as well as you, I don't know."

The sinews stood out in her slender arms as she clenched her fists.

"The truth is often unkind. But it is what it is, and we just have to put up with it. In the grand scheme of things, a man torn between two women is hardly news, especially if he's sleeping with only one of them." He paused to allow his words to sink in. "He was with her three nights ago. I saw him go in and I saw him come out, and at one o'clock in the morning I don't think they were playing backgammon."

Lilian was visibly upset now, doing her best to hide it.

"Maybe with time he would have told you about her. Between you and me, I think he would have. Sadly, we'll never know."

# DAY NINE

There was no sudden awakening. He came back to consciousness slowly, on a building wave of pain. It carried him inexorably toward the shore and dumped him in a heap onto the beach. Only, it wasn't a beach, because there was a wall and something lying on top of him, pressing down on his leg.

He remembered now: the stick of bombs converging on him, the motorcycle sliding away, then flying, weightless, airborne . . .

As his eyes adjusted to the pale wash of moonlight, he saw that he was lying at the bottom of a steep bank, jammed up against a stone wall, his left leg caught beneath the motorcycle. How long he'd been there, he didn't know. There was a smell of gasoline, and the thought of the precious liquid leaking away stirred him into action.

Once he'd freed his leg, he was surprised to find he was able to stand. He checked himself over with his hands, his palms raw and throbbing. The bleeding seemed super-ficial — lots of grazes and some deeper cuts on his legs. There was also a large bump on the back of his head, congealed with blood. He couldn't place too much weight on his left ankle. It didn't feel broken, though, just badly sprained.

He was more worried about the motor-cycle, but she also seemed to have survived. There was still air in both tires, and al-though the handlebars were slightly out of alignment, the steering felt fine. From the sound of it, there was also enough gas in the tank to see him to Valetta.

He made his way up the bank, trying to piece together what had happened. He had come off the road at a bend. He hadn't seen it at the time, and it wasn't the reason he'd hit the back brake so hard. He had braked because some survival instinct had told him it was better to be close to the ground when a bomb went off. He could make out the large crater the bomb had torn in the shoulder of the road. He'd been lucky. The bend had probably saved him, the steep bank shielding him from the blast as he'd left the road.

The airfield at Luqa was recovering from the onslaught. He could see a few fires still burning, and every so often a delayed-action bomb would go off.

He turned at the sound of an approaching vehicle, traveling fast. He guessed what it was before he saw it — an ambulance racing to the scene. They were about the only things left on the roads since gas rationing had been tightened, and he often joked with Freddie that he and his kind were a bloody menace to other drivers.

He was right. It was an ambulance going hell-for-leather. He was about to flag it down when something stayed his hand — something Elliott had said to him, something he hadn't thought about since.

The question isn't *where* he took Carmela Cassar, but *how* he took her there.

He tried to reject the idea taking shape in his head, but it refused to be budged. The thought ripped through his brain, touching and changing everything in its path. The world as he'd been looking at it blurred into nothingness, and when it fell back into focus, he was no longer on the outside looking in. He was right at the heart of it, able to see things from all angles with a crisp and terrifying clarity.

"Oh my God," he said quietly.

He knew there were seventy-two steps because he'd counted them before. He counted them now, not for old times' sake but because each one sent a sharp pain shooting up his left leg. Maybe the ankle was broken after all.

He knew there was a good chance Lionel would be there — his last night on the island — but Max didn't care. He didn't even pause on the landing before knocking.

Mitzi eventually answered the door looking like something out of Dickens, with a dressing gown tightly tied at her waist, and carrying a chamber candlestick.

He was leaning against the doorjamb for support.

Her face fell. "My God, Max, what happened to you?"

"Who did you tell about us?"

"He's here," she said tightly.

"Who did you tell about us?"

"Max . . . ," she pleaded.

It was too late. Lionel materialized from the gloom behind her.

"I say, old man, are you all right?"

Max ignored him. "Who did you tell?"

Mitzi turned to Lionel. "He's obviously not himself."

"I'll say. What's going on? What do you mean?"

Max stared at them both. He saw the silent pact that had brought them together and the emptiness hanging between them, the lies. He could change it all in a moment. He could take it from them. He could hand the hurt straight back to Mitzi. It was so easy. Too easy.

"I've been seeing a girl in the office," he said finally. "She's Maltese. She's also married. I made the mistake of telling your wife here. It now seems that half the bloody garrison knows."

"Are you drunk?"

"A little. Enough to crash my motorcycle."

Lionel edged past Mitzi protectively. "I think you should leave."

Mitzi placed a restraining hand on Lionel's arm.

"Freddie," she said. "I told Freddie."

There was gratitude in her eyes for the lie he'd concocted.

"When?"

"Oh, for goodness' sake —"

"Shut up, Lionel." Mitzi looked back at Max. "A few months ago, maybe more. January, I think."

Max nodded his thanks, and she turned and wandered back to the bedroom. Lionel wasn't done with him yet, though.

"You're a bloody disgrace to your service!"

"Am I, *Ken?*"

He saw a satisfying flicker of alarm in Li-

449

onel's eyes.

"I know about you and Mary Farrugia, and I'm guessing you also brushed with Loreta Saliba and Carmela Cassar."

"I have no idea what you're talking about."

"Yes, you do. They're all dead. Murdered."

"Murdered?"

"Don't worry. I know it wasn't you."

He turned and hobbled off down the stairs.

He had never given his service revolver much thought — he strapped it on each morning, removed it before bed — but now he felt naked without it. Finding a replacement wasn't going to be easy at five o'clock in the morning. There was an obvious place to start, though. It was also on his route.

He was surprised to find the boys at the Bofors gun site near his flat already up and about. They were peering down over the bastion wall into the dark abyss of Grand Harbour. It was another half hour till sunrise, but way to the east, beyond the harbor mouth, the sky was already brightening.

"There!" said one of them, pointing.

It was just possible to make out the dark form of a ship sliding through the gloom toward them.

"It's the *Welshman*. She made it!"

There were cheers and slaps on the back, and that's when they noticed they had company.

"It's only me," said Max.

"You see that, sir, the *Welshman* got through!"

"Cigarette, sir?"

"Cup of tea, sir?"

"Foot rub, sir?"

The joker got his laugh. Max was in favor with the Manchester men since their heroics had been reported in the *Weekly Bulletin,* as he'd promised they would be.

"Just a quick word in private with Sergeant Deakin, if he's around."

"Right here, sir," came a voice from the darkness.

Max led Deakin a little way off. "I don't have time to explain. I need to borrow your gun."

"My gun?"

"Your service revolver. I wouldn't ask if it wasn't important."

"You know I can't, sir. It's against regulations."

"It's a matter of life or death."

"That's the truth. The CO'd 'ave my guts for garters if he found out."

"What if I took it off you by force?"

451

"You're welcome to give it a go, sir, but if you don't mind me saying, you're not moving too good."

"Okay," said Max, "here it is. My friend, my best friend, is probably a German agent. He's also planning to kill a girl I care very much about. For all I know, she's dead already. So you see, I'm going to have to give it a go whatever."

"Holy mackerel," said Deakin softly. "Are you sure you're all right in the head?"

"Never better. Actually, that's a lie. But what I've just told you is the truth. You have my word on it."

After a few moments, Deakin handed over his revolver.

"You're a good man, Sergeant."

"Yeah, well, just remember to bring that up at my court-martial."

The road to the naval hospital at Bighi skirted Grand Harbour on its southern side, taking him through the Three Cities, right past the dockyards. He thought about stopping off and enlisting the support of the military police, but procedures would have to be followed, phone calls made, authority sought. Precious minutes, hours even, would tick by. Besides, the situation might call for the kind of behavior not exactly endorsed by the rule book. He had no problem with that, but officialdom would see things differently.

No, this was a personal matter now — or rather, it had been all along. Only his self-absorption had kept him from grasping that fact earlier. It had been right there in front of him, not just staring him in the face but prodding him in the chest, kicking him in the shins.

The notion that the coincidence had been anything more than just that — the capricious hands of chance at work — had never even occurred to him: a killer on the loose, a crew member from the *Upstanding,* which just so happened to be the submarine commanded by the husband of the woman with whom he'd been having an affair.

He hadn't made the connection before because he'd assumed that no one else knew about Mitzi and him. But she'd set him straight on that. Freddie knew; Freddie had known since the beginning of the year. Freddie, who had drawn him into the intrigue in the first place. Freddie, with his talk of left-handers and *Have you ever wondered if it's Lionel?* Max could almost see Freddie laughing to himself as he tinkered with their sick little triangle of deceits and clandestine affairs, the puppet master surveying them all from on high, pulling their strings, jerking their limbs. Maybe Elliott had been right, maybe Freddie was a moralist at heart — one who had no scruples when it came to his own behavior.

Where Elliott fitted, he didn't yet know. Why had he helped Max, nudging him toward the answer? Did he already know the truth? Had he suspected all along? For now, Max was happy to forgo the answers. All that mattered to him was finding Lilian. That one goal consumed him. It also scared him, because he saw just how far he was willing to go to get her back. Freddie had made the rules, and Max was ready to play by them.

The naval hospital at Bighi stood square, squat, and ugly on the tip of the cliff-girt promontory beyond Vittoriosa, near the mouth of Grand Harbour. Like the other hospitals on the island, it had suffered at the hands of the Luftwaffe in the past month. Unlike some of them, it was still operational.

The nurse at the main desk couldn't say for certain where Freddie was, so she directed Max to the surgeons' sleeping quarters. This was after she had offered to summon the duty medical officer to check him over, assuming that he'd shown up in search of treatment.

He hobbled his way to the low run of stone huts on the grounds near the east wing of the building. A slumbering doctor, not happy at being woken, directed him to Freddie's digs two huts down.

Freddie wasn't there, but his roommate was.

"You just missed him. He's headed for the docks."

"The docks?"

"To help with the wounded from the *Welshman*. She hit a couple of mines on her way in."

Nearing the hospital, Max had passed a small fleet of ambulances racing down the hill in the opposite direction. This put him no more than fifteen minutes behind, if he stepped on it.

"I'd keep well clear of the docks, if I were you. They're sure to have a pop at her come sunup."

As Max hurried back through the grounds to his motorcycle, the first sliver of the new sun appeared out of the eastern sea, illuminating his path.

At first, he thought the *Welshman*'s precious cargo must be alight. A dense gray-green cloud was rising over the dockyards, spreading like some malevolent fog. He slowed the motorcycle, listening for the accompanying crackle of exploding ammunition, but heard nothing. A smoke screen, he realized, put up to throw off the aim of the enemy bombers. Moments later, he was swallowed up by it.

Chaos ruled along French Creek, much of it caused by the swirling smoke belching from the generators. With visibility reduced to a matter of yards, Max abandoned the motorcycle and set off on foot, searching for the ambulances. The unloading was already under way, and the quayside was a logjam of trucks waiting to bear off the cargo. Men moved through the miasma, appearing and fading like ghosts to a chorus of muffled shouts and orders. These increased in volume as the *Welshman* loomed into view, long and trim and battle-worn, with streaks of rust staining her flaking paint. She had her own cranes for loading, which was fortunate. Those on the quayside stood broken and twisted like crippled giants.

Max barged a path up the gangway onto the ship. He collared a crewman and asked for the sick bay. A peculiar stillness descended on him as he made his way below-decks. He felt utterly divorced from the frenetic activity unfolding around him, focused on the imminent confrontation.

Freddie wasn't in the sick bay, but a man on a bunk with a big bandage on his head mumbled some directions to the forward dressing station where the wounded were being tended to.

A couple of them hadn't made it. They lay covered in blankets in a corner of the room. The others were on stretchers, patched up and ready to be moved. Freddie was in the thick of things, administering an injection of morphia to a howling sailor whose thigh was swaddled in blood-soaked rags.

Was that how he did it? Was that how he subdued the girls, with pharmaceuticals?

Freddie seemed to sense Max's thoughts, turning as he got to his feet.

"My God, Max, what are you doing here?"

"I need to talk to you."

"Hardly the time or the place."

Freddie gestured the waiting orderlies forward. "Okay, let's get them out of here."

Max could only look on as Freddie marshaled his men, leading the party of stretcher-bearers through the belly of the ship. Max brought up the rear, doing his best to keep Freddie in his sights.

The air-raid siren heralded their appearance on the upper deck. This gave them seven minutes at most before the bombs would begin to fall. Somewhere up ahead, lost in the blanket of smoke, Max heard Freddie call, "Clear the gangway! Make way for the wounded!"

Max imagined Freddie slipping away in the man-made fog, but he was waiting at the bottom of the gangway, seeing the party safely off the ship, pointing a path through the torrent of men and clattering carts loaded with crates.

"Where is she, Freddie?"

"What happened? You look terrible."

"I know it's you."

"And you're not making a whole lot of sense."

Freddie turned to follow the train of stretcher-bearers across the quayside. Max held him back by the arm. Freddie shook himself free, angry now.

"I don't know what's got into you, but there are men there who need attention. So — if you don't mind — I've got a job to do."

Max hadn't spotted the ambulances on the quayside because they were parked in the streets of Senglea, just back from the docks. Senglea was a ghost town, long since evacuated by order of the governor. If anything, the smoke sat thicker there than on the quayside, undisturbed by the urgent passage of men.

There were four ambulances in all, but only three were required for the wounded men. Freddie sent them on their way before turning his attention back to Max. They were alone now, and Freddie was still angry.

"Okay, what the bloody hell's going on?"

*Don't be fooled by the indignation,* Max told himself. *You're dealing with a practiced liar, a dangerous man.*

"Where's Lilian?"

"Lilian?"

"Tell me where she is!"

"How the hell should I know?"

Reaching for his gun seemed the right thing to do. Taking his eyes off Freddie for a split second as he did so was definitely the wrong thing.

The fist caught him square in the mouth, snapping his head back. His knees buckled and the world seemed to recede around him. He was dimly aware of the air-raid siren and the taste of blood in his mouth and the sound of an engine starting. He forced himself back to consciousness in time to see the remaining ambulance disappear into the smoke.

He stumbled off in pursuit, pulling the

revolver from its holster. That's when the Grand Harbour barrage opened up. It hadn't been heard in months, not on this scale, not since the March convoy. The restrictions on ammunition had clearly been lifted, and guns were letting off from every quarter. The shattering cacophony didn't assault just the ears but all the senses. The street shivered before Max's eyes; his legs felt leaden, numbed to the bone by the reverberations.

He didn't hear the ambulance until it was almost on him, materializing in a moment, its blunt nose bearing down on him head-on.

He hurled himself to the left, landing hard in a pile of rubble. The ambulance veered to crush him, and it might have succeeded if a large chunk of stonework hadn't deflected it from its course. The front wheel struck the block with a sickening crunch, and the vehicle reared up, flashing him its dark belly as it passed over him, teetering on two wheels.

Because of the smoke, he didn't see it roll over, but he heard the sound, even above the thunder of the barrage and the scream of diving Stukas.

He groped for the revolver among the rubble, pushed himself to his feet, and set off after the ambulance.

The vehicle lay on its side, its engine still running. He didn't bother to check the driver's compartment because he saw Freddie staggering off through the smoke. Max wasn't capable of breaking into a sprint, but he did his best under the circumstances and was closing in when Freddie cut right, up some steps.

They led to a church, or what was left of it. A large section of the front façade was gone, and the entrance doors hung drunkenly from their hinges. A small voice told Max to holster his weapon before entering the building. He ignored it.

Freddie had made no attempt to hide. The roof had collapsed into the nave, and he was scrabbling his way toward the back of the building over the twisted beams and broken tiles. Max fired a warning shot, the report echoing off the walls and stopping Freddie in his tracks. He stood upright, turning to face his pursuer.

Outside, the crumping barrage began to fade, the first phase of the raid over. Max picked his way through the rubble. Within the four walls of the church, the smoke seemed to hang in the air like incense at a Catholic Mass.

"Is she alive? Tell me she's alive."

"She's alive."

"Where is she?"

"In a basement."

"Where?"

"Within a two-mile radius."

They both knew what that meant. Grand Harbour's toothy huddle of cities and towns was reputed to be the most built-over place in Europe.

"You'll never find her, I can promise you that, not if you pull that trigger. She'll die a slow death, a horrible death, the worst kind. Starvation and dehydration — is that what you want for her?"

"Why, Freddie?"

"Why?" He gave a short laugh. "My God, that's a question and a half. How long have you got?"

"I don't understand."

"I don't expect you to."

"We were friends."

"You mean we aren't anymore?"

He seemed almost to be enjoying himself, untroubled by the gun leveled at his chest.

"Tell me where she is."

"You think you can make me with that popgun? Go ahead, try. Better still, don't bother. There's no point. I'll never tell you, not you, not anyone." He spread his arms wide. "Here before God I give you my word."

"You're bluffing."

"You don't know me," said Freddie darkly. "It'll be my little victory. Go on, do it. She's dead anyway."

Max lowered the gun sharply, aiming at Freddie's leg, his finger tightening around the trigger.

A shot rang out around the church and Max was sent reeling, as if clubbed in the arm. He stumbled and fell, gripping his shoulder, feeling the blood, the shock giving way to a searing pain and the vague realization that he'd just been shot.

Elliott stepped into view from behind a pillar — his gun, his eyes, trained on Max.

"Is he alone?" Elliott asked.

Max was on the point of replying when Elliott turned to Freddie and demanded, "Is he alone?"

"I think so," replied Freddie, slowly coming out of a crouch.

"You think so, or you know so?"

"I'm pretty sure."

Freddie's confusion was becoming more evident with each response.

Keeping his gun on Max, Elliott recovered the revolver from the ground before backing away.

"What are you doing here?" Freddie asked, bewildered.

"My job," said Elliott. "Covering your back. I work for Tacitus too."

Tacitus? The significance of the word was lost on Max, and for a moment the same seemed true for Freddie. But then he began to laugh.

"You think it's funny? You see me laughing? I wouldn't have to be here if you hadn't screwed up."

"Elliott?" said Max pathetically.

"Shut up."

Elliott turned back to Freddie and nodded toward the main doors. "Get out of here."

Freddie edged his way past Elliott. "What are you going to do with him?"

"Use your imagination."

"Goodbye, Max," said Freddie.

The words sounded almost heartfelt.

Max stared at them both, incapable of speech.

Elliott advanced on him.

"Elliott . . . ," he pleaded.

"Lie down."

Max kicked out with his feet, trying to keep him at bay.

It couldn't end like this. It wasn't possible.

His efforts to defend himself were rewarded with a crippling boot to the solar plexus. Gasping for breath, he looked up at Elliott, vaguely aware of Freddie — a dim shape in the smoke, watching from near the entrance.

"I'm sorry," said Elliott, dropping to one knee and placing the muzzle of his revolver against Max's temple. "But as the old saying goes, 'It is appointed unto man once to die.'"

The words chimed with some hazy memory. He knew that they had made him laugh at the time, but he couldn't remember why. Something to do with snow and an old man . . .

He was still groping for the details when Elliott pulled the trigger.

# LONDON

## MAY 1951

"Shall I pour?" said Elliott, reaching for the wine bottle.

"Why not?"

Elliott filled their glasses before raising his own in a toast. He took a moment to settle on one he was happy with.

"To all those who didn't make it."

"All those who didn't make it."

They clinked glasses tentatively, as if the weight of their shared history might shatter the crystal.

"They told me *you* didn't make it."

"I know," said Elliott. "Remind me — how did I die?"

"You went down in a plane off the French coast," replied Max.

"I hope it was quick."

"They said Freddie died in the same crash."

"What else did they say?"

"Is he alive?"

The idea that Freddie might still be walking the planet somewhere tightened his stomach.

"Not unless he sprouted wings." Elliott paused briefly, lowering his eyes. "I threw him out of a Lodestar over the Bay of Biscay."

"You threw him out of a plane?"

"You make it sound easier than it was. He fought me like a tiger all the way."

"I don't understand."

"That's why I'm here. What do you want to know?"

"I thought you were a German agent."

Elliott rolled his eyes. "Jeez, they really didn't tell you anything, did they? I'm beginning to understand the frosty reception."

It was true, they had told Max almost nothing. In their efforts to hush the whole thing up, they'd flown him off the island the moment he'd been fit to travel. There'd been a desk job waiting for him back in London at the Ministry of Information, but he'd recognized it for what it was: a bribe to keep him quiet and onside while seeing out the war with some modicum of respectability.

"But you shot me."

"Only cos *you* were about to shoot *him* in

the leg, and I couldn't trust you not to hit an artery. I needed him alive."

"What, so you could throw him out of a plane?"

Elliott shrugged. "I changed my mind."

"Why?"

Elliott pulled a black hardback notebook from his jacket pocket and laid it on the table. It was old and scuffed.

"It's all in there. Everything. Going back years. He started young. Freddie Lambert was the sickest sonofabitch I ever came across, and I've been around the block a few times since Malta. I haven't lost a minute's sleep over what I did. He went out that door screaming like a stuck pig, and that's exactly what he deserved."

"Judge, jury, and executioner?"

Elliott slid the notebook across the table toward Max. "Read it first. And when you're done, burn it. You'll want to."

"Why did you want him alive?"

Elliott lit another cigarette before replying. "There's only one thing more valuable than an agent, and that's a double agent, assuming you can be sure of his duplicity."

"You knew he'd killed three girls and you were still happy to work with him?"

"Not exactly dancing a jig, but nothing beats feeding the enemy what you want

468

them to hear. Yes, I knew what he'd done. I also knew what he could do for us. My job demands a certain pragmatism. Not everyone has the stomach for it."

According to Elliott, the British authorities on the island hadn't been happy with the idea, and it had made for tension between him and Malta Command.

"You see, we knew the Germans had an agent on the island. We'd known for a while. We didn't know who he was, but we knew exactly what he was up to, and why. I was all for finding him and using him. They were all for sitting tight."

"Sitting tight?"

"Doing nothing. They had their reasons — good reasons." He paused. "This isn't public knowledge, and it won't be for a while yet, so keep it to yourself. We'd cracked the German codes by then. Well, a bunch of your experts had. Hell of an achievement. Probably swung the war our way. It sure as hell made all the difference on Malta. We knew where and when they were running their convoys to Rommel. We knew when the Luftwaffe was leaving Sicily for the Russian front and when they were returning. Remember the Italian E-boat raid on Grand Harbour? We knew it was coming. We were ready for them. That's why

469

they didn't stand a chance."

Max remembered it clearly. It had been a rout, a predawn massacre.

"The only trouble with having the heads-up is you've got to be careful how you use the intelligence."

"Because you'll give the game away."

"Exactly. That's just what it is — a game. Defense Security didn't want to risk moving on the Germans' agent because they might have figured out we were deciphering their signals."

"The lives of a few Maltese girls — who cares, right?"

"I didn't say it wasn't a dirty game. No one enjoys doing the math on these things. And like I said, I didn't agree with them."

"That's why you helped me."

"I gave you a few pointers."

"You used me."

"We were watching your back."

"He wasn't after me. He was after Lilian."

Elliott glanced down at the notebook. "Read the book. You'll find you're wrong. You were part of the big plan too. He just never got a chance to see it through."

"You were playing with our lives."

"Look, I didn't come here for forgiveness. I came here to tell you how it was. I did what I thought was right at the time, and with limited resources. You can't legislate for everything in those kinds of operations. Like Busuttil. Smart fellow. That's why we had to remove him. We were trying to contain the situation, and he was running around town making too many waves. Hasn't held him back, by the way. I heard he made chief inspector."

"I know. We're still in touch. I even went to his wedding."

They were interrupted by the waiter, looking to take their order. They hadn't given their menus a second thought, so Max picked a couple of the restaurant's signature dishes for them.

For all their talk, they seemed to have skirted the central issue: that Freddie, their friend, had been a traitor and a murderer. Elliott had obviously come to terms with that fact, but Max needed to talk about it. He was still haunted by images of that ruined church wreathed in smoke, of Freddie standing amidst the rubble of the fallen roof, arms spread wide, an almost Christlike figure. Neither his eyes nor his voice had been those of the person Max had known, almost as if he'd been possessed.

"Did you ever suspect it was Freddie?" Max asked.

"It crossed my mind, but no, I didn't read

471

the signs."

"So what were you doing at the church?"

"I got a call from Mitzi. You'd just been at their flat. She was worried about you."

"Why call you?"

"Because I'd asked her to. We'd lost track of you at that point. She said you'd been asking after Freddie, so I called the hospital at Bighi, found out where he was, figured you had too by then." He paused. "Dear, beautiful Mitzi, God rest her soul."

She had never made it to Alexandria. The seaplane she'd been traveling on had strayed too close to Crete and been shot down by 109s. It was something Max thought about a lot but never talked about. Now was no different.

*Yes, God rest their souls,* he thought.

"I sometimes wonder what would have happened if she hadn't called me."

"You would never have got to shoot me in the head, for starters."

"A little to one side, I think you'll find."

"Close enough to leave a scar."

Elliott shrugged. "A small price to pay for Lilian's life. It was done for her."

Max gave an incredulous laugh.

"It's true. He said it himself — he was never going to reveal where he was holding her. My only chance was to persuade him I was on the same team and hope to get it from him that way." Elliott crushed out his cigarette in the ashtray. "Which I did, I might add."

"Tacitus . . ."

"His German contact. He had to fall for it. He didn't know we'd broken the codes. The idea was inconceivable to him."

Max could see it now. He was no longer squinting at the picture, struggling to make sense of it.

"If what you say is true, then the moment you mentioned Tacitus to him, it was all over."

"Over?"

"For you and your double agent. I can't see you using a man who knew the codes had been broken."

"That would have been . . . imprudent."

"Which means you threw it all away, right at the end, everything you'd been working for."

Elliott spread his hands. "Turns out you're not the only sentimentalist in the world."

When their food arrived, they talked about Elliott's line of work. He didn't reveal much, only that he still drew a government salary and had spent a lot of time in Moscow in the intervening years.

"Twenty million Soviets died fighting for

the same cause as us, and now they're the enemy. Go figure that."

His bleak prognosis was that things were going to get a whole lot worse between the USSR and the West before they got any better.

Assisted by the excellent food and another bottle of wine, they relaxed and talked of happier things, of places they had traveled to and others they hoped to visit, of their new families and old friends.

Ralph, Max informed Elliott, was now a commercial pilot with BOAC, flying Stratocruisers on the long-haul routes.

"Still moaning about 'the machine'?"

"Different machine, same moaning."

Elliott was far more surprised to hear that Hugh had gone on to become the headmaster of a prep school in Sussex.

"I didn't see that one coming."

"Nor did Rosamund. She told him she'd divorce him if he took the job."

"And did she?"

"What do you think?"

"I think I should look them up next time I'm in the country."

"Do that. I know they'd like it."

Their plates were being cleared away when Elliott mentioned, "By the way, I saw your house in a magazine."

"It's not my house."

"I'm sure as hell glad it's not mine. Where'd you get your inspiration from — a fish tank?"

"It's called modernism."

"That's not what the guy who wrote the piece called it."

Max laughed. "You can't please everyone."

The glass and concrete villa had been his first private commission since qualifying as an architect. The best that could be said of it was that it had "divided the critics."

"Well, at least you've got a wife who's made something of herself."

She appeared as if on cue, being led by Mario toward their table. She was wearing a strapless silk taffeta evening dress that Max had never seen before. As ever, he gave silent thanks for his good fortune.

Elliott caught his expression and turned. "Oh yeah. I forgot to say, she's joining us for coffee."

They both got to their feet, and Elliott stooped to kiss her hand. "You look radiant."

"You do," said Max, kissing her on the cheek.

"Friends again?" she inquired.

"You'll have to ask your husband."

Max looked long and hard at Elliott. "I

don't see why not."

Lilian smiled.

"That's good," she said. "That's very good."

# HISTORICAL NOTE

The fly-in of new Spitfires on May 9, 1942, marked the turning point in Malta's fortunes. The following day, sixty-three enemy aircraft were shot down over the island. A German broadcast declared, "Malta can be reduced by other means." It never was. In 1964 the island finally gained independence from Great Britain.

While trying to remain as true to the period as possible, I have, inevitably, taken certain liberties for the purposes of the story. My apologies for these, and for any other errors I'm not yet aware of. The majority of the characters in the book are entirely fictitious. Those who aren't bear no relation to their real-life counterparts, whose impeccable wartime records speak for themselves.

# ACKNOWLEDGMENTS

As ever, I owe a big debt of gratitude to my agent, Stephanie Cabot, for her tireless enthusiasm and support. I would also like to thank my editors, Jennifer Hershey and Julia Wisdom, for their expert insights and guidance. My thanks also go to Bara Mac-Neill.

Of the many books I read while researching the story, I would like to make special mention of *Malta Magnificent* by Francis Gerard, as well as *Fortress Malta,* James Holland's vivid and entirely compelling account of the island's wartime trials.

# ABOUT THE AUTHOR

**Mark Mills** graduated from Cambridge University in 1986. He has lived in both Italy and France and has written for the screen. His first novel, *Amagansett,* was a national bestseller and also won the British Crime Writer's Association Award for Best Novel by a debut author. His second, *The Savage Garden,* was a number one bestseller in the UK. He lives in Oxford with his wife and two children.